HUNGRY LIKE A WOLF

JESSICA LYNCH

Copyright © 2019 by Jessica Lynch

All rights reserved.

No part of this book may be reproduced in any form or by any electronic or mechanical means, including information storage and retrieval systems, without written permission from the author, except for the use of brief quotations in a book review.

Cover by Jessica Lynch

PROLOGUE

On the subject of broken unions:

1. All Paranormal unions (also referred to colloquially as *matings, claimings, bloodings, soulmates,* etc.) are final so long as both parties sign a notarized certificate ("Bonding License") stating a "bond" exists between them. The penalties for fabricating this claim are up to and including incarceration at a state-run facility.
2. In the event that one party becomes deceased, this Ordinance requires that, should the remaining party be a Paranormal, the broken "bond" must be neutralized in order to keep the Paranormal from becoming a danger to the rest of society.

3. As of the latest revision for this Ordinance, the surviving Paranormal has three options: a) voluntary incarceration in a state-run facility until rehabilitation; b) voluntary dissolution of the existing "bond" by a government-employed witch; c) in the most extreme cases, when rehabilitation is not deemed possible, a state-sanctioned execution.
4. Rehabilitation is conditional. If the surviving Paranormal breaks any of the clauses outlined in this Ordinance following release, the penalty is further incarceration or, in severe cases, execution.

— Ordinance 7304
Section IV

1

Colton Wolfe tapped his fingers against his leg, grateful that his claws hadn't made an appearance yet. Grateful and a little surprised, too. Shit. His control was holding out better than he expected.

Maddox would be proud. He always said Colt's temper was too explosive.

Yeah, well. Guilty as charged.

It really didn't take much to set him off. One of his tools missing from its specific spot in his work shed. Traffic snarls, he fucking hated those. Another wolf having the balls to mark in his territory? It was a struggle to keep to two legs instead of four. Even something as simple as his soda going flat before he had finished it tested him.

He couldn't help it.

Shifters were known for having a short leash, with Colt's notably shorter than most. He always snapped first, asked questions later. It was one of the reasons he was glad his brother was four years older. Even if they were both born alphas, Maddox had the bad luck to be his father's second-in-command, the next in line to be Alpha, if only because he was the eldest.

He would lead the pack one day if Colt could finally convince Mad that he didn't belong behind bars.

Last month, Colt didn't even bother trying. He'd given up after his first few visits, knowing that he'd never be able to change his stubborn brother's mind.

But that was last month.

Last year.

Hell, that was *yesterday*.

Not today, though. Not with this recent knowledge buzzing around his skull, making his inner wolf yip frantically with excitement.

He needed to get to Maddox.

Too bad the cop wasn't making it easy for him.

Colt's temper was primed to go off like a rocket. The smirk, the damn smirk on the cop's face, was enough to provide a spark if he wasn't careful.

Because if there was one thing that guaranteed an appearance by his beast? It was someone deliberately screwing with him. And the smarmy, smug bastard on the other side of the bulletproof glass wasn't just screwing with him—he was wearing a shit-eating grin while he did it.

"I don't know," the blond officer drawled, squinting

at the P.I.D. card Colt had just passed through the one-inch gap in the partition. "You sure this is you?"

Colt swallowed his growl, his claws scratching at the tips of his fingers, begging to be let free. "It's me."

"Don't know about that. It doesn't look like you all that much."

"That's my picture," Colt said through gritted teeth. "That's my name."

"You don't say. Huh."

Ah, hell. How had he forgotten? Officer Wright thought he was some kind of comedian, only his tired routine had gotten old the first time he pulled it almost a year ago.

Damn it. Did Colt have to put up with this crap every time he wanted to visit his brother?

He exhaled roughly through his nose. A quick shake of his shoulders, settling inside of his skin. Wolfing out while at the Cage was the quickest way to get thrown *in* one. "Come on. It's me. You know it is."

"Name says 'Wolfe'," the officer noted, purposely drawing out the last word. "'Shifter type: Lycan'. Yeah?" He made a point to squint a little as he took in Colt's tall, lean frame, frowning as he eyed the shifter's clean-shaven face, his closely cropped light brown hair. "I just don't think I buy it. Shouldn't you be hairier or something? Where's the fangs, pretty boy?" Wright let out a derisive snort. Colt bit down so hard, he nearly split his tongue with the fangs he purposely kept just out of sight. "Your kind should come with a warning label, not just some stupid card."

Okay. *Pretty boy* he could handle, he'd been called worse by his brother, but the way the cop spat out *your kind* as if Colt was somehow less because he was a paranormal? He locked his jaw, smartly staying quiet in case he snapped something that guaranteed he'd never get in to see Maddox.

Flaring his nostrils, he took another deep breath, struggling to retain his hold on his furious wolf.

Because another thing that made him lose it? Nobody Ants like Wright who thought they were better than Paras.

When he was confident he wasn't about to shift on the spot, Colt relaxed enough to unscrew his jaw and speak again. No matter what Wright thought, his trip to the Cage wasn't a waste of time. He had a damn good reason for coming back so soon and, as tempting as it was, squashing this Ant wasn't it.

Later, though. He'd remember this later.

Nothing he could do now anyway. The glass protecting Wright's worthless hide wasn't just bullet-proof. He could tell from the way the hairs on the back of his neck stood up that the glass was also enchanted to be Para-proof. Claws and fangs and brute strength were powerless against the warding spells.

Fucking witches. He fought back another snarl. Alpha, how he hated them.

The ones who turned their back on their fellow

Paras to sell their spells to the government were the absolute *worst*. Just the thought of them made his skin itch, his gaze icing over as he fought the urge to shift. They were traitors, in his opinion, all of those who chose to side with the Ants.

He might be forced to interact with asshole humans like Wright because it was his duty to keep in touch with his brother; as long as Maddox was trapped in this hellhole, Colt would be there. Witches did it solely for the money. Without all of their enchantments and their wards, the Cages probably wouldn't even exist.

Colt was reminded of that every time he came back here.

Wright flicked his blunt pointer finger against the edge of Colt's identification, back and forth, back and forth. The rasping of his skin against the plastic set Colt's teeth on edge. He had a sudden longing to shove his P.I.D. down Wright's throat.

They both knew that the cop was going to let him in—Colt was on the shortlist approved to see Maddox and, regardless of what Wright implied, his identification was legit—but the game was to see how long he could keep Colt waiting. And how close he could get the wolf shifter to going rogue.

Too damn close, and the bastard knew it.

Colt figured Wright had something against the Wolfe brothers, even if he couldn't put his claw on the why. As a pack animal, Colt was born with an innate knowledge of alpha males and hierarchies. It was obvious that nothing would make the arrogant officer happier than to see Colt rotting in the same cell as Maddox and fuck if he would give him that satisfaction.

He pulled all of his aggression back and, with a grin that lit up his boyishly handsome face, he leaned in toward Wright. A dimple popped in his left cheek.

Then he remembered being called *pretty boy*. His grin turned feral, his fangs lengthening until they bit into his bottom lip. Wright went as pale as a ghost. And, since Colt's best friend was one, he considered himself an expert.

"You questioning my government-issued P.I.D.? *Again*? Maybe you should call your supervisor down here. Get a second opinion. Check if I'm allowed to see my brother or not." His grin widened as he made sure to bare his fangs. "It's okay. I'll wait."

In response, Wright slapped Colt's identification on the counter before shoving it roughly back through the glass partition. Irrationally pleased, Colt pulled his wallet out and put his P.I.D. away while Wright leaned over. With more force than was necessary, the cop slammed his palm against the red button off to his side.

Even though the alarm sounded on another floor, the piercing shriek was still too much for Colt's sensitive shifter hearing. He point-blank refused to let Wright see how much it hurt, though, so, like he usually did, he swallowed roughly until the ringing in his ears became more tolerable.

It didn't matter how many times he heard it, the shrill whistle never got any easier. He decided long ago that it was on purpose.

He grumbled under his breath. Fucking Ants.

A few minutes later, a bald-headed officer about twenty years Wright's senior appeared behind the glass partition. He nodded at Wright. The younger man scowled and jerked his head at Colt. Some color was beginning to return to Wright's face; a nice, angry red, Colt was glad to note. The bald officer appeared surprised and almost happy to see the wolf shifter standing at attention in the waiting area.

Colt relaxed a little further. Okay. Now *that* was the kind of welcome he liked to get.

This time, when Colt offered Officer Bennett a smile, he hid his fangs again.

He liked the older cop. Since the Cage was technically considered a very dangerous prison—whether a majority of the inmates were "voluntary" or not—the government refused to staff them with ordinary correction officers; except for the civilian warden, a never-ending rotation of tenured police officers ran the place instead. No matter what department they were from, what precinct, each and every cop had to do at least one year's time in a Cage as a reminder that "protect and serve" referred to paranormals, too.

Bennett seemed like an honest man. Even Maddox

had a good word or two for the officer over the years and, considering his brother didn't like too many people, that was saying something. Bennett did his year about a decade and a half ago and decided to stay even when he didn't have to. And, unlike Wright, he didn't give Colt any grief whenever he came to see Maddox.

Bennett already had his keys in hand when he left the guards' side in favor of joining Colt. "Hey, Wolfe," he greeted genuinely. "How are you?"

There was a door built into the far side of the waiting area. It was locked, since it led further into the maximum security facility, and Bennett needed two separate keys from the ring—plus a palm print—to open it. Once he had, he swung the thick door in before gesturing for Colt to step through.

"I'm fine."

"Good. Good. Say, didn't I just see you not too long ago?"

Colt was wondering if anyone would call him out on that. He was aware his visits drained Maddox so, on his brother's orders, he kept them to once a month. And, like Bennett noted, it had only been a handful of days since the last time he took the trip out.

"Something came up," he grunted.

"Pack business?" Bennett asked. There was no trace of disgust or irony in his question. He was actually interested.

Shaking his head, Colt told him, "Personal, but

important. It couldn't wait until next month. I know it's late." No thanks to Wright giving him the runaround, he thought. Colt rolled his head on his neck, his fingers stretching and cracking. "I'll try to be quick."

Bennett nodded and, while curiosity colored his hangdog face, he left it at that. His ring of keys tucked securely onto his belt again, the older cop led the way down the empty, dark hall.

Not that Colt needed a guide. Even without his tracking senses, he could find his way through the hidden nooks and less-traveled paths of the Cage blindfolded.

In the three years that he'd been visiting his brother, Colt lost track of how many times he'd gone down this empty hall. It always smelled strongly of chemicals—probably the industrial cleaners the maintenance crews used—and he snuffled gently, trying to keep the acrid stench from burning his nose. Between that and the way the hall narrowed continuously as he walked, he knew that it was a subtle warning for paranormal visitors, especially shifters.

Damn if the Cage wasn't a true cage, even the part of the prison that allowed civilians. It was designed to be a constant reminder that there was no freedom here: no windows, save for the artificial light streaming down from the fluorescent bulbs hanging overhead, and absolutely no fresh air.

Colt had to resist the urge to shift and take off. Just run. His wolf was all for it.

Another scent suddenly filled the stuffy corridor. It was faint, barely noticeable against the caustic stench of the cleaner, but he recognized it in a flash.

Colt was well acquainted with the sour tinge of fear. He was making Bennett nervous.

And that's when he realized that he was growling under his breath and, yup, those were his claws. He hadn't been able to keep them back after all.

He took a deep breath, held it, pushed it out through his nose. Again.

Maddox was his older brother and, though not much got to him anymore, his protective instincts were often triggered when he saw that Colt was having a hard time holding it together. Right then? He needed Maddox calm. Which meant he needed to calm the fuck down himself.

Bennett was an honest man, a good man—and he was a pretty brave man, too. Despite the flare of unease in his scent, he turned, daring to look Colt straight in the eyes. Not long enough that it was a challenge, Colt couldn't deny that it was a reminder. Officer Bennett was a cop, an experienced Cage guard, and the gun his hand was currently resting against? Colt would bet his left nut that it was full of silver bullets.

"You doing alright, Wolfe?"

Colt jerked his head in agreement. "Yeah. Sorry. Just anxious to see my brother."

"Wright should've already called him down to the

visitors' block. Good chance he's there, waiting for you."

Part of Colt wondered if Wright was going to dick him around some more. He hoped not. The annoying prick seemed to respect Bennett so maybe, for once, he'd do his job without giving Colt an even harder time. Or maybe Colt's threat to go over Wright's head had hit its mark. Didn't matter. The only thing that did? When Bennett got through the locks that led into the visitors' area, just how relieved Colt was to find Maddox slumped on a stool behind the glass.

The square room was the same one Colt always met Maddox in. About twice as large as the waiting area on this floor of the Cage, it had three grey cinderblock walls and a fourth made up of glass that separated the brothers. A mirrored row of stools sat on both sides, a seat each for the inmate and the civilian. Behind the inmate, there was another solid cinderblock wall and a door that would bring Maddox back to his cell.

Colt had never seen his brother's cell before. He tried not to think about Maddox living locked up behind bars like a common criminal. Locked away for the crime of loving his mate, then losing her.

It only made Colt want to howl his rage at the unfairness of it all.

As soon as Bennett slipped back into the hall— followed by the soft *snick*ing of the lock behind him— Colt knew that this illusion of privacy was all he and his brother were going to get. His senses didn't pick up anyone else in the room, but he wasn't fooled. He remembered the position of every camera, knew there was always someone watching.

Colt snorted out loud. He didn't care if the cameras picked it up or not.

Voluntary.

Right.

Maddox heard the snort. Colt knew he did, just like Mad's shifter hearing would've picked up on the door opening, closing, then locking. He pretended he didn't, though, the other man refusing to lift his head, leaving it bowed, his chin tucked into his chest as if he were praying.

Colt's hands flexed, deadly claws unsheathing all of the way without a sound.

It did a number on him, seeing his older brother like this. He always left the Cage with the urge to hunt down whoever was responsible for turning a once proud wolf into this sad, sorry shadow of a man.

Too bad that there was no one to blame. The *Claws Clause* said Maddox had to choose, yeah, but he never should've been forced to make that decision in the first place. It all came down to one terrible night, some awful bad luck, and that bitch, Mother Nature. How did you fight against *that*?

Of course, that was before this morning. Now... now he knew better.

2

The lighting was surprisingly brighter than the back halls, especially when he took the coarse, solid, pale walls that surrounded the room into account. Still no windows, but the wattage in the overhead lights was almost blinding.

Between the cameras, the lack of shadows, and the glass partition that was doubly as warded as the one protecting Wright, Colt couldn't come nearer than two feet to his brother. No doubt that level of security was why the cops felt comfortable leaving them "alone".

That, and the locked door. Colt didn't have to check it out to guess that the knob was also enchanted. Like everything else, the audible click of the lock was just one more reminder. If he tried grabbing that handle without Bennett's keys in the lock, he'd singe all of the fur off his paw.

And it wasn't like he needed the reminder that his

brother was a dangerous alpha wolf. Even through the thick glass that separated them, he could feel the overwhelming presence and strength of Maddox's more dominant beast.

Colt only submitted before two males—his older brother and their father—and his own wolf was whining inside of his head in confusion. Rather than meet his gaze and assert his authority as Alpha, Maddox kept his head down which meant that Colt's wolf was torn between either lying on its belly in submission or snapping its teeth in challenge.

After all of these years, it was getting harder and harder to heed the hierarchy in their pack. Colt might only visit Maddox monthly because his brother asked that of him. He had to admit that he agreed for purely selfish reasons.

The rational part of Colt's brain—the man part—knew that Maddox was still suffering from the pain of losing his mate. But it wasn't just that. As Colt stayed back, waiting for Maddox to acknowledge him, his eyes narrowed on the thick collar locked around his brother's throat.

The *silver* collar.

He hated that damn thing. And he knew there was no way he could get it off of Maddox, even if he somehow got past the glass. He'd burn his hands raw anyway because it was *right*.

The blazing light from above flashed against the gleaming metal, mocking him.

Fucking silver. And the humans called *his* kind monsters.

So what if the inside of the collar was treated to keep from burning a shifter's skin? It never worked. The outside was pure silver, potent and terrible enough to not only keep Maddox trapped in his human skin, but to weaken him significantly. No wonder Colt's beast wanted to take Maddox's role in the pack. The silver was messing with him almost as much as it was draining Maddox.

Too soon. This visit was too soon. Colt's shoulders jerked and hunched, his body primed to shift. It was a hard fight to push back. The tendons on his arms stretched and his feet arched off of the ground seconds before he slammed his full weight back on the tile. He huffed and grunted, relaxing only when he felt his human form settle back into place.

That's when Maddox finally decided to look up.

Hell.

No matter how many times Colt saw him like this, it always took him by surprise.

Maddox was a big man, standing a couple of inches taller than his younger brother and Colt was no slouch. But the pounds fell away from him the first year in the Cage and he never managed to gain many back. He looked older than his thirty years, his skin paler than its normal tanned hue, his hollow face creased with worry and despair. His once vibrant eyes were dull, as were his blunt human teeth.

His face was expressionless, as if at first he didn't recognize his visitor, then he couldn't be bothered when he did.

"Oh. It's you again." Maddox's brow furrowed. "Hang on. It hasn't been a month yet, has it?"

Colt kept his hands curled into his fists at his side as he shook his head. His damn near miraculous discovery couldn't have come at a better time. Maddox might not have chosen to be put down after the accident. The result would end up being the same since the Cage sure as hell was killing his brother.

Maddox huffed. "Didn't think so."

His voice was hoarse and listless. That wasn't new. It was all part of the sad, sorry routine. Maddox went through the motions during Colt's monthly visits, knowing that as soon as he did, Colt would leave him alone to his misery.

Since he lost his mate, that was all he had left—or wanted.

Not for the first time, Colt was grateful he hadn't found the one woman meant for him. If this was what he had to look forward to if he ever lost her, he'd much rather never find her in the first place.

"The pack all right?" Maddox asked. Just like he always asked. At least he still cared that much.

"Pack's fine."

"Dad okay?"

He didn't bother wasting any words to ask after their mother. Both brothers understood that, so long as their father was still kicking, Sarah Wolfe was safe and sound. The day something happened to her, they'd be digging two graves.

"Old bastard's still hanging in there," Colt said with a hint of a wistful smile.

Their father was the most ornery old bastard he knew, but his wolf was undefeated. He wasn't kidding when he said Terrence Wolfe was hanging in there. Colt believed his father lived on spite and the desire to kick ass until his oldest son was back with the pack. Once that happened, Terrence could finally step down to retire someplace remote and wooded with his mate.

Every predatory shifter in the state knew that Maddox was supposed to be the pack's next Alpha... only he couldn't do that while he was stuck in the Cage. Enterprising shifters had tried to challenge Terrence and failed. Their father decided three years ago that he would lead the pack until he died or Maddox got out. Up until that morning, Colt didn't see either of those things happening any time soon.

But now—

That wiped the smile off of Colt's face. "Listen to me, Maddox. I... look. There's no easy way to say this so I'm gonna just spit it out. Okay?"

When he received a listless shrug for an answer, Colt realized that that was the best he was going to get. He took a second to brace himself. On a shudder, he said, "I've come about Evangeline."

Maddox stiffened, strung as tight as tension wire. It

was a knee-jerk reaction whenever someone dared to say her name out loud. Colt knew that well.

At least he had his brother's attention now.

"What about her?"

The entire ride back to the Cage, Colt tried to figure out the best way to tell his brother what he had accidentally discovered. But he'd never been all that good with words, and he hated wasting time beating around the bush, so, in true Colton Wolfe fashion, he was honest, brash, and to the point.

"Your mate isn't dead."

And there it was. A sudden spark in his gold-colored eyes that said, no matter how deeply buried it was, the old Maddox was still in there somewhere.

Instinct hit Colt like a sledgehammer. He immediately lowered his gaze, watching the way Maddox's hands flexed and cracked. He subtly tilted his head to the right and offered his throat. Colt was an alpha wolf, damn it, and even he recognized the danger rolling off of his brother.

"Say that again," whispered Maddox.

"She's not dead." Colt purposely made his voice as gentle as possible. Rousing Maddox's beast, probably not the smartest plan. Sure, the collar kept him from shifting, and the Para-proof glass kept them separated.

Tell that to his whining wolf.

His brother's answer was halfway between a snort and a snarl. Flecks of spit dotted the glass when he snapped out, "Bullshit."

"I saw her myself this morning, then rushed here to make sure you knew first thing. And, let me tell you, she's got too much color to be a ghost. She's got a pulse. A scent. She's fucking alive."

A warning grumble started deep in Maddox's chest. "Stop lying to me."

Colt's wolf demanded he obey the Alpha's command. He was, though—he just needed to convince Maddox of that fact.

"You know I would never lie to you."

"No. What I *know* is that my Angie is dead. Gone. Trying to convince me otherwise is an insult to her memory and to me. Now get the fuck out of here before I make you. And if you know what's good for you, don't come back."

Colt bristled. Okay. Sure. He knew this wouldn't be easy. It still stung that Maddox thought him capable of lying about *this*.

Trying hard to hold onto his temper, he stayed where he was. Until Maddox got it through his thick head—or Bennett returned to drag him out—Colt wasn't going anywhere.

"It's true," he insisted. "First I scented her, then I saw her—"

Maddox's growl raised in pitch.

"It's the Alpha damn truth!"

His brother snapped his pathetic human teeth. "Don't make me tell you again."

Colt sank down onto the stool opposite of his

brother. Though he was careful not to make any eye contact that could be taken as a challenge, he wanted Maddox to see his earnestness. "Listen to me. I wouldn't have come all the way back here and fucked with you like this if I wasn't a hundred percent positive it was her."

"She—"

"I can't explain it, I don't know what the hell is going on, but Evangeline is abso-fucking-lutely alive. You know I'm telling the truth. It's your mate, Maddox. You can trust me on this."

Colt poured as much sincerity into his words as he could. He didn't need to have a mate to understand that there were just some things you didn't screw around with.

The growl subsided at last. Colt dropped his gaze, waiting for Maddox to process the bombshell that had just gotten dropped on him. When enough time had passed and his brother was still eerily silent, Colt peered up through the thick fringe of his eyelashes, watching him through the glass. Maddox had to believe him. He *had* to.

It took a couple of tense minutes full of heavy breathing and wild eyes for Maddox to finally digest what Colt had said. In the end, he must have realized that Colt was probably the only one he *could* trust right now.

Maddox shook his head, the quiet broken up by a keening whine that escaped from the broken man on the other side of the glass. Colt understood, his own wolf anxious to answer his Alpha's mournful call.

Because if Colt wasn't lying... he could see the struggle play out on Maddox's weathered face.

"No... she... then that means—"

Colt exhaled roughly. "That your mate is out there. And she is. I swear it."

He didn't expect it to sink in right away. Colt might be a heartless bastard when it came to the idea of mates, but the bond he shared with Maddox was just as sacred. He could feel his brother's pain, and the blossoming hope that maybe the impossible had happened.

Three years was a long time to mourn and grieve; it wasn't easy to turn that off like a switch just because Colt had told him that Evangeline was miraculously still alive. But when he did understand, Colt expected Maddox to be anxious and happy and desperate to get back to his mate.

What he got instead was unbridled fury.

Before Colt could even react, Maddox surged to his feet, pounding the flats of his palms against the wards on the glass. Though it didn't shatter, the glass *did* shake which told Colt that Maddox was even angrier than that. Rage spilled out of him like fire. Unwilling to pour any gas on it, Colt got up from his stool and took a hesitant step away.

"What the—"

"Fuck me!" Maddox roared. He smashed at the glass again.

Colt jumped back, landing in a crouch, sparing a glance behind him before facing the obvious threat in front of him. He expected one of the Cage cops to barge in at any second. He couldn't have that. If he didn't calm Maddox down, his brother might be tranqed.

Remembering the silver bullets in Bennett's gun, Colt gulped.

"Mad, you gotta cool it," he cautioned.

"Cool it? How? She's not just out there, she's alone! My mate's all alone while I'm dicking around in here. Fuck me!"

The roar that tore out of his collared throat was completely animalistic, both a demand and a plea from Maddox's caged beast.

It finally dawned on the frantic shifter that smacking the glass partition wasn't getting him anywhere. Before Colt could cry out another warning, Maddox reached up and grabbed the silver collar around his neck. Colt immediately smelled the acrid stench of burning flesh as Maddox's fingers pried at the untreated silver that protected the collar. If his brother felt any pain, though, he didn't show it. He yanked and pulled and twisted as Colt howled at him to stop.

Where the fuck were the cops in this place? Forget the protection spell—too much exposure to the raw silver could kill Maddox.

He thought about all of the damn cameras covering this room. Someone had to be watching this scene with Colt as Maddox struggled with the collar on the opposite side of Para-proof glass. And there wasn't a damn thing Colt could do to stop him.

It wasn't until Maddox burned away nearly all of the skin from his fingers and his palms that his rage finally ran out and he seemed to give up. Knees buckling as he toppled over, he barely landed on the stool, panting heavily as his head hung in defeat.

Colt realized he was breathing just as hard, his claws digging deeply into his palms. Rivulets of blood dripped, dripped, dripped onto the pristine floor.

There wasn't a single mark on the fucking collar.

"That was stupid," Colt spat out harshly. He snuffled, trying to get rid of the stink. It didn't work. And that made him angrier—which only made him more reckless. What was Maddox thinking? "The power of that collar could've killed you. You're no good to Evangeline dead, Maddox. You *know* that."

Maddox kept his head bowed as he mumbled something.

Screw his enhanced shifter senses. All Colt could hear was the rush of blood in his ears and the erratic thrum of his heart.

"What?" he demanded.

Despite the power of the collar, when Maddox met Colt's fierce gaze, Colt was looking back into the glowing, golden gaze of Maddox's wolf. And that, more than anything else, calmed him.

Snarling, Maddox repeated himself —

"I said, get me the fuck out of here."

3

Evangeline Lewis was a creature of habit. She had to be. It was the only way she could hold on to her sanity.

Every morning her alarm went off at precisely 7:35 a.m. After she negotiated with it for another eighteen minutes—two complete snooze cycles—she shoved her covers back, stumbled into her bathroom, and took a piping hot shower.

On mornings when she slept soundly through the night, her shower was quick; ten minutes, tops. Then there were the flashbacks to her accident when she stayed underneath the spray until the water turned cold, hoping to finally rinse the lingering aches and pains and bad memories down the drain.

And then there were the mornings after *he* visited her dreams.

Evangeline had no idea who he was. The same tall,

dark, menacing figure had a starring role in her nighttime fantasies—and, she secretly admitted, they *were* fantasies. Despite how graphic and vivid those dreams were, she never saw his face. He was always hidden in the shadows.

The only things she ever remembered were a pair of glowing golden eyes and strong, calloused hands that were surprisingly gentle and amazingly wicked.

Those mornings? Nothing less than an ice-cold shower would cool her down before she could start her day.

After she was dressed and ready, she checked her e-mail and assessed her workload as she ate breakfast. If it was a light day, she gave herself until noon to take a walk around town and get any errands done; if she was coming up on a deadline, she made sure she was back at her apartment by eleven. Evangeline was new to Grayson, having only moved to the predominantly human community at the beginning of the spring. She was still finding her way around and enjoyed taking her daily walks around its small downtown area.

Evangeline was grateful to be able to work from home. She was an editor for a small publishing house, one who communicated mainly through e-mail. Her boss would shoot over the manuscripts she was assigned; so long as she finished her edits on time, no one cared where she did her work. It was such a change of pace from the hectic position she held at another agency before her accident. The sky-high office building in Woodbridge was always so frantic and busy. In Grayson, things seemed calmer.

Just what she needed.

Though there were quite a few leftovers from the accident—her dreams, a constant headache, the twinge in her right hip that wouldn't go away—her enjoyment for her work was the same as before. Evangeline lost herself in her edits for hours each day until 6:30 when she closed the lid on her laptop and made herself a quick dinner.

And it had to be quick. Because, at 7:00 every night like clockwork, Naomi Lewis called her daughter for her daily check-in and, as Evangeline learned a few months ago, if she didn't eat before that phone call, she wouldn't be eating at all.

Sometimes, she thought wryly, that was one part of her routine that made her question her sanity.

Evangeline knew her mother would call. She always did. If Evangeline didn't answer her the first time, she dialed twice more before she convinced herself that there was some sinister reason behind her daughter's silence. God forbid Naomi leave a message on Evangeline's voicemail, or wonder if perhaps her adult daughter was too busy to answer the phone.

It would never occur to her that Evangeline might be avoiding her, either. Oh no.

The first time Naomi had the police stop by for a welfare check, Evangeline learned it was much easier to grit her teeth, paste a fake smile on her face, and answer the phone whenever her mother called.

She was just finishing her plate of pasta when the phone rang that night. Without even looking to see who was calling, she answered as she always did.

"Hi, Mom. Yup, I'm still alive."

Naomi's soft sigh was the only sign that she didn't appreciate her daughter's morbid sense of humor.

Skipping over any pleasantries, she asked after Evangeline's day—though demanded might have been a better word for the rapid-fire questions she let loose in a barrage of well-meaning.

What did you do today? Where did you go? What did you eat?

If Evangeline's answers were satisfactory, Naomi would then move on to the heavy hitters.

Did you have any nightmares last night, honey? Any sudden headaches? What's today's date? I hate to ask, but you know Dr. Morris said that we have to... are there any new blanks in your memories?

And then, no matter how many times she said no, her mother always had to add one last question.

Are you ready to come home yet?

Evangeline played her part by telling her mother what she wanted to hear—whether it was the truth or not—in the hopes that it would get Naomi off the phone faster. Except for that last question.

She always said no. Even if her wards failed and something happened to her building, she would rather live in the woods than spend one more night living under her parents' roof. It had been a major blow to her pride to move back in after her accident. It took nearly three years before her mother and father agreed that she could live on her own again.

She would hold onto that scrap of independence with her teeth if that's what it took to keep it.

Naomi's obvious disappointment when Evangeline refused to consider moving back to East Windsor usually signaled the end of their phone conversation. She would suggest that perhaps Evangeline was tired and should head to bed. Desperate to end the conversation, she would agree.

Not that night, though.

"Oh, Eva, sweetie. Can't believe I almost forgot to mention it... guess who I saw the other day."

Evangeline winced at the nickname. She'd never liked it when she was younger, though she gave up trying to tell her mother that ages ago. "I don't know, Mom. Who?"

"Fiona's son. You remember him, don't you?"

Evangeline tightened her grip on her phone. She had to remember that, if the call suddenly died because she mangled her phone or "accidentally" smashed it, then she would only have about a ten minute head start before her mother sent the cops to come break down the door to her apartment. When they found her—and they would—after the cops dragged her kicking and screaming back to her mother, Naomi would still insist on this chat. She was certain of it.

Better to get it over with now.

"You saw Adam?"

You remember him, don't you?

The Wrights had lived down the street in the neighborhood where Evangeline grew up. Like Evangeline, Adam Wright was an only child. They were the same age and, since their mothers liked to drink coffee together and gossip, it was inevitable that they would be friends.

At least, that's what Naomi used to call him. Eva's little friend. Ha. To Evangeline, Adam Wright was a terror with an angel's smile.

When they were in elementary school, Adam got a kick out of chasing her on the playground, pulling her pigtails, even trying to get a peek at what was under her skirt, all while she squealed and ducked away before throwing rocks at him.

In middle school, Adam was the most popular boy in their class; dark blond hair, warm brown eyes, and an innocently handsome face made him a hit with the teachers and the hormonal teen girls who all scribbled Mrs. Wright on their binders. Evangeline didn't fall for it. Even so, he was her first kiss during an awkward game of spin the bottle, and Adam never let her forget it.

By the time they were in high school, both of their mothers had this brilliant idea that the two of them were meant to be. Evangeline—who, even at seventeen, scoffed at the idea of fate—gave in to her mother's not-so-subtle hinting and went on a few dates with Adam. They only lasted until she got wind of a reputation that Adam tried desperately to hide from her.

He had the angelic face, the innocent expression down pat. It was Evangeline, though, who was the naive one of the pair. When she listened to the gossip in the girl's room, she realized that Adam was only after one thing. Since she didn't want to be just another conquest for him, she broke things off.

In the years since, Adam had tried countless times to get her to change her mind. She refused. She wouldn't let him try to charm her again—and charm was the right word for it. Adam might have sworn he was as human as they come, but sometimes she wondered if he had a little witch blood in him. He could be too persuasive. There was a reason she hadn't seen him in ages.

How many years now? Not since her accident, and that was three years ago. Four? Maybe five? That sounded about right.

Did she remember him, though? Evangeline stifled a snort. How could she forget?

"I did. He asked about you."

She was sure he did. "That's nice."

If Naomi heard the edge in Evangeline's voice to drop it, she pretended she didn't. Like a bulldozer, she still kept coming, ready to knock over everything in her path.

"He's been getting updates on your... mm... your progress from Fiona. They're very worried about you."

"Tell them I'm fine."

"I did. Both Adam and his mother were glad to hear it. And then he asked if you were seeing anyone."

And there it was.

Evangeline could've guessed it was coming. The carefully stated comment still made her stomach drop.

She loved her mother. She really did. But it was hard to remember *why* exactly when Naomi started to meddle. Was she seeing anyone? No. Her mother knew that, too. And since Evangeline hadn't been on a date since long before her accident, it wasn't even as if she could blame her reaction on the crash.

Because there *was* a reaction.

Her stomach tightened. She wasn't surprised and she couldn't control it. It happened every time someone asked her why she was still single, or whenever her mother started to matchmake again. She couldn't explain it—especially not to Naomi—but just the idea of talking to a man, spending time alone with him in an intimate setting... it made her feel like she was going to hurl.

Seriously.

There was a twist in her gut, a burn in the back of her throat, and a shaky feeling that always came over her. Dating? Yeah. Not gonna happen. Even if it was only catching up, even if she'd known the guy since kindergarten, it didn't matter. It filled her with a dread that was irrational.

She blamed it on the accident. It left her so many different shades of messed up that it was easy to fault the crash and her recovery for how much she had changed over the last three years.

Swallowing roughly, Evangeline knew she had to say something. "Mom—"

"Of course I told him you weren't. He could hardly believe it, pretty girl like you still unattached. You should have seen the look on his face. You know, I think he's still harboring that little crush on you."

"Mom," she tried again, with a touch more urgency this time. "I really don't—"

Naomi continued as if she didn't hear her. "You would enjoy yourself, Eva. Fiona is always raving about what a good boy Adam is."

Adam was a grown man. Maybe he'd matured as he hit his late twenties, grew out of his womanizing ways. Evangeline doubted it. In her opinion, Adam hadn't been a "good boy" since the time he tried to talk her into losing her virginity in the darkroom during senior year photography. Ten years ago, she got him to back off by splashing him with stop bath. Had he changed all that much since then?

Her mother seemed to think so.

"—and, you know, he's made something of himself.

He's constantly moving up in that job of his. Fiona tells me he's due for another promotion soon."

That caught Evangeline's attention. "Wait a sec, Mom. Doesn't he… didn't you tell me not too long ago that he works at one of the Cages?"

Cage. Technically that wasn't the politically correct term for the magic-free prisons created for dangerous paranormals—that would be "voluntary incarceration facility"—but "Cage" was what most everyone called them since a majority of the inmates were animal shifters who were kept locked away because they weren't tame enough to be allowed on the loose. It wasn't nice. It wasn't fair. Still, even Evangeline had to admit it fit.

She didn't mind the Paras. She had no reason to. When she was a little girl, her best friend had been an untrained witch with the loveliest lilac eyes. Some of Evangeline's fondest memories involved all of the trouble two girls could get into when magic was involved.

It was a shame that their friendship didn't last. Once they graduated to middle school, Morgan was sent to a Para academy to learn to control her powers and Evangeline—at her parents' insistence—attended a local human-only private school.

If she was being honest? Though she got along with humans and Paras alike, there was one race of paranormals that… that just made her nervous.

Shifters.

And it wasn't because each of the shifters walked around with some kind of animal inside of them that could spring out without a moment's notice.

It was the whole 'mates' thing.

Everyone—human or not—knew all about how certain Para races believed in fated mates. It was the whole basis behind the Bond Laws that got passed right after the world learned that the paranormal races had always existed alongside the humans.

But shifters? They were the worst. Supposedly a shifter could tell their mate from one single sniff.

What kind of shit was that?

Seriously. What about the chosen mate? They could have a job, a life, even another family that maybe wasn't touched by magic, but was just as important. Didn't matter, according to the shifters. Fate chooses— which meant that, a lot of the times, the partners didn't get to.

That bothered Evangeline, even more now. She shuddered. There had been so many things that were out of her control lately. Fated mates? Lifelong bonds? Nope. Just the idea that she might have no say in who she would spend the rest of her life with made her want to hole up in her apartment and never leave.

After everything she had gone through these last three years, Evangeline was done with letting anyone else make decisions for her.

Even her well-meaning mother.

Naomi was still talking. Evangeline realized that

she was trying to explain how respectable it was to be a police officer doing his year's time as a Para prison guard. Great. So her mother hadn't given up on convincing her that she should give Adam a shot.

With a softly murmured, "Mom," she finally managed to interrupt her mother's pleasant voice.

"He— oh, Eva? Did you say something?"

"Didn't we decide that it was time for me to try living on my own?"

"Well, yes—"

"And shouldn't that mean that it's up to me to decide if I'm ready to date again or not?"

"Of course," Naomi said, "but I—"

"I haven't talked to Adam in years. Is there a reason why you're suddenly throwing him at me now? If I wanted to go out on a date, I could. I'm happy, Mom, or at least I'm getting there. Where is this coming from?"

Naomi let out a soft sigh. Evangeline, sensing victory, tightened her grip on her cell phone and waited.

"I know, sweetie. It's just... I worry about you. Me and your dad both do. It's been a long, hard road, watching you recover yourself. You've started working again and you've moved out on your own. You're moving on. And Fiona made it seem as if he was just waiting for you to get to this point before he tried reconnecting with you again. I thought Adam might be... oh, I don't know. I'm sorry, Eva. I won't mention it again. Promise."

Evangeline closed her eyes briefly.

Oh. Her mother was *good*. Because, if her recovery had been hard on Evangeline, it was pure hell for her parents. She'd come so close to death—no one even really knew how she survived the crash as it was—and her parents seemed to blame themselves from the moment she woke up in the hospital. They were with her every step of the way, ready and willing to support her if she even looked like she might stumble.

So maybe her mother was telling the truth. Maybe Naomi was just trying to be helpful. On the flip side, Evangeline would do just about *anything* to satisfy her mother.

Even break a promise to her seventeen-year-old self.

Screw it. What was one more date with Adam Wright?

"Okay," she said. She'd hate herself in the morning, but if it made her mother happy... "Okay. You know what, Mom? I'm free next week. If you think it's a good idea, pass my new number on to Adam. We'll see what happens then. Alright?"

And maybe, if she was still drowning in guilt, she might actually answer the phone.

But there was no way that Evangeline was going to let him into her pants—or, she knew with a certainty she couldn't explain, her heart.

4

Naomi worked quick.

It hadn't even been a half an hour after Evangeline finally got her mother off of the phone that it rang again.

She stared at the screen, tempted to drop it in the toilet.

Oops, sorry, Mom.

Evangeline shook her head. No. It wouldn't work. Hell, now that she knew for sure that Adam was a cop, she wouldn't put it past her mother to send him over to check on her personally if she pointedly refused to answer this call.

Might as well get it over with.

She glanced at the screen again. The phone number was unfamiliar. She didn't recognize it and wasn't even a little surprised. The only contacts in her phone were her mother, her father, her primary care physician, and her boss. The area code was local, though.

Evangeline grimaced, took a deep breath, then swiped to answer her phone.

It was Adam.

Of course it was.

To her absolute surprise, the phone conversation was actually kind of nice. Although it had been years since the last time she spoke to Adam Wright, it wasn't awkward at all. It was like falling into an old rhythm, his deep voice washing over her, asking her how she was doing, telling her about what he was up to. And if it was obvious that Naomi had coached him? Evangeline let it slide.

He asked her about her new apartment, her new job, how many diamonds the local witch charged to create the wards for her. He pointedly avoided the topic of her accident, the memory lapse she suffered after the crash, or her long road to recovery. Adam was courteous, charming, and kind.

By the time he smoothly steered the conversation toward getting dinner some time, Evangeline was the one who boldly said, "How about tomorrow?"

She immediately regretted it. The words left a bad taste in her mouth, as if some part of her knew she shouldn't be making a date with this man. She swallowed roughly, shrugging off her discomfort.

Her mother was right. She deserved to be happy. Moving out to Grayson was only the first step toward a future she never thought she'd see again when she woke up in that hospital bed, the right side of her body nearly crushed and her poor memory full of holes.

She remembered Adam, at least.

It was a start.

Another point in his favor? Adam Wright was punctual. She was just pulling a pair of black flats out of her shoe closet the next evening when her buzzer went off. Glancing at the clock on her mantle, she nodded in approval.

Eight o'clock on the dot. Right on time.

Jamming one foot into her flat, then the next, Evangeline hobbled over to her intercom button and pressed it. "Yes?"

There was a crackle, and then: "Eva? Is that you?"

Her finger slipped off the button. Eva. She wished he hadn't used that name. If it was a choice between being called Evangeline or any shortened version of it, she'd always choose the full length of her name over being called Eva. Sure, her name was a mouthful, but Eva always made her think of some high-class chick with five-hundred-dollar shoes and a glass of white in her hand. She'd tried to go by Angie when she was younger—she definitely identified more as an Angie—but it had never stuck.

She let her mother get away with calling her Eva

because, well, that was her mom. Adam using it just felt weird. Then again, her stomach went queasy when she imagined his rich voice murmuring "Angie" through the intercom.

He wasn't supposed to do that, but hell if she could remember why.

No. Evangeline shook her head, letting her long, dark hair settle over her shoulder. Tonight wasn't going to be about the things she lost, the memories that had slipped away from her. It was about reconnecting, about new beginnings.

She jabbed the button with her thumb. "Yes. It's me. Adam?"

"That's right. Hey, look, I was gonna come on up and surprise you but your wards are crazy strong. I can't get past the second floor of the building. Do you think you can remove them for me?"

She rarely had visitors to her new apartment. She'd forgotten all about the wards. It was one of the two conditions her parents gave her before they felt comfortable letting her move out on her own again. Not only did they insist that she live in a predominantly human part of town, but her apartment had to be warded up the wazoo. If you weren't a Lewis, you weren't getting in unless Evangeline either let you in or had you coded to the wards.

Since she wasn't sure that Adam would be coming back, she didn't need to have him coded in. Dropping the wards for a few minutes would be enough.

"Sorry about that. Give me a second, okay?"

"Sure. No problem."

Now where did she put that stupid thing?

The last time she had lowered the wards was last week when she let the pizza delivery guy up—

Ah ha!

Evangeline hustled into the kitchen and pulled open her menu drawer. The small timer was tucked toward the front.

Gotcha.

The witch who set up the wards tried explaining the magic inherent to the spell to Evangeline. She said it was easy if you only knew how to tap into it; magic was a raw force with so much potential that you could make it do whatever you wanted to. All Evangeline had wanted was a strong set of wards to put her mother's mind at ease. But since she also didn't plan on giving away any of the precious shreds of freedom she'd managed to claw back, the witch gave her the timer. A flick of the wrist and the wards were down for as long as it took the sand to fall.

Evangeline turned the timer over and placed it on the mantle before heading back over to her intercom. "Okay," she said. "You have about ten minutes before the wards go up again."

Despite her apartment being on the sixth floor, Adam was knocking at her door in less than five. She fluffed her hair, checked to make sure that her sweater covered up the majority of her cleavage, and took a deep, calming breath. Then, with a smile as shaky as she suddenly felt, she opened the door.

And there he was.

"Come on in."

Adam took two steps into her apartment and froze. He stared at her long enough to make Evangeline feel even more uncomfortable—did she suddenly sprout a massive pimple in the middle of her forehead or something?—before he gave his head a clearing shake and grinned.

"Wow," he said, visibly stunned. "You look beautiful, Eva. Just like always."

Really? Because this whole thing had seemed wrong the more she thought about it, Evangeline had barely tried. A touch of mascara and some pink lip gloss, that was all. And her sweater looked like something she might have worn back in high school. At least she filled it out better now—a fact that Adam seemed to appreciate as his warm brown eyes lingered on her chest.

She was glad she went looking for her flats, though. At only an inch shy of six feet, there weren't many men she met tall enough that she could wear her heels around them without dwarfing them. Adam wasn't a small man by any means, but this was a flats-type of night out.

He looked good. Really good. Better than she expected, and more than she had hoped for. Evangeline figured his work as a police officer helped him with his muscular physique, and he wore his wavy blonde hair cut shorter than he used to when they were kids. When he smiled at her, she saw the dimple in his right cheek. That sure had been a panty-dropper for him growing up. She almost felt insulted that he dared use it on her the minute she let him into her apartment.

Lucky for him, he held a small box in his hands. A present. That fiendishly charming dimple was forgiven at once.

Adam must have caught the acquisitive glitter in her eyes because he chuckled. He jerked his chin at the box. "As you can see, I brought you a gift."

"You didn't have to," Evangeline told him. That didn't stop her from reaching for it with greedy hands.

"My mother taught me never to come calling on a lady without something to offer. I could've brought you flowers, but that seemed too easy. You deserved something special." His boyish grin sharpened, his dimple deepened, and Evangeline could feel her cheeks turning pink at the way he continued to stare. "Besides, I used to go to your birthday parties, Eva. You always got a kick out of a good present. Maybe, if you like mine, you won't make me wait ten more years for another date."

She had wondered if Adam would mention the few times they went out when they were in high school together. Choosing to ignore his comment—and just what he was implying—she busied herself with opening the small box. And, hey, if Adam wanted to call it a date, that was his business. As far as she was concerned, this was dinner. That was all.

That didn't mean she was going to turn his present away. Growing up an admittedly spoiled only child, Evangeline knew a bribe when she saw one. As she lifted the lid and peeked inside, she hoped it was a good one.

Nestled inside on a bed of cotton was a small violet bottle with a stylized glass rose as a stopper. Liquid sloshed back and forth as she gave it a little shake. In tiny, pale purple print, it said: *eau de parfum sorcière.*

"Perfume?"

"Yeah. The girl I bought it from guaranteed it."

Evangeline removed the stopper and sniffed. It was a soft perfume, some blend of vanilla, lilacs, and baby powder that seemed to calm her. It was exactly the sort of perfume she'd choose if she ever bothered to wear any.

"It's lovely, Adam. Thank you."

She was putting the stopper back in the bottle when he said, "Why don't you try it on?"

"What? Right now?"

He nodded. "Why not?"

Once again, Evangeline had a vaguely unsettled feeling in the pit of her stomach, as if there was some reason why she shouldn't. Shoving it aside, she shrugged her shoulders and dabbed some of the perfume onto her wrists.

"You know where else you should put some? Let me show you."

Then, before she could say no, Adam gently lifted the bottle out of her hand and, using his pointer finger as a stopper, sprinkled some of the perfume onto his skin. He stepped around her, scooping up her hair with one strong hand, settling it neatly over her shoulder. Once her neck was bare, Adam ran his finger along the back of it.

His touch was more like a caress, his voice gone impossibly deeper as he asked, "How's that feel?"

Evangeline stiffened, and not entirely because of his unsolicited touch. With Adam pressed up against her back, she felt enveloped by his scent. And it wasn't like he smelled bad. He didn't. He smelled like freshly clean male, a combination of his shampoo, his soap, and his strong cologne. But that was just it—it was too much, almost like he was trying to cover something up. Breathing him in, she couldn't shake the feeling that it was so, so wrong. She'd always liked a man who wore his musk proudly.

He had never—

The sharp, stabbing pain attacked her mid-thought. It was a pulsing migraine on steroids, ripping Evangeline from the present and throwing her into a silent, black void where the only things that existed were Evangeline and her agony.

It never lasted long—a few seconds at most—but it

felt like an eternity before she recovered enough to open her eyes again.

Adam had moved. He was in front of her now, his hands reaching out to her, his concerned face only inches away from her. His eyes were wide and worried; the brown almost looked hazel this close, the golden flecks a small reminder of the man who haunted her dreams.

Gold. *His* eyes were the most beautiful golden color. *He—*

The room started to spin. The pain reverberated against her skull, pulsing, pounding, aching. She was more prepared this time. Clenching her jaw, pushing through the worst of the pain, she waited until the sensation had passed again.

She didn't know how long he'd been calling her name. She figured that was the buzzing in the back of her head that abruptly stopped as soon as Adam saw that she was conscious and coherent.

He let out a sigh of relief, the rush of his breath tickling her nose. "You're okay. Tell me you're okay."

"I'm fine," she lied. If she hadn't been fine in years, he didn't need to know that. Besides, she could fake it. How else had she been able to convince her parents to let her live on her own? "I— wait. Am I on the floor? How did I get on the floor?"

"You started to drop," Adam told her, his voice wavering slightly. Her little spell had rattled him. "I didn't want you to get hurt so I brought us both to the floor."

It took her a second to focus beyond his worried gaze. Adam was kneeling in front of her and, yup, they were both on the ground. The perfume bottle—with its stopper back in place—lay on its side by his right boot. The lilac and vanilla blend seemed stronger now that it was on her skin, with Adam's scent lingering all around her.

Evangeline had the sudden urge to get far, far away from him. She started to sit up so that she could climb back to her feet. That was when she realized he was still holding onto her by her shoulders. As if he'd been touching her all of this time.

Okay. That was *too* close. She started to shake—even though she couldn't say why she did—and Adam's frightened expression came rushing back. He got to his feet, gently easing Evangeline up until she was standing again. He didn't let her get away, though. Tucking her into his side, he began to guide her further into her apartment.

"Come on, Eva, let's get you down on the couch before you start to faint again."

"I didn't faint," she protested weakly. Might have been more convincing if she didn't sound like she was about to pass out. "I'm alright. Please let go."

"When you're sitting, I will."

"I'm fine, Adam."

"It's okay. Listen, your mom said something about

how you used to get headaches. I'm not gonna push when you obviously don't feel well. We'll go out another time."

Adam managed to get her halfway across her living room before his words sank in. She shook his hands off of her, panic flaring up as the rest of the pain fled in its wake. "No, no. Not a headache, just a twinge. It's nothing to worry about."

They had to go out now, no matter how she felt. She'd never hear the end of it from her mother otherwise. And considering she'd told her parents, her therapist, and her doctors that the night terrors had stopped and she hadn't had a headache in months, she couldn't explain *why* she canceled. She could only hope that Adam forgot all about it by the time dinner was done. If he snitched... well, she knew her mother had her room waiting for her. If Naomi ever discovered the extent of her fudging the truth, she'd be moving back home before she had time to blink.

That settled it. She was going out with him if it killed her.

"Hey," she added, skirting around him when he tried to reach for her again. The adrenaline shook off the last of the pain, making her alert and determined. "I'm dressed, it took me half an hour to find my shoes earlier, and now you've got me wearing fancy perfume. You promised me dinner, Adam. I won't let you take it back now."

Evangeline held her breath as she waited for his

answer. His brow was furrowed in a concern she wished he didn't feel, but a few seconds later his lips quirked up into an amused grin. "I did promise, didn't I?"

It took everything she had not to let her breath out in a rush of relief. "You did."

"And you're sure you're feeling up to it?"

Evangeline could barely remember what had brought the headache on so suddenly in the first place. Of course, that was the problem. They said the strange holes in her memory would close up in time. Eventually she would learn her triggers and be able to avoid them.

She was sick and tired of waiting.

She was sick and tired of feeling all alone.

Adam Wright wasn't the man in her dream. Still, he would do.

"Are you trying to get out of dinner?" she dared him.

"I wouldn't dream of it, Eva."

"Then let's go."

And when Adam dared to place his hand on Evangeline's shoulder again to help her into the hallway, she let it stay there.

Even if she really, really wanted to shove it off.

5

It took more than a month before Maddox was finally released from the Cage.

As his brother so eloquently put it during one of their now weekly meetings: *voluntary incarceration, my hairy ass*. If it wasn't for Colton's testimony that he was the one who scented Evangeline first, then actually saw her with his own two eyes, Maddox doubted they would have even *had* a hearing.

Even more notably, Colt managed to rein in his wolf throughout the hours-long process, biting back his snarls as he told his story over and over again to the board. They brought in a witch to test him, to see if Colt was telling the truth. Colt passed with flying colors.

Bureaucracy was bitch, though. So what if Colt's testimony proved that there was no reason why Maddox deserved to be locked up? It took weeks to cut through the red tape before Bennett finally got the okay to remove the silver collar from around Maddox's throat. Once the veteran guard escorted him back to the outside, Maddox had only one goal in mind.

Find his mate.

It broke his fucking heart that doing so wasn't going to be as easy as it should've been. Ever since he found out that she was still alive—that, for the first time in years, there was *hope*—Maddox expected some part of his bond to come back.

It, uh, it hadn't.

After the accident, their mate bond had been razor-sharp, both jagged and raw from where he believed her death had severed it. And while he refused to let any of the prison's witches try to take it from him, he had buried it deep down inside of him as he suffered all alone in the Cage.

The remnants of their bond were all he had left of Evangeline—of his Angie—and he treasured it. No doubt about that. But it was too painful to experience around the clock, and he tucked it deep where he could hide it and kept it close without being reminded that it was abruptly broken when she died.

Only she wasn't dead. And now that he needed it? It was impossible to recall it. It was almost as if it was gone. It wasn't, he could still sense it tucked away, but there was no way he could use their missing bond to lead him to where his defiantly *not dead* mate was living without him.

When Maddox admitted that to Colt during one of their last visits before the board hearing, his brother told him not to worry. That, as soon as Maddox saw Evangeline again, the bond would return. It had to. Maddox and Evangeline were fated mates who developed a bond over a year's courtship. They might not have been formally bonded, and he'd forever regret not claiming her for his wolf when he had the chance, but the bond was there.

Don't worry?

Ha.

Maddox didn't just worry about their muffled bond—he *obsessed* over it. It was the only lead he would have when he got out and Colt knew it. That's why his brother tried to track her down before Maddox's release. The way Colt figured it, if he dragged Evangeline to the magic-free prison, even the stubborn board couldn't deny Maddox his freedom.

One problem, though. And it was a biggie.

Evangeline was gone.

Colt had gone back twice to the place where he spotted Evangeline and found no sign of her. Her earlier trail was too muddied to follow and Colt couldn't find a hint of her soft vanilla scent anywhere nearby. It was as if she had disappeared in the time since he first scented her. Colt might not have been all that attuned to Evangeline's scent—she wasn't his mate, after all—but he remembered it vividly from the times when she was his brother's mate. Colt's wolf had some of the strongest senses of the pack. If he couldn't track her, that was a big fucking problem.

Not only that, but Colt had to resort to using human tech to search for her. No luck there, either. Her phone number had long been disconnected. The house she grew up in? It had been bought by a newlywed couple more than two years ago. When he asked, they couldn't offer any information on the Lewises except for a forwarding address that was another dead end when Colt chased it down.

Evangeline Lewis hadn't just disappeared after the car crash that supposedly killed her; it was like she didn't exist at all. True, Colt hadn't found an obituary for her anywhere online, but Maddox's mate didn't have *any* social media presence. No facebook, no twitter, nothing. If she was hiding, she was doing a damn good job at it.

But *why* was she hiding?

It was obvious that Colton had his suspicions. He refused to acknowledge them, though, and would change the subject whenever Maddox brought it up. Considering how Maddox nearly bit his head off when Colt told him she was missing, he didn't blame his brother for evading the topic.

After a couple of tense visits, Maddox stopped talking about it, focusing all of his energy instead on getting out. All he was doing was torturing himself while he was still trapped in the Cage and, eventually, it didn't matter. Both of the Wolfe brothers knew that, despite whatever had happened to sever it in the first place, as soon as the mate bond snapped back into place, Evangeline would never want to leave Maddox's side again.

Of course, that meant nothing until he managed to find her again.

So, fresh out of the Cage and without his mating instincts or a fully formed bond to guide him to her, Maddox had to do something no self-respecting bonded shifter ever wanted to do: he had to ask for outside help in finding his mate.

There was only one place that would be authorized to help him.

He groaned just thinking about it.

If you thought the D.M.V. was bad, you'd obviously never been to the D.P.R. Short for the Department of Paranormal Registration, the D.P.R. was a government-run agency that kept track of all blood bonds, matings, and claimings, issued and regulated Paranormal I.D.s, officially changed a ghost's birth certificate into a death certificate... basically, if, as a Para, there was something that you had to take care of, the D.P.R. was where you went to do it.

You just better make sure you have all day to spend there.

Once he walked inside the sterile building with its plastic chairs and warded glass enclosure, all Maddox wanted to do was grab one of the D.P.R. workers and have them use their fancy computers to give him Evangeline's address. He knew it wasn't going to be as easy as that, but he hadn't been prepared for all of the administrative bullshit.

It was almost enough to make him homesick for his cell.

First, while attempting to sign in with the receptionist, Maddox discovered that he no longer had a valid P.I.D. Before he could even ask about Evangeline, he was sent to Window C with a stack of paperwork about two inches thick. He struggled to answer the increasingly ridiculous and invasive questions—how the hell was he supposed to know how old his grandfather had been during his first shift?—and finally just started to jot down the first thing that popped in his head, accurate or not.

After he was done, he was off to Window A, where they snapped his picture and created his Paranormal I.D. The Maddox glaring back from the stupid piece of plastic looked pissed off. Pretty spot on. His mood only worsened from there on out.

Window H was next. The woman perched at that counter gobbled him up like he was a piece of candy. There was a come hither look in her big blue eyes that made Maddox's wolf sit up and snarl because they weren't Evangeline's forest green shade. This woman wasn't his, and his wolf took the arousal it scented through the thick glass shield separating him and the D.P.R. worker as an insult.

Once he wrangled his beast back, he managed to explain his situation through clenched teeth while she listened *too* attentively to his request. The blonde leaned forward, pushing her breasts up high as she crossed her arms right beneath them. Maddox could feel her lust like an oil slick coating his fur. He shook it off, reminding himself that this woman might be able to help him find Evangeline.

She was interested in what he had to say for the first few minutes, only to cut him off when he mentioned that he was a shifter looking for information on his missing mate. Which she would have known if she asked to see his P.I.D but, after the time he spent getting that squared away, not one damn person asked to see it. Almost ruefully, she sent him off to Window F. He loped away from her window, his wolf yipping at him to put some distance between the pheromones coming off of the woman.

After waiting over an hour for the pointy-faced man at Window F, Maddox walked up and opened his mouth—then never even got the chance to say a single word. The little man looked him over, swallowed loudly, and shook his head. His beady eyes were locked on Maddox's bared teeth.

Maybe it wasn't the smartest idea to show this clerk his sharp fangs. He'd admit that. But he couldn't help it. The weasely man's whole countenance shouted 'prey' and the predator in Maddox responded.

"Window B," the man squeaked out, pointing at a window across the crowded room. "Next!"

Maddox knew a dismissal when he saw one. Plus, the reek of the man's fear was even worse than the blatant way the human female at the other window had openly lusted after him. With a dirty look that caused the clerk to tremble noticeably, Maddox stormed his way back over to the first bank of windows.

At least fifteen others were leading up to Window B, a motley mix of shifters and vampires waiting anxiously. One sniff told him that his wolf was the most dominant animal in line. Too bad pack didn't mean nothing when it came to bureaucracy; no matter how badly he wanted to bully his way to the front of the line, he couldn't.

Even worse, with so many vampires nearby, the tangy rust of blood and dead meat assaulted his senses —a bloodsucker's scent both tantalizing and repulsive to a shifter—and he was forced to breathe shallowly through his mouth before he gave in to his instincts at last, wolfed out, and attacked.

There was at least another hour's wait ahead of him. His wolf let out a long, mournful howl and, honestly, Maddox didn't blame the beast one bit.

. . .

"Next."

Maddox realized with a start that it was finally —*finally*—his turn. He took a step forward, then watched as some smarmy vampire tried to cut in front of him. Oh, *hell* no. It didn't matter that he was dealing with a more docile Dayborn instead of a ferocious Nightwalker, he reacted the same: with a deafening snarl that left spit on the vampire's smooth alabaster cheek. The vampire hissed, wiped the spit away with the back of his hand, and bared his fangs in warning at Maddox.

But when Maddox lunged forward, the bloodsucker took a hurried step back. Maddox didn't even blink. The vampire's fangs were only half an inch long. A mere fledgling. He wasn't even worth a second look as Maddox stalked over to the open station and the bored human standing behind the glass partition.

At least, the human male had looked bored before the shifter appeared before him. The second he got an eyeful of Maddox, his eyes widened and he gulped. Now he just looked alarmed.

Maddox resisted the urge to snarl at the clerk, too. Not another one. This was the fourth line they had sent him to and each of the D.P.R. workers acted as if they'd never served a Para before. This clerk alone, in the last hour, had helped six vampires and nine shifters—one of which was a fucking bear. Was his wolf that scary? Shit.

He huffed and waited for the human to regain his

composure. As long as the Ant didn't ship him off to another line like the last one, Maddox could spare a few more seconds before he said fuck it and let his wolf take over, screw the consequences.

Would it have killed them to have a worker who didn't flinch every time a dominant Para approached a window?

The D.P.R. tended to hire Ants because, as they discovered shortly after its inception, there was something about the menial tasks, the paperwork, and the tedium that just called to human workers. Sometimes the agency would make a mistake and hire a Para, but after the last time a witch got frustrated and blasted a Para civilian who complained about their P.I.D., they secretly adopted a very pro-human hiring policy. Normally that wouldn't bother him. But his patience had worn thin the instant he walked into the D.P.R. and now he was seconds away from losing it.

A month back, Colton's news had caused a drastic change in Maddox. It didn't matter that he couldn't sense Evangeline yet, just knowing she was out there was enough for the moment. His appetite came back triple-fold—and, for a shifter, that was saying something—and his boundless energy made him manic, considering he couldn't give his beast free rein. While he was still in the Cage, the warden gave orders that he had to wear the silver collar, but the urge to bust out into fur and claws and break free simply manifested itself in another way. He exercised. He ran laps and lifted weights. He did sit-ups until he fell asleep and woke up in a push-up stance. In the cozy darkness of their bedroom, Evangeline always loved to run her hands along his defined muscles as she murmured how hard he felt. She already owned him, heart and soul. He wanted to give his body back to her, too.

Maddox had to admit that he probably looked better now than he had at any point in the last three years. Taller, stronger, and deadlier. There was no denying he was a powerful alpha shifter who would stop at nothing to get what he wanted.

No wonder the Ant on the other side of the counter was staring at him in ill-disguised terror. That's how humans always seemed to react whenever they had seen him with Evangeline. Looked like he was going to have to get used to that all over again. Fine. It was a miniscule price to pay to have his mate back—even if he was finding it kind of hard not to spring at the glass and watch this Ant piss his pants.

Maddox had to give this clerk credit since he did recover much faster than the others. He didn't quite resume his bored expression—Maddox could feel the tension that surrounded him even through the enchanted glass—but he sounded like a true professional as he actually attempted to help Maddox.

Hallelujah, he had found the right window at last.

6

"Name? Last name first, please."

"Wolfe, Maddox. Two 'd's, one 'x'. There's an 'e' at the end of Wolfe."

The clerk turned to look at the screen in front of him. It was positioned so that, even with Maddox's shifter eyesight, he couldn't see a damn thing. There was the fierce tapping of keys and then a brisk nod.

"Thank you, Mr. Wolfe. Now what can I do for you?"

"They told me that this was the window to ask about mates. Is that right? Because I'm beginning to think someone's giving me the runaround here."

"Hmm... okay." The clerk tapped his computer screen, his lips moving as he read something to himself, then pressed a couple of more keys. An instant later, he frowned. "That's interesting. I think I see what's going on here."

"What's interesting?" The air suddenly shifted and Maddox tensed. The human wasn't so much afraid as he was suddenly very, very anxious. "What's going on?"

The clerk pretended not to hear Maddox's demand. "What was the name of your mate?"

Was. Maddox didn't like the sound of that. There must have been something about his three-year incarceration or the *Claws Clause* on that screen.

"Her name's Evangeline Lewis."

The clerk looked up from his computer. "*Her* first name is *Lewis*?"

"No— oh, that's right. Last name first. Sorry. It's Evangeline. Lewis, Evangeline. And Lewis is spelled L-E-W-I-S."

Maddox's wolf bristled as he spelled her name. He knew his other half was desperate to assert its claim on his mate and, before he thought better of it, he found himself adding, "It should be Wolfe, but she didn't get the chance to change it legally after we got hitched before..."

He let his gruff voice trail to a close as he thought back to that night three years ago. Of course she didn't. The car crashed the night they got married. One bad turn in a freak storm on their way to their honeymoon cabin. They never even got the chance to consummate their union, his wolf edgily reminded him, or finish the claiming.

That was something that would change as soon as he got his claws back into Evangeline.

He couldn't wait.

"Hmm..." More clacking. "Oh, I see. Let me just..." A tiny twitch above the clerk's right eye. More clacking. The stink of fear started to seep back into his scent. He kept glancing back over at Maddox, his eyes locked on Maddox's throat. "Okay. Hmm."

Maddox wasn't a patient shifter at the best of times. While he had more control over his wolf than most—including Colton and his notorious hair-trigger temper—there was no denying the fact that this Ant was, in his wolf's eyes, the only obstacle between him and his mate.

"Stop it with the damn 'hmm's, alright? Is she in there or not?"

"Can you verify her date of birth for me?"

If answering stupid questions got him to Evangeline quicker... "March 22nd. She just turned 27."

"Thank you, sir. If you'll just excuse me one moment."

The clerk abandoned his computer. Maddox braced his hands on the granite countertop, scowling as he was forced to wait. The enchanted glass that separated him from the D.P.R. workers was the same shit they used in the Cage which made the whole thing worse. It didn't matter that he was finally free again; he was free in name only. The trapped feeling still followed him, and his wolf whined. It wanted out almost as bad as it wanted Evangeline.

The clerk wasn't gone long and, when he returned,

he wasn't alone. He brought back with him a tall, stern woman with slicked iron-grey hair and eyes so dark they were nearly black. She could've been anywhere from forty to sixty and, from the look of disgust on her thin face, she hated everyone and everything for every single one of those years. She had the word 'supervisor' written all over her.

She spared Maddox a quick, dirty look, sniffed audibly, then followed her employee's point to something written on the computer screen. Turning sharply, she looked back at Maddox and, as the clerk had before, she narrowed her focus on Maddox's throat.

That's when he realized what all of the humans were staring at. He had worn a silver collar around his throat the entire three years he was in the Cage. When they finally removed it, he found out that they were full of it when they said that the treated side of the collar kept the silver from harming him—he just hadn't *felt* it as it ate into the skin around his neck. Reaching up, Maddox anxiously rubbed the raw patch of ruined skin where the collar had left its mark. Thanks to the silver, that was one injury that would never heal. Anyone who saw the scars knew exactly why he had them.

The Ants didn't need a computer to tell them that he'd been in the Cage. Maddox was all the proof they needed. No wonder he alarmed them all. They probably expected him to go rabid at any moment.

And, he admitted to himself, they weren't wrong.

The supervisor turned back to the computer screen. She hit a couple of keys, peered closely at the screen, then pressed the enter button. Maddox's hackles rose as a tiny glint of satisfaction lightened her expression. Something told him that meant bad news for him.

"What's going on?" His stomach tightened as the old familiar weight of despair settled back into place. Maybe Colt was wrong. Maybe the warden made a mistake and Evangeline was…

He shook his head and gripped the countertop in front of him again. "Is it Evangeline? Is something wrong?"

"That, *sir*, is none of your business."

Could she have sounded any snider if she tried? He doubted it. "She's my mate. Everything about her is my business."

"That's where you're wrong. According to our database, Ms. Lewis is listed as one hundred percent human. She's never bonded with any paranormal. At least," the supervisor added, and there was the smallest of smiles as she did, "not officially."

Screw despair. This was absolute panic. Maddox caught his outraged howl just in time, though his fingers flexed and he gripped the edge of the countertop with all of his strength. The granite was no match for a furious shifter. With a loud *crack*, the edge shattered as if it was made of clay, rubble and sand and broken bits of counter falling at his feet.

Was she fucking serious?

Three years ago not one damned soul gave a shit that they had never visited the local Bumptown to get a stupid piece of paper signed. After the accident, it was clear to everyone that he was both a bonded male and highly unstable without Evangeline so they immediately invoked the *Claws Clause*. As soon as the human cops got word that she was DOA at the hospital, Maddox was given his three choices: life in a voluntary incarceration facility; he could undergo a mystical lobotomy that would rip Evangeline from his soul; or be put down like the animal they clearly thought he was.

No one ever asked him to see their bonding license when they were cuffing him in silver and transporting him to the Cage.

Now though, now that he had discovered the truth —the impossible, glorious truth—that damn piece of paper was everything. No bond, no rights. That's what this Ant was telling him. All because of the ridiculous *Claws Clause*.

No fucking way.

"She's my mate," Maddox said, pushing away from the damaged counter before he broke off the rest of it. "You have to tell me where to find her."

"Actually," the supervisor shot back, "we don't." There was a finality to her tone that told him he could argue until the moon turned blue and she still wasn't budging. "Franklin, please explain to this…

gentleman how the bonding laws work. Quickly now, we have a line to get through before we break for lunch." She turned her nose up at Maddox and waved her hand at the mess. "And make sure to take his information. We *will* be sending him a bill for repairs to the counter."

The clerk, Franklin, waited for the woman to walk away before he leaned in. Though he lowered his voice, Maddox picked up every word through the haze of his denial. "Sorry about that. Unfortunately, she's right. Agency's a real stickler when it comes to the Bond Laws."

The *Claws Clause*. If he ever came face to face with the lawmakers who made up those ridiculous laws, he'd love to show them how much damage a real pair of claws could do. Because that damn ordinance had done a number on him. He figured he could return the favor.

Maddox kicked roughly at the mess at his feet. He had to make him understand. "I don't care if she's right. I just want to know where my mate is and get her back."

"I wish I could tell you, but... look, between you and me, I get it. I really do. I've had girls run out on me before, too. It sucks. But if this ex of yours found a way to get out before the two of you actually bonded, there had to be a reason."

No, Maddox thought as he shook his head. Not his Evangeline. She loved him. She married him. Before the accident ripped her away from him, they couldn't have been more bonded—

"She didn't want to go anywhere before the crash. We were already bonded," he snapped through gritted teeth. His gums began to burn, his fangs begging to lengthen again, before he forced his change back. He had to. More ridiculous laws for Paras to follow. Just like vampires weren't allowed to bite in public and witches couldn't cast spells within twenty-five feet of public buildings, there wasn't any unauthorized shifting allowed within a federal facility. "She's *mine*."

The clerk flinched—based on the way his vocal cords stretched and his voice sounded like gravel, Maddox could only imagine the distortion of his features locked in the beginning stages of a shift—but refused to back down. If Maddox wasn't so frustrated, he might have been impressed.

"Not according to the government, she isn't. Our records are foolproof and you know the law, Mr. Wolfe. Without the bonding license, you can't invoke any of the clauses in Ordinance 7304. I can't give you any further information on Ms. Lewis. There's simply nothing else I can do for you in that regard. Please don't make me get my boss again."

"Mrs. Wolfe," he growled out. The words were almost unintelligible, slurred out behind an overlarge tongue and a set of canine fangs. He'd lost the battle with his teeth the instant the clerk used Evangeline's maiden name. Let them fine him for losing control. He didn't care. "The second I get the bonding license signed, she's changing her fucking name. I promise you that."

"So you say, sir. Just remember that you can't actually force anyone to be bonded to you."

Maddox didn't even dignify that with a response. He let the flash of his wolf's glare and a hint of fang let the clerk know that he'd gone too far with that last comment. He wouldn't have to force his mate to do anything as soon as the bond snapped back into place and anyone who knew anything about the mating instinct knew that.

This time, when the clerk flinched again, Maddox knew he rattled the poor Ant. A wave of sudden terror hit Maddox in the snout, burning the inside of his nose. Okay, Maddox allowed, watching as poor Franklin pushed his chair back away from his station, called out that he was going to the bathroom, then scurried away. Maybe he might have shifted a little more than he thought he had.

Whoops.

Biting back his frustrated growl, Maddox took a deep breath and forced his features to return to normal. Then, because there were no other windows he could go to and no one left to help him at the D.P.R., he left. He nearly slammed the door on his way out except he could tell the entrance's glass wasn't protected like the glass partitions. If the glass door shattered, he would have to pay for it. Bad enough he was already looking forward to a bill for the counter.

Wonderful.

Standing in front of the D.P.R., Maddox took stock of his situation. His bond was still eerily quiet, which meant he couldn't track down Evangeline on his own. The D.P.R. did jackshit for him. He had the clothes on his back, twenty bucks in his wallet, a brand spanking new P.I.D., and that was it—

Well, no, he admitted. That wasn't quite true. He had Colton, and while Maddox refused to let the rest of the pack know what was going on—including his parents—until he had formally claimed Evangeline entirely, he knew that Colt would help him with whatever he asked.

And it wasn't like the trip to the D.P.R. was a *complete* waste of time.

Evangeline was undeniably alive. He didn't realize how much he was harboring a quiet fear that Colt was wrong, that the warden and the prison board had made a mistake, until the clerk confirmed that she was, at the very least, still alive. Not married, not bonded, but breathing... he'd take it. It was some kind of closure.

And based on where Colt spotted her in the first place, he had a starting point. Fuck if he didn't have every little thing about her ingrained in his very soul. Maddox didn't actually *need* those bureaucrats to find her. He was just trying to be nice. Law-abiding. A fucking Ant.

But he wasn't an Ant. He was an alpha wolf shifter who was going to do whatever it took to track down his mate and revive their mating bond. Starting with going to the last place he knew she had been.

After he went to see Colt, that was. He'd refused Colt's offer to come pick him up when they finally let him out of the Cage. His brother had done enough already and Maddox needed to prove he could do something for himself.

Now, though?

Now he had no choice.

Maddox didn't have a vehicle of his own, not since the crash. He would have to borrow Colt's truck. And then, for the first time in three years, he'd have to climb behind the wheel again with the nightmare of his Angie's last screams still haunting him.

But he would do it.

For Evangeline, he would do anything.

7

Colton lived in a Bumptown about an hour's drive out from the Cage—or, in Maddox's current shape, close to a two-hour run.

Bumptowns were what you got when too many Paras settled close together. They were neither planned nor officially sanctioned; they just sort of happened. First a vampire would move in, then maybe a shifter family or a banshee, and boom! There went the neighborhood. Humans fled and Paras took the area over.

Just like Paras referred to human-only neighborhoods as Ant Farms, Paras found sanctuary in aptly named Bumptowns. Because that was where things went 'bump in the night'. Fucking humans.

Ah, well. At least it was better than Ant Farm.

The ruling government—the powers that be that supposedly controlled the entire population, both humans and paranormals—liked to think that there was a seamless blend of both factions in society so they turned a blind eye when Bumptowns sprang up. The closest they got to acknowledging them was by making sure each settlement had a delegate on-site to sign off on bonding licenses; after a while, they were the only places where you could find one. So, even if you were like Maddox, who chose to live in a cul de sac with both human and paranormal neighbors, you visited a Bumptown eventually. Because his brother insisted on living in one, Maddox actually visited Colt's Bumptown pretty regularly—at least, before his time in the Cage, he had.

Maddox had always felt uncomfortable heading into the strictly Para-only settlements. It was no secret that he was the more human-friendly wolf in his family, and it was no surprise when his mate turned out to be human herself. To him, the image of Bumptowns conjured up some idyllic scene of the different paranormal races living in peace together. What bullshit. Get too many predators living in close quarters and it was like a powder keg ready to explode. He would never expose his Evangeline to that.

Colton, on the other paw, seemed perfectly at ease living in the Bumptown. Though everyone who lived there was some sort of paranormal, even the residents chose to segregate themselves based on their kind. In Colt's settlement, the Dayborn vampires lived on Sunset Boulevard; the Nightwalkers hid out in the dark corner they called Little Transylvania. The ghosts haunted along Cemetery Row.

And the shifters? They built their houses on the edge of a 5,000 acre plot of federally protected woods, perfect for a shifter who wanted to burst out of their skin and just run free for a while without worrying about a backside full of buckshot. Due to the mix of predator and prey shifters who seemed to co-exist somewhat peacefully, that corner of the Bumptown was referred to as the Zoo. Maddox almost bust a blood vessel laughing the first time he found out.

Even now, even with all of the thoughts and worries warring in his head, he had to smirk to himself as he loped easily through the protected trees. The Zoo. Well, it made sense. What were shifters anyway if not their animal?

It had been three years since he last ran this trail. Not much had changed while he was in the Cage. Maddox caught a whiff here or there of several new predatory shifters on a tree or a bush, but he could tell that Colt was still the top Alpha in this Bumptown.

Maddox stopped only once to add his own marking. There was an old oak tree that he liked to visit whenever he made this run. Colt thought of these woods as part of his extended territory so he didn't overdo it. Just a little piss to show the rest of the Zoo that big brother was back before he ran through the trees and followed his nose to Colt's backyard.

When he was in his skin, Maddox recognized the

back of Colt's house by sight rather than relying on the power of scent. The wide wraparound porch, the weathered shingles that gave the two-story house a rustic feel, the piles of wood and stacks of lumber that Colt hoarded in case inspiration struck. In his fur, he followed his wolf's nose. And his brother marked his immediate territory with a fervor that had even Maddox's wolf thinking twice before breaching the border.

Deciding it might be better to approach Colt's den on two legs instead of four, Maddox spit out the bundle he was carrying securely between his teeth before crouching low in the dirt and preparing himself for the shift.

He'd heard his dad explain to an Ant once what shifting felt like. The human thought shifting must be painful, but Terrence described it more like a sting. Like a rubber band snap, he had said, where the anticipation of the shift was worse than any other part of it. That's why most shifters went full shift without thinking about it. It was partial shifts, or when a shifter was trying to hold the change back, that the sensation grew annoying. That, he explained, was more like an itch you couldn't scratch.

When Maddox was done, he stretched, arching his back and exhaling roughly as he chafed against the feel of his human skin. His wolf whimpered that his time out wasn't anywhere near long enough. After three years without a shift, his beast wanted to run for days reveling in the grass underfoot and the feel of the wind threading through his grey and white fur.

Later, he told his wolf. Evangeline first.

Mate first, his wolf agreed. There was only a hint of grumbling before the other part of himself curled up to wait. Without the mating bond for his instincts to follow, his beast knew that this was a job for the man's brain.

As soon as he was sure his wolf was calm—it would be pointless to dress right away if his wolf would burst through again, turning his clothes into tattered rags—he reached for the bag at his feet.

When he was out on a run, Maddox didn't usually bother carrying around a spare change of clothes like a pack mule. Shifters were too used to nudity to be bothered by mostly human concerns like modesty so long as there weren't any pesky Ants around waiting to cry out about indecent exposure. He couldn't tell you how many times he burst naked into Colton's house, only to remember later when he felt a breeze on his cock that he was sitting bare-assed naked on one of his brother's chairs.

Evangeline had tried to talk some modesty into him when they started sleeping together six months into their relationship. It hadn't worked. Maddox was a stubborn wolf who couldn't understand putting on clothes when he was going to have to take them off again to shift. She tried pointing out that if he was sitting bare-assed on the chair, how many other asses had sat there before him? That predictably led to a comment about where he'd like *her* bare ass to sit. Hint: nowhere near anything of Colt's.

It wasn't until his sweet Evangeline growled at him and told him that she hated the idea of anyone else seeing what was hers that Maddox promised to be naked only in front of her. Because possessiveness... *that* he understood.

Normally he would just borrow something of Colt's rather than tote around a bag between his teeth. But these clothes were special. He was wearing the same shirt and jeans the last time he saw Evangeline—it was what he'd gone into the Cage wearing, and the only personal belongings Wright grudgingly handed over upon Maddox's release. Even after all of this time, if he breathed deeply enough, he could still smell his mate on the fabric.

Until they were together again, he wouldn't wear anything else.

He didn't have any underwear so Maddox went commando as he took special care to zip up his jeans. The black tee stretched tight over his chest, another clue that he was even bigger than before. He strode across Colt's backyard barefoot, making a mental note to borrow a pair of his brother's boots. He would need them when he took Colt's truck.

Pausing on the back of Colt's porch, Maddox listened for some sign of Colt in the house. The buzzing coming from somewhere off to his left told

Maddox that his brother wasn't inside but, instead, busy working in his private shed on the far side of the property.

His brother was a talented architect who not only drew beautiful houses on blueprints, but he could build them with his own two hands while working for Wolfe Construction. That was his job. Constructing wooden furniture from scratch, carving a structure and staining the pieces before selling them off to the highest bidder... that was his labor of love. Not many people knew of his skill—Colt was quiet like that—but his "hobby" brought in more than enough to keep the pack wealthy on top of their family's construction business.

Maddox found Colt hunched over some monstrosity inside of the massive shed. The structure was about half as big as the cabin in the woods that the pack owned, that was how much of his free time Colt spent there. Tools hung precisely in their proper place on pegs lined up along the wall, half-finished pieces of furniture stood against one wall while a large rectangular table held about fifteen different cans of stain. Colt's carving knives were spaced exactly a half an inch apart, sized largest to smallest. A broom was propped in one corner; Maddox didn't see a single speck of sawdust on the entire cement floor. The two bay windows on opposite walls allowed in enough natural light to reveal the pristine state of Colt's workshop.

Maddox looked on with pride. Ah, Colt's anal-retentive attention to details. Thank Alpha some things never changed.

Even with the sander going and his protective headphones covering his sensitive ears, Maddox had no doubt that Colt knew he was there. His brother would have picked up on his arrival as soon as he approached the shed, then decided whether or not Maddox was a threat to him. Since he wasn't, Colt kept his attention on his work.

Ten seconds later, Colt finished sanding the corner of his project, turned the sander off, and removed both his safety glasses and his headphones. There was a peg for both. He made sure to put them in their right place before he turned around to face Maddox.

Colt's movements were slow, precise. That... that was different.

"Hey," his brother said, a strange look on his face when he nodded at Maddox. "Wasn't expecting you so soon. I bet Dodge the warden would dick you around some more, find a reason to delay your release. I'm glad to see I was wrong."

He took a ginger step toward Maddox, winced slightly and stepped again, obviously favoring his left leg. For Colt to show even that much of a reaction to pain, it had to be excruciating.

Maddox froze, his senses focused on Colt's left ankle. He could actually feel the heat radiating off of it. If it wasn't broken just then, it had been shortly before.

Hungry Like a Wolf

Considering how fast a shifter's natural healing abilities worked, it had to be one hell of an injury if it was taking so much time and power to heal.

Whoever did this to him, whatever caused his brother pain… Maddox had the sudden urge to chase them down and rip out their throats with his fangs. Coarse grey fur tinged with white sprouted along the length of his arms. He swiveled back and forth, to and fro, searching out any immediate threats.

Only two people in the world roused Maddox's protective instincts. One was his mate. The other? Colton.

He knew it was ridiculous. Colt was only four years younger than he was, an alpha wolf in his own right, and he'd proven time and time again that he could take care of himself. It didn't matter. Try telling that to Maddox's wolf. His dad was the only wolf in their pack more dominant than Maddox, and since Terrence fiercely protected his mate, Maddox knew his mother was in good claws. But ever since he was a young pup, his dad had pounded the notion that it was up to Maddox to look out for Colt into his thick skull.

He took that job very seriously.

"What happened to your leg?" Maddox demanded when his surveillance revealed that they were the only two on the property.

"Don't snarl at me, Mad. I'm glad to see you, but I'm not in the mood. My leg's just fine. It's nothing."

Maddox wasn't about to let Colt brush him off. "It had to be bad if you're still limping. What happened?"

"I said it's nothing. Drop it."

"I'll drop it when you tell me why you're walking on a broken ankle, Colt. And don't you fucking dare say 'nothing' again. You should've healed already if it was nothing."

"You don't think I feel like an idiot already without you badgering me?" Colt snapped. "It was a dumb accident. I dropped a dresser I was delivering on my foot and crushed my ankle, okay? But the bone's already knitting back together. I'll be a hundred percent by tomorrow. There are more important things to worry about than my fucking clumsiness, you know. So I'll say it again: *drop it*."

Maddox pointedly continued to ignore the warning in Colt's tone. "Clumsiness? Since when are *you* clumsy?"

Colt's icy blue stare went nearly glacial as he glared up at his older brother. "Since now, I guess. How the hell would you know, anyway? When did you ever ask about me when you were in the Cage?"

Forget imaginary threats—suddenly he had a real problem right in front of him that he couldn't pretend didn't exist. Maddox's wolf sat up a little at that barked comment, bristling at Colt's tone and eyeing Colt's burgeoning snout and elongated fangs with interest. Sometimes it was a bitch to be an alpha, especially when his beast was seriously thinking about ripping

Colt's throat out for what it saw as a clear challenge. But if Terrence refrained from killing his boys over the years, Maddox could indulge his younger brother.

Now wasn't the time to assert his dominance after an absence of three years. That could wait until after he found Evangeline.

Colt must have realized how close to the edge he was at the same time that Maddox made a conscious effort to not notice Colt's attitude. His brother took a deep breath and dropped his stare. Turning his back on Maddox—an obvious sign of submission and trust—he picked a sheet up off of the floor and shook it out before covering his project. When he turned around again, he looked embarrassed. And entirely human.

"Sorry about that," Colt said, running a hand through his short hair. His downcast eyes were back to their bright blue color. "I didn't mean it."

"Don't worry about it."

"No, it's just—"

Maddox shook his head. "Colt, no. You're absolutely right. I have a lot to make up for. But first—"

"First you have to find Evangeline. I know. While I was waiting for you to get here, I've been trying to figure out what to do next. I'll do anything I can to help you."

"*If* I ever find her." Maddox exhaled. All of his adrenaline rushed out with his breath.

Suddenly the weight of his expectations, the strenuous run to Colt's Bumptown, and, of course, the disastrous visit to the D.P.R. came crashing down on him. He grabbed one of the wooden chairs waiting to be stained, dragged it closer to him, and sank down into it.

Hanging his head, Maddox rubbed the ruined skin around his throat.

Colt froze.

Staring across the workroom over at Maddox, the sight of his brother slumped in the chair disturbed him. The pose was too eerily similar to the way Maddox reacted while he was still in the Cage. Colt immediately pushed his own troubles and the nagging pain in his stupid ankle away as he perched on the edge of the stool closest to Maddox.

It was easy to fall back into the old routine, Colt the savior trying to draw some sort of positive reaction out of Maddox.

"We talked yesterday, when they said they were letting you out as soon as the release came through. There was no *if*. What changed, Maddox?"

Defeated. That was the only way Colt could describe the way Maddox sounded as he told him about his disastrous trip to the D.P.R., including the lustful clerk, the strict supervisor, and the tangle of red tape that meant that no one at the agency was going to give Maddox any information about Evangeline beside the fact that she was alive, unbonded, and still used her maiden name. Maddox refused to delve too deeply into his hellish hours there, but Colt knew his brother well enough to be able to read between the lines.

"That's bullshit. I can't believe they can pull that and get away with it."

"Believe it. The D.P.R. was no help at all. Seems like I didn't need to show my bonding license to go into the Cage but, without it, they won't tell me where to find Evangeline."

"Fucking *Claws Clause*," snarled Colt. "I told you you should've signed the bonding license before the marriage license."

He had. A hundred times before the accident and probably a thousand more since Maddox had been incarcerated. But Evangeline was human and had human values and human beliefs. Maddox was so eager to do things her way to make his mate happy. His brother had no doubt that she felt the bond just as deeply as he had. And while Evangeline had said she recognized that claiming was even more final than marriage to a shifter, she had point-blank refused to be legally bonded before she was legally wed.

So Maddox brought her to the courthouse and married her. Getting the bonding license notarized in a Bumptown was an afterthought. The honeymoon was supposed to come first—but they never made it to the cabin.

"Yeah, well, hindsight's a bitch," admitted Maddox.

"Coulda, woulda, shoulda. Now I got to find her the old-fashioned way."

"Nose to the dirt?"

"And paw to the pedal."

"Take my truck," Colt offered. "You're going to need wheels to get around, and I can use my delivery van if I have to head out of town. Unless you want me to try tracking Evangeline again. I can put any orders on hold for a couple of days, no big deal."

Maddox was his brother, his packmate, and the man who would be his Alpha as soon as their father handed the pack over to him. He would do whatever he could to help him.

Considering it was partially his fault that Maddox was missing his mate, he would do so gladly.

Maybe then fate would finally quick taking potshots at him.

Maddox's head jerked up.

He felt the little hairs on the back of his ruined neck stand at attention. Something... something wasn't right. He could tell. Without the silver collar dulling his senses, he was finally picking up on it. Colt was a pro at hiding what he was thinking, what he was feeling, but Maddox was his brother.

Something definitely wasn't right.

Like the calm before the storm, something was

brewing within Colt. His brother was doing a damn good job shielding it from Maddox and his wolf, but that right there roused his suspicions more than anything else—even more than when Colt lost his head before and nearly invoked a challenge.

Colt had a lot going for him, but while he was loyal to a fault, this sudden bout of generosity wasn't like him. Maddox knew he was taking Colt's truck—he just expected to have to pull rank to get it. And putting orders on hold? Colt's work was his life. He was the best brother a guy could ask for, but he wasn't a fucking saint. Something was off and right after he finally cemented his bond with Evangeline, he was going to do whatever *he* had to to find out what.

When Maddox didn't push, Colt relaxed just enough for Maddox to take note. Before he could change his mind, Colt reached into his pants pockets, pulled out his keys, and tossed them at him.

"For the truck," Colt said.

Maddox looked at the keys in his palm. He peered up at Colt, cocked his head. "Were you serious when you said you'd help me?"

"Whatever you need, it's yours. I'll do whatever I can to help. I know what she means to you." A strange expression flashed across Colt's face. Maddox never got the chance to try to read it. Seconds later, Colt's usual glower was back in place.

Maddox debated for a second if it would be worth asking Colt about his reaction. It was... *off*. Before the accident, Colt rolled his eyes at the idea of mating and refused to accept it might happen to him. Now, he actually seemed to understand. Part of Maddox thought it had to do with how hard the last three years had been on the whole family.

For the first time, though, he began to wonder...

"So the truck's all yours. What else do you need?"

Colt's question distracted Maddox from his train of thought. He shook his head. Evangeline. This was all about getting back to his mate. Everything else could wait.

"First, boots. I had sneakers, but I left them behind after I shifted by the D.P.R.—I'll probably need a couple of cheap pairs in case that happens again. A cell phone, if you think I'll need one of those. You're the only one I'm talking to right now so if you won't call it, don't bother. Money, definitely—my account's still frozen from my time in the Cage, but you know I'm good for it." Maddox held up his hand, ticking off each item as it came to him. "Let's see... oh yeah, speaking of the D.P.R.... either I've got to pay someone to fix that damn counter, or maybe you could just do it for me. That would help. And, of course, I'm going to need the coordinates of the last spot you caught her scent."

Colt had picked up a pen and pad from his tabletop and was currently jotting down his brother's list when Maddox got to the last one. He glanced up, his brow furrowed. "I'll give it to you, no problem. It's just... you know I wasn't able to track it again, right? It's like her scent just up and disappeared."

"I know, but I figure she passed by there once, she's bound to do it again. You know Angie, she likes her routines. Besides, it's the only lead I got. I'll live on the street corner if I have to, if it means I might see her again."

"Just don't do anything stupid. I lost you once to the Cage and, now that you're out, I don't need you giving anyone a reason to lock you up again." Then, as if he could guess the direction of Maddox's thoughts, Colt raised his eyebrow. "And, yes, sniffing random humans to see if they carry her scent counts."

Maddox laughed out loud. It was the first time he'd found anything to laugh about in years which made him realize something important. "I missed you, bro. Really missed you, Colt. I know I saw you when I was locked up but…" He cleared his throat. "Well, you know. It's good to be out and I know I'll never be able to repay you—"

"Don't mention it. You'd do it for me in a heartbeat and we both know it. Now, let me make sure I got everything here." As if he was eager to avoid dealing with Maddox's embarrassing gratitude, Colt glanced down at the notes he'd scribbled on the page in front of him.

He blinked. "Hey, Maddox?"

"Yeah?"

"Truck, sure. Boots, got it. But, uh… counter?"

"Yeah."

"Why do you need me to fix a D.P.R. counter?"

Maddox's golden eyes flashed, an amber sheen rolling over his pupils. "Because I broke it."

Colt pursed his lips. "Do I want to know *why* you broke it? Or when? I mean, considering you only went to the D.P.R. after the warden released you, should I just be glad that you're not halfway back to prison already?"

Maddox climbed out of Colt's chair. He placed a heavy hand on his brother's shoulder before saying solemnly, "I'm never going back to the Cage, Colt. If they give me the choice again, they'll have to kill me this time."

8

Evangeline was dreaming about the accident again.

It had taken her a while to tell the difference between a flashback and a nightmare. For the first few months of her recovery, she relived the terror of the crash every minute of every day. It felt like she was stuck in an endless loop, trapped in the minute the truck slipped and skidded around the slick curve of the mountain before it flipped end over end down the craggy, rocky side.

She didn't remember the actual impact. Just the fall. Her doctors theorized that she must have blacked out from fear before the vehicle actually ran right through the rusted guardrail and started its descent; if she was already limp, it made her unlikely survival a little more understandable.

The hole in her memory frustrated her because she

felt like there was more to it than that. There was… there was something else she should be remembering.

When she fell asleep and the nightmares found her, she realized that the some*thing* was a some*one*.

That was how Evangeline was finally able to tell the difference between her memories and her dreams. Because, logically, she knew that she had been alone in the car when it crashed. Her parents assured her that her broken body was the only one trapped in the wreckage of the truck she'd been driving. She tried once to tell them that she didn't even remember owning a vehicle like the one they found her in—or, for that matter, *driving* one—but they just sighed as they held her hands and promised that she would remember it all in time.

In her nightmares, Evangeline replaced her missing memories with her own twisted version of how the accident must have happened. It was raining, the sky dark and overcast. A hint of sweat, musk, and pine lingered in the small cab of the truck, caressing her senses and making her feel at ease despite the butterflies fluttering in her stomach.

She was sitting in the passenger seat—*he* was driving, his hands beating a happy rhythm on the steering wheel. It was supposed to be a shortcut, the two of them desperate to get wherever they were going. The rain made the curve in the road dangerous, but he assured her that he had taken this path hundreds of times before. It was supposed to be safe.

That lull, that sweet certainty that nothing bad could happen when she was with him... it was the last thing she remembered before she was blinded by a bright purple flash. Lightning? Maybe. The truck swerved, as if it had been struck by it. The driver yanked the wheel sharply to the right. The truck didn't respond. In her nightmares, it never did. Like a suicidal jumper, it took its swan dive over the side of the mountain, crashing right through the pitted, old guardrail as if it hadn't even been there.

Strong arms yanked Evangeline right out of her seat, pressing her against a broad chest. There was only enough time to duck her head under his chin as he wrapped himself around her like a protective cocoon before the truck started to flip over and over.

His name was always the last thing she screamed—the *only* thing she screamed. Over the squeal of the tires and the groan of the truck's metal frame folding around them, Evangeline could never make out what she was yelling before she was suddenly jolted awake from her disturbed sleep.

For almost three years she suffered from the same nightmare. As her body healed, her bones mending, her fear of heights less crippling with time, Evangeline still dreamed of the crash. Nothing ever changed. Despite knowing the identity of the shadow man while she was dreaming, she could never remember it as soon as she was jerked awake.

That night was no different.

Sweat plastering her long, dark hair to her forehead, her fingers clutching the sheet with a death grip, Evangeline looked wildly around her bedroom. The magic hum in the air told her the wards were still up. The sun streaming in through the window said she slept in later than she wanted; it wasn't night any longer, but late morning at the earliest. She gasped and tried to get control of her breathing.

Because she shouldn't be awake. Not yet. That wasn't the end of the dream.

So what had woken her up?

It took her a minute to figure it out. The answer?

No pain.

Evangeline shoved her sweat-soaked hair out of her face, marveling at that realization.

She'd had the same dream over and over again and it never ended until another blast of purple energy hit the car and she was violently ripped from her savior's embrace. Then there was an excruciating pain. It shocked her, paralyzed her, and made her wish she was dead.

But she wasn't dead. She survived the crash that terrible night, just like she continued to survive reliving it ever since.

That morning was the first time she had woken up from her nightmares without the pain consuming her first. As she panted, her entire body tensed as if expecting it to hit now. But it didn't. Instead, she could've sworn she still felt the heat of the other passenger in the car as he tucked her into his side, protecting her as they fell. It felt as real as it had in her dream, as if she'd had a guardian angel who protected her as her car careened down the mountainside.

In her dream, the angel had a name. She knew it then; ripped awake before he disappeared, it was on the tip of her tongue. She scrunched her forehead, struggling to remember. It seemed so important. M... M-something.

Her heart, which had calmed, suddenly began to beat a wild tattoo inside of her chest at another realization. This was the closest she'd come to a breakthrough in years. She normally woke up with nothing but the memory of the pain and the empty lonely ache she suffered so much from, yet worked so damn hard to hide.

M-something... Mmm. Matt? Was it Matt? No. Not that.

Max? Max... Evangeline rolled the name around her head, forcing it to work harder. Not quite it, but close.

Very close.

The 'x' sounded right, but she felt like there was a 'd' in there somewhere. Something like Mad-something. She wanted to scream in frustration—*screaming* seemed to be key.

Why was she screaming for—

Madison? Madden? Maddo—

Her phone rang and the name slipped away like

the grains of sand in her timer. She struggled to hold onto it, gave in to her urge to scream just the once, then cursed loudly when the remnants of her dream—the name, his scent, his protective heat—simply faded away, leaving her alone.

She *was* alone. And she hated it.

Picking up her phone without checking to see who was calling, she answered it by snapping, "What?"

"Eva? What's wrong, babe?"

Adam. She should have known. Who else would be calling this early in the morning? At least her mother always waited until after dinner.

Leaning back in her bed, Evangeline let her head fall against the pillow as she shielded her eyes with her arm.

"Hey, Adam. Sorry about that... nothing's wrong. The phone woke me up just now. I guess I'm pissed at myself for sleeping in so late."

"Is that why you weren't answering? Lazy bum," he scolded lightly, with enough humor in his tone that Evangeline decided it didn't warrant her snapping at him again. "I've been trying you all morning. I was just getting ready to head out and check in on you. You know I like to make sure you slept well."

Translation: *I like to make sure you didn't have any nightmares.*

She hated to admit it, but she thought his open concern was kind of sweet; he didn't make her feel as smothered as her mother did, either, so that was a huge plus. Adam wanted to be the last voice she talked to at night, and the first she heard as she started her day.

At first, she suspected he was doing all of that because he wanted her to sleep with him. After dating exclusively for more than a month now, Adam hadn't spent the night yet. He never even pushed for her to do more than kiss him. And when he sensed that she was hesitant to do even that, he backed off.

He didn't need to touch her to show Evangeline how much he cared. He did so in a million other ways.

Due to his hectic work schedule, they saw each other maybe three times a week. Adam still made sure he spoke to her at least twice every day, more when his fourteen-hour-long shifts at the Cage allowed him to use the phone. He brought her dinner when she admitted she hadn't eaten, and he liked to shower her with gifts. The perfume was only the beginning. And, sure, it kind of seemed like he was buying her affection.

Oh, well. It was working.

It warmed Evangeline how Adam followed her lead when it came to their relationship. The slow pace didn't frustrate him; he seemed happy and content that she was willing to continue to see him romantically. She had to admit that Adam Wright might have grown up after all.

Evangeline remembered her tantrum and grimaced. At least one of them had.

"I'm sorry if I worried you. I must've slept through my alarm clock and"—she pulled her phone away from her ear, pressed a button, and checked her missed calls. Wincing, she said—"and your seven phone calls."

Adam groaned. "That many? Shit. Sorry, babe. I'm at the window again, so I was dialing in between visitors, hoping to get you on the line. I didn't mean to be so obnoxious."

"Hey. Don't worry about it." Seven was nothing. When she first moved out, she would sometimes wake up to twelve missed calls from her mother. "I'm glad you did. Sleeping in wasn't on my agenda today. I guess I was more tired than I thought."

"I should've known better. It took you... what? Three days to crank out the edits on that last manuscript? I'm surprised your eyes aren't bleeding by now."

It was her first big test, a massive editing project that had a turnaround of only three days. Three days since she left her cramped apartment. She ordered in meals when she could take a break from her work, and went without when she couldn't. Adam came over last night with take-out from the Chinese place down the street. She'd barely been able to eat half of her sweet and sour chicken before he was tucking her into bed, risking a chaste kiss to her forehead, and replacing her wards on his way out of her apartment.

She winced when she remembered how hard she

had crashed. "I wasn't much company last night, was I?"

"It was nice. Quiet, but nice—just what I needed after a long day in the Cage. I'd love to do it again the next time they give me a night free. Sometimes I feel like I'm locked up with those animals, the hours they want me to work. Crazy, right?"

There was a sneer in Adam's voice whenever he mentioned working at the paranormal-only prison that she couldn't ignore; he never brought it up and she never mentioned it, but Evangeline got the vibe that he wasn't a fan of the paranormal part of the population. She knew he was counting the days until his year was up and he could rejoin the ranks of the Grayson PD.

Even though he didn't live in town himself just yet—he was house-hunting in his limited spare time—Grayson was his home precinct. Evangeline thought that was strangely suspicious until Naomi admitted that part of the reason she didn't fight the move was because Adam's mother, Fiona, had recommended Evangeline's part of Grayson as a mixed human city with a low crime rate and no real need to drive.

Perfect for Evangeline.

Just the thought of riding in a car again made her panic; it had gotten so bad that her mother gave her a sleeping pill before her father drove the moving van into Grayson. She refused to risk the chance of another car crash. Right after they finally let her out of the hospital, she sold her car and took her old six-speed bicycle out of the garage. The fact that she didn't remember anything leading right up to the crash, but had no problem riding a bike, told her that the damage to her memory was only short-term. She might be missing almost a year of her life, but she could still pop a mean wheelie.

Adam cleared his throat, reminding Evangeline that it was her turn to say something. Too bad she had no idea what the last thing Adam had said was.

Something about work, maybe?

"Are you gonna be working all night?" she asked. "I only have a couple of pages to proof today. I can cook something to make up for conking out on you yesterday. You could come over again."

"I wish I could, but they have me pulling an all-nighter. I'm looking forward to tomorrow, though."

Tomorrow? Evangeline racked her brains, trying to remember what tomorrow was. That was the biggest problem with always suffering from the sensation that she forgot something: so consumed with remembering to remember, she tended to forget even the littlest things.

"Um... tomorrow?"

"Yeah. You remember, Eva. It's date night."

She managed to bite back her groan in time. "It's Friday already?"

Date night was Adam's genius idea. After she agreed to the first dinner, he asked her to lunch. Then another dinner. A movie that Friday. By the afternoon walk around Grayson on Saturday, Evangeline had to admit that she was dating Adam Wright. It just sort of happened.

The next Friday, Adam proclaimed it date night. It was the one night of the week that he was always free and he wanted to spend it with her despite their busy schedules. So far there had been three date nights. She hadn't been able to dissuade him from any of the nights out yet, though she always tried.

Evangeline knew she was being ungrateful. She genuinely liked Adam and enjoyed spending time with him—when they stayed in for the evening before Adam went home. The anxious feeling that something wasn't right nagged her whenever she left the apartment on one of their special 'dates'. But she didn't dare tell him—or, God forbid, her mother—that being seen with the handsome cop in public left her feeling short of breath. Both of them treated her fragile enough already. If she admitted that she was only getting worse, the next thing she knew she would be cocooned in bubblewrap.

For her own safety, of course.

Oblivious to how she was already trying to figure a way to get out of this Friday's date night, Adam chuckled. "Wow. These last few days worked you over good, didn't they?"

"I guess. But at least that job's over and done with

now. The next one'll be a walk in the park compared to it."

"Is that what you're working on today?"

Evangeline hesitated. His tone hadn't changed. Adam sounded as concerned and interested as he usually did and that, she decided, was the problem. It was bad enough that she felt like she had to account for her every move to her mother. Recently, she couldn't shake the suspicion that Adam expected her to do the same for him.

"That was the plan. Get up, take a shower, get dressed. I slept through breakfast, so I thought I might pick up a muffin or something and get some coffee before I start my work. That sound okay to you?"

If Adam heard the sarcasm she couldn't quite keep out of her short tone, he didn't act like it. "I don't know, Eva—"

"What's wrong with my plan?"

"Don't you have coffee in the kitchen?"

She did. But it wasn't the same. "The coffeehouse is only a couple of blocks away. Plus, they have muffins."

"Babe—"

"I'm just going to get coffee and come right back. It'll be fine."

"Hang on. I was about to go on break," Adam told her. In the background, she heard the squeak of his desk chair as he stood up. A moment later, the jangle of his keys came through loud and clear. "Wait for me to get there. I'll take you out."

He had to be kidding. "What? No! I mean… you don't have to do that."

"I was on my way already. When you didn't answer, I got Bennett to okay an early break. I'll be there in fifteen."

Evangeline closed her eyes, prayed for patience, then said, "Adam, don't be ridiculous. I could walk to Mugs and back before you got here. And Grayson is harmless, right?"

She had to believe that. Even with Fiona and Adam's endorsement, Naomi had researched every inch of the town before she approved Evangeline's move. Its crime rate was almost nonexistent. Evangeline attributed that to its proximity to the Cage. About ten miles away, it was too close to draw many criminals. Paras wouldn't want to catch the Cage's attention, and human crooks feared the threat of being thrown inside with paranormals regardless of what the laws said.

Adam's voice gained a hard edge. "You can't think like that, babe. No place is harmless. Something could happen at any moment. You, of all people, should know that."

Evangeline knew his heart was in the right place. Still, she hated when anyone tried to take her choices away from her. If going out to get coffee was the one thing she could control in her life then, damn it, she was getting that cup of coffee.

"Careful, Adam. You're starting to sound like my mother."

"That's because I love you, too, Eva."

She winced. He'd started up with that during their last night out together, right before she started the editing job that, okay, she might've offered to take because it gave her an excuse to avoid Adam for a few days. Afraid that he was just using the words to soften her up so that she would invite him to spend the night—and terrified he might mean it after only a month together—she refused to say it back.

The words held weight for Evangeline. She would only say them when she meant them. And, as much as she was growing to care for Adam, she didn't love him. Not yet.

"I'll be safe. How about this? I'll bring my phone with me, grab my breakfast, then call you when I get back to my place. Better?"

Adam started to say something, stopped, then sighed. "Since you're probably halfway out the door now, I guess that's fine. I'm going on record saying that I don't like it, though."

"Duly noted, Officer."

"*Eva.*"

His stern voice might have counted for more if he didn't punctuate it with a sexy little chuckle. Between that and his handsome face, strong body, the charming dimple... she wished she knew what it was that Adam saw in her and why he was wasting his time when he could probably have half the population of Grayson with only a wink.

Evangeline was glad he couldn't see the way her cheeks heated up. No matter how she tried to discourage him in the beginning, he was adamant about seeing her. She didn't understand it, but she'd be lying if she said she didn't like the attention. He was kind, considerate, good-looking as hell, and willing to bend over backward for her. In her darker moods, she wondered if her mother was paying him to watch over her. But then she caught sight of the way he would look at her as if *he* was the lucky one and she had to smile.

"I'll talk to you in a little bit, Adam. Promise."

"Okay." He sounded resigned, though he didn't argue again. "Love you."

Blowing him a kiss with her lips pressed against the mouthpiece—that was the most she could offer him. She disconnected the call a second later and tossed her phone away from her. Holding her breath, she waited to see if it would ring again.

It didn't.

Evangeline exhaled softly.

Adam was overreacting, she decided. As a police officer, it was his job to be wary and prepared. But that didn't mean that his mother hen routine was going to keep her from living her life. She went to Mugs nearly every day and maybe she hadn't mentioned that, but what did it matter? Sure, Adam was a protective guy—

that was the cop in him—but to drive all the way into town to walk her two blocks over? That was pushing it, even for him.

Besides, she wondered as she finally climbed out of her bed, what could possibly happen to her in the ten minutes it took to get coffee?

9

At first, Colt hadn't wanted to tell Maddox where he was when he first scented Evangeline. Maddox couldn't figure out why. When he was in the Cage, it wasn't that important. Knowing that his mate was inexplicably still alive was enough.

Now that he was back on the outside? He desperately needed the coordinates.

Colt kept putting it off. Without any sign that she'd been back to that spot, he argued that it would only be a waste of time to focus on one single location. Maddox disagreed. It was the only lead he had and, with a little bit of brotherly persuasion, he went about convincing Colt to spill it.

A heavy hand to the back of Colt's head, a few barked threats, and Maddox had a name.

Grayson. He couldn't fucking believe it. While Maddox was locked up and rotting the rest of his life away, Evangeline had started over in the well-known mixed city less than ten miles away from the Cage.

So close, but not close enough.

Where was she now? Colt didn't know. Neither did Maddox. She certainly wasn't at the local Quick Stop set on Grayson's main thoroughfare.

But she had been.

Colt swore to Maddox that that was the spot. A month ago, he followed Evangeline to the convenience store. After catching her scent on the breeze, immediately recognizing it despite how impossible it seemed, Colt traced it to a shy, leggy brunette as she entered the Quick Stop on the corner.

Torn between grabbing her, shaking her, demanding she tell him where she'd been for three years or running straight to Maddox, Colt tapped into his beast. He went straight into hunter mode. Staking out the corner on the opposite side of the street, Colt decided to watch and wait and see if he could figure out what was going on before he confronted anyone else with the truth.

Even with the distance, he could sense that at least five other humans were shopping inside the Quick Stop, all of them human. Knowing Grayson's anti-Para reputation—despite a good chunk of the population being paranormal—Colt kept his wolf under lock and key, unwilling to reveal himself as a shifter before he saw Evangeline again.

Only one problem.

He never did.

After leaning against the corner lamp post, eyes narrowed on the front door of the convenience store for close to half an hour, Colt finally realized he'd been duped. Maybe she saw him and was trying to avoid him. Maybe she simply took another way out of the store. Didn't matter. Either way, when Colt braced himself and stormed inside, only her scent lingered. And while he had half a mind to chase after her—that was his wolf's input, at any rate—Colt knew what he had to do. Hopping in his truck, he headed right out to the magic-free prison to tell Maddox.

More than a month later—and two days out of the Cage—Maddox wished Colt had tracked Evangeline out of the Quick Stop. Knowing his mate, she would never be walking around the downtown area so late in the afternoon if she didn't live nearby. Colt had been so sure that he would be able to pick up her scent trail again; since he hadn't, Maddox was left wondering if maybe he was wrong.

He really hoped not.

There were no laws against Paras entering cities like Grayson where humans nominally were in charge. Since humans and paranormals had the same rights—at least, on paper they did—where one was allowed, the other one was as well; ideally, society was fully integrated these days. That didn't stop Bumptowns and Ant Farms from springing up, though. It might not be illegal for Maddox to stroll into the predominantly human Grayson, advertising the fact that he was a bonded shifter fresh out of the Cage, but he knew he wouldn't be welcomed, either.

He was proven right the second he walked into the Quick Stop. A big, burly redhead with a bushy mustache stood behind the register, his arms crossed over the ill-fitting yellow uniform shirt he wore. A satisfied smirk disappeared underneath his mustache as he surveyed the handful of customers milling around the store.

His eyes fell on Maddox, dipping to the scars that circled the base of Maddox's throat. The big man stayed quiet, moving closer to the counter. His shoulder shifted. Maddox could tell that his hand was reaching for something.

Gun, bat, or witch's protection spell, Maddox didn't give a shit. He'd walk through fire to get Evangeline back. This Ant thought he could stop him?

Not in this lifetime.

Loping to the counter, Maddox pointedly ignored the gasps from some of the other shoppers. Whispers filled the air and then, almost as one, the shoppers put down anything they were holding and eased toward the door. Within a minute, no one was left inside the store except for Maddox and the clerk.

He'd give the human credit. The big guy bristled, a hint of nervousness seeping into his scent, but he didn't back down. Instead, with a flat look, he rumbled, "You're not supposed to be here."

No. Probably not.

Too fucking bad.

Maddox reached into the back pocket of his worn jeans, pulling out a photograph.

Since his disastrous trip to the D.P.R., Maddox decided to skip going to his old home. It was too painful with Evangeline in the wind somewhere. Colt had a spare room and Maddox took it over.

Maddox was relying on his brother for everything: his truck, his clothes, his money, his old cell phone. And now this. It was a good thing Colt had a picture of Maddox and Evangeline in his junk drawer that he was willing to lend him, saving Maddox an agonizing trip out to Wolf's Creek.

Folding it over so that she was the only one visible, Maddox showed it to the clerk.

"I won't be here long," he said. "Look at this picture. I just need an answer. You know this woman?"

"No."

"Look closer. She's shopped here before. Has she been in recently?"

The clerk made a display of peering at the photo. After a second, he gulped, then shook his head. "Never seen her before in my life and I work most shifts 'cause I manage the store. She's never been a customer of mine."

Maddox's wolf had a sense of smell that was especially keen. He'd always been able to tell when someone was lying to him. It was hard to explain to a non-shifter, the way dishonesty had a sour tang like curdled milk. Some witches had the same power, but that was just magic. Maddox, like most shifters, relied on his nose.

Snuffling, he blew the stink from his nostrils. "You sure about that?"

"Damn sure."

"You're lying," Maddox said softly.

He didn't mean to do it. It just happened. Narrowing his eyes on the human, he stared without blinking. A true predator's stare. From the way the Ant lost all of his color, Maddox was willing to bet his eyes flashed like liquid gold, a warning rolling across his shuttered expression.

The human took a step away from the counter, followed by another until he was forced to back into the wall behind him. His hands were shaking. So was his voice as he pointed to the exit. "I answered your question. I think it's time for you to go."

"Maybe when you give me an answer I like I will."

The blotchy patches on the clerk's beefy neck started to match the color of his unruly hair. He raised his arms, showing empty hands. "I'm not looking for any trouble here."

"I didn't say I was looking for trouble, either. I said I was looking for her."

Another gulp. "And I said I've never seen her before."

The scent of deception was even stronger, mingled

with noticeable fear. He didn't back down, though. Jutting his chin, maintaining eye contact with Maddox's burgeoning fangs, he pointed at the exit again.

Maddox let his wolf peek through. A rumble deep in his chest, the beginning of a warning growl—

"I've got a panic button under my counter. If you don't leave right now, I'll press it."

It was a threat—and a good one, too. Maddox could probably leap over the counter and take out the human manager before he pressed it, but what if the big guy was faster than he looked? No way he could break through emergency wards if they slammed down, leaving him a sitting wolf for the Cage cops to pick up.

Getting out of the Cage was a one-shot deal. If he went back, no amount of pleading or proof would get the board to release him again.

With one last snarl, Maddox snapped his teeth at the Ant before crumpling the photo in his fist, shoving it back in his pocket, and storming for the door.

THE ANT MIGHT HAVE BEEN ABLE TO FORCE HIM TO LEAVE the shop, but that didn't mean he was going to get rid of Maddox so easily. Unless he was willing to go toe to toe with the wolf, he had to put up with Maddox pacing back and forth on the street corner right outside of his store.

Maddox prowled the same stretch of sidewalk for four straight hours before the human manager finally grew a pair and, from behind the safety of his closed door while waving the phone clutched tightly in his grip, threatened to call the local police and tell them that Maddox was loitering.

Scowling, Maddox debated whether or not it would make him feel better to shift into his wolf and mark his territory all over the jerk's trash cans. He ultimately decided to take the high road and cross the street where he could glare at the Ant while continuing to keep a vigil for any sign of his mate.

When the woman who ran the shop he was now pacing in front of came out to see what was going on, she took one look at his scars, his scowl, his frantic pacing, and went back inside. A few minutes later, she came back with a bottle of water for him.

Bertha was a doll, and he didn't just think that because she owned and operated Hello, Dolly, an antique doll boutique set directly across from the Quick Stop. A handsome woman in her early seventies, she didn't mind when Maddox took up his spot looming right outside her door. After the water, she offered him a slice of pie and stopped for a little conversation before she locked up for the night.

She was as human as they come, from a time before the paranormals had revealed their existence to

Hungry Like a Wolf

the whole world. But love was love, she said, and she told him that her dear Harold had worn the same expression as Maddox during their courtship more than fifty years ago. Bertha didn't recognize Evangeline's picture, but she fed Maddox, offered him advice, and even stuck her tongue out at the Quick Stop manager whenever she saw him peeking over at them from his window.

Despite having a stretch of territory to stake out, it still felt like he'd taken a step back, another roadblock in the search for his mate. Innate stubbornness kept him from moving further than a block from the shop even if he couldn't pick up on a single sign that Evangeline had been by in the last month.

Utter exhaustion eventually had him finding shelter in a local motel Bertha recommended for the handful of hours he allowed himself to rest and recover since running back to Colt's Bumptown was out of the question. Only the thought of how Evangeline would react if she found him exhausted, dirty, and smelling like roadkill enticed him to sleep, shower, and air out the clothes he refused to change.

Her scent was fading fast. Maddox tried not to let that bother him, but it was tough.

He would find her again. He had to.

There was no other choice.

Day three. The weather was still holding out, and Bertha brought him a slightly stale banana nut muffin when she opened her shop that morning. It was the only thing he'd had for hours and, while he was grateful, it was kind of dry.

Maddox didn't want to offend her. Since he stubbornly took up his post in Grayson, Bertha was one of the few he encountered who didn't freak when they saw him. Most of the humans crossed to the other side of the street to avoid him. Any Paras making their way through gave him a wide berth, recognizing a bonded shifter on the hunt. Bertha was the only one who treated him like a person instead of a dangerous beast.

Maddox made it about an hour before he couldn't take it any longer. He hated the idea of leaving the block during daylight hours. It was barely ten o'clock and if Evangeline wanted to make a pit stop at the convenience store before work, this was the prime time.

But, hell, if he choked to death on a muffin because a piece of walnut got stuck in his throat, he'd never see Evangeline again.

His mate was *everything*. Even with the dry, stale muffin nagging him, his thoughts were only for her.

There was a coffee place a couple of blocks away. Mugs. Bertha would close her store for an hour every afternoon for a cup. She told Maddox they had the best coffee in all of Grayson and he tucked that nugget away, knowing that he'd never go.

There was only one coffee shop that he was fond of. A small, family-owned joint in Woodbridge, it was the place where he first made his move on Evangeline, four years ago. Wolves were nothing if not loyal. When he got her back, he'd take the trip out there just for old times' sake.

Of course, that wasn't helping him now. And coffee sounded pretty fucking good right about then. It was hot, he was exhausted, and the muffin was pissing him off.

A couple of minutes. He'd only be gone for a couple of minutes. Five, maybe, depending on how busy the shop was. Run to Mugs, get a cup for him—and maybe one for Bertha—and he could be back at his post before anyone knew it.

Running his hands through his unkempt, shaggy hair before resetting his sunglasses on his nose, Maddox cast his gaze around the calm street. He reached with his shifter senses. No hint of Evangeline on the late summer air.

Go.

He made it to Mugs in less than three minutes. Narrow and long, with dark wood paneling and burnt orange tabletops, it was a bustling hotspot with a mixture of clientele. Mostly human, but there were more Paras inside getting their caffeine fix than he'd met on the street these last few days. He caught a glimpse of a pair of witches in one corner, and a predatory shifter who made a row of booths his immediate territory. A sniff revealed that the male shifter was a tiger, cunning and quick, but less dominant than Maddox's wolf.

The tiger started to rise. With all the humans surrounding them, Maddox doubted he was about to defend his claim. He was probably conceding it to the Alpha.

No need for that. He met the tiger's dark eyes, nodded, then pointedly looked away. The tiger sat back down, assured that no one was being challenged.

The Ants milled around Mugs, oblivious to Para politics at play. One or two did pause and stare as Maddox passed by, but he was used to it. Since no one stopped him from ordering his coffee, using Colt's cash to pay for it, or claiming the furthest corner for himself, it was fine. Better than he expected, actually.

The coffee was piping hot, the air conditioning cranking. He sprawled in his seat, waiting for the coffee to cool enough to swallow without burning the shit out of his tongue. Leaning his head back, he closed his eyes—

They snapped open.

A chill coursed up and down his spine as he sat forward, all senses on alert. His wolf perked its ears open.

He didn't know why. His nose hadn't caught a whiff of anything beyond the coffee brewing, pastries being heated, and the scents of each individual patron inside of Mugs. But he learned long ago to rely on his gut and, as if his instincts knew something he didn't, he found himself zeroing in on a tall woman with long, dark hair who was accepting her cup from the barista.

There was no reason why she should have captured his interest so suddenly like that. It was the weirdest thing. From behind, there was nothing about her that set her apart from anyone else in Mugs except for her height. He took a deep breath, searching for that familiar scent ingrained in his soul. Rich vanilla and something that was uniquely Evangeline.

Even with his nose clamped shut and a thousand different scents to process, he could've picked his mate's out in a heartbeat. It wasn't there.

The woman was intriguing, but that's all she could be.

Her back was to Maddox. She murmured something, then turned.

Maddox got his first look at her face. She was beautiful, from the pout of her lips to the elegant slope of her freckle-covered nose. Drawn to her like a magnet, he met her gaze through the shield of his sunglasses.

He froze on the edge of his seat.

"Holy shit," he breathed out.

Her eyes were green. Forest green, dark and wild and full of life. So what if they were shadowed, her lips turned up slightly in the smallest of haunted smiles? He would know those eyes anywhere.

His cock punched to life so fast, he swore there would be zipper treads burned into the length by the time his erection finally went down again. *If* it ever went down again.

Evangeline.

By the time he got over the shock of seeing his mate in the flesh for the first time in years, she was halfway out of Mugs. So stunned, he didn't even realize it when she looked away from him or when she started to leave him behind. But as the soft tinkle of the bell over the door rang and he caught a glimpse of her long legs as she walked away from him, Maddox's predatory instincts awakened.

He was a beast, his beauty the prey.

The chase was on.

Abandoning his own cup, Maddox trailed behind Evangeline. It went against every instinct he had not to simply swoop her up in his arms and run off. It was *her*. His mate. He was absolutely certain it was. Only... her scent. He couldn't get over how her scent had changed.

No. Not changed.

Disappeared.

The warm vanilla scent he adored simply wasn't there.

It was *gone*.

He breathed again, his wolf whining with confusion. Maddox *saw* her. That was undeniably his Angie. His sudden hard-on, his first one in more than three years, was proof enough.

But what the hell happened to her scent?

No wonder Colt couldn't track her down. Except

Hungry Like a Wolf

for the slightest hint of a sickly sweet scent that made his nose twitch, Evangeline left no scent trail. Once she stepped outside, the stronger odors of car exhaust, asphalt, and trash drowned out her meager scent.

His nose was out. Maddox had to rely on his keen animal sight to track her as she walked about a block ahead of him.

He followed her to an apartment building two blocks away from the coffee shop. Pretending he was interested in the bakery across the street from the building, he watched her reflection as he looked past the scones in the window. When he was certain that she was going inside this particular building, he struggled to wait another few minutes before heading straight toward the front door.

That was as far as he got.

The instant his hand closed on the handle, he was zapped. It was a mild jolt, a quick sting that warned him against touching the door again. Maddox ignored the warning. After shaking the sting out of his hand, he grabbed the handle and yanked, pulling the door open. He felt the pulse of magic as it traveled up his arm, the ache causing his entire right side to go numb before he tore his hand away.

Snarling under his breath, he folded his injured hand and tried to force his way inside. His boot kicked up against resistance; it felt like he walked into a brick wall. Maddox pressed his good palm against the patch of space in front of him and pushed. No go. He shoved and punched and growled and didn't even move an inch inside of the entryway. His brute strength might have been enough to open the door, but even his shifter abilities were no match against Para-proof enchantments.

And that's when he realized he was in bigger trouble than he first thought. Because Evangeline's apartment? It was warded and there was no way he could get any closer to her.

Evangeline kept her drink in one hand, her cell phone in the other. She tried to keep her pace leisurely, looking like she didn't have a care in the world as she strolled down Main Street. Inside, she felt like her heart was doing the mambo against her rib cage.

With only the tiniest of peeks over her shoulder, she glimpsed a big, dark figure loping quietly not more than a block behind her. Black shirt. Dark jeans. Sunglasses. It was the man from the coffee shop. She was almost positive. He was built like a linebacker, but moved like a freaking cat.

And he was *following* her.

Okay, she couldn't say for sure that he was following her. There were probably thousands of reasons why he had appeared behind her as soon as she made her escape, her iced caramel macchiato in hand. They'd locked eyes for two, maybe three seconds when she was heading out of the coffee shop—and that was assuming he could even see her through the thick, dark shades he had on.

Evangeline wanted to think it was the sunglasses that caught her attention. Who wore sunglasses inside unless they had something to hide, right? Of course she was curious.

In fact, for one terrible moment, she had to wonder if he was a Nightwalker before she chided herself for jumping to conclusions. The human-turned-vampires wore sunglasses around the clock, the shades a trademark for that dangerous type of Para—but that didn't make her dark stranger a vampire. He couldn't be. Nightwalkers were dust if they stepped into the sun and that guy? He had no problem following her home. Plus, his skin was a delicious golden color; Nightwalkers, no matter what they looked like when they were still alive, all paled considerably after their death.

So... not a Nightwalker. Did that make him human? Evangeline didn't know.

And then there was his size. Freaking hell, he was *huge*. This was a man who could make *her* actually feel petite.

She wanted to think all of that. The shades. How difficult it was tell if he was Para or human. His size. Yet, even as she worried about him stalking only a few steps behind her, she knew she was absolutely full of shit.

She couldn't explain it—didn't even begin to

understand it—but in the few seconds when she looked right at this dark stranger, she felt as if she knew him. Almost like an invisible thread stretched between them, tying them to each other as if no one else in the coffee shop existed. And that... that's what made her want to run. She'd never felt such a strong attraction in such a short period of time before and that scared her so bad she had to get out of there before she did something she would regret.

Somehow, she didn't think Adam would like it if she flung herself into another man's arms. And before she scurried out the door? That was something she actually thought about doing.

He wasn't supposed to come after her.

Another peek. She gulped, her hands shaking. Her coffee splashed on the sidewalk.

He'd closed the gap considerably.

Just get home, she told herself. The second she entered her apartment building, the wards would protect her. Hers were strong enough to keep this big guy out, and even if her neighbors' weren't and he made it inside, no one was getting on the sixth floor unless she let them.

When there were maybe ten feet separating Evangeline from the front door to her building, she abandoned all pretense of keeping it cool. Her leisurely pace turned into a sprint as she bolted inside.

Her heart was racing as she dashed up the stairs, so frazzled that she forgot all about the elevator. By the time she made it up the five flights, she figured she had made a close escape.

But, she wondered, escape from *what*?

Evangeline was still shaky. It took three tries before she got her key into her apartment door, slipping inside as if that one barrier had the power to keep the dark stranger out.

She locked the door behind her, placed her drink on her mantle, then ran to the window in her living room that overlooked the street below. Kneeling on her sofa, she moved the curtain aside with her free hand and pressed her forehead against the glass.

There was no one standing in front of the bakery.

He was gone.

Evangeline exhaled, twisting her body as she sank against the arm of the sofa. He was gone, and she wasn't sure how she felt about that.

Glancing at the phone she was still gripping tightly, she wondered why she hadn't called anyone when she feared that she was being followed. Safe in her apartment, she had to admit that it might have been concern that made her leave the shop, but she hadn't been afraid as he stalked behind her.

No, that hadn't been fear. She was almost... *exhilarated.* And what did that say about her?

It took her ten minutes before she remembered the reason she was still clutching her cell phone. By the time she was finally dialing Adam, she decided not to tell him anything about the man from the coffee shop.

She had just about convinced herself that she had overreacted—that it was all one big coincidence. Just because he got up and left the shop shortly after she did didn't actually mean he was following her home.

Maybe he was done with his coffee. Maybe his path had taken him this way. It didn't matter. He was gone now, and if he had somehow felt the strange connection that Evangeline had, there was no way she would ever know.

She didn't know how she felt about that, either.

10

Maddox burst into the front door of Colton's home like a tornado. A six foot four, bulky tornado with glowing gold eyes and a face sharpened from the vestiges of his last shift. Claws curled from a mangled mix of hand and paw, stretched arms hanging down past his hips as he stood hunched in the doorway. And then there was his constant erection, mocking him. Weeping from the tip, the head a deep purple, the damn thing pointed due north without any sign that it was going down anytime soon.

The door swung off its hinges, the knob punching a hole in the wall as it connected and stuck. Colt glanced up from the laptop in front of him, got one look at his brother's monstrous half form, then raised his eyes to the ceiling as if asking some higher power for help.

As if praying would help either of them.

Maddox spent three hours prowling outside of

Evangeline's apartment before he gave up, shifted to his beast shape, and ran the entire way to Colt's Bumptown. At least he knew where she lived and, while the wards kept him from entering, he knew what route she took for her coffee. He would be able to find her again, no doubt.

But what good would it do when she didn't recognize him?

Because she hadn't. During his long run when he pushed himself as much as he punished himself, he couldn't stop remembering how she glanced at him, almost unseeing, then took off.

She ran from him.

Fucking *ran*.

His mate never would've run from him.

No doubt that was Evangeline. But without her scent, without her forest green eyes lighting up with love whenever she looked at him, Maddox was forced to accept the truth.

That was Evangeline, but she wasn't his mate.

Not anymore.

As Maddox continued to stand in Colt's doorway, eerily silent and obviously livid and way too naked, Colt sighed, closed up his laptop, and set it on the coffee table. Then, because his brother's cock glaring at him was all the proof he needed, he said wryly, "I'd ask if you found her, but something tells me you did."

Considering Maddox's state, Colt knew it wasn't fair of him to take his rotten mood out on his brother. Then again, Maddox had just broken down his front door. Any other day, Colt would have been all for giving him a hard time. But then he thought about the hard-on Maddox was sporting and he felt a little guilty for not being all that sympathetic.

Not having control of their dicks... *that* was the true curse of the werewolf. Forget silver—the biological need to produce a generation of pups that would survive meant that a shifter could only procreate with their fated mate. Foolish romantics, some Ants had gotten it in their heads that shifters mated for life because they *wanted* to.

Yeah, right.

They had no choice. Female shifters didn't ovulate until they found their mate, and male shifters couldn't even get an erection. Was it any surprise that, once a shifter found the one person they could mate with, they held on as tightly as possible with both paws?

The mating instinct—and, later, the mate bond—was the pull between two people who could best love each other and only screw one another.

It was just one more reason why Colt never wanted to go searching for his mate in the first place. He didn't understand how sex and love went hand in hand like that. And when your mate was a human...

Humans mated who they wanted, when they wanted. Sometimes they did so because they wanted children. Most of the time, it was all about connection, sensation, and pleasure. From what Colt understood, human mating had very little to do with actual mating. It was fucking, plain and simple. Two people coming together to feel good without any lifetime commitment behind it.

Colt knew that changed whenever a paranormal and a human bonded. Just like the Para, the human would want nobody else—but that was with a bond. Colt's fingers curled into tight fists. Without a bond, human mates could do whatever the fuck they wanted—

Maddox cocked his head to the side. The move was decidedly canine. "Are you growling at me?"

It was one thing to be snarky. It was another to challenge an infuriated, aroused, *lonely* wolf shifter. Colt would be lucky if Maddox only kicked his ass if he kept on provoking him. His brother was wound so tight, he was almost vibrating in place. One wrong word. That's all it would take. Maddox would pounce, and not even the fact that they were blood would save him if Maddox's wolf got control.

Colt let out a rough exhale before dropping his gaze. "No. Just clearing my throat."

"You sure?"

"Positive. So, you gonna come in and tell me what's

going on? Or was mooning the whole Bumptown the reason behind your unexpected visit?"

"Mooning? Ah, fuck! My clothes!" Maddox finally stepped inside the house, grabbing the doorknob and jerking it roughly until it wasn't stuck in the drywall. His flashing eyes gleamed dangerously as he slammed the door shut behind him. He stalked toward his brother. "I wasn't even thinking when I shifted. And after I carried them all the way out of the Cage, too. Jesus, Colt, I'm a fucking moron. I forgot all about my clothes."

Shifters went through a ton of clothes. Something about the momentum of the shift, the final snap as the body traded one shape for another, made it impossible to keep clothes in one piece if you didn't strip first. The material burst at the seams, shredding into unwearable tatters.

Colt couldn't understand why one pair of clothes mattered to Maddox more than another, but recognized that this wasn't the time to ask about Maddox's sudden attachment to a particular outfit.

"Here," he said, leaning over the edge of his couch and pulling a pair of crumpled jeans from an overflowing laundry basket. He'd been meaning to stop by his parents' house and see if his mom would take pity on her poor son, but after everything that had happened lately, laundry wasn't at the top of his to-do list. Throwing them across the room, he hit Maddox squarely in his heaving chest. "Put those on instead.

I'm tired of that thing winking at me. And you can keep the jeans, too."

Maddox was still breathing heavily as he jammed one leg into the pants. "Jealous, little brother?"

Colt thought of his situation and shook his head firmly. "Not even a little bit. Now tell me what happened. Three days I don't hear from you and suddenly you're back, huffing and puffing and blowing my damn house down."

Maddox's expression went dark, his brow furrowed, lips pulling into an angry snarl. "I saw her. I saw Angie."

The monster hard-on had already clued Colt into that. But the mutinous expression, the fury that had Maddox tied up in knots? Add that to the fact that Maddox was in his house instead of busy claiming his mate again and something was wrong.

"That's good news. Good news, Mad... isn't it?

"It should've been. It was supposed to be easy. Find Angie, claim Angie. Only..." Maddox shrugged helplessly, his golden eyes wild. "Her scent was gone," he admitted at last. "And her eyes... she looked right through me. She acted as if she didn't even know who I am."

Colt nearly choked on his breath.

So it wasn't just him, was it?

Maddox's head snapped in his direction. "What was that?"

Colt swallowed roughly. "What was what?"

He didn't give anything away in his scent, he was sure of it; born an alpha wolf to the Alpha, Colt learned how to keep his emotions locked up tight so that nothing gave him away. He was working on twisting his words enough that no one could pick up on the rare times he didn't feel like being honest. Apart from that strangled gasp, there was no way Maddox should have been able to guess that Colt was suddenly rattled.

Except that Maddox was his older brother. So what if he spent the last few years in the Cage? Colt didn't stand a chance against him.

Maddox moved carefully across the room, picking his way around the furniture, never taking his predator's gaze away from Colt. "What aren't you telling me? What the hell is going on, Colton?"

Colt winced. Colton. Maddox sounded just like their father—just like the Alpha—whenever he barked out Colt's full name like that.

He couldn't help it. He immediately went on the defensive.

"Okay. Listen. You can't blame me. I thought it was a fluke. I mean, she's not *my* mate."

"What's that supposed to mean?"

"When I found her scent, right? When I followed her to the store in Grayson? She saw me. I know she did. She had to have known I was waiting out front, too. Why else would she sneak out the back? But… here's the thing, bro. She acted like I was a stranger. No recognition. She had a blank stare, a sad smile, and the same scent that used to be embedded in your skin. I knew it was your Evangeline, only she didn't know it was me."

Maddox glared at him. A rumble built up in his chest, growing louder and louder before his accusation came out in a mix of snarl and spit. "You didn't tell me any of that!"

Colt held up his hands. "Hey, I was hoping to be wrong. I'm not the one who bonded with her. I figured she had no reason to remember me. But you... she loved you, Mad."

"She might have once, but now she doesn't remember me. My *mate* doesn't remember *me*!"

Colt dared to meet Maddox's angry gaze. "What did you expect? She would see you, the bond would spring back, and you'd be busy making pups as soon as you got her back home?"

From the frustrated look on his face, that was exactly what Maddox had expected.

"That's what you told me would happen!"

"How the fuck would I know? Who died and crowned me the mating king? I told you what you needed to hear to keep from going full wolf the second you got out of the Cage."

Sometimes Colt wished his wolf didn't have that all-consuming need to obey Maddox's because, shit, what he wouldn't have given to be able to lie straight to his face.

Because the second the words were out of his mouth? Colt hated himself for telling the truth.

And when Maddox snarled before lunging straight at him, Colt didn't try to evade or submit to him without giving Maddox the chance to blow off some steam. Why would he? Whatever came next, he knew he deserved it.

Still… this was going to *hurt*.

The fight was fast and furious, a flurry of fists and fangs as each of the Wolfe brothers engaged in a partial shift. It was how they had always fought since they were pups: not a challenge or a real attempt to hurt each other, but a scuffle between brothers. In their human shape, Maddox was taller, though Colt was faster and wasn't afraid to hit his brother as hard as he possibly could; as wolves, Maddox had the full advantage because of his dominance. Halfway shifted, they were more evenly matched.

Colt was a single-minded fighter who fought dirty when he had to. Maddox had his missing mate bond to fuel him. While Colt got in a few good hits, it was no surprise that Maddox wiped the floor with his younger brother.

In fact, the floor was where they both ended up when the fight was over. Colt was flat on his belly, Maddox perched on Colt's back, forcing Colt to keep on submitting. There was blood on Maddox's knuckles and Colt's right eye was swollen shut, but while they both panted from a combination of exertion and adrenaline, the injuries were already starting to heal.

It was easy to let a good right hook do the talking when the damage done would fade away in minutes due to a shifter's metabolism. Their tendency to use a fistfight to solve all of their disputes used to drive their poor mother crazy, especially when Terrence jumped in and fought alongside his boys.

Colt ran his tongue along the inside of his mouth, checking his teeth. He could've sworn that last punch knocked a couple of them loose. Luckily for him, they all seemed to be accounted for. Not too bad. When they last fought years ago, Colt lost two molars and chipped a fang.

He felt Maddox's weight shift on his back. Peering over his shoulder, he found Maddox leaning forward, rubbing the rough, ruined skin on his neck with both hands. Colt didn't even think Maddox was aware he was doing it.

The scars from the silver collar reminded Colt how much the Cage had cost Maddox, and what was at stake. Colt knew his brother couldn't stand to lose Evangeline again. Discovering she didn't remember him was bad enough. If they couldn't fix this and fast, who knows how long before Maddox self-destructed?

Colt cleared his throat. "Hey? You feeling better now? Ready to start working on your bond again? Or do you want to go another round, maybe let me knock some sense into you first?"

Colt decided not to take it too personally when Maddox chuckled. He never thought he would hear that sound again, even if it came at his expense. And then Maddox told him, "My dick's so hard I could use it to hammer nails but, other than that, yeah. I think I'm okay now. Thanks, Colt. I needed that. And, hey, at least I know the mating instinct is still working for me."

"Don't mention it," Colt told him. "I know I'm trying to forget how much I know about your dick."

"Whatever, pup. I still think you're jealous."

Colt groaned as he pressed his face against his carpet. In this position, with Maddox purposely weighing him down, he was stuck. He couldn't do anything except wait for Maddox to get his ass off of his back. He was just grateful he'd been able to get his brother to put jeans on before their skirmish.

It was bad enough Colt had to deal with his own erection. Dealing with Maddox's... that just added insult to injury.

Maddox took over Colt's spare room again. It was either that or spend the night sleeping in the vacant alleyway near Evangeline's apartment building. With the revelation that, for some terrible fucking reason, his mate didn't recognize him, heading back into Grayson would cause more harm than good.

He couldn't get to Evangeline. He couldn't make any sense of what was happening. Being so close to her would be a tease his wolf didn't deserve.

So Colt, nursing a fading black eye and wearing a scowl, reopened his home up to Maddox. Until they could figure out what was going on—until Maddox could find a way to fix it—it made sense for Maddox to stay over at the Bumptown.

It threw him back to almost four years ago, right after he first found Evangeline. It had been pure luck—and a big ol' dose of fate—that led Maddox to his mate that first afternoon. He'd been out for a run, choosing to take the drive to Woodbridge because it was open land that didn't belong to any pack in particular. No dominance issues, no territory lines, just a good, honest run.

The wooded area surrounded a park that was popular with Paras and humans alike. He tended to stick to the trees, taking to the rougher terrain to give his wolf a challenge. Evangeline, he discovered, was the reserved type. On her days off from work, she liked to lay out on a blanket in a more secluded part of the park, reading a book while keeping to herself.

When Maddox caught her rich vanilla scent on a breeze, it was like a punch straight to the chest. It tripped him right out of his shift, going from wolf to man in an instant. For twenty-six years he'd been searching for a mate. He found her in a gorgeous brunette who shrieked when she first laid eyes on him.

Hungry Like a Wolf

At least he was already doing better this time around. Evangeline might have dashed into her apartment before he could confront her, but she hadn't screamed. That had to count for something, right?

Getting Evangeline to agree to be his mate had taken ages. When he wasn't prowling around outside the back of her home in Woodbridge, taking to the trees that bordered her yard, he stayed in Colt's home since the Bumptown was closer to Woodbridge than Maddox's place in Wolf's Creek was.

Just like how the Bumptown was closer to Grayson.

Without bothering to change from his borrowed jeans, Maddox sprawled out on the king-sized bed his brother kept around for when he came to stay. He stared up at the ceiling, his thoughts racing.

He made Evangeline fall in love with him once. She was still his mate. His bond might not be as strong as it was, but it wasn't completely severed like he'd feared. There was no denying the presence of his mating instinct; his erection didn't go down until after the fight with Colt, when Maddox had to accept that getting his mate back wasn't going to be as easy as he thought when he was waiting to be let out of the Cage.

The tether between them was fragile, weak, but it was there. Why else would he have picked up on her presence in the coffee shop? She locked eyes with him, too. She saw him.

Did she sense him?

He really fucking hoped so.

She ran, though. Maddox couldn't forget that. Her scent was so muted, he could barely pick up anything other than the sickly sweet smell that clung to her faintly, but he could've sworn there was a rush of... of *something* right as she bolted for the glass door.

At first, he thought it was fear. When he forced himself to back away from the crackling wards, he almost talked himself into believing it was a burst of excitement.

Not the way he wanted his mate to react when he finally found her again.

But, then, she wasn't his mate, was she?

Filled with sudden fury, Maddox unleashed his claws, slashing at the royal blue sheets that covered Colt's guest bed.

She used to be. She *should* be. Just like the bond should have snapped back into place.

Only it hadn't. And, as much as he didn't want to, he had to face the reality that, if he wanted Evangeline back with him as she should be, he was going to have to do something about it.

Struggling to regain his control—he didn't want to destroy anything else of Colt's because he couldn't maintain his hold on his anger or his wolf—Maddox let his thoughts turn to what it was like centuries ago, when witch burnings were a thing and it was all "shoot the wolf full of silver bullets, ask questions later when it shapeshifted back into Old Man Jenkins". Paranormals chose to keep their world segregated from the humans—not because of any great secret, but because the brutal truth was that the alternative could mean genocide.

But the world wasn't stagnant. It's always changing. First there were newspapers and radio, television and then the internet. Paras couldn't hide anymore and they didn't really want to, either.

Fifty years ago, they stepped into the light and they never left. It wasn't as easy as that, though. It took until humans stopped looking for monsters on every corner before the paranormal community finally revealed itself little by little, making strides, building relationships until having a law-abiding Dayborn vampire neighbor wasn't just accepted, but encouraged because they made excellent neighborhood watch captains.

Back then, though, mates were mates. None of this *Claws Clause* bullshit. If you found your mate in a village, you ran off with her and prayed the torches and pitchforks didn't follow behind you. Sometimes the village would mourn the loss of a woman of marrying age before writing her off as a sacrifice that kept the things that went bump in the night happy. And finding his mate made a paranormal male *very* happy.

But as more Paras found their mates in humans, the government inevitably stepped in. Realizing it was futile to try to keep a paranormal from his or her mate, they passed and enforced Ordinance 7304: the Bond Laws.

Or, as Paras snidely whispered to each other, the *Claws Clause*.

Not only did the strict set of laws prevent against forced matings—and the disasters that always followed when a mate wasn't given the choice—but the *Claws Clause* was a shield against the calamity that occurred whenever a bonded paranormal was left without their mate.

Shifters were the most unstable. Maddox would be the first to admit that. That's precisely why he had Colt lock and barricade him inside the spare guest room. Sure, he could knock down the door if he gave in to his urge to see Evangeline. It might be a little harder to get through the three chairs and a solid mahogany dresser Colt stacked up against it.

He needed to use the brain in the head on his shoulders instead of thinking with his cock.

Maddox got Evangeline to fall in love with him once. If he couldn't force her to bond with him, he'd have to convince her that she wanted to.

He banged his head against the pillow, trying to shake loose a brilliant idea or two.

Convince his mate to *be* his mate?

How the hell was he going to do that?

Come on, come *on*—

And then it hit him.

Mugs. The coffee shop.

Maddox exhaled roughly, lying flat on his back, slowly working his way through the fledgling idea.

When he was first courting Evangeline, he hid that he was a shifter for the first couple of months. Pretending he was human, Maddox orchestrated an "accidental" meeting at the coffee shop down the street from the offices where Evangeline had worked.

A week after he made that initial contact, they were dating. It was exclusive from that moment on. Two months later, when Evangeline called him out on being a Para, he confessed that she was his mate.

But it all started that afternoon with a fancy cup of coffee.

Hell. It worked once, didn't it?

Tomorrow, Maddox decided. He would head back to Mugs tomorrow, and every day after that until he could see Evangeline, scent her, and come up with a way to make her his once again.

11

After what happened the day before, Evangeline promised herself that she wasn't going to return to Mugs anytime soon. Mainly because she kind of really wanted to.

The lure of the stranger was that strong.

She couldn't explain it and that was after only a quick glance across the crowd. All through that day, she couldn't go more than ten minutes without thinking about him. At night, she rushed her mother off the phone and pointedly refused to tell Adam about her shadow home from the coffee shop.

She barely slept. Every time she closed her eyes, she inevitably fell into another of her wicked, sexy dreams. The only difference? The shadow man with the golden eyes had a face now. The sharp, sculpted features of the dark stranger from Mugs followed her into her dreams just like he followed her to her apartment.

In her dreams, he looked the same as he did that afternoon. Black t-shirt. Dark denim jeans. There was only one small difference. He wasn't wearing any shades, leaving her to drown in his molten golden gaze before the dream turned into another fantasy that left her feeling guilty when she woke up.

Because, when she was sleeping, Evangeline never remembered Adam.

Her dreams hadn't stopped yet and she didn't harbor any illusions that they would now; almost every night for months she'd had one. The shadowy figure seemed to follow her whether it was a nightmare or a fantasy. He seemed closer every time she dreamed of him, and in the few moments when she was trapped between sleep and awake, she wished that she could run to him—even if it meant leaving Adam behind.

Once she was fully conscious, she regretted her irrational impulse. She shouldn't want a dark stranger as much as she did and she felt guilty for being drawn to him.

Just like she tried to ignore how much that man from Mugs had affected her.

That morning, Evangeline was up and dressed before eight. The cold shower cooled her raging hormones enough for her to pull up her most recent manuscript and get to work.

Hours later, as she struggled to make sense of the

paragraph she was working on for like the fifteenth time, she chalked it up to caffeine withdrawal. She was missing her coffee. And, sure, she could've gone into her kitchen and brewed a pot, but why should she have to? She liked the way Mugs made her iced macchiato and one strange encounter wasn't going to keep her from it.

Besides, it wasn't as if he was going to be there again. And if he was? Maybe it would help to confront him and ask him if he had meant to follow her yesterday.

Evangeline grabbed her purse, made sure her wallet, phone, and keys were inside, then set her jaw. She knew she was reaching. She also knew she wasn't fooling herself.

That didn't stop her from heading back to the coffee shop.

MADDOX YANKED ON THE COLLAR OF HIS TURTLENECK.

Remembering how the Ants at the D.P.R. treated him after they noticed his scars, he had Colt run out and buy him a bunch of cheap shirts to hide his neck before he left the Bumptown. He already decided to approach Evangeline as human now that he knew she didn't remember him; after all, that had also worked for him before. He then made a conscious effort to hide his paranormal features until he was sure he wouldn't scare her off again. He borrowed another pair of sunglasses from Colt—in a bid to hide his Para eyes—and the turtleneck covered up the marks from the silver collar.

He despised the shirt. It was tight and confining, nothing like the t-shirt he had destroyed when he lost control and shifted a few blocks away from Evangeline's apartment. Maddox admitted that he hadn't been thinking clearly after walking right into her wards, but at least he'd had enough brain cells to wait until he was further from her door before he went wolf. The last thing he needed was for her to find a pile of his ruined clothes right outside her home and wonder how they ended up there.

He was still pissed at himself for that. Not so long after he vowed to hold on to the last reminder of her scent, Maddox went ahead and let his shift destroy it. It wasn't like he could replace it anytime soon, either. Not while Evangeline managed to hide her scent from him.

Then there was the undeniable fact that he hadn't been able to even approach the front door to her apartment building yesterday. Wards. He scowled as he nursed his coffee, clinging to the prop as some explanation why he was haunting the coffee shop. Her place was warded so heavily that he could throw everything he had at it and it would mean nothing because he wasn't getting in.

Just like Colt had a hate boner for witches, Maddox couldn't stand their wards. It wasn't natural, being separated from his mate like that. To see her, but not smell her. To know where she slept at night, but to leave her to sleep alone.

He slammed his half-empty coffee on his tabletop, yanked on his collar again, and huffed. For everyone's sake, she better be sleeping alone.

That was it. His biggest fear seeping its way into his thoughts despite how desperately he tried to ignore it. Gritting his teeth, he attempted to push the terrible suspicion out of his head only to fail miserably. Three years she was out there. Three years without any kind of mate bond.

It had been pure torture for Maddox while he was incarcerated, but at least he had his memories. After yesterday, Maddox was almost positive that Evangeline didn't even have that much. If she was faking, if she had recognized him and just pretended not to, he would've been able to tell. No. She looked *at* him—then looked right *through* him.

What would he do if Evangeline had started a new life without him?

Just the *idea* was so painful, Maddox had to clamp his jaw shut to keep his wolf's keening cry from escaping into the crowded coffee shop.

It wouldn't matter, he assured his wolf. Evangeline was his. He knew it. Fate knew it, too. They were made for one another. He was as much hers as she was his and Maddox would do anything to prove it.

Even sit at the same table for more than four hours

in the hope that he might get the chance to do more than stalk her home.

After he ordered his first cup of coffee and tipped the trio of baristas a twenty, they left him alone. He went back and had them refill his cup twice, his shifter metabolism burning through the caffeine before he even felt so much as a twinge.

No, it was the anticipation that had him twitching in his seat.

Where was she?

Though Evangeline might not know him any longer, Maddox refused to believe that she was a stranger to him, too. His Angie was as reliable as the sun. Once she developed a routine, you could set your watch by it.

It was barely noon yesterday when she walked into Mugs. He scrabbled for his last receipt. He bought a croissant because he needed something to chew on and—*there*. 12:13. That was maybe ten minutes ago.

Where *was* she?

The door swung outward, the bell tinkling gently. Like he'd been doing for most of the morning, Maddox glanced toward the front.

He went absolutely still.

Angie.

She turned her head to and fro, obviously searching for something. Searching for him? Maddox didn't want to risk getting his hopes up when, suddenly, their gazes locked from across the room.

Evangeline froze, like a deer in headlights as she stared. There was no other word for it. She simply stared.

Maddox had to tell himself that he was still wearing his sunglasses, otherwise he'd wonder if she could see his shifter's eyes flash and glow in the coffee shop's dim atmospheric lighting. His wolf was as attracted to Evangeline as he was. The mating instinct was hell. Just the thought of her could make him hard, a constant ache that wouldn't go away.

Now, if only he could get her to remember him. Knowing that he wouldn't be able to trigger the bond if he let her slip back to her apartment, he decided to treat Evangeline like the most skittish of prey.

In the hours that he'd been loitering inside of the coffee shop, Maddox had plenty of time to fine-tune his plan. He couldn't approach her straight out—that would only engage her fight or flight response. For this to work, she would have to come to him.

Trust him.

Though it was one of the hardest things he'd done in a while, Maddox broke the stare. He picked up his coffee, took a sip, turned his attention toward a different corner of the crowded shop.

There were at least twenty other patrons inside, enjoying their drinks, having a quick bite, using the free wi-fi. A soft, quiet sort of unmemorable muzak piped in through speakers scattered throughout the entire place. Conversations hummed. Machinery buzzed and frothed and beeped as the baristas worked the counter.

Over all of the din, Maddox still managed to make out her soft sigh.

He was already so attuned to her. As she got on line, Maddox obsessed over that sigh. What was the reason behind it? Relief? Or something else?

He didn't know—but he was sure as hell going to find out.

He watched her out of the corner of his eye. His sunglasses hid the way he followed every move she made. As she ordered her drink, paid the barista, went to stand on the far side of the counter to wait for her coffee.

His Evangeline was tall, and so beautiful that she stood out from any group. She kept a good distance between her and the next person, her arms crossed, almost like she was hugging herself.

Maddox watched her closely.

Colt told him that, the only time he saw her, she seemed distant and sad. Lost in her own thoughts. Maddox understood exactly what his brother meant.

Something... something wasn't right.

As if she could sense his scrutiny, Evangeline dared another glance over at him. He couldn't have stopped himself from reacting even if he wanted to.

Lifting his hand in a lazy wave, Maddox gestured to her.

He almost expected her to pretend not to see him.

She didn't. Instead, she glanced around her, checking to make sure she really was the one he was waving over. Evangeline obviously didn't believe it. Her eyes widened as she met his gaze again and pointed to her chest.

Maddox nodded.

He held his breath, careful not to make any sudden moves. If he did something to spook Evangeline now, he'd have to find a way to kick his own ass.

"Evangeline? Order's ready."

She started at her name, too distracted to remember why a female voice would be calling for her.

Her thoughts were too wrapped up in the same dark stranger from yesterday. How easily he lorded over his corner of Mugs, and just how casually he had gestured to her. She couldn't believe it. One second, she was waiting for her coffee—

Her coffee!

The blonde barista with the pixie cut was holding a cup of coffee in her tiny little hands. She wore an automatic smile, nodding when Evangeline rushed forward to take her drink.

Evangeline started to say thank you, but the words caught in her throat when she realized that the barista wasn't even looking at her. Nope. She was taking a second to openly gawk at someone across the coffee shop. Evangeline followed the barista's line of vision, not even a little surprised to find that the girl, barely out of her teens, was drooling over the dark stranger who had to be more than a decade her senior.

She bristled, her back going right up; though she knew she was being ridiculous, seeing the barista stare at him rubbed Evangeline the wrong way. She'd only ever encountered him herself the one time before but, in between yesterday and today, she'd thought about him so often that she built up an imaginary relationship in her head. She didn't know him—it just felt like she did. And it bothered her more than she wanted to say that someone else was eyeing him like he was a piece of meat.

Maybe that's what made her do it. Taking her coffee with the fakest of smiles, Evangeline thanked the barista. Then, before she could think about what she was doing, she straightened up to her full height and headed right toward the man.

He was just as foreboding and—okay, she'd admit it—as rakishly handsome as she remembered. He'd traded his tight t-shirt for a turtleneck that did even more to highlight his sculpted body and his broad chest, though he was still wearing the shades.

What was up with the shades, she wondered again.

She couldn't ask him that. Instead, pausing when she was near his table, she said, "Umm... hi. I saw you waving. Is there something I can help you with?"

"You were here yesterday."

She briefly thought about denying it, then decided against it when she realized that his words weren't even a question. That was definitely a statement. "I was."

"You come here often?" he asked.

"Is that the pick-up line you're going with?" Evangeline couldn't keep back her small smirk. All that time she spent obsessing over this man... and the first chance he got, he came at her with the lamest line in the book. Really? "Wow."

He chuckled under his breath. The rough rasp of his low laugh sent chills running up and down her spine. "Not a pick-up line. Just curious. I'm... I'm new to Grayson. I stopped in for coffee yesterday, liked it so much I came back today. Since I remember seeing you and you're another regular, I must've made the right choice. It's good stuff. Much better than what I was used to."

"I like it," she told him.

"Then we already have something in common."

Evangeline blinked, but didn't say anything else. She let her incredulous expression do the talking for her.

Another chuckle. "Don't worry. I'm still not trying to pick you up. Just trying to be friendly. Promise." With the heel of his boot, he nudged the chair in front of him away from the table. "If you've got the time, why don't you join me for a second? You seem to have good taste. I'm not all that familiar with the area.

Maybe you could tell me where else I should plan on stopping by."

"Oh, I don't know—"

"Sit. Please. Unless I make you uncomfortable... if I do, I'm sorry. I mean nothing by it. I just... it'd be nice to have a conversation where people didn't take one look at me and run the opposite direction." He gave her a crooked, tight-lipped smile. "Since I came to town, you're the first person who even tried to look me in the eyes." Tapping the rim of his pitch-black lens, he shrugged. "It was nice."

Evangeline felt her heart breaking for this poor stranger. Was she so paranoid now that she saw villains everywhere? He probably had just finished his coffee yesterday when she left and was leisurely exploring the town like she'd been doing the last few months. Look at her, getting herself all worked up, convincing herself that he had meant to follow her.

He seemed like a nice guy.

It couldn't hurt.

Right?

"Okay," she said, placing her coffee down across from him. "I guess I can sit with you. For a few minutes anyway."

A FEW MINUTES TURNED INTO HALF AN HOUR BEFORE Maddox knew it. He kept the conversation going anyway, starved for her company and eager to keep her close. He was well aware that Evangeline was only sitting and talking with him out of a blend of curiosity and pity.

That was fine with him.

And maybe he was going to rot in hell for plucking on her heartstrings the way he had. Oh, well. Desperation did that to him. He would've said anything to get her to sit and stay for just a little longer.

It was easy. *Too* easy. As soon as the awkwardness of the first few minutes was behind them, they fell into an easy rhythm as Maddox asked her about Grayson, hoping that he might learn something about Evangeline in the process. Not many people had a second chance to have a first date and, no matter what she thought she was doing, Maddox decided this counted.

Whatever he had to do to get Evangeline back, he would do it—even if it meant starting over.

When she mentioned the work she had waiting for her back at home, Maddox offered to buy her a drink for the road. She hesitated for a few seconds, then agreed when he said he needed another refill himself. Evangeline accepted the coffee graciously but, before she could excuse herself and leave, he quickly asked her about her work.

That was ten minutes ago. Oblivious to the time, Evangeline told him about her job as a copy editor. Her passion made her carefree and she spoke energetically, waving her hands to illustrate some point or another in between taking sips of her iced drink.

Maddox always loved that about her, the way she could lose herself in something that made her so happy.

He made her that happy once. And, he vowed, he would do it again.

She clearly enjoyed her work. Maddox was glad to see that that hadn't changed, even if she worked from home these days rather than heading into the office. Evangeline spared no details when it came to the publishing house she worked for, or what it was she actually did.

He had a much harder time trying to get her to tell him anything about her personally, but that didn't surprise him. Evangeline had always been guarded. Maddox knew he met his mate the first time they accidentally bumped into each other more than four years ago, but it took months of convincing before Evangeline would even call him her mate. She didn't take him home for almost the whole first year. For her to open up as much as she had, he considered that a miracle.

Maddox had spent the entire time trying to work up the nerve to ask if she was free for dinner—while trying not to think about how ludicrous it was to have to ask his *wife* out on a dinner date in the first place—and recognized that his window of opportunity was quickly shrinking. Because, all too soon, the conversation started to dry up. He was just trying to think of a

Hungry Like a Wolf

way to stretch it out when Evangeline's lips suddenly thinned. Maddox recognized the look of annoyance that flashed across her lovely features.

He was willing to bet he knew what caused that expression. An annoying buzz had been going off almost non-stop for the last ten minutes. It wasn't his phone—Colt was the only one with the number and he knew better than to bother him—which meant it had to be hers.

And she'd finally caught on to the fact that it was ringing.

"Something wrong?" he asked, keeping his tone light.

"What? Oh. No. I just—" She picked her purse up from its place on the floor and propped it on the edge of the tabletop. After fishing around inside of it for a few seconds, she pulled out a cellphone. It was vibrating loudly. "I thought I heard something," she murmured, more to herself than to Maddox. She glanced up at him. "I'm sorry. I... I should really take this call."

Evangeline kept the screen angled toward her. He didn't know if that was on purpose or not, but it didn't matter. Maddox couldn't see who was calling her and, while he didn't want to share, he had to remind himself that he didn't have a real claim to Evangeline.

Not yet, anyway.

"I understand," he lied. He choked down a sip of his cold coffee, acting as if it didn't bother him one way or another that she was choosing to talk to someone else.

And then she answered the phone.

"Hello?"

"*Eva.*"

Maddox's hand shook so hard that he spilled half of the mostly untouched coffee onto the tabletop.

A man's voice. That was *a man's voice*.

Evangeline looked up at him again, her eyebrows raised as she caught sight of his mess. "Hey. What's up?"

"*Where are you, babe?*"

And there went the other half of his coffee. Babe. That faceless bastard just called *his* mate 'babe'.

Evangeline leaned over and grabbed a handful of napkins from the dispenser. Covering the mouthpiece of her phone with one hand, she murmured, "Clumsy," and handed Maddox the napkins before getting up and taking a few brisk steps away from their table. As he made a half-assed attempt to mop up the spilled coffee, he was focusing on every word she exchanged with the mysterious man on her phone.

Thank fucking Alpha for shifter hearing.

"I told you what my plans were for the day," she said softly. "I'm getting coffee right now. Then I'm going right back to work. Remember?"

She might have been keeping her voice down. Maddox thought her words were clipped. She was clearly annoyed. Evangeline had always hated it when she felt she was answering to someone else which made for quite a few arguments early on in their courtship. Possessive shifter versus headstrong human, it had taken Maddox some time to learn how to care for Evangeline without smothering her.

This dumbass certainly hadn't.

"*I tried calling you a couple of times while I was taking lunch. Then just now. You didn't answer.*"

"The coffee shop is loud. I must not have heard it. Is anything wrong?"

Maddox thought of the way Evangeline's eyes had strayed toward the floor a few times during their conversation. He had heard the vibrations before and ignored them, so intent on listening to what she was saying. It made him a little bit happier to know that she might have done the same.

His happiness deflated like a balloon when the man started to speak again.

"*No, nothing's wrong. I just called because I wanted to remind you that it was Friday. You seemed a little iffy about the days yesterday. Didn't want you to forget about date night.*"

"Yes, Adam. I remember. I'll be ready by eight, like usual."

"*And maybe we can head back to your place after for some coffee.*"

"We'll see, okay?"

"*Okay.*" There was a pause. "*You sure you're feeling okay, Eva? You sound a little... off.*"

"I'm fine. I was just getting ready to leave. I've got a couple of pages to proof before I get ready for tonight. Then I'll be free."

"I'm looking forward to it. Eight o'clock... see you then. Love you, babe."

Maddox was stunned.

He could hardly believe what he was hearing.

No. No, that wasn't true. He *could* believe it, except that didn't mean he wanted to. Or that he *would*.

Sure, his mate was sitting there, having coffee with him, smiling at him—*bonding* with him—but only for this one moment in time. For a few precious minutes he had been able to pretend she was his again before reality smacked him in the face.

There was no bond. His Evangeline didn't know him from Joe Schmoe down the street.

And she was going out with some bastard named Adam.

Eight, as usual. There was a *usual* involved. This Adam fucker kept insisting on calling Maddox's mate 'babe' like he had the right. No. He refused to believe it. Something might have happened to break their bond, but it was going to come back stronger than ever.

It *had* to.

Keeping one ear cocked for the rest of the conversation, Maddox had been writing Adam's obituary in his head, already figuring out where he could hide the body if he ever got his claws on the bastard, when he heard Adam clear as day: *Love you, babe*.

Yeah, not if he knew what was good for him.

Maddox stopped breathing, waiting to see how his Evangeline would react. If she said it back...

And that's when she did something that made the fur sprout along the back of his hand in a total loss of control. After a small, almost imperceptible sigh—imperceptible to a human, not a shifter—Evangeline brought her phone's speaker up to her mouth before she smacked her lips softly into it.

Kissy noises.

Fucking *kissy* noises.

To another man.

It didn't matter that she rolled her eyes as she did it, or that she sighed again as she ended the call and slipped her phone into her bag. The damage was already done.

Because that little display meant one thing to the jealous wolf she'd unwittingly just provoked.

It meant that, despite her eye-rolls and tight voice, Evangeline wasn't being forced into another relationship. She was choosing to be with Adam when she'd already made her choice years ago to marry Maddox. To mate with him. To *bond* with him.

Except what the fuck did that mean when she obviously didn't remember?

Before any of the Ants in the coffee shop saw, Maddox jammed his furry claw-tipped paws into the pockets of his jeans an instant after he shoved away from the table and climbed to his feet.

Sure, it could have been worse. She could have said "I love you" back.

But *kissy noises*?

That did it. No more Mr. Nice Guy. No more lovesick puppy dog gazes, hoping she would throw him a bone. No more sitting and waiting and hoping she would remember and the bond would come back.

It wouldn't come back until he *made* it.

Without a word, and leaving a sopping mess of napkins and a visibly startled Evangeline behind him, Maddox stormed out of the coffee house. His borrowed turtleneck was already pulling at the seams as he fought his body's urge to shift. Because even his beast knew what was going to happen next.

Evangeline had sealed her fate the second she answered that phone. From there on out, she wouldn't be facing off against the man he'd been pretending to be.

Nope, she'd be dealing with the big, bad wolf.

12

It felt good to break out into his fur for a change.

Of the two of them, Colton was more in tune with his wolf than Maddox. He always thought it had something to do with being the second son of an Alpha leader. Accepting that he would have to fight two tough challenges to lead the pack and knowing that he would never challenge his father or his brother, his role was secure. He didn't have to bother with all of the politics so it didn't matter if he wore his fur on his sleeve. Give him his wood and his tools and his small patch of territory in his Bumptown and he was content.

Of course, that was all before Evangeline and the accident. Maddox never realized how much Colt's life turned upside down the night their car rolled over. With one stupid, reckless comment to the wrong person—because, even if he never admitted it out loud, he blamed himself for it every day—everything changed.

Evangeline was gone, Maddox was locked up, and Colt was suddenly his father's second, next in line to be Alpha of the pack.

To make matters worse, Maddox refused to let anyone else see him in the Cage except Colt. So Colt was reminded every damn time he drove out past Grayson that he had a paw in doing this to his brother. He would've given up everything, done *anything* to take back his careless words and fix this. When he stumbled on Evangeline, he thought he had his chance to make things right.

He was still trying.

It had been days since the last time he allowed himself to shift. Too much was going on and the more Maddox lost his control, the more Colt struggled to maintain his. It was bad enough he could barely fight his impulses while he was walking around like a man. If he even dared to shift away from his territory... well, maybe they hadn't found anyone to fill Maddox's cell yet.

Because that's exactly where Colt would end up if he couldn't get a hold of himself.

His wolf wanted him to head into the city. Colt was still strong enough to refuse to leave the Bumptown, no matter how much he wanted to. He eventually settled on a compromise that satisfied both him and his beast: a few hours in his fur and maybe he'd be too tired to go for a drive.

Colt *needed* to shift. The howling was driving him crazy. He finally gave in and let his wolf out in the sanctuary of the woods behind his house. He'd been holding a tighter leash than usual these days; if his wolf had its way, Colt wouldn't be available to help Maddox at all and, no matter what, the man part of him insisted that family came first. Pack before anything else. And if his wolf wanted to argue semantics about words like 'family' and 'pack', then it was going to be kept caged up tight for as long as it took for Colt to remember himself.

He ran for hours. Long after the Nightwalkers retreated to their coffins, the Dayborn vampires changing shifts as they went out on the hunt, Colton ran through the acres surrounding the Bumptown. It was a perimeter patrol as much as a chance for him to roam. Colt never went far, though, even if his wolf keened a lonely song as it flew through the trees.

There was too much anxious energy. Colt didn't cut short his run because he was tired. If he let his wolf off its leash, no doubt the beast could run all the way to Grayson without even a hitch in its stride.

He cut his run short because, when he sped past the border of his immediate territory, he picked up a scent.

Slowing down, Colt put his snout to the ground and snuffed. Recognizing it at once, he bolted for his house. He switched shapes once he was on his own land, ducking into his shed to throw on a pair of jeans and a tee. There was a cloying, sweet smell mingled with his brother's scent that warned Colt that he'd want to be fully dressed for this conversation.

He went inside, following the scent into his living room.

Maddox was sitting in Colt's favorite armchair—in the dark. And while shifters had amazing night vision, no one would choose to sit in the dark without a good reason.

The reek of grain alcohol was a pretty big clue that Maddox thought he had one.

Colt recognized it instantly. Whiskey. Hell.

Well, he figured, it could've always been worse. At least his brother hadn't started with the sappy power ballads yet.

Just like when he was in the Cage, Maddox had to have picked up on Colt entering the room. But he kept his head bowed, his eyes on the floor. His legs were spread, bracing his big body as he perched on the edge of the armchair.

Colt zeroed in on the pile between Maddox's boots. He rolled his eyes.

Wonderful. Forget a good reason. For this reaction? It had to have been a catastrophe.

A shifter's metabolism made it difficult for them to get drunk. To feel a buzz, Maddox would have to down an entire bottle straight; to get drunk, he would need another two bottles, easy. Colt's quick glance revealed that Maddox was surrounded by no less than three bottles at his feet, with another half-empty one hanging from his limp fingers.

Considering the shit Colt was dealing with on his own, walking into this mess was the last thing he wanted. His run had just about worn his wolf out, taking the edge off of him, but now it was clawing at the inside of his chest, desperate to break out again.

At least he had something else to focus on. Taking care of a drunk Maddox—while not at the top of his list of fun activities—would distract him for a while. He just hoped he had gotten to Maddox in time.

Because, if his brother managed to get enough drink in him, the alcohol made Maddox melancholy and whiny. It got so bad when he was first bonding with Evangeline that Colt and Dodge went through the house and cleaned it out of any liquor. Maddox always managed to sneak in his own. Colt could never understand it, since Maddox was never a big drinker, but there was something about his feelings for his mate that did that to him.

Maddox told him once that, when he thought of Evangeline, it was like a balloon filling his chest. She took up every bit of space inside of him, lodged forever in his heart, and when she rejected him, the balloon popped. It was agony. Maybe it wasn't the healthiest reaction, but the alcohol numbed his pain.

Colt always thought his brother was being a pussy.

A mate just *was*. The perfect half, the other side of their soul… there was no need for messy feelings to get involved. You find your mate, you claim your mate—it was supposed to be easy.

Colt learned the hard way that he was fucking *wrong*.

And that was the only reason why Colt didn't walk over to Maddox and snatch the whiskey bottle from his lax grip like he wanted to. Instead, he maneuvered his way past Maddox and flipped the switch on the other side of the room.

As soon as the light flooded the space, Maddox threw his head back and let out a pained howl.

"Are you done?" Colt asked dryly.

Maddox blinked rapidly, getting his sight back against the bright light. When the amber sheen rolled away, leaving the rich golden gaze staring up at him, Colt knew his brother was still in a state where he could make sense of this.

Of course, that just meant that Maddox was teetering between anger and whatever it was that did this to him.

He opened his mouth. No fangs in sight. The wolf was there, but it wasn't riding Maddox. Colt would've preferred dealing with Maddox's beast. The hierarchy was easy there. When Maddox let the man be in control?

Anything goes.

Maddox didn't say anything for a few seconds. It

was like he was searching for the words when he shrugged. "I— damn it to hell, Colt. She found someone else."

Colt tried not to wince at the news. It was super difficult.

Ah, *fuck*. That would explain it.

Maddox shook his head. "So that's it, I guess." He lifted his hand, brought the bottle to his mouth, *missed*, then tried again. After a few pulls off the whiskey, he wiped the back of his mouth with his other hand and slumped back into the armchair. It looked like it was trying to swallow him whole. "I have to accept that the bond's not coming back."

Oh no. No, no, no. Drunk Maddox declaring he was giving up was a very bad thing. Because, when he sobered up and realized he couldn't have Evangeline, he would be back on his way to the Cage—if he was lucky. Colt remembered the way Maddox told him he would never willingly go back to the prison.

Maddox would choose death this time. Colt was sure of it.

Hell no.

Crouching down, careful not to meet Maddox's gaze straight in case his wolf felt like it was being challenged, Colt kept his voice calm. Reasonable. "Listen to me. Do *you* feel the bond?"

"Yeah. It's not as strong as it was, but it's come back since I saw her myself. Doesn't mean shit."

"Like hell it doesn't. You feel it, she's gotta feel it,

too. If not now, soon. Give her some time. It took you ages last time before you even talked to her, and even longer before you guys were dating. Remember? Sneaking around her house, following her to work, spending nights apart? You nearly drowned in all those cold showers."

Maddox didn't crack a smile or even wince at the reminder.

"You don't get it," he said, a slight slur noticeable. "You've never been bonded. Once you find your mate, it's not that you don't want anyone else—it's like you don't *see* anyone else. You only want her touch, you only want to hear her voice... everyone can just fuck off and you'd still be happy. Angie made me wait because she was scared, but she never mated with anyone else. She is now. It's over, Colt. I lost her."

"You don't know that."

"I heard—"

"With your ears. What about your nose? Did you smell a man on her?"

"I can't even smell *her* scent anymore."

"That's not what I asked," Colt said firmly. "Does she smell like someone else is fucking her?"

Maddox growled, probably from the image Colt had purposely put in his head. "*No.*"

"So don't give up yet. You said you wanted her. Grow a fucking pair and take her. She's your mate. If you don't want anyone else to touch her, do something about it."

"I had a plan," Maddox told him. There was a whine in his voice that couldn't quite hide his slur. Nope, still wasted. "I was gonna take my time, make her fall in love with me again. It was a good plan."

"A good fucking plan," Colt agreed. "It worked once before."

"But she's with someone else. She wasn't then."

"Does it matter?"

Maddox blinked, thinking long and hard about Colt's question. "It should," he said at last.

"But it doesn't."

"No, it doesn't," Maddox admitted readily. He sighed, tilted his head back and brought the bottle to his lips. In three oversized gulps, he downed the last of the booze before hiccuping once and groaning softly. "That's why I got the shiws-key... the *whiskey*. Because I want it to matter. I want Evangeline to be happy and, fuck it, Colton. Maybe she is." He shuddered. The bottle dropped, landing with a thunk against the wooden frame of the chair as Maddox kept a tight grip on it. "Kissy noises, brother. *Fuck*."

Colt wasn't sure he heard that right. "What?"

"I said *kissy noises*." Maddox smacked his lips together, spraying his spit all over the place. "She gave those to her precious *Adam*. I never got them." He slumped in the chair, the empty bottle swaying and clanking. "So she's gotta be happy."

"She's not," Colt stated flatly.

"How do you know?"

"Because she's not with you. Kissy noises? Come on. You don't need to make noises when her tongue was halfway down your throat most of the time. So you might have given up, Maddox, but I sure the fuck haven't. She's your mate—no one can make her happy but you. You *know* that. If you weren't too busy getting shit-faced in my house, you'd realize that and make your move. Evangeline fell for a wolf, not a pussy."

When he saw the warning flash in Maddox's golden eyes, Colt realized he might have pushed him too far. It was hard to gauge how firm he needed to be, the alcohol throwing them both off. When his brother started to snarl, showing a hint of his fangs, Colt decided to retreat a little. Just a little, though. The more wolf Maddox revealed, the faster his shifter metabolism would burn the whiskey off.

That's exactly what Colt wanted. He needed Maddox sober.

A beating from a ferocious older brother he could handle. If a drunk Maddox started sniffling and singing power ballads from the '80's again, Colt was summoning Dodge and letting him take over. Sure, he was loyal, but he wasn't suicidal. A plastered wolf shifter howling along to Def Leppard's "Love Bites"? Pass the silver bullets, please.

Maddox leaned forward. His grip tightened on the neck of the empty bottle, as if he'd like to bean Colt over the head with it. "I haven't given up on nothing, you dick. But what do you want me to do? She doesn't feel the bond—"

"There's something wrong with your bond, we both know that. A normal bond, it would never have broken without a reason, and broken bonds mend pretty fucking quick between mated pairs. You keep acting like it's something you've got to do but, well..." Colt took a deep breath. "Here's the thing. There's something I've been meaning to tell you. I've been thinking—"

"Nothing good ever comes after 'I've been thinking'," Maddox observed, scowling. His eyes were still flashing, like a pair of high beams cutting through the darkness.

"Fuck you," Colt snapped back automatically, his voice lacking heat. He almost couldn't believe how nervous he felt since he didn't know how Maddox was going to react. Always unpredictable, this might set him off. "Your bond. After the accident, they offered to let witches remove your bond. How do you know... maybe they removed Evangeline's instead."

"She would never have wanted them—"

"She was hurt, Maddox. Bad. When they brought her to the hospital, no one knew if she would survive. But she was still one hundred percent human then, and... they wouldn't have needed her permission to remove her bond. Her parents could have given the okay. And if they did... well, you felt it when she 'died'.

Maybe... maybe that was the bond being severed on her end."

"You're telling me..." Maddox blinked, trying to understand. Confusion gave way to fury as what Colt just said seemed to hit home. He tensed, leaning forward, his free hand reaching up to pull at the front strands of his hair. "I... I hear you, but all this whiskey in me, I'm not sure I know *what* you're telling me. Damn it!"

With a sudden angry roar, Maddox reared back and threw the empty bottle. It screamed by like a bullet, whizzing past Colt until it hit the opposite wall, shattering on impact.

Raising his eyebrows, Colt said, "You better clean that up."

13

"Later," snapped Maddox. His eyes glowed with deadly focus. Still glazed, still drunk, but he was trying his hardest to pay attention. "Now explain to me exactly what you're trying to say."

Colt tried. He spoke softly, surely, explaining his suspicions. How, without a bonding license, Ordinance 7304 didn't apply to Maddox and Evangeline's mating. Nobody would've invoked the stipulations in the *Claws Clause* that said that bonds were sacred. With Evangeline on the edge of death, her parents could have chosen to sever the bond and no one would've stopped them.

Especially since they had no idea that their daughter had eloped with Maddox that morning. Only Maddox's family knew. Maddox would've told them all —the cops, the paramedics, her parents—except the crash knocked him out upon impact. He didn't stay out long, but enough time had passed that Evangeline had already been whisked away to a human-only hospital before he came to again.

They told Maddox she was dead on arrival. Someone had obviously lied. But why? And, the more Colt thought about it, the more sense it made. A mate bond was so powerful, Maddox should've been able to follow the bond inside of him and know that she still was alive.

Unless a witch was involved.

Colt had to work to bite back his snarl.

He fucking *hated* witches.

Maddox listened to everything Colt laid out. When Colt was done, Maddox climbed out of the chair, scattering the empty whiskey bottles from his path.

"It's just something to think about."

"They always hated me. Her mother especially. It didn't have anything to do with *me*, not really. It's my wolf. They hated the idea that Evangeline was a shifter's mate." Maddox stopped pacing. There was a little wobble in his step so the whiskey was still affecting his body. His mind, though? He was getting it. "If Evangeline was hurt, they would've blamed me in a heartbeat. They had the money to get the diamonds to hire the best witch in the state. They could've done it."

"Someone *did* do it," Colt said. "I don't know who for sure, but I'd be willing to bet anything I've got that they're responsible. Gonna make family dinners kind of awkward in the future."

Maddox didn't seem to appreciate his joke. Scowling, he said, "What family dinners? Evangeline chose someone else. The fucking *Claws Clause* is clear. She might be my mate but, unless she chooses to bond with me, I'm shit out of luck."

"Then screw the *Claws Clause*. Take her. If she's not around her parents or that other guy, maybe the bond will come back. She's *your* mate, Mad. Take her and prove it."

"Yeah, right. The Ants will have me thrown in the Cage so fast, my ass'll leave skid marks on the floor of my cell. Be serious, Colt. Hell, I thought I was the drunk one here."

"I *am* serious. It's how an Alpha always did it. Stupid *Claws Clause* didn't even come about until... what? Fifty years ago? For centuries, a shifter found its mate, claimed its mate, and doted on its mate. It never failed before. The bond knows. Even the humans admit that after a while. Besides, Evangeline chose you once before. Give her the chance and she'll choose you again."

Maddox blinked. "You... you mean this. Really mean this. What happened to 'that's kidnapping and it's against the laws'?"

"What are you talking about?"

"I distinctually... no, *distinctly*... I distinctly remember that. When I first met Evangeline and I knew she was my mate. You said not to take her, 'cause the Ants consider that kidnapping."

That sounded like something Colt would've said. But that was before.

Before he watched Maddox and Evangeline fall in love. Before Colt saw just how happy his mate made Maddox. Before—

"So? It's not like whoever had your bond cut didn't already go against the laws. You're just evening the playing field."

Shaking his head, Maddox muttered, "Oof. There's still way too much whiskey in my gut for me to listen to this shit."

"Why? Because you think it's too risky?"

"No. Because I'm beginning to think you've got a point. Evangeline already agreed to be my mate once. The bond's coming back... for me, at least. And we're still fucking married. It... it wouldn't be taking her, right? Just bringing her back home."

Colt could tell that Maddox's drunk brain was reaching. And, while he made a very excellent point, they both knew that the law wouldn't see it that way.

Know what?

Fuck the law.

Evangeline was Maddox's mate. And Colton Wolfe was going to do anything and everything he could to bring them back together.

"Exactly."

THE NEXT MORNING, AFTER MADDOX SLEPT OFF HIS whiskey binge in Colt's spare room, he wanted to believe that Colt was kidding. That, while Maddox was too inebriated to retaliate, his brother was deliberately fucking with him.

Taking Evangeline? Paras didn't see it the same way —not when it came to a mate—but there were so many Ant laws against it, Maddox would be risking his neck if he even tried it.

It had to be a joke.

Only it wasn't.

Laying on his back, remembering most of the conversation from last night, Maddox realized that Colt was serious when he said they could do it.

He was only too willing to help, too.

At first Maddox thought it might be the whiskey talking, but it wasn't long before he couldn't blame the booze any longer and, over lunch, Colt was *still* explaining how easy it would be to just run off with Evangeline.

Sober, aware, and missing his mate painfully, Maddox began to buy into the idea himself. And the more they plotted and planned and connived, it became clear that his younger brother got a kick out of trying to beat the *Claws Clause*.

He eagerly offered up the continued use of his truck, and even suggested using his house as a base of operation. Grateful for the offer, Maddox had to tell him no. He couldn't risk involving his family or any of his extended pack with this crazy idea. Something also warned him against bringing Evangeline to a Bumptown. The temptation to get that stupid piece of paper signed once and for all would be hard to resist, but he couldn't do that, not when Evangeline didn't even recognize him.

Besides, he had a place of his own in mind. The house he shared with Evangeline in Wolf's Creek would be too obvious, so that one was out, but the cabin... apart from his pack and his mate, no one had ever been there.

It was the cabin his father had offered up to Maddox and Evangeline for their honeymoon. Even though their wedding had been intimate—with Colt as the only witness at a quick courthouse wedding—his parents arranged for the newly married pair to spend a week at the cabin just outside of Woodbridge, the town where Maddox and Evangeline had met.

It was pack property, set beyond a small mountainous area, with plenty of land to roam on—and as much privacy as they would need for the final claiming that would make their bond permanent.

They never made it to the cabin. A freak rainstorm seemed to follow them through the trees and onto the narrow path that led through the mountains. With less than fifteen minutes left before they would've arrived at the cabin, the road gave way, the car ran through the old guardrail, and the crash tore Evangeline from his arms for the next three years.

No one would think he would take Evangeline there. Even Maddox thought he was tempting fate. But he had to do it.

It felt right.

Colt tried arguing. Of course he did. Maddox hadn't expected anything less. If he allowed him to, Maddox did not doubt that Colt would run out to Grayson and bring Evangeline back as easily as if he was picking up a gallon of milk from the corner store. He had to think quick, which wasn't easy considering his head was still foggy and running on whiskey fumes.

"I need you to do a huge favor for me."

Colt hesitated, obviously torn between wanting to do whatever he could to help Maddox and suspecting that Maddox was just trying to get him out of the way. His brother was smart like that. And while Colt already called Terrence and arranged for the cabin to be empty —without telling his father exactly *why*—he was wary of what other favors Maddox would need.

He sighed. "Okay. What is it?"

"Hunt down a witch."

Colt's brilliant blue eyes went suddenly icy. "What's the catch?"

"Catch? Well, you can't actually hunt the witch, for one. It was a figure of speech."

His brother huffed. "It's not nice to tease the wolf."

"I mean it, Colton. Once I get Angie"—because now that he signed onto this plan, it wasn't an *if* he went after her again, but *when*—"if you're right, if there's magic at work here, I'm gonna need a witch. If a witch can remove a bond, maybe they can figure a way to put it back the way it was on Angie's end."

It made sense to him. Maddox figured, if the government witches could take bonds away, he could pay a freelance witch even more to replace it. There wasn't time to seduce Evangeline, to remind her why she fell in love with him in the first place, and rebuild their mate bond. He didn't want to wait a second longer than he had to because, every second he wasn't with her, was another second that *Adam* might be.

It was as sound a plan as he was going to get. The D.P.R. wasn't going to help him. The Bond Laws left him with his paws tied. He needed that consent decree signed, the bonding license filed, which meant he had to do whatever he could to bring that bond back. It could only be notarized when both mates swore that there was a bond.

A witch was his last hope.

"Maybe get in touch with Cilla, if she's still around, but I'm not picky," Maddox said. "Anyone who knows the craft and can help me. I'll get the diamonds if you get the witch. I want the best and I trust you to do that for me."

Sending Colt to find one was a stroke of genius to his still half-inebriated brain. Not only was Colton the only one he could trust to be his partner in this crime, but—in the very likely scenario the plan got shot to

Hungry Like a Wolf

shit—he didn't want his brother around for any of the fallout.

His parents were safe. After twisting his brother's arm, Maddox got Colt to swear he wouldn't tell Terrence and Sarah Wolfe about his sighting of Evangeline until Maddox had claimed her for real. The days following the car crash were hazy, but he knew how much it killed his parents to watch him voluntarily walk into the Cage, knowing there was little chance he'd ever walk out again. Until he was sure that he wouldn't be going back, he refused to give his parents hope that things would be different. That they would be better.

It was for the same reason he refused to let them visit him when he was incarcerated. Maddox had only endured Colt's monthly visits because he knew that his brother would've torn down the damn place brick by brick if they tried to keep him out.

After all Colt had done for him over the last three years, Maddox owed him everything. At the very least, he wanted to make sure that Colt didn't get mixed up in his desperate scheme.

Even if it *was* his idea in the first place.

"Take Dodge with you," Maddox suggested, bringing up Colt's best friend. Dodge McCoy was a ghost with magic of his own. He could go invisible, walk through doors, and never forgot anything. Ever. "Maybe he'll help."

Colt's expression shut down. "Dodge doesn't leave

the Bumptown much anymore." He paused for a moment. Then, in an emotionless tone, added, "It's getting closer."

Maddox winced. "I'm sorry. I didn't know."

"Hey, I always knew he had an expiration date. I mean, he's a ghost. He died once."

"Maybe the witches will be able to help him, too."

"That's what I thought." Colt shook his head. "He tried. No luck. When it's time, it's time. Dodge always knew that."

Maddox raised his hand, rubbing away at the back of his neck. He was suddenly super uncomfortable. "Hey, uh— is there anything I can—"

Colt stopped him. "Go. Find your mate. I'm gonna chalk your little chick flick moment here up to the whiskey still in your system. I'm a big boy. I'll miss Dodge, but if you're waiting for me to start sniffling..."

"You're such an ass, Colton."

Colt's lips quirked upward just enough to be considered a grin. "Doesn't it make you happy to know that not everything has changed?"

14

She shouldn't be back at Mugs.

It was a bad idea.

Her mother would have her head, and Adam would totally lose his if he knew.

Good thing neither of them did.

Evangeline entered the coffee shop. She intended to get in, get her coffee, and go. Just one quick look, that was all she was going to allow. And even that was ridiculous because who would continue to go back and spend the day away drinking coffee like they had nothing else better to do?

Well, except for her, of course.

Before she opened the door, Evangeline took a deep breath. She tried to pretend that she didn't care one way or another if he was inside. And then, when she entered Mugs and found that he had claimed the same seat he had on Friday, she tried to fool herself into thinking that her giddy excitement that caused her belly to flip-flop was just hunger pangs because she'd missed breakfast that morning.

As if he'd been waiting for her, his head jerked up the instant Evangeline moved through the doorway.

He waved.

Go to the counter, she told herself. Go to the counter, order your drink—

Her feet betrayed her. While she was still in the middle of talking herself into avoiding her coffee date from last week, her lower half didn't seem to be on board. Before she realized it, she'd veered off to the right, heading straight toward him.

Evangeline smiled when she stopped next to his table, butterflies flapping nervously in the pit of her stomach when his lips curved in a sexy, answering grin.

"Um, hi... I wasn't sure if you'd be here today. You kind of ran out without saying goodbye last time."

"Sorry about that. I got a buzz while you were on the phone. It was a family emergency." He paused for a second, then added, "My brother. Colton."

Evangeline got the strangest feeling that he expected her to know his brother. Come to think of it, it dawned on her that, despite the hour-long chat they had before the weekend, she didn't even know *his* name.

She was just about to ask when he got up from the table. Holy Christ, she hadn't imagined his size. The guy was huge, but in an absolutely delicious way.

"I hoped I'd see you again. Here." He leaned past her, pulling the extra seat out. "If you have a second, I'd love to hear more about the story you were telling me last time."

Evangeline glanced at the empty chair. She wanted to sit. Wanted to take a load off, pretend that he could be a friend she met for coffee every now and then. She wasn't that naive, though. If she felt the connection between them, he probably did, too.

Which was why she had to decline.

"I wish I could, but I'm pushing a deadline. I really just ran in to get my coffee. I can't stay."

"I was just about to get some more myself. Let me buy you a cup."

"Oh, no. That's okay. I don't drink actual coffee."

"I know. You get that iced thing," he said. "Don't worry about it. I got you. Consider it my treat for humoring me the last time I saw you. I owe you for some of your recommendations. That Chinese place you told me about? It was delicious. Least I can do is get you a drink."

When he put it that way…

"Okay. Thanks."

"Wait here. I'll be right back."

Evangeline stayed by the table while he stalked right over to the counter. No one else was waiting to place an order and she watched as two baristas—one male and one female—had a quick, silent argument over who had to take his order.

For a second, she felt her heart break for him again. She remembered him telling her how she was the first one who wasn't put off by the glasses or his size. Feeling awful, she took a few steps toward the counter —only to pause when the male barista pouted, then stormed toward the backroom. The girl had a noticeable smirk on her pretty face as she turned to face the man.

Evangeline paused.

Oh. So she had read *that* situation wrong.

He braced his hands on the counter, leaning in to smile at the barista. "Hi, Kimmy. Can I have another refill?"

"Straight up black, right?"

"Right. You know I like to add the sugar myself. And, uh, how about one of those macchiato drinks? Caramel. Iced. The biggest one you got."

"Coming right up."

Evangeline was surprised yet pleased that he remembered that much of her drink order. She had a complicated one, she'd be the first to admit it, but it was still touching that he had noticed she had an iced caramel macchiato, even if he didn't ask for almond milk or a pump of vanilla syrup. The thought was there.

As soon as his order was done, he took both of the drinks over to the milk and sugar bar. As he tended to his coffee, Evangeline dared a peek over to the counter. Just like on Friday, the cute blonde barista with the pixie cut—*Kimmy*—was following every move he made.

And, just like on Friday, Evangeline discovered that, for some inexplicable reason, she really, really didn't like that.

She shouldn't do it.

She shouldn't do it—

Evangeline joined him at the milk and sugar bar just as he put the lid back on his to-go cup.

Glancing up, he shot her a quick grin when he saw who it was. "Hey." He picked up the cold drink, holding it out to her. "Here you go."

"Thanks." Evangeline took it. He had already put a straw in her cup. She took a sip, savoring that first taste as he finished cleaning up his mess. She did a double-take when she noticed the small bag next to his big hand. "What's that?"

"This?" He picked it up. About half the size of a sandwich baggy, it was full of a crystallized white powder. "It's mine. I can't have real sugar, so I use a sugar-free sugar in my coffee. Some small indie shops have it, but most don't. I guess I've gotten used to carrying around my own."

Evangeline wrinkled her nose. "Sugar-free sugar?"

He laughed, the sound a rumble deep in his chest. It was nice. "I know how that sounds. You ever heard of stevia?"

She shook her head.

"It's like a sugar substitute. It's super sweet, but it

comes from a plant. No calories and it doesn't cause my blood sugar to spike. I always bring some with me in case I stop for coffee." He held the bag out to her. "Want to try?"

"Thanks, but I'll have to pass." Evangeline took another sip. "This one's pretty sweet already."

He nodded, then tucked the small baggy into the front pocket of his jeans. "Maybe next time."

Maybe.

"Well, thanks again. I'll have to get yours next time I see you."

He grinned. While the dark shades highlighted his dangerous air, his wide grin managed to soften his sharp features. "Until we meet again."

It was too easy to talk to her dark stranger.

Or maybe she just didn't want to leave.

Evangeline stood near the doorway, edging closer to the exit as she struggled to convince herself that she needed to go. Ten minutes after he bought her coffee, she still hadn't left Mugs.

She wasn't even sure how it happened. He made a comment right when she turned to go, Evangeline paused, then answered him. One question led to another and, suddenly, they were engaged in a full-blown conversation. She kept trying to find a way to ask him his name, then gave up; it was already awkward that, after talking to him twice, she still didn't know it.

She kept hoping he'd ask her for hers. He didn't.

It didn't seem to bother him. Evangeline tried not to let it bother her.

Her macchiato was down to the ice before she realized that she'd stayed far longer than she meant to. He was still talking but, for some reason, she was finding it a little difficult to concentrate. Her head felt cloudy, her eyelids heavy. The sleepless nights were finally catching up with her.

Holding up her finger, gesturing that she was moving toward the trash while he continued to talk about... *something*, Evangeline took two steps before stumbling.

He was right there to catch her.

"Hey. You okay?"

"Wha— oh. Yeah. Sorry. I'm just feeling tired all of a sudden. It's so weird. And you got me a large drink, too. That much caffeine, I should be"—Evangeline couldn't stop herself from yawning widely—"oof, *wired*."

"That's my fault. You said you had to hurry back and here I am, yakking your ear off."

Evangeline tried to tell him that it wasn't him, it was her. Strangely enough, she couldn't form the words. She ended up nodding, then felt terrible, almost like she was agreeing.

He didn't take any offense. Instead, after easing the

empty plastic cup from her suddenly lax grip and tossing it in the trash, he slung his arm around her shoulders. Evangeline knew there was a reason why he shouldn't be tucking her close into his side like that but, for the life of her, she couldn't figure out what.

He smelled so yummy. Just like a man should smell.

If he noticed the way she nuzzled him, he didn't say. He just slid his hand up her arm, comforting her. "Let me help you get out of here."

She started to tell him that she was fine, that she didn't need his help, but the words got lost along the way. Another heavy yawn ripped out of her as he opened the door, ushering her onto the street.

Evangeline blinked in the sunlight. Her eyes were too sensitive after the darkness inside of the coffee shop. The bright light was almost piercing and she clamped her eyes shut to escape the pain.

Her legs felt weak, like she was dragging. The strong man at her side carried her easily. It dawned on her that he was bringing her somewhere and she was just letting him. Was she crazy? She needed to head back to her apartment.

There was no way he knew where she lived. So where was this stranger taking her?

She opened her eyes just in time to see a shiny black two-door truck parked down a side street. Her stomach jolted. Unless she was wrong, he was leading her right to the vehicle.

God, she hoped she was wrong.

In case she wasn't, she tried to pull away from him. Impossible. The arm that had been so sweetly laid over her shoulder had turned into a chain that kept her tethered in his embrace.

What... what was going on?

He made a bee-line straight for the truck. Without letting go of Evangeline, he opened the passenger seat. Then, while she was too stunned to do anything to fight back, he picked her up easily and sat her in the seat.

No.

She shook her head weakly.

No!

"Shh. Everything's gonna be okay. I promise." He reached over her, yanking the seatbelt across her chest before fastening it with a decisive click. "You can trust me."

Like hell she could. She wanted to scream. Screaming seemed like something she should be doing. But her tongue was too big to fit in her mouth, dry and thick. She tried to open her jaw and felt her head lolling back instead.

A soft whimper escaped her.

He touched her cheek, tucking her into the seat, securing her as if he thought she could go anywhere other than where he put her. "You'll understand sooner or later. I had no other choice."

The door closed gently, trapping her inside.

Not the truck...

She tried to beg. Tried to plead. Tried to tell him that she never wanted to ride in a vehicle again. Even incapacitated, she knew better than to willingly stay in this truck.

Her hand wouldn't work. She reached for the handle, missing it by a mile. Before she could try again, the bastard climbed into the cab beside her. In her fuzzy, heavy head, she reached out and slapped him, fighting him off before she made her escape.

In reality, he tucked her flailing hand into her lap, then reached down and lifted Evangeline's purse so that it was in the seat between them. The last thing Evangeline remembered was the dark stranger rifling through her bag and pulling something out of it.

After that, there was only blackness.

15

For the fifteenth time, Adam Wright dialed Evangeline's cell phone number. And, for the fifteenth time, it went straight to voicemail.

It was off.

Her phone was off.

A muscle ticked in his jaw, his boot slamming down on the gas pedal.

It was *never* off.

And, okay, so maybe she didn't always answer it as often as he would like. She got touchy when he questioned her, and Adam was working on the urge. He didn't want her to think he was constantly checking up on her. That would only lead to her wondering *why* Adam was so worried about her when, on the outside —and based on what Eva said herself—there was nothing for anyone to be worried about.

When it came to hiding the truth of Evangeline's

missing year, Adam had long been skeptical. The more he got to know this Evangeline, the more he came to adore her, he began to think that maybe she should be told what she'd forgotten.

Or, better yet, *who*.

Wolfe.

Adam sneered as he pushed his cruiser faster than was legal. He thought about turning the sirens on before deciding against it. If his hunch proved to be something more than just his overreacting imagination, he didn't want to give Wolfe any advanced warning.

Ever since the prison board voted to let the animal out, Adam had been waiting for something like this to happen. Didn't matter that the perks of the Bond Laws were worthless since there was no record that Evangeline had bonded with that beast. He'd spent the last year working at the Cage. He knew what those monsters were capable of—and how much danger she would be in when he found her and she didn't remember him.

If Wolfe believed that Evangeline was still his mate, nothing on Earth was going to stop him from going after her. If she knew the threat that lurked out there for her, she could be at least be prepared.

Her mother insisted on the secret. Eventually, Adam agreed, mainly because he knew he would do whatever he had to to keep her from learning all about Wolfe.

The animal lost her once. He couldn't be allowed to get his paws on her again.

Adam made it his personal mission to keep Evangeline safe away from Wolfe. So he watched from a distance, helping Naomi and Paul Lewis support Evangeline during her recovery. When she was ready to move out again, he suggested that she move to Grayson because it was his precinct.

He was supposed to protect her. It was his duty as a police officer, and it was his privilege as Evangeline's boyfriend. As far as he was concerned, her *fling* with Wolfe ended the day Wolfe lost control of his truck and Evangeline nearly died.

Whatever bond they had that day was broken. Adam doubted one had existed at all. When she finally woke up from the hospital, she didn't even remember the Para.

It was the best news Adam had ever heard.

Adam had been halfway in love with Evangeline Lewis for years. When he was a kid and she didn't want to give him the time of day, he talked himself into believing it was a harmless crush. Nothing serious. Each went their separate ways: Evangeline went to school to study English and became an editor while Adam headed straight for the police academy.

But he never forgot his Eva.

He was a couple of years into his time on the Grayson PD force when he learned that Evangeline had hooked up with a wolf shifter. Maddox Wolfe, next in line to run the biggest pack in the state. That nearly killed Adam. Not only did he lose his woman to a Para, but Wolfe was a powerful bastard, too.

But power only went too far. Laws were laws for a reason. When the bond snapped, when it was touch and go for Evangeline for a while, Wolfe exhibited signs of a bonded shifter without his mate and got thrown into the Cage. The lack of a bonding license worked to everyone's advantage because, when she pulled through, no clause said that Wolfe needed to be informed that she hadn't died.

She wasn't his mate.

She *wasn't*.

She was free. With no bond to tie her to that monster, Adam saw his opportunity and he took it. Sure, he'd had to wait while Evangeline recovered her strength. The accident was so bad, PT alone took months. And her parents were so traumatized, they started treating their only child like she was a girl again instead of a woman in her mid-twenties.

Then came the day that Wolfe's pretty boy brother showed up at the Cage. It was the moment Adam had been dreading since they forced him to do his year inside. Colton Wolfe had discovered that Evangeline was alive.

And Adam had to make his move.

With her mother's help, Adam finally got his chance to show Evangeline how much he cared for her. At the same time, he vigilantly kept tabs on his girlfriend, protecting her without telling her *what* he was protecting her from.

When it came to taking care of Evangeline, her parents were firmly on his side. Adam knew it was because he was human, but he didn't care. Naomi was as invested in keeping Evangeline away from her old "mate" as he was.

Which was why, when Evangeline went for more than an hour without turning her phone back on, Adam contacted Naomi. Evangeline's mother already knew that something was up. When she couldn't get her daughter on her cell phone, she tried the apartment. No answer there, either.

So then Naomi tracked her.

Adam pulled the cruiser up to the curb in front of Mugs. The coordinates for the point where Evangeline's phone last broadcasted a signal was about a half a block away, but Adam knew it was an approximate guess at best. Since Evangeline was a caffeine fiend who visited Mugs as often as she could, his best bet was to check the shop.

Probably because it was still early afternoon, Mugs was crowded. It took Adam a few minutes to march through the place, checking each table, each face, for Evangeline. When he assured himself that she wasn't there, he headed straight for the counter.

The girl who stood at the register was all of maybe twenty years old. She was cute, in a kid sister way, with short blonde hair and big brown eyes. She looked puzzled when he cut in front of a college-aged kid about to order, then smiled when it was obvious the kid wasn't going to argue.

"Hi. Welcome to Mugs. What can I get you?"

He had his phone in his back pocket. Because this was his afternoon off—which was the excuse he was going to use for trying to get Evangeline on the phone since he wanted to go see her—Adam was wearing a button-down shirt and khakis. He grabbed his phone, showing the girl at the counter the picture on his lockscreen.

He'd taken that photo of Evangeline during their first date night. She had no idea. It was a three-quarter profile, with Evangeline looking at something in the distance. A sad smile tugged on her pretty lips, her eyes almost lost.

Adam turned it so that the girl could see. "Was she in here today?"

"Uh. Yeah. I recognize her."

"From today?"

She nodded. "Most days, but today for sure. Like an hour ago, maybe two. During the lunch rush, definitely."

"Who was she with?"

"What?"

"This woman. Was she alone or was she with someone?"

The girl hesitated.

Trying to hide his mounting frustration and

Hungry Like a Wolf

growing worry, Adam leaned in and gave the barista a strained grin. He glanced at her name tag. "Look, Kimberly, this is important. If you know something, I need you to tell me."

"I'm not sure if I should—"

Wrong answer.

He yanked his badge off of his belt, slamming it against the counter. The girl jumped, and he tried to force himself to dial it back.

"You're police," she squeaked.

"I'm her boyfriend."

Kimberly's big brown eyes went wide. "You are? Then who was that guy she left with?"

As if she realized what she said, she lifted her hands, covering her mouth. Too late. The damage was done.

Adam felt his stomach drop down to his shoes. "I need a description of the guy. Now."

She told him. For whatever reason, the coffee shop girl had gotten a pretty good look at the man who left Mugs with Evangeline. Her description talked about how big he was, how handsome he was, how nice he was. Generous, too. Dark hair. Rugged features. Sunglasses.

By the time she mentioned that he was wearing a tight turtleneck, something that caught her attention because it was so warm out, Adam had to work to keep his fear back. There was only one reason the dark-haired man in sunglasses would also be wearing a turtleneck.

Maddox Wolfe left the Cage with the tell-tale ring of scars.

And now he had Evangeline.

Through gritted teeth, Adam forced himself to thank Kimberly for her time. He remembered to offer her one of his cards with the express instruction that, should she see the guy again, she needed to call Adam right away. He doubted Wolfe would return to Mugs—why would he if he managed to leave with Evangeline—but he needed to cover his bases.

Then, thinking about the coordinates where Evangeline's phone had pinged last, Adam left Mugs and turned right. At the end of the block, there was a side street that was just secluded enough to catch his attention. And it just so happened to be the exact spot where Evangeline's phone was last at.

He made a sharp turn, searching the side street. At first, he didn't see anything out of the ordinary. Adam didn't realize how much he was holding out hope that she had just let her phone run out of battery and was mingling downtown, coffee in hand, until he was met with an empty street.

No, he realized a heartbeat later. Not empty.

A stray sunbeam managed to break through the shadows of the side street, glancing off of a pile of mangled metal pieces lying in the middle of the empty road. Adam broke into a jog, heading straight for it.

Crouching down next to it, it didn't take a puzzle-master to recognize what he was looking at. It was the broken remains of what used to be a cell phone.

Evangeline's cell phone.

He immediately reached for his own. It didn't matter that it had barely been an hour since she'd been taken. Evangeline was gone, and she was most likely at the mercy of a shifter who wouldn't take no for an answer.

Forty-eight hours be damned. Officer Wright called it in.

Whatever Maddox gave her, whatever he dosed her with... it was some powerful stuff.

The sedative had been another one of Colt's ideas. He even went out to get it himself, returning less than twenty minutes later with a bag of powder and a guarantee that it would calm Evangeline down long enough for Maddox to spirit her away.

Because Colt was gone and back so quickly, Maddox suspected the powder came from someone in the Bumptown. He made a point not to ask what exactly it was; despite a hint of bitterness that whispered out when he sniffed at it, it seemed as innocent as baking powder.

Yeah. It definitely wasn't.

Not only did it work way faster than he expected,

but it knocked Evangeline on her ass. If Maddox hadn't been there to load her into the truck, she would've dropped to the sidewalk.

She didn't even twitch the entire drive out of Grayson. Maddox floored it as soon as they crossed city lines, heading straight for pack land. He didn't want to risk Evangeline waking up before they got to the cabin.

Turned out that was a pointless worry. The day had slipped by him, it was closing in on sunset, and Evangeline seemed as if she'd be sleeping forever.

Maddox knew he probably should leave her to it. Though she appeared to be peaceful, it wouldn't last. He accepted that. Finding him hovering over her when she finally woke back up would probably make it all worse.

He tried to leave after he assured himself for the countless time that she was still breathing. His wolf wasn't having it. Claws shot out, a snarl ripping out of him as his two halves battled over their next move. Spit sprayed the floor. Maddox left a gouge along the wooden doorjamb.

His wolf won.

Deep down, Maddox admitted that he didn't fight his beast as much as he could have. So long as his wolf had its mate in its sight, it was content to wait for Maddox to let it out again.

So, with his wolf caged, Maddox struggled to keep from going feral. The longer Evangeline's eyes stayed closed, the harder it was.

He paced the length of the room, careful to make sure to keep at least a good five feet between him and the edge of the wooden bed frame at all times. As soon as he had laid Evangeline out in the center of the oversized bed, he covered her with a thin sheet then backed off. He had to touch her to carry her inside but that was it. When he placed his hands on her again, he wanted it to be because Evangeline let him.

If she was anything like the mate he remembered, staying on the opposite side of the room wasn't just smart. It was *essential*. Maddox didn't know exactly how she was going to react—nothing had gone the way it was supposed to since they let him out of the Cage— but odds were that it wasn't going to be all that positive.

While she was still out, Maddox spent hours planning what he would do when she came to again. How he would grovel if he needed to, beg if he had to, anything to make Evangeline see that she had nothing to fear. That he had no other choice.

He hadn't. To a human, this was definitely kidnapping. Paras didn't see things in black and white like the do-gooder Ants did. Especially when it came to shifters, it was all about instinct. The mating instinct was almost undeniable. He wasn't about to climb on top of his poor mate and start rutting on her—he had more control over his animalistic urges than *that*—but there was no right or wrong when it came to being with his mate.

Evangeline was a human. There was a pretty good

chance that she wasn't going to see it the same way as he did.

There was still some light left outside, but night was quickly creeping in when his ears pricked. He heard her breathing change, the deep pulls turning shallow as she struggled to resurface again. Her legs stretched, toes pointed, the sheet beneath her rustling as she twisted, going from her back to her side.

Maddox froze, then quickly backed into the corner. Because if he didn't? He wasn't sure he could stop himself from rushing toward her and that just wouldn't end well at all.

He crossed his arms over his chest, heart racing, fangs lengthening, and he waited.

It took longer than he liked for Evangeline to fully return to consciousness. So in tune with every move she made, desperate for her to look at him, to realize he was standing right there, Maddox could tell when it finally hit her that something wasn't right.

That something was off.

Slowly, ever so slowly, Evangeline flipped so that she was laying on her back again. She didn't see him right away. Her eyes were open, though, big, green eyes staring up at the ceiling as she let out a soft moan.

His hackles rose. The growl was out before he could swallow it.

Evangeline turned toward the sound. Letting out a squeak of surprise, she lifted her head enough to spy him lurking in the corner of the room.

Her mouth dropped. She took a deep breath—

Maddox leapt forward, dashing toward her, closing the gap between them before she could even fill her lungs. He held his hands out, pleading. "Don't scream. Please don't scream."

She strangled the scream, turning it into a panicked gasp. Her eyes darted his way, shooting to his left, his right, taking in the room that had to be entirely unfamiliar. She saw the door.

He'd throw himself in front of it before he let her get to it. One glance at his face, and she could tell.

Evangeline struggled to find the right words. "What is... what are you—"

"It's just you and me here. You're safe, I swear it. I had to take you with me. You'll understand if you just give me a chance to explain."

She trembled. Terror mixed with pure disbelief as she stared up at him. A spark of recognition filled her wild green eyes. For a second, he had hope, when she said softly, "Wait. I know you. You're the guy from Mugs."

Shoulders sagging, Maddox nodded.

Her voice dropped to a whisper. "That's where I was... but where am I now? Where did you take me?"

"Listen, I can explain."

She didn't want to hear it. "I was drinking coffee. It's the last thing I remember. I couldn't have blacked out again... there was no headache. How did I get here?"

"You didn't black out," Maddox told her. He didn't know what she meant by headaches or blacking out, but he didn't want Evangeline to think there was something wrong with her. "It was me. I just needed you calm."

"Calm?" Her voice rose so high on that one syllable, the pitch could've shattered glass. "Calm? I am *not* calm. You can't *expect* me to be calm. Where am I? Who *are* you? What the hell is going on?"

Then, as if just realizing that she was laying in an unknown male's bed, Evangeline's back went ramrod straight as she jerked upright, pulling herself in a sitting position. The sheet pooled around her waist. Her attention dropped to her chest.

Relief pulsed off of her for a split second as she realized that she still had on the pale pink v-neck tee that she'd be wearing when she went to the coffee shop.

The relief didn't last, though.

Shoving her hair out of her face, Evangeline looked over at him, shock plus confusion—and a heavy dose of pure accusation—twisting her pretty face into a look he never wanted to see her shoot his way again.

She swallowed roughly. Her voice, normally so throaty and enticing, was emotionless when she spoke again.

"I don't remember getting here. I never would've come. I know there's no way in hell I'd agree to go anywhere with a stranger, let alone end up in his bed. What... what did you do to me?"

He opened his mouth.

She wasn't done. Her eyes widened, her bottom lip trembling. "Make me calm, you said. It was the coffee, wasn't it? You... you *drugged* me? Why? Why would you do that?"

Because I had to.
You're safe.
You're with me.
Because I love you.
I missed you.
And I need you to remember me.

Any one of those statements would have expressed his thoughts and emotions and motivations in that very moment—except that's not what Maddox said.

He took a deep breath, old habits leading him to pull her scent into his lungs. A lifetime of being able to control a situation by using his nose meant he was trying to pick up on strong emotions she never would confess to.

Was she angry? Sad? Scared?

One breath was all it took. If he hadn't been locked down tight already, the punch of attraction coupled with the certainty that this woman was absolutely, undeniably his mate might have caused him to go feral. He had to have this woman and only his ironclad control kept him from joining his mate on the bed.

Instead, Maddox backed away from her, savoring her scent.

Vanilla.

For the first time since he found her again, Evangeline smelled like vanilla.

There were so many things he could have said to her. What came out of his mouth was—

"You smell... *different*."

Oh, fuck. He couldn't help it. Couldn't stop his reaction, either. Already he felt the blood rushing to his groin. He thought the erection he got in the coffee shop was bad? Maddox was just about to sprout a third leg.

And she was glaring at him.

Well, at least she wasn't trying to scream again.

He understood why as soon as she retorted. Reining in her fear and confusion, Evangeline was fucking *pissed*.

"I'm sorry," she snapped, angrily kneading the edge of the sheet. She looked like, if she could get her hands around his throat, she'd be strangling him. "Guess it didn't occur to me to refresh my perfume when I left the house this morning. Never expected I'd go out for a cup of coffee and end up *abducted*. Silly me."

"That's not what I meant. You smell like *you* now."

She blinked up at him. Fury faded just enough for incredulousness to slip in. Evangeline looked like she thought he was nuts.

And maybe he was.

Because he was smiling.

That last comment she made? The sarcastic retort that almost seemed out of place considering he'd done just what she accused him of? Maddox *had* abducted her. He'd stolen her away from her home, her friends, her family, and her life, tucking her in a secluded cabin with just him.

And he was smiling because a comment like that was quintessential Evangeline.

She was spooked.

She probably hated him.

That was okay. She was still Evangeline. Still his mate.

Good thing that, as often as he used to piss her off, she could never stay mad at him for long.

16

This... this couldn't be happening.

It was one thing to be secretly attracted to a man she met a couple of times. In some ways, he was everything that Adam was not. Dark—tanned, rugged skin, black sunglasses, dark brown unruly hair—where Adam was fair. Big. Visibly dangerous.

Adam was as law-abiding as they come. A freaking cop. This guy looked like he'd done some serious time. And, since abducting a woman was one hell of a crime, it looked like he'd be doing a lot more.

If she got out of this in one piece. If she managed to live long enough to testify against him.

Keep calm. Don't agitate him. Guy already looked like he was on the edge and that was before the way she smelled seemed to set him off. *Don't give him a reason to decide you're not worth it.*

Maybe she shouldn't have snapped back at him. She didn't know him. She didn't know what he was capable of—

Well. *No*. That wasn't right. Her dark stranger was obviously capable of drugging her and grabbing her off the street in broad daylight.

If he could do that and not show any remorse when she threw it back at him...

Evangeline struggled to stay calm. Don't piss off the big, scary man, she told herself firmly. If only he'd take off those damn sunglasses. She wished he would. They covered his eyes and half of his rugged face, making it impossible for her to get any idea of what he was thinking.

She wasn't sure that he *was*.

The man she'd innocently had coffee with last Friday had kidnapped her. Drugged her first, then brought her to this place. No denying that.

But why? She didn't know. And he didn't look like he was about to tell her.

Thank God Adam *was* a cop. He called her so frequently, constantly checking in. How long would it take before he realized that something had happened to her? That she was missing?

It couldn't be long. She had faith that Adam would find her, too. He loved her—he was always telling her that he loved her. Nothing would stop him from coming after her.

She just had to survive long enough to give Adam a chance to track her down.

Don't set off the unpredictable stranger... she could do that.

Right?

In a slow, careful voice, she said softly, "Who else am I supposed to smell like?"

THE SMILE SLID OFF OF HIS FACE.

He was going to *kill* Colt.

Take her, he said. She's your mate, he said. Once she's with you, the bond will snap back.

Horse shit.

Who was this woman in front of him? It was Evangeline. Of course it was. But the Evangeline he knew— the woman he mated, then married—had never gentled her voice around him. She said what she was thinking when she was thinking of it.

He expected screaming. Ranting. Fury. If she picked up the lamp on the desk and heaved it at him, he was prepared to duck; he already made a mental note that he'd probably have to replace it after they left the cabin.

This woman was acting super weird. Not like his Angie at all. He'd done what no Para was allowed to do: he'd run off with his mate. And, instead of shouting bloody murder, she obeyed him—actually did something she'd never do, and *obeyed* him—when he begged her not to scream. Now, she sounded like she was just commenting on the weather or something.

No. No, no, no.

He had a plan.

A good plan.

Why did his fucking plans never work?

Maddox cleared his throat. He purposely kept the distance between them. "I'm sure you have questions."

"You could say that."

A hint of fire. He felt hope, only to have that dashed when Evangeline seemed to remember herself. She pulled the sheet up again, as if trying to shield herself from him.

Protect herself.

Shit.

Maddox backpedaled, swallowing his snarl as he reached up, yanking the obnoxious collar of another turtleneck that seemed eager to strangle him. It wasn't a game. This was his life. His future was at stake.

He had to fix this. Short of releasing Evangeline—because, if he did that, he was sure he'd never set eyes on her again—Maddox desperately needed to do something that would prove to her that he wasn't a threat.

If that meant giving her space, then that would be what he did.

For tonight, at least.

"I'll answer them all, I promise. Just not tonight. Not now." Maddox pulled the keys out of his pocket. "It's late. You've had a scare. I don't blame you—"

"Blame *me*?"

He continued as if she hadn't interrupted. "—but I think it's best that I leave you be for a bit. I won't go far. My room is the next one over. I'll be right there if you need anything."

Her eyebrows rose. "After all the trouble you went through to get me here, you're just gonna leave me all alone? Not that I want you near me, but I could walk out of here and you would never know."

"Yeah, not quite." Maddox showed her the ring of keys. "I'm going to lock you in. If you need me, shout. I'll hear you, and I can assure you that, where we are, nobody else will."

Evangeline paled. In her eyes, he could just about see the visions of her grand escape going up in smoke.

"So I'm a prisoner, is that it?"

"I didn't say that."

"You're locking me in. What, so I can't get out?"

"More like I figure you'll get used to this room easier if I'm not in here with you. This way, you know you're alone, even if you can't leave just yet." When she just stared at him in open disbelief, he shrugged. "And, okay, maybe because I feel better having you somewhere where I know you're safe."

"But how do *I* know I'm safe?"

Maddox set his jaw. "One day you'll understand how deeply you just cut at me. You're upset, and I'm sorry. But, I swear to you, Angie, you've never been safer than you are here with me."

It was a slip. He didn't mean to use that name. Not yet. Not when she wouldn't have any clue what it meant between them.

She caught it. Her fingers clenched the sheet, bunching the material tight. "What did you call me?" she whispered.

Maddox had two choices: deny it or own it. He went with the latter because, hell, he'd already fucked this up as bad as he possibly could. "I called you by your name."

"You don't know my name!" The words exploded out of her like bullets from a gun. Whatever Maddox had done, he'd broken through her icy and careful shell. She picked up a pillow and chucked it across the room. "You don't know anything about me!"

The pillow missed. Badly. It fell about five feet short, and two feet wide from where he was standing.

Maddox frowned.

It was one thing to know that she didn't remember him. It was another entirely to have Evangeline act as if she was as much a stranger to him as he was to her when it was just the two of them alone together.

The words were out before he could think better of it.

"Your name is Evangeline Lewis." Wolfe, he added to himself. She wasn't ready to hear that yet; still, that didn't make it any less true. "You're twenty-seven years old. Your favorite color is orange. You love it when it rains because you think it's God's way of crying and that means it's okay to be sad sometimes."

Her mouth fell open. Evangeline blinked, then shook her head as if that was enough to get him to shut up.

"You're addicted to caffeine. You get this fancy frou frou drink, always iced, even in the winter. Almond milk, too, not because you have a problem with real milk, but because you're convinced it makes your drink taste a bit nuttier."

"Stop it—"

Maddox couldn't.

"Your mother is Naomi. Your father is Paul. They never liked me. If they knew you were here... if they had any idea I had you, all hell would break loose. It's one of the reasons I had to do it this way. I'm sorry, but I had no choice. You'll see. One day, you'll understand why it had to be this way."

For both of their sakes, Maddox hoped it was sooner than later.

Evangeline's mouth hung open, gawking up at him. No fear. No shield. Just pure shock.

"Who... who *are* you?"

"My name is Maddox. And I know everything there is about you."

"How? How..." Evangeline shook her head. Her hands were shaking. Quickly, she shoved them under the sheet. Too late. Maddox picked up on the reaction. "The coffee shop... you really did set me up. Me. You picked me out on purpose, didn't you?"

"Angie—"

"How long have you been watching me?"

"It's not like that."

"Then how is it? You drugged me. You brought me here, wherever *here* is. I met you, what? Like five days ago? But you seem to know so much about me, I bet you could tell me the name of the hamster I had when I was twelve."

"Rupert the Survivor," Maddox said. The answer just popped out. "He had no teeth and you fed him birdseed that he managed to gum down, piece by piece. He lived for close to four years, even after he went blind in one eye. You cried so hard when he died that you swore you would never have another pet again."

He always thought that Evangeline's irrational phobia about loving another pet was ironic. There she was, swearing she'd never get attached to another animal, and what happened? Fate decided she was the mate of a wolf shifter. In one fell swoop, she got a husband in Maddox and the most devoted pet ever in his beast.

Maddox didn't know what it was that did it. She

stared him down within seconds of taking stock of her situation. When her temper got the better of her, she lashed out, even though she had no idea that she had nothing to fear from Maddox. She tried to manipulate him into thinking she was harmless, even unaffected beyond an icy shield.

But showing her just how much he remembered about her, about his mate... that did it. Tears filled her eyes, making the green go glassy. She gulped and, for the first time since she discovered him in the room, Evangeline looked away.

"Get out." She curled up on the bed, her legs tucked protectively under her as she turned away from him. "Turn the lock, I don't care. Keep me prisoner. Just go."

He sucked in a breath. He got another taste of her scent. Even that wasn't enough to make the guilt subside.

Maddox never expected to break her. What happened during the last three years? The fire and the venom and the anger, that was okay. He'd been expecting that. But this?

What the fuck had he done?

Nothing that he wouldn't have done if given a second chance to do it all over again.

She didn't understand. She didn't know.

Maybe—

Maybe it was time he told her.

"Evangeline?"

"What do you want from me?" Her voice was throaty. Raw. If she wasn't sobbing yet, she would be soon.

That broke his heart and hardened his resolve. "I want you to look at me. I want you to *see* me."

"I—"

He removed his sunglasses.

She gasped.

He knew what she saw. Golden eyes. Hints of amber rolling across his pupils.

Shifter eyes.

"I'll be just on the other side of the door," he reminded her. "When you're ready to talk... when you're ready to listen... to *remember*, you let me know. I'm not going anywhere, either."

The big bastard made his escape so fast, Evangeline barely had enough time to process what she was seeing before he was gone. She had no doubt that he made good on his promise to lock her in the room. She had to check anyway.

A quick tug assured her that she was still trapped.

Golden eyes. She didn't think a pair of peepers like that actually existed in this world.

Not the real world, at least. In her dreams, the man who haunted her—who loved her—had a pair of eyes like that. But he was a dream, a fantasy. The big shifter who kidnapped her was a monster, and not only because he was a paranormal.

Para or human, nothing gave him the right to do what he did.

He... he *stole* her. At least, now that she knew he *was* a Para, it made the tiniest bit more sense. Everyone heard stories about a friend of a friend who got involved with the paranormal races. Picking a woman off of the street—or out of a bustling coffee shop— just because they had the urge to seemed like something a shifter would do.

In the back of her mind, Evangeline felt a niggling panic about what that could mean. It was easy to drown it out. The panic that she was trapped with a dangerous man whose inner beast made him even more formidable? Yeah, she was definitely focusing on *that* one.

She lifted her hand, gnawed nervously on her thumbnail. It wasn't just his size and his dark aura that she had to worry about now. A human woman was no match for a shifter, no matter what kind of animal he shifted into. Heightened senses, increased speed, crazy fast healing... those were just the perks she knew about. This guy... this *Maddox*... he already had the upper hand simply because of what he was. Throw in the terrifying fact that he knew so much about her *and* had managed to separate her from anyone who could have helped her...

It was going to be up to Evangeline to help herself.

She couldn't stay. That was out of the question. He promised her answers, but he could shove those answers up his furry ass for all she cared. He might think he had a good reason to steal her away from her home. Fine. She could learn all about it when he went on trial.

First, she had to get the hell out of there.

Evangeline searched the room again. Every inch of it. There were two doors: the locked exit and an empty closet. Three windows. Wary of how he could probably hear every step she made, she tiptoed over to the two small windows on the far side of the room.

Shit. Locked.

Okay. Fine. There was still one more.

She gripped the edge lightly, her heart in her throat. It eased up gently with barely a whisper.

Yes!

Once she'd opened the window, Evangeline poked her head out. A warm breeze caressed her face, her hair flying all around her. It carried the scent of a forest with it, a mix of dirt and moisture and wood. A rich cotton candy sky peeked through the rare gaps between branches and towering trees. It was sunset.

Evangeline blinked. What time *was* it? It had been barely afternoon when she set out of Mugs for her apartment. So she'd lost hours while she slept, if not longer than that.

Great.

She immediately reached for her pocket, searching for her phone. It surprised her that she hadn't thought to look for it before; probably because, deep down, she knew her captor wouldn't have been so stupid to leave her a way to call for help. Grabbing it if only to check the time? It was a habit.

And she was crushed all over again to realize that he left her with nothing.

No phone. No purse. No wallet. No keys.

Evangeline let out a soft sound that was a mixture of a laugh and a sob. At least he didn't strip her of her shoes.

She was going to need them.

Poking her head out of the window again, she took a deep breath and looked down. A bed of crisp green grass was below. One problem, though: it wasn't *directly* below. About fifteen feet kept her from the ground.

He'd stowed her in a room on the second floor.

Of course he did.

It wasn't going to be so easy to get away from him as that. No wonder he felt confident enough to leave one of the windows unlocked. The shifter thought he knew everything about her. He never would guess that she'd risk a broken leg rather than stay with him.

Gritting her teeth, Evangeline was going to prove him wrong.

She was tall, but she was slender. Without a screen, it was only a matter of a couple of minutes where she maneuvered her body so that she was perched on the ledge of the window. She didn't believe him when he said that he was going to leave her alone. Sooner or later, he was going to check on her. There was no time to waste.

She had no idea where she was. Help could be on the other side of the trees, or she could be swallowed up in the shadows within minutes, forever lost.

Evangeline glanced down, swallowing back her nerves.

It was a pretty big drop. No way she was going to make it without hurting *something*.

She started to second-guess herself. Would it be so bad to see what it was he wanted? He... he had seemed so nice, so *kind,* whenever she met him at Mugs. Except for the time she was afraid he had followed her home, she'd never felt any fear or trepidation in his presence. She knew better now. If he'd been watching her long enough to know every last detail about her, no doubt he *had* followed her home. Even so, she still couldn't shake the feeling that he was harmless.

And that was fucking insane.

He *kidnapped* her. She didn't honestly believe he was so hard up for a dinner date that he had to abduct one. As intimidating as he was, as terrifying as this situation was, Evangeline would be lying if she said that the spark of attraction between her and her captor had been snuffed by his actions.

That scared her more than free-falling out of a second-story window.

Golden eyes. This Maddox had golden eyes.

One part of her wanted to stay. That was even crazier than anything else. One small part of her, the part she tucked away, the part that was too painful to live with following her accident... it wanted her to stay. It wanted to hear what he had to say, and it wanted to drown in those familiar golden eyes.

Good thing it was easy for the rest of Evangeline to drown out that voice, too. Dealing with a hole in her memory made it easy for her to compartmentalize. She'd unpack all her baggage way later on.

Now?

It was time to go.

Evangeline braced herself on the ledge. As impossible as it was, she tried to relax. If she hit the ground hard while her body was all tensed and tight, the risk of hurting herself was even higher.

"It's going to be okay," she whispered to herself. "I'm gonna be fine."

Then, once she was as ready as she was going to get, Evangeline lowered herself along the rough siding of the rustic cabin.

It was smart to get as close to the ground as possible instead of jumping straight out. She twisted her body as she slowly dropped, hand over hand until she was facing the cabin, her arms extended.

The fifteen-foot drop was less than ten now. Hopefully the grass would be enough to break her fall without breaking any part of *her*.

Right before she let go, she closed her eyes and fervently wished she had been born an Othersider.

At least then she would have had wings.

17

This was going to have to be the fastest shower of his entire life.

If he could have avoided it, he would have. Nope. It was necessary. Torn between wanting to lick the salty tears from her cheek while pulling his mate close or flipping her onto her belly so that he could mount her, Maddox stepped into the second bedroom and headed straight for the shower.

The cabin had running water. It had a water heater, too. Maddox refused to use it, jerking the knob to the right until the icy stream beat down on his tense back.

As he washed up, he avoided his erection. He was so primed, one touch would be all it took to go off. The damn thing was nearly raw, he'd rubbed it that often since he first caught sight of Evangeline again. Just the thought of her was enough to make him go instantly hard.

Having her in the next room over, lying in a bed? He knew he had a snowball's chance in hell that she would ever invite him to join her. That didn't stop his wayward cock from acting up.

He washed his body, his face, his ass, his feet. He scrubbed his hair and brushed his teeth. The cold water did nothing for his hard-on. A shock of pure pleasure made his body tighten, his toes curl, when he accidentally brushed the head with the back of his palm. It felt so good, yet so wrong. Only a thin wall separated him from his delicious mate.

This was a bad idea.

A fucking awful idea.

It was hard enough already to keep his paws off of her. Why tempt himself?

Then again, maybe if he took the edge off, got it out of his system, he'd be calmer when he returned to his mate to feed her a late supper. She had to be starving and nothing was going to stop him from providing for all of her needs.

That settled it. As the water poured off of his bowed frame, Maddox braced one hand against the wall, grabbing his cock with the other.

He grunted as he stroked himself. Each pull was more of a yank. It was fast, furious, and vicious. It felt amazing, but it wasn't about the pleasure. It was about the *need*. He wanted nothing more than to claim his mate, bite her, bond with her... *anything*. He'd kill to get back inside of her—but that wasn't going to happen anytime soon. He accepted that.

And he rubbed one out instead.

The orgasm came quickly. It started low, his knees shaking, his ass tightening as his sac drew up. He bit into his hand in a vain attempt to muffle his shout as ropes of thick, milky white spend shot out of his cock, hitting his belly. He kept stroking. He kept coming.

When he finally finished, he pulled his mouth away from his hand. Blood mingled with seed as the shower water continued to flow over him.

And that's when his senses picked up a voice coming from the other room.

"It's going to be okay," Evangeline whispered. "I'm gonna be fine."

His heart stuttered to make out the despair in her soft voice. He could just see it: Evangeline curled up on the master bed, tears in her eyes, the long dark curtain of her hair shielding the angry and lost expression on her beautiful face. He was hurting her and it was fucking killing him to do that. But he had to.

This was the only choice he had left.

His cock went limp, and not because he ran out of seed; as a bonded shifter, he could've easily jerked off again and again and still be hard. He let it slip from his hand, his cock slapping into the side of his inner thigh before hanging between his legs. Maddox let it settle, even when it started to come to life again with the tiniest of twitches.

It didn't seem right to focus on his own pleasure when Evangeline was so upset with him. He grabbed his soap, roughly washing away the last of the cum that painted his belly white. The puncture wounds from his fangs had already sealed up. By the time he was done with his shower, he'd be completely healed.

He would be.

What had been pleasure immediately turned to pain when a sharp ache filled his chest—and not all of it was his. Maddox didn't know what, but his mate had done something to hurt herself. Through the meager bond that existed between them, he felt it, and he bit out a curse between sudden fangs.

Angie.

He focused his senses, stunned when he realized that the warm vanilla scent that belonged to his mate was fading. Oh, it lingered, and his wolf wanted to burst out and roll around in it, but the source of it?

It was gone.

She was gone.

His ears pricked open. If he strained, he could just pick up the sound of Evangeline as she crashed through the trees and crushed the foliage underfoot.

Holy shit. She actually did it. She *escaped*.

The metal shower knob creaked in protest as his hand gripped it angrily. Hell no! He slammed down on the misshapen knob, killing the stream of water before hopping out of the shower.

Pausing only to throw on his jeans, Maddox burst

from the bathroom. He inhaled deeply as he flew down the hall. Her rich scent clung to the air, but it was only an echo. His wolf's anguished cry only confirmed what he already knew. The second he jumped in the shower, Evangeline was gone.

Not for long, though. He would get her back or die trying.

There was no way he could survive losing her a second time.

Running on a sprained ankle was pure hell.

With every step, every stride, the shock of pain radiated all the way up to her hip. It was agony, but at least it wasn't broken. She never would've been able to bolt if the bone had splintered.

Adrenaline helped. It cushioned the pain enough that it was bearable; it wasn't easy to move, but she was so determined to escape, she pushed past it. Gritting her teeth, Evangeline dashed through the woods, putting more weight on her left foot. The right one was weak, her ankle throbbing, and the uneven terrain was terrible to navigate. She fell once, cursed under her breath, then scrambled back to her feet.

He would chase her. She knew that with every fiber of her being. The stranger would chase her as soon as he realized she was gone.

She had to put enough distance between them so

that it wouldn't be that easy for him to track her. If luck was on her side, he wouldn't be a predatory shifter with excellent tracking skills. Of course, then she remembered his gold eyes, the air of danger and dominance that surrounded him, and she realized she was *screwed*.

But she wouldn't give up. She had to try. Three years of recovery following a crash that should have killed her... she didn't go through all of that only to end up a shifter's plaything.

Branches whipped past her. The trees were so close together, it was a tough fit. At some point she got snagged by one of the rougher branches, tearing right through the flesh of her upper arm. Compared to her aching ankle, the slice was nothing but a sting. No, it was the blood she was freaking out about.

Why not just leave a big, honking arrow that told him she'd run this way?

Pausing only to slap a patch of mud on the dripping gash, Evangeline wiped her hands on her shorts before forcing herself to continue. She purposely avoided thinking about things like dirt and infection. It was all about the escape.

It wasn't long before she realized she'd run out of time.

The howl split through the air. It was loud, ear-piercing, a baying-at-the-moon type of wail. It sent a chill coursing through her and Evangeline stopped running. She just *stopped*. The howl was paralyzing, a deep-throated cry that seemed to reach inside of her and press the pause button.

She couldn't move.

The echoes of the stark animalistic howl reverberated in her skull, pulsing in time to the frantic beat of her heart. Because that howl? She knew without knowing how that it was a cry meant for her. The shifter male had already started the chase, calling for her with the help of his beast.

And he wasn't all that far from where she stood like a dope, just waiting for him to find her.

Before she could pull herself together and take off, he burst into the trees.

Evangeline almost expected him to be wearing fur. He wasn't.

Maddox, uh, wasn't wearing much of anything.

Jeans, yeah, but that was all. He was entirely shirtless and, now that the shifter was out of the bag, he didn't bother with his shades any longer, either.

Her eyes were immediately drawn to his sculpted chest. She'd have to be blind not to notice how ripped he was. He was strangely hairless, considering he was part animal, and she found herself staring at one pec in particular.

Drawn in a silver-laced ink so that it was permanent, Maddox bore a tattoo right over his left pec. Right over his heart. A string of numbers, Evangeline stared at the tattoo in confusion.

She knew that date.

Why… why did he?

Tearing her gaze away from the marking he shouldn't have, Evangeline did a double-take. Every time she met with him at Mugs, he wore a turtleneck. Now, though, she finally got a glimpse of what he was hiding apart from his tattoo.

His throat.

Growing up in mainly human neighborhoods, Evangeline didn't know as much about the paranormal races as those who lived in the more integrated communities. She still recognized the scars and raw skin that left Maddox's lower neck visibly destroyed.

Those were the marks of a silver collar.

Only shifters who were thrown in the magic-free prison were forced to wear collars like that. From how ruined Maddox's skin was, he must have been wearing one for a long, long time.

But he wasn't in the Cage any longer.

He was there. Chasing her. Stalking her.

Watching her.

"No," she whispered. "Leave me alone."

"You know I can't do that."

Evangeline clasped her trembling hands to her heaving chest. "Of course you can," she pleaded. It was one thing when he was just another shifter. But a shifter who used to be in the Cage? That was like letting a man on death row loose. No one *ever* got out of the Cage. "I won't tell. Just let me go."

He set his jaw. Eyes like molten gold flashed as his

attention was riveted on the rise and fall of her breasts. His voice, when he spoke again, came out hoarse. "You misunderstand. I should've said I *won't* do that."

She swallowed her frightened moan. "Why? Why me? What did I ever do to you?"

"Angie—"

"Don't call me that!"

Maddox held his hands up. "I'm sorry. Evangeline."

Why didn't that feel right, either?

"Maybe if I explained before, told you what was going on, you wouldn't have felt like you had no choice but to run. I should've expected that. You've got spunk, my m— Evangeline. You always have."

She sneered in a bid to hide how nervous he made her. "Yeah? How would you know?"

The shifter didn't answer her. He lifted his hand, rubbing his scars with his fingers. She flinched when he drew her attention back to the mark.

"I already told you, I know everything about you. And, when you accept that I had good cause to whisk you away, we'll laugh about this. You're safe with me. In the woods, not so much. Come back to the cabin."

"I'm not going anywhere with you."

"I'll throw you over my shoulder if I have to. I won't let you stay out here all night."

"You can't stop me," she dared.

Maddox called her bluff when he stepped toward her.

Evangeline trembled, but she kept her voice strong

now that she had found it again. "If you touch me, I'll never forgive you."

His expression went pained for a heartbeat before he clenched his jaw. Another step closer. "You will," he growled. He sounded certain of it, too.

"*Never.*"

"It's whatever happened to your memories. Something's not right, I've already figured that out. You don't remember me. It's why I had to bring you here, remind you of what we are to each other—"

It was like a sudden buzz in the back of her skull drowning out his words. She didn't want to hear him, didn't want to acknowledge that there was a method to his madness. He didn't take her because he *could*. He had a purpose for it.

And, if she let him, he'd tell her. Only Evangeline didn't want to know.

It was so much easier to hate him if she didn't know.

"Listen to me," she said, raising her voice so that she could hear herself over his stupid, pointless explanation. Nothing he could say would make this okay. *Nothing.* "There is no 'us'. There is no 'we'. We, me and you... we are *nothing* to each other because, and I will tell you this again and again if I have to, *I don't know you.*"

Her words seemed to slam into him like a mack truck. His body jerked, then bowed at her heated denial. His eyes glowed, glittering viciously.

And he snapped.

"Remember me, damn it!"

Whoa.

In the echoes of his deep-throated roar, Evangeline realized that, for the first time since she woke up less than an hour ago, she was terrified. Before, she'd been angry. Pissed off to high heaven that he managed to snatch her and she'd been so trusting and naive that she had let it happen. Deep down, she hadn't been afraid because she never suspected that he would actually hurt her.

She wasn't so sure now. He insisted he knew her. She had no idea who he was.

The ruined scars surrounding his throat were a tell-tale sign he used to be a prisoner in the Cage.

He had a jailhouse tattoo on his chest commemorating the day of Evangeline's crash.

That last one scared her more than anything else.

Maybe he did know her. Maybe there was a reason behind why she felt so drawn to him. It didn't matter. She had received a second lease on life and hell if she wasn't going to live it the way she wanted to. No growly shifter was going to stand in her way.

She had to get away from him.

With a squeal, Evangeline let her fight or flight instinct take over again. No way she could take on an enraged shifter. Even now she could see the fury and the pain that caused his eerily golden eyes to shine as he locked on her.

This Maddox expected something of her that she simply couldn't give him. With so many gaps in her memories, how did he expect her to remember a man she'd been sure she had never seen before?

That only left her one choice: flight.

As soon as she stopped running before, the pain in her ankle came alive with a vengeance. She pushed herself too hard, too fast. Now, when she needed it the most, her body betrayed her.

Evangeline turned to dart away. Her ankle buckled, her knee gave out, and she took one quick step before she started to drop.

"Ang, no!"

"Stay away," she gasped out. She landed on her knee, another jolt of pain coursing through her. The impact was rough. She hit, then fell back onto her ass. As soon as she was down, she threw her hand up. "Don't come any closer."

He listened.

And he frowned.

"Oh, Angie, I'm so sorry. I didn't know."

The sorrow in his tone hit her right in her gut. She'd rather take the anger, the certainty that he had a right to do this to her. To feel sorry that she was in pain made her insides twist. If he came any closer to her, she thought she might spit in his handsome face.

"Stay away from me," she warned.

"Let me help you—"

"*No.*"

She leaned forward, pushed up off of her hands, and landed on her knees again. Evangeline could almost sense the desperate need he had to lunge forward and help her up. She wouldn't give in to him. Shaky and more scared than she'd been, she climbed up on one foot, then the next.

Easy does it. Now that she was prepared for the ache, she babied her swollen ankle. Running was out. She kind of figured that. But hell if she didn't want to be able to walk away from him.

She took a step.

Her ankle held her weight for all of three seconds before pain shot up her shin and her leg gave out from underneath her. Evangeline had just enough time to realize that this was going to *hurt* when she hit the ground before she was tumbling down again.

But the impact never came this time.

With her nose inches from the dirt, the shifter screamed toward her, wrapping her up in his arms and holding her close as he dropped to a predator's crouch.

Damn, he was *fast*. No wonder he was able to track her down like that.

He might not have expected her to bolt before, or maybe he hadn't chased her again right away because he knew she couldn't get far. There was no way he could have known that her ankle was already tweaked from when she jumped from the window. And yet, after she twisted it again and tried to rise, he was there in an instant to hold her against his chest.

His very naked chest.

This was the closest they'd been. Even through her t-shirt, she could feel the blazing heat coming off of his bare skin. She shivered and the bastard tightened his hold on her. Maybe he was offering her warmth, maybe it was comfort, but Evangeline wouldn't let herself buy into it. He'd kidnapped her, damn it.

She refused to become another victim of the Stockholm Syndrome.

"Let me go," she told him, shoving against him. It was like trying to bend steel. His arms weren't going anywhere.

Instead, he slipped his hand between their pressed bodies, taking her defiant chin gently between his claw-tipped fingers. He tilted her head back, careful not to scratch her.

"Look at me," he demanded.

Stubborn to a fault, Evangeline closed her eyes. "No."

He exhaled. Warm breath fanned her cheek, a delicious musk surrounding her. Her body wanted to fall into his embrace. Evangeline refused to let it.

"You're tired," he rumbled. "You're hurt. You're scared. Look at me, Evangeline. Recognize who I am. I'll never hurt you."

She quirked one eye open. He seemed so earnest, so sincere.

He was absolutely full of it.

"Why should I believe you?"

Maddox ignored her question, though she did notice that it was his turn to tremble. But, when he spoke again, his voice was firm and commanding. "Look at *me*."

She refused. "I told you no. You stole me, you monster. You took me from my family, my friends. My home. I won't do a damn thing you tell me to. I'd rather die first."

"I'd die myself before I let that happen again."

Evangeline found her eyes darting back to the tattoo on his chest. This close, she couldn't deny it. She couldn't pretend. Those numbers... that *date*—it was the day of the accident. *Her* accident.

She almost died once before herself. And the way he said 'again', almost like he knew...

How did he know?

Maddox took a deep breath. She felt his chest move. In, then out. In. Out. His skin brushed against hers and, as if she expected what was coming, she braced herself.

"Look at me, Angie." His voice resonated with a power she couldn't describe. Or understand.

That name again. She hated that it felt so right for him to call her that. She hated that he thought he had the right to call her that.

Against her better judgment, she looked over at him.

His golden eyes. The same glowing golden gaze that haunted her dreams and gave fuel to her every fantasy. Familiar and alien at the same time, Evangeline was drawn to him like a moth to a flame. She knew it was foolish. She knew it was dangerous. She couldn't seem to stop herself anyway.

Could it be just a dream? Those eyes were so familiar. And, though she was too shaken to admit, so was he.

Her fingers ghosted over the numbers etched into his skin. The date of her accident. When she'd died— and been given a second chance at life. He rumbled again, but it wasn't from anger or exertion this time. It was pure pleasure that she touched him.

She took her hand back. His eyes flashed, an amber sheen turning the gold a darker shade.

Evangeline didn't know this man. She *didn't*. But she was almost sure she knew what he was.

The strength, the speed, the power. The howl. The ability to track her through the woods. The inhuman hearing. The amber eyes.

She knew he was a shifter. That was undeniable. Some part of her had been hoping he was something safe and sweet, like a pussy cat or a bunny rabbit.

Of course not.

"You're a— you're a…"

Maddox grinned ruefully, the full length of his canine fangs extending past his bottom lip.

"I'm yours, that's what I am. And the sooner you remember that, the better off we'll both be."

18

He was *fast*.

Evangeline already knew that. Even with her aching ankle, she'd had enough of a head start that she should've been able to put some kind of distance between the two of them. How long had she been running for? Five minutes? Maybe ten?

He must have booked it through the woods to catch her before she found her way to freedom. Then, as soon as she wobbled and fell, he proved that he was even faster than she thought. A blur of black jeans, tan skin, golden eyes... he was in front of her, then he wasn't.

Before she even hit the dirt, he scooped her up, cradling her against his brawny chest.

The shock and awe didn't last. As soon as he started to rise to his full height, Evangeline shifted her weight, shoving against any part of his body she could reach.

"Let me go!"

"First Colt, now you," Maddox said, as if he hadn't heard her. He certainly didn't loosen his hold at all, carrying her as easily as if she was weightless. "Seems busted ankles are catching."

Evangeline didn't know what he was talking about. She didn't care. Still pushing, she snapped up at him, "If you hadn't been chasing me, I wouldn't have run on it and my ankle would be fine."

"If you hadn't escaped, I wouldn't have been chasing you."

She wanted to scream. It would only be a waste of energy; her brief escape proved that he hadn't been kidding when he said there was no one else around for miles.

She had to do something, though. She had to make her kidnapper realize that what he was doing was wrong.

"You can't keep me locked in there," she told him, gentling her voice. She'd resorted to slapping at him before giving up. It was like slapping at an unmovable brick wall anyway. "Come on. Just… just let me go. And I don't mean right now. Let me go home. This isn't right and you know it."

"I can't do that." His voice was an apologetic rumble. "I'm sorry. I know you don't believe me, but I *can't.*"

Remembering what he said, she repeated, "Won't."

Her body lifted slightly. Fell. He had shrugged. "It's

the same. You know what I am. You know what it means when I tell you that you're my mate."

Evangeline went cold.

This was it. Her nightmare come true, her deepest fear brought to life. No control. A shifter could tell their mate from first sniff. Was that what happened? That first day at Mugs—had he gotten a whiff of her and planned this very abduction to force her to mate with him? Forget her parents, forget her boyfriend... Evangeline would have to give up everything that she'd worked so hard to reclaim because some... some *animal* liked the smell of her?

Not in this lifetime.

"This is crazy!" She jerked in his hold, suddenly furious again. "*You're* crazy! You can't do this. You're not allowed. I know the laws, I know my rights. You can't just... just take me from my life and think I'm gonna be a part of yours." Evangeline threw all of her strength behind the punch she managed to land on his upper arms. She wanted him to hurt, and if he dropped her? At least he wouldn't be touching her. "Get your damn paws off of me!"

MADDOX TRIED TO REMAIN CALM, THOUGH THE WAY SHE squirmed in his arms was making it harder and harder for him to hang onto his control.

The pure, rich, honest scent of her—despite the

fear and pain that overlaid it and damn near broke him into a million pieces—was a balm to his soul. The way her soft skin brushed against his, even as she hit him, was driving him insane. It was so damn hard to keep his mind out of the gutter when, every time she twisted, her delectable ass brushed up against the bulge in his jeans.

So distracted, so consumed by her presence, it took a second for Evangeline's words to sink in. When they finally did, it dawned on him that she wasn't simply squirming in his arms.

She was *fighting* him.

The realization hit him like a bat to his skull and, for once, his cock decided to behave. He had his mate in his arms and she really, really didn't want anything to do with him.

She gasped, struggling to get in enough air to breathe. Shaking her head frantically, she clawed at his arms, scrabbling to get out of his unbreakable hold. Maddox still refused to let go. He was too afraid she would hurt herself again if he did.

"Angie, calm down," he said. He laced his voice with the power of an alpha wolf in an attempt to get her to submit to the predator in him.

It didn't work.

"No— *no*! I won't do it. You can't make me. This is *my* life. I get the choice. You don't get to tell me that I'm yours and that's that—"

"I'm not going to make you do anything you don't

want to. It *is* your choice."

She stilled, hope filling her voice. "Then it's simple. I choose to go back home."

"No."

"So it's not *my* choice after all, is it?"

Maddox didn't answer her again. Instead, he tilted her in his arms, holding her tight in a fireman's carry, her cheek pressed against the heat of his bare chest.

He started back for the cabin.

"What do you think you're doing?" demanded Evangeline. "Put me down!"

"On a sprained ankle? No. I'm taking you back and we're going to put some ice on that."

With the adrenaline coursing through her, she barely noticed the throbbing. She'd be lying if she said it wouldn't slow her down. But, even if she couldn't run away from him again, she refused to let this overgrown caveman treat her like an invalid. "It's fine. I can manage on my own."

"Angie," he growled her name, an obvious warning.

It didn't faze her. Not now. She left her fear back where she fell. With the sudden understanding that he believed she was his mate, she knew he wasn't kidding when he said he'd rather die than hurt her.

Pity she didn't feel the same way for him.

"I don't need anything from you." Then, aware of

how he winced whenever she corrected her name, she added with a touch of vindictive glee, "And it's Evangeline."

Maddox stopped moving but she felt his torso tremble as another growl built its way up his chest. Glaring down at her, his shifter's eyes flashed, suddenly glowing like a nightlight, while his jaw clenched in obvious anger. It lasted for a few seconds before he let out a shaky breath. Evangeline did the same, and only then did it occur to her that she'd been holding hers.

Okay. Maybe she was still a tiny bit afraid.

The spike of fear in her scent irritated him. She'd never been afraid of him before, not even when she first found out she was destined to be a wolf's mate.

Why was it so hard this time around?

Maybe it wasn't the smartest idea, but Maddox finally let some of his frustration slip out.

"Evangeline," he said, purposely using the name, "I'm not going to hurt you, but I'm not going to let you hurt yourself, either. You're my mate, and I'm going to do everything I can to take care of you. I suggest you get used to that. I'll do what I think is best for you until you're back to normal. You might not like it, but you'll deal."

She stiffened in his arms again. "As soon as my ankle is better, I'm gonna run."

That's not what he meant by *back to normal*. Too bad Evangeline didn't know that.

"And I'll chase right after you," Maddox vowed. "My wolf is stronger and faster than you are. It knows these woods and can follow your trail wherever you go. It won't stop. Remember, I'm not some fucking Ant who's gonna give in to your temper tantrums and let you have your way. I'm a bastard, but I'm *your* bastard. Like I said, you'll deal."

"I won't," she said solemnly. Blissful silence followed for maybe five seconds before she demanded, "And what is that anyway?"

Still battling back his fury when it came to her insistence that she could escape, Maddox was looking forward to a quiet walk back to the cabin as he reflected on all the ways he'd fucked this up so far. He was so focused on having her near, it took him a second to realize she was waiting for his answer.

"What's what?" he asked. What was she even asking him?

"Ant. When you say it, I think it means one thing and it's not good. What is it?"

Maddox's body gave a start at the question.

Oh, *shit*.

He'd said 'Ant', hadn't he?

He jerked, then tightened his grip on Evangeline. Talk about déjà vu. Maddox had had this exact same conversation with her more than four years ago, shortly after she finally accepted that she was his mate. It was their first real fight back then and something warned him against answering her.

He should've listened.

"You, uh, you've never heard anyone say that before?"

"If I had, do you think I would be asking?"

She had a point.

"Ants... it's kinda like how humans call paranormals 'Paras' when they're referring to us as a group. They know that there's countless different races, but they can't be bothered to differentiate so there's a catch-all term. Paras think of humans in the same way, I guess. They look around and see humans everywhere, and it reminds them of worker ants. Strong and resilient, good at mindless tasks, but"—and he winced, knowing that it sounded bad, yet unable to stop himself from adding—"ultimately there are way too many of them, easily replaced and, um, easily"—don't say killed, don't say exterminated, don't say—"*squashed*."

Evangeline's gasp of outrage and the spike of betrayal in her scent were like a knife to his heart.

Bravo, Maddox. Genius fucking move, there.

He kind of expected her reaction; it was exactly the same as it had been. That didn't mean he had to like it as she said, "Is that how you see me?"

Her voice was soft. Too soft. He would've taken the

brunt of her lectures or her shouts gladly. But this dangerous quiet was a million times harder to hear.

Ah, hell.

If it was even possible, he fucked up *worse*.

Maybe it wasn't too late for some damage control.

"Ang— *Evangeline*, no. I—"

She tucked her chin into her chest, refusing to look at him. He could've sworn he saw ice crystals billow out with her breath as she wondered coldly, "Why would you ever want to mate with something so useless?"

Nope. Too late.

Still, Maddox knew Evangeline better than she would ever expect. That was one of the only advantages he had. She might insist that they'd never met before this week, but they'd had a whole life together before the accident. He knew how she liked her eggs, how she cried over ASPCA commercials with puppies and kittens, how she refused to sleep with anything less than four pillows, and how she used a sharp wit as battle armor coupled with her soft voice as a shield. When she got like this, Maddox always backed off and let her win.

But that was before. After they were bonded, she could win any fucking argument they had. *After* they were bonded. Until then, no matter how dirty he had to play, he was going to win. Losing wasn't an option. Evangeline was his and, with certainty ringing in every word, he told her exactly that.

"Because you're *mine*."

Evangeline clamped her mouth shut, didn't respond. As far as Maddox could tell, she had resigned herself to being brought back to the cabin. Not that he expected she'd given up on trying to escape—his Angie had always been a fighter—but his wolf finally stopped in its frantic pacing once the cabin was back in his sights.

She started to struggle a bit as he opened the back door, stopping when she realized that he had no intention of letting her tackle the steps that would lead up to the second floor. Evangeline sighed softly, her breath tickling his overheated skin. His cock twitched, a reminder that he was still as hard as a fucking rock.

He was super grateful that Evangeline hadn't caught on to his arousal yet. Her beautiful scent was finally free of the taint of fear. If for only a few minutes, he wanted to pretend she wasn't afraid of him.

Though he couldn't help but feel an ache down below as he brought Evangeline back into the bedroom.

Maddox placed her on the bed gently, warned her not to move, then disappeared through the bedroom door. Evangeline was just working up enough strength to test her weight on her ankle again when he returned, carrying a bag of ice in one hand, a glass of water in the other. He set the glass on the night table before opening his fist.

There were two tiny white pills nestled against his palm.

She held up a slightly shaking hand, warding him off. "Oh, no, no, no. After what happened with my macchiato, I'm not gonna swallow anything you give me ever again. Who knows if I'll wake up at all next time."

He frowned, careful not to clench his fists too tightly in case he crushed the pills. "That was necessary. I'm sorry I had to do it but, make no mistake, I'd do it again if I had to. I just want to help you... but if that's how you feel, I get it. I do. You don't want to take something for your pain, I'm not going to force you. But don't cut off your nose to spite your face, thinking you're getting back at me. It won't change anything, and you'll just be more miserable. If it helps any, I swear I'll never force you to do anything you don't want to do."

"Except stay here against my will, right?"

Maddox set the two pills down next to the glass; if the pain got too bad, he wanted her to be able to take the medicine after he left. Swallowing back a frustrated growl, he told her honestly, "I keep hoping that you'll change your mind and want to stay with me."

"That's not hope, you brute," Evangeline snapped. "That's delusion."

As hard as it was to refrain from snapping back—while they were mated, a good argument often turned into great foreplay that led to out-of-this-world make-up sex—Maddox decided to try another tactic. Losing his patience with Evangeline wasn't going to make her want to stay with him.

"Here, at least put some ice on your ankle." When Evangeline opened her mouth to refuse again, he cut her off with a sad smile and an enticing shake of the bag. "If you're going to try to run again, you'll need your ankle healed up right."

That got to her. Snatching the bag out of his hand, she slammed it against her sore ankle. It had to have hurt like hell, the way the ice clanked against the bone, but she was too stubborn to let him see how much.

She didn't need to. He could sense her pain like a jagged line that nearly split his soul in half.

Maddox's eyes flashed, his golden irises glowing a vibrant yellow. He'd been hiding it for too long. It felt good to let his wolf peer out at its mate, even if she was purposely looking anywhere but at him.

"I'll be outside, patrolling the grounds," he said gruffly. Her pain wasn't fading and it killed him that he couldn't make it better for her. She'd never let him. Not now. "Feel free to explore the cabin if you like. It's as much yours as it's mine."

Evangeline refused to comment on that last part as she finally dared to meet his earnest gaze. "You're not going to lock me in this room again?"

"What's the point?" Maddox asked, snorting. "I know now that locks won't keep you out or in, but that ankle might. And if you try to run again, I'll introduce you to my wolf. Trust me, he's dying to say hi."

She crossed her arms over her chest. As if that would stop him from picking up on how fast her heart was beating all of a sudden.

"I hate you."

For a split second, Maddox wanted to howl in agony. His mate was the other half of him. No matter what he had done to deserve her anger, she wasn't supposed to be *able* to hate him.

And that's when he caught the slightest sour tang to her scent. Curdled milk mixed with warm vanilla.

She was... she was *lying.*

Maddox had hope. It wasn't a lot, and he knew he had a tough road ahead of him, but he clung to that hope like it was the edge of a buoy and he was fucking drowning.

"If you need me, stick your head out through the window and holler. I'll hear you." Maddox paused, pulling his phone out of his back pocket. "As I'm sure you realized by now, no one else will. Shame, huh?"

He waited to see if she would say anything else. When she turned to look away from him, he frowned, then shook his head. He thought about his phone and the next step to his crazy plan. Of course, he hadn't meant for it to happen this way, but desperate times called for drastic measures. Calling up Colt and admitting how badly he'd messed up already—yeah, he was pretty desperate.

"Take it easy on that leg," he said, lifting the phone to his ear after he pressed a single button. He could hear the beeps echoing around him as the phone automatically dialed. "I'll be back before you know it, then I'll cook dinner for us."

She stuck out her chin. "I won't be hungry."

He sighed. Somehow he knew she would say that. "Hungry or not, you'll sit and eat with me. I won't let anyone think I can't provide for my mate."

"I don't think anyone will care since I'm *not* your mate."

His wolf howled at the flippant way she denied them both. His claws appeared at the end of his fingers, scratching against the glass protecting the front of his phone. He tightened his grip and probably would have crushed the stupid thing if it wasn't for the fact that the ringing suddenly stopped.

Because this time?

When Evangeline said she wasn't his mate, she was telling the truth.

"*Hello? Mad, you there, bro?*"

Maddox's eyes flared as he looked down at his contrary little mate. It was a good thing that Colt answered the phone when he had. He was two seconds away from showing Evangeline just how wrong she was and, despite the man part of his brain knowing damn well that he needed her to remember him before she could acknowledge their bond, the wolf didn't care. If it had its way, it would make a new bond when it claimed her for good. She couldn't deny them when she wore his bite proudly on her skin.

"Hold on," he snarled into the phone. He narrowed his gaze on Evangeline, his expression one of sensual heat and a promise of retribution. At that moment, biting wasn't that far off the table. "I will see you for dinner, *mate*. If you change your mind about the pills, they're harmless. Just aspirin. I hate seeing you hurt so please think about taking them."

Then, before she could say anything else that might provoke him, he stormed from the room.

19

Okay. So maybe she might have pushed him too hard. But, well, hadn't he deserved it?

Evangeline blamed it on the pain. The adrenaline that pushed her to do something so stupid as to try and escape from a room on the second floor had worn off while Maddox carried her injured ass back to the cabin. Her ankle was throbbing when he brought her to her prison cell and it made her feel worse when he came back with the aspirin and the ice. Sure, she wouldn't have been hurt if she hadn't been trying to flee from him, but did he have to be so nice about it? It would make it so much easier to hate him if he didn't seem to want to take care of her.

Of course, that was because he thought she was his mate. She couldn't forget that. While he was wrong about any bond they might have, she had to admit that she was going to take advantage of that belief for as long as she could. If he planned on treating her like a shifter's mate, then that meant she had nothing to fear from him except, well, being forced into a loveless mating with a man who had drugged her in a coffee shop.

The second Maddox left the room, she jumped up from the bed. She was willing to bet he knew, but she didn't care. Hobbling and trying her best to ignore the way her poor ankle screamed in pain, she put her ear to the door.

Maddox must have stopped right outside of her room to have his conversation because she could hear his growl through the closed door. Part of her was happy to hear that she wasn't the only one he growled at; at least the animalistic sound made a lot more sense now that she knew he was a shifter. The other part of her—the twisted part that responded to her kidnapper way more than she should—was inexplicably jealous. She purposely quashed that part as quickly as she could, straining to make out what he was saying now.

"Hey, it's me. Yeah. Sorry about that. She's... she's adjusting." Maddox paused. "How's it going? Colt, let's just say it could have gone better."

Colt again. Colt sounded like a man's name, something that Evangeline tried to pretend didn't matter to her at all. Besides, Maddox had mentioned the name before, when she hurt her ankle, and now he was calling him for help which meant that this mysterious

Colt obviously knew all about her kidnapping. Evangeline made a mental note to hate him on principle, too.

Now, if only she could convince herself that she *did* hate Maddox. She definitely *wanted* to, and she had when she first discovered she was trapped, but he was luring her in with his golden eyes. They were just so familiar; it only made it worse that he seemed to think they'd met before, when Evangeline couldn't shake the same impression. And then he went and sprung this mate baloney on her as if that excused his lawbreaking.

A wolf. The bastard was a *wolf*.

It was bad enough he was a shifter who was using their supposed status as mates as an excuse to keep her locked in a cage. But why did he have to be such a… such a *predator*? She might've been able to handle a rabbit shifter, or a harmless little hedgehog, or even something sweet like a puppy dog if the circumstances had been different. But a wolf? Territorial, possessive, and with a skill at tracking he'd already proven.

She was so screwed.

"Yeah, yeah. I know. But I called for a reason, not because I wanted another lecture, alright?"

A pause.

"Good. Listen, turns out that the cabin's a wash. She doesn't remember it and she's already made a break for it once. It's too dangerous. It's making my wolf restless, too. It knows what was supposed to happen here and it just doesn't understand why we both have to wait."

Evangeline cringed, then pressed her ear closer to the door. It was smashed up against her skull and still she pushed, eager to hear what he was saying.

Now that she knew he thought she was his mate, she could guess what his wolf was waiting for.

Hell freaking no.

Maddox sighed loudly. "Sure. Okay. But, listen... remember when I had you get that stuff from Wolf's Creek? Uh-huh. You got it? Thank fucking Alpha. It's a back-up plan, but the only one I've got, so this is what I want you to do—"

The heavy cadence of his steps echoed and faded as he started down the hall again. His voice became nothing but a buzz of murmurs and muttered orders before Evangeline couldn't hear anything from him at all. A few seconds later, she heard the door slam. He'd gone into his bedroom.

That was one good thing.

Evangeline stepped back from the door, a strange feeling—an empty feeling—washing over her.

A good thing... *right*?

She shook her head, hobbling back toward the bed. She was stuck, just like she figured, all alone in an empty cabin out in the middle of the woods. It was like the set-up to a bad horror movie. No one would be able to hear her scream. But if she managed to get her hands on his cell phone...

Evangeline's pulse settled. She felt a lot better knowing that at least one of them had a phone. The second he let down his guard, she'd snatch it from him, then she'd get the hell out of there.

Because now that she knew why he wanted her so badly? She had to escape before she started to buy into his obvious delusions.

Colt hung up his phone and slipped it into his pants pocket with one hand. He pinched the bridge of his nose with the other.

One day. His brother had followed their plan for *one day*. Not even a day. Now he wanted to give up on the cabin, trading it for the only home that anyone could trace to him? He had to be kidding.

Only Colt recognized that tone. That was Mad's Alpha voice which meant that he was deadly serious. That was his *obey-me-or-else* voice. As soon as Colt finished this late night meeting, he'd have to check in on his brother and see if Maddox could be reasoned with.

Slamming his truck door shut, Colt snorted.

Why the fuck had he thought Maddox could keep a clear head around Evangeline? His brother was thinking with a head, all right, but it certainly wasn't the one sitting on top of his shoulders.

He should've known better. To be honest, pushing

Maddox to run off with Evangeline was a clear sign that *Colt* probably wasn't doing his best thinking, either.

What he was about to walk into? Probably the biggest hint that, somewhere in the last week or so, he'd lost his ever-loving mind.

The building he was standing in front of was one of a trio of skyscrapers that lorded over the city of Coventry; aptly named for the main power in town. His instructions were to go to the middle one and stop at the receptionist desk. So long as he had payment, he'd be let up to the top floor.

If you were oblivious to the witches' presence and power in the large integrated city, no one could blame you for not knowing that the building was the headquarters for the local witch's coven. Except for the purple accents displayed throughout the first floor, there was no other clue that this was coven territory.

Well, if you were oblivious *and* an Ant. As a shifter, Colt picked up on the magic before he even stepped a toe inside. The sweet scent of baby powder overlaid everything, coupled with a jolt of electricity that made his fur stand on end.

Shaking it off, he headed straight for the young male witch at the desk. Like every other witch Colt had ever met, this witch proudly wore his purple eyes out in the open. In the years since the Paras stopped hiding who and what they were, the witches had earned the best reputation. They didn't have to hide anymore and most didn't.

"Can I help you, sir?"

"I'm here to see Luciana." Colt flashed the diamond in his palm. "She's expecting me."

It was a full carat, worth more than three grand. It should've been enough to hire a handful of witches except, for some reason, his name came up on the coven's blacklist. Not a single witch would take his job. And since he couldn't get in touch with Maddox's witch, his brother's longtime friend Priscilla Winters, Colt had to do something he absolutely hated.

He had to grovel.

To add insult to injury, just arranging to meet with the head witch of the local coven was obscenely expensive. She wouldn't even let him make an appointment to see her without the promise of payment. And a witch didn't take cash.

The male witch nodded. Colt was willing to bet that the guy knew the worth of the rock in his palm at a glance. It was nice to see he passed muster.

"Take the first elevator to the top floor. Madame is waiting for you."

Colt folded his fist. "No stairs?"

"Just the elevators, sir. They're run by magic, though. You don't have to worry about them going out."

That wasn't what he was worried about.

"Yeah." He ran his hand through his short hair. "That's fine. Thanks."

A short elevator ride later—that seemed longer with his wolf whimpering at the metal confinement he could rarely tolerate at the best of times—Colt found himself entering one hell of an office.

It was made of windows, each one warded with enough magic to make his back teeth ache. Everything inside was either black, white, or gold; no need to overdo the purple when one look at the woman sitting at the massive black desk in the center revealed that she was a powerful witch. At least twelve other witches were in the room, some at desks of their own, others milling nearby in case their *Madame* needed them, but Colt easily picked up on the biggest, baddest, most dominant predator of the bunch.

Ah. The head witch.

He'd never met her face to face before. Luciana la Sorcière was almost a boogeyman in Para circles. Everyone heard of her, but she spent most of her time running her coven like a multi-billion dollar company; she was rarely caught in public. If other witches served as the face of the race, Luciana was the beating heart of the coven. Without her, they just wouldn't work.

Her eyes drew his attention first. They were purple, of course, and they were shrewd. She might be wearing a smile on a pair of lips so red, it was like she painted them with fresh blood, but her eyes were sizing him up, too.

Smart witch.

Luciana was wearing a suit: white blouse, black blazer. If she got to her feet, he knew she'd have on black slacks and heels. It was the same uniform all of her people wore, with the male witches moving easily in boots that matched the female witches' stilettos.

The other witches all kept their hair short or plaited out of their face. Not Luciana. Her hair was a vibrant red shade, cascading in perfect waves down her back. She smelled like an earthy combination of baby powder and fire. It should've been off-putting. Strangely, it wasn't. He wondered if she wore her hair like that on purpose. When she nodded in greeting, the light from above rippled on her long red hair, making it seem like a dancing flame.

She was also exceedingly beautiful, but Colt had been expecting that.

Witches were nothing if not a contradiction. If they trained in it, they could be as good a lie detector as a shifter, using magic to sense a deception rather than sniffing one out. But, because of how they could use their magic, most witches tended to glamour themselves. Luciana had been the head witch of this coven since before Colt was a pup. She didn't look a day over twenty-five. She was a walking lie.

He had to remember that. She could lie to his face by keeping her glamour up. If he so much as tried to tell a fib while in front of her, she'd make him pay.

Fucking witches.

Colt strode forward, forcing himself to remember why exactly he was doing this again.

He wouldn't even be there if it weren't for his brother. Finding a witch to check on the status of Maddox and Evangeline's bond was exceedingly important and if it kept him from dwelling too closely on his own troubles, that was fine with him.

Luciana folded her hands, finger over finger, resting them on the edge of her desk. The epitome of a business professional about to make a deal.

See? Just another day at the office.

"Did you bring the diamond?" she asked.

He showed the witch what was in his hand.

Her painted lips pulled upward in a satisfied smile. "It's mine? Meant for me and no one else?"

Colt nodded.

More witchy bullshit. The diamonds had to be freely given otherwise they were worthless to their spells. It was why the witches sold their magic to the government and those who could afford their steep prices. If making off with a sackful of precious diamonds left their inherent power intact, there would be a rush of gorgeous jewel thieves with purple eyes. Since they had to earn them—and buying them with their own funds didn't seem to work, either—spells and wards cost a pretty diamond.

Luciana held out her hand. Soft purple light bathed her palm in an otherworldly glow. She closed her eyes, hummed, then opened them wide.

The diamond was nestled in her palm.

Colt glanced at his. Completely empty.

He hadn't felt a thing.

His wolf bared its teeth. Just in case he gave in to the same urge, Colton clamped his mouth shut. Probably not a good idea to accidentally threaten the witch.

As if she even noticed his reaction—or maybe she did and didn't care. She laughed joyously at her prize, dipping her hand down to one of the pockets in her suit. As soon as the diamond was gone, Colt knew she'd taken his payment. For as long as she wanted to humor him, he had an audience with Luciana.

Well, then. Better make the most of it.

20

"I need a favor."

Luciana leaned back in her desk chair, the very picture of a regal queen in her throne. "Go on."

"A witch severed one side of a mate bond. I'm willing to pay as much as you're asking to put it back together again."

"Interesting. Tell me… was it your witch?"

His back went up. A heartbeat later, his wolf lunged to the forefront. Fur sprouted along his arms, his neck, his throat. He struggled to force the partial shift back, but it was almost as hard as his poor, unfortunate dick.

But *his* witch? Colt didn't have a witch.

Luciana pursed her lips. "Your eyes go blue. Almost icy blue. That's… unusual."

It was. He was the only shifter he knew whose eyes

did that. In the case of wolf shifters, even if the two-legged shape didn't have the golden eyes common to his kind, the wolf did and his shifter's gaze turned a mix between amber and yellow.

Not Colt.

While pure-bred wolves in the wild didn't have blue eyes, shifters could—but only the man, never the wolf. Colt was the only one he knew whose gaze went icy blue when his wolf was in control. He'd given up trying to understand why.

And he *hated* it when someone pointed it out.

Almost as much as he hated someone telling him that he had a witch when he most definitely did not.

For Maddox's sake, he didn't snap. It wasn't easy.

"The mate bond is my brother's," he grumbled after a moment. "Maddox Wolfe."

Luciana tapped the bottom of her chin with one of her long nails. To nobody's surprise, it was painted purple. "Name's familiar."

She gestured toward one of the witches watching from the side. A stout witch with her raven hair done up in twin braids came rushing over.

Luciana murmured something.

Colt was barely six feet away from her. His shifter senses should have picked up on the murmur—but they didn't. He didn't catch a single word. It was like someone had shoved cotton in his ears.

The other witch whispered something back.

Luciana nodded. With a careless wave of her hand, the magic lifted.

His ears cleared in time to hear an understated, throaty growl. Shit. It was coming from him.

"Sorry about that," Luciana said. "Coven business. I'm sure you understand."

In an instant, Colt was thrown back to the day he found Evangeline and ran straight to the Cage. Pack business. That's how he described his reason for returning so soon. So, yeah, he understood.

Didn't mean he liked it, though.

"My apprentice reminded me of your brother's sad tale. He lost his mate, didn't he? Then chose to wallow in the dreadful prison rather than let one of mine relieve him of his heartache."

"Yeah," Colt said dryly. Not the way he saw it—or Maddox, for that matter—but who ever said that witches were like normal folk? "Only it seems as if someone got the wrong memo. His mate isn't dead now."

One perfectly arched eyebrow quirked skyward. "That's wonderful news. But what does that have to do with me?"

"His mate isn't dead, but his bond is."

"Oh."

'Oh' was right.

"I know you witches work with the Cage guards. You ward the windows, make the cells Para-proof. If a bonded Para chooses to break their bond, there's a witch on duty to perform surgery on the poor sap's soul. I don't know what happened to my brother and his bond. No one does. But, we're thinking, if a witch can cut a bond, maybe they can heal one."

It made sense to Colt. To Maddox, too.

One look at Luciana's regret-filled expression and Colt realized that he didn't know jackshit when it came to magic.

"I wish I could tell you that it would work like that. A bond that needs to be removed, it's child's play to snip it in half. But the reverse…" Luciana shook her head. "A bond heals on its own or it doesn't. Unless there are other forces at play, there's nothing I can do."

Colt seized on the last thing Luciana said. "Other forces? Like what? What's that supposed to mean?"

"Magic is a fickle thing. You spend decades learning it, then it switches suddenly because it's in a mood. Do you know why we use diamonds?"

Strange segue, but Colt had to admit he had no clue why the witches did anything.

"It's because a good diamond is hard and it's cold and it's strong. The perfect conduit for spells that require a little more oomph. With enough power, anything is possible. I could give you your deepest wish"—Luciana's purple eyes lit up, a true shocking violet—"I could make her notice you at last, even make her lust after you, if I had enough diamonds. I could make her forget you, too. But I could never make her bond with you. Love… there are things that are more powerful than magic. You understand?"

Colt might have—if the witch hadn't used his nonexistent bond as an example.

This time, when he went full wolf, he was a hair away from shifting totally on the spot. Only the reality that he'd either have to march through the crowded downtown in his fur or strut to his truck bare-assed naked kept him from the final snap.

It didn't stop him from snarling at her.

"I'll take that as a yes," she said, a hint of amusement in her tone.

The room crackled with magic. Everyone and everything took on a pale lavender tinge. Every single witch in the room—male and female—had a spell at the ready. Colt needed to calm the fuck down.

It took a second. He grunted and shook, adjusting his shirt before he popped his collar. His wolf continued to prowl around inside of him, torn between wanting to run to his mate and following Colt's lead that she be left alone.

He never should have come into the city. It wasn't Grayson, but it wasn't home, either. At home, Dodge could shield the house, trap Colt inside whenever he thought he was going feral. When Colt was younger, Dodge was still strong enough that he could track Colt down, haunt his furry ass all over the state. Now that he was fading, Dodge couldn't even leave the Bumptown—which meant that Colt was on his own for this one.

He had to get the hell out of there.

"Know what? I'll think about what you said. I'm still gonna find a way to fix my brother's bond. If love won't heal it, maybe enough diamonds will."

It was hard to talk around his extended canines. His claws and his fangs revealed the precarious state of his mind.

The other witches were primed to throw magic at him if he made any sudden moves.

Luciana continued to smile across her desk at him. "I like you. Too bad another of my kind has already got her hooks in you."

He went still. "She's not a witch."

"Tell yourself that if it makes you feel better. It's faint, but it's there. You've definitely been touched by a witch."

No. It wasn't possible. She didn't have the signature purple eyes, and she spent every day downtown running some kind of hippie shop in Grayson. What kind of witch worked retail for cash when she could be guaranteed true diamonds by working with the coven?

She wasn't a witch.

She wasn't his mate, either.

Colt had had enough. Time to get out of the building before he lost his temper, the witches retaliated, and he ended up a toad or something equally as embarrassing.

"Thank you for your taking the time to see me," Colt said solemnly. "Appreciate it."

"I really do like you. Pity about your mate. If she won't help you, you can always come back to me for your next favor." Her lips curved. "And it'll only cost you a .25 carat."

"I'll have to keep that in mind," he said. Sure, he was lying, but he was leaving so he didn't think it mattered all that much. "You're a real gem."

"A diamond, dear wolf. A diamond."

Evangeline tried to pretend she wasn't hungry, even going so far as to hum to drown out the rumble of her stomach.

She made it maybe three hours.

Her body clock was all thrown off. Night had fallen fully since her captor returned her to her cage. It was dark, she still didn't have any idea what time it was, but it had to have been close to twelve hours since she'd had something to eat.

At first, she didn't even feel any hunger; stress and anger and nervousness tended to do that. But as the night wore on and she realized that a dangerous shifter believing she was his mate meant that she was the safest she had ever been—since Maddox would save her from everyone and everything, including himself

—her stomach started to remind her that it had been hours since the fateful coffee.

She was *starving*.

Well, he did say that he was going to prove himself to her. And he had mentioned something about dinner.

So maybe she had thrown it into his face that she would never sit down and have a meal with him. That was back when her appetite was missing. Now? She needed nutrients to keep up her strength if she wanted to try escaping again.

Besides, her ankle was still screaming with pain. Evangeline had finally given in and taken the aspirin about thirty minutes after he left her alone. It helped a little, but the harsh aspirin wasn't sitting right in her empty stomach. She'd always had to swallow her painkillers with a meal; going without meant feeling nauseous and weak until it worked its way through. Better than outright pain, but not by much.

Careful not to put her entire weight on her swollen ankle, Evangeline limped over to the door. He promised that he wouldn't lock it again. She didn't even bother to check. What was the point?

She banged on the door. "Hey! You! Are you just going to leave me to waste away in here?"

The door knob turned within seconds. Maddox was there, like he'd been waiting out in the hall for just this moment.

"Finally hungry, my mate?"

Ugh. The way he called her his 'mate' so easily almost stole her appetite away. It seemed as if he was taking a new approach, too. She was going with acting like the biggest bitch around so that he reconsidered keeping her with him. Maddox? He was all "act like she *is* his and maybe she will be".

Yeah, right.

Not gonna happen.

Crossing her arms over her chest, leaning on her good ankle, Evangeline scowled. "I didn't say that I wouldn't eat dinner. I just said that I wouldn't eat it with you. If you're gonna keep me in here, the least you can do is feed me, you jerk."

He smiled. The bastard actually smiled. "Of course. Give me a second. I'll be right back."

Maddox pulled the door behind him before he left. He didn't lock it. She was kind of surprised.

Evangeline thought of the aspirin she finally swallowed, and the last of the water that was probably warm and stagnant by now. She cupped her mouth with her hands, shouting through the door. "A glass of water, too, if that's not too much to ask of a kidnapper!"

Maddox heard her. He returned a few seconds later, carrying a fresh glass. "Here," he said, offering it to her. "I figured you'd get hungry before long so I already made you a plate. I'm just warming it up now. Get comfy. I'll bring it to you."

He was as good as his word. Evangeline had just resettled herself on the bed when Maddox was coming back, carrying a platter with him in one hand, a tray table in the other.

Her mouth immediately started to water.

He made her steak and a monstrous-sized baked potato for dinner. It was one of her favorite comfort meals, and one she didn't have often because she could never find the time to bake the potato for long enough. Not to mention that, every time she tried to grill a steak inside of her apartment, she tended to overcook it.

This one looked perfect. There was even a pat of butter sitting on top of the potato, melting down the salt-encrusted skin.

Just how she liked it.

Why wasn't that a surprise?

He held the tray table out to her. Evangeline snatched it from him, settling the table over her legs; she had her ankle elevated on a pillow. Maddox placed the platter on top of the tray, then added a fork and knife he pulled out of his back pocket.

She yawned.

Maddox noticed. "Feeling tired?"

It probably wasn't the smartest idea to admit to a prospective weakness. It just slipped out. "Yeah, I just... that's so weird."

Maddox chuckled. "That's okay. Escape attempts take it out of a girl. You and your ankle will feel better after a full night's sleep, promise."

There was a twinkle in his eyes, a spark that made him even more attractive. As if *that* was hard. He might be a no-good kidnapper, but he was a gorgeous no-good kidnapper.

Damn it. It wasn't fair.

As soon as her meal was arranged so that she could eat it, the bastard had the nerve to perch on the edge of the bed, leaning up against the bottom post. Forget gorgeous. The easy position, the stray lock of hair falling forward... he was sexy as hell.

Still wasn't fair.

Her stomach flip-flopped. "Are you planning on sitting here and watching me eat?"

"I've just given you a knife. Gotta make sure you don't try to use it to stab me in the back or anything." He paused, obviously teasing, though there was nothing but earnestness in his tone when he added, "You'd only regret it when you remembered me."

Evangeline snorted. If she could have any wish, it would be that she could remember everything she'd lost over the last handful of years. Wouldn't it just twist his tail if he discovered that she still had no clue who he was?

Even if his eyes—and that sly smirk of his—were so annoyingly familiar, glancing at his face was like an itch she couldn't scratch.

She shrugged, trying to push her burgeoning uncertainty aside. "Watch me. Whatever. It's just food."

"You'll enjoy it. I made it just the way you like."

Pointedly ignoring his comment, she was reaching for the fork when a thought occurred to her.

"Wait." Evangeline shoved her plate toward him. "You first."

Maddox cocked his head.

She jerked her chin at the fork still lying on the tray table between them. "I remember something alright—I remember what happened the last time you made something for me. Your 'calming' drugs were in the coffee, right? You never confirmed that."

Maddox's lips thinned. Okay. Seemed as if he *still* wasn't going to admit to it.

Fine. "How do I know that you didn't do something to this dinner?"

"You don't."

"Exactly. You take a bite first. From the potato and the steak. Until you do, I won't eat a single bite. I'll starve first."

For a second, she thought he would refuse. He didn't. Locking eyes with her, Maddox grabbed the fork. He used the edge to slice off a piece of steak, then popped it in his mouth. A forkful of the baked potato followed. He chewed. Swallowed.

He placed the fork back onto the plate. "There. Perfectly fine. Now eat."

Evangeline didn't like being told what to do. However, she was so hungry that she chose to take up the fork on her own. Within minutes, she'd polished the entire steak, eating half of the potato before she picked up her glass of water again.

She drank, then set the glass on the nightstand so

she could turn her attention to demolishing the rest of the potato.

Maddox let out a soft rumble that seemed like contentment. Did wolves purr? Evangeline didn't know, but it's what the sound reminded her of.

"I know you don't remember this," he murmured, "but I've always loved watching you eat. It makes me happy."

Evangeline nearly choked on her bite. She snatched at the glass of water again, draining the rest of it in three gulps.

His eyes glittered innocently. "Was it something I said?"

"No. It just went down the wrong pipe."

"Mm."

She meant to glare at him. The effect was ruined when, as she narrowed her gaze on him, a huge yawn ripped out of her. Her eyes were so heavy, they were like sandbags weighing on her lids.

Her hand went limp. The fork fell onto the sheet.

And that's when she realized why this stupid, dozy feeling felt so familiar.

"You..." Evangeline glanced down at her plate. It was hard to do any strenuous thinking since her head felt like it was stuffed with cotton candy, but she could still put two and two together. "The food— *you drugged me again?* How? You ate some!"

"You've always been smart, Angie. I knew you'd expect something like that in your meal."

It dawned on her. "The water. It was in the stupid water."

Maddox nodded.

"This time I mean it," she slurred, her head drooping. "I really hate you."

"I know, Angie. I know."

21

Evangeline was sleeping.

At least, she thought she was.

She'd been waiting for Maddox to come back after the way he stormed off last night. If she knew how to find him, she would've chased after him. She had a thing or two to say to him, especially since a relationship wouldn't work if there wasn't an open and honest communication. Too bad he left his stupid phone behind when he left or she would've already let him have it.

The night wore on. As it did, her anger turned to worry when he didn't return to Wolf's Creek. She thought about giving up and driving home to Woodbridge—they'd talked about moving in together a couple of times, though she still had her house—and decided that she'd give it a few more hours.

She must have fallen asleep because, next thing she

knew, she was being nudged gently awake by a strong, warm hand.

"Angie?"

That was her name—no. That was what Maddox called her.

Maddox.

She came to slowly, stretching her arms, her back, her toes before shifting from her side to her back. It was brighter than it had been. She blinked a few times, then focused on the handsome beast of a man crouched next to her.

Evangeline smiled. There was no one in the world she'd rather wake up to than Maddox Wolfe. "Hey."

Relief flashed across his face. "Hey. What are you doing on the couch?"

She was quiet for a moment, thrown back to the night before. The argument when Maddox sprang an impulsive proposal on her, and the awkward discussion when it came to becoming his bonded mate. He asked her to marry him because he wanted to bite her, wanted to claim her fully. Evangeline was down with mating—she wanted to hump him so bad, it wasn't funny—but she had insisted that they get married by human officials before the claiming.

A paranormal through and through, her shifter mate balked at the idea.

Evangeline stood her ground.

Maddox left the house, probably to cool off, then hopefully realize what a massive, hypocritical dick he had been. But he was back now. Whatever his reason, he came back.

That didn't change the fact that he left her.

Evangeline's smile slid off of her face. "Oh. I was waiting for you to come back home. I guess I fell asleep. Sorry about that."

"You could've slept in the bed."

Without him in it? No, thanks.

"I wasn't planning on sleeping," *she told him, purposely turning away.*

The long night weighed on her shoulders and she started to yawn. She stifled it with the back of her hand before shrugging. For some reason, it seemed important not to let her big, bad wolf see how much his abandonment hurt her. Because now? Evangeline couldn't find it in her to be angry, even though she was. Maddox was her mate. The one who professed to love her. He wasn't supposed to run away.

He wasn't supposed to leave her alone.

They had a bond. All that was left was the final claiming, and the two certificates that would make them married and mated in the eyes of all. She already gave him everything: her love, her hope, her dreams, her future. When he was ready to take her, she'd give him her body.

All she wanted was him—

There was so much more that should have happened. Like the strongest sense of déjà vu, Evangeline had the feeling that she had lived this exact same scene once before. Maddox would apologize, the two would work out their feelings, and then... *something* would happen.

Something *did* happen.

The room flooded with a cloud of thick smoke. It wasn't dark, more of a pale purple, and it moved like thunderstorm clouds across the sky. Within seconds, Evangeline was surrounded. She felt it reaching for her, washing over her, pushing her down like a wave crashing over her. She was blinded by it, consumed by it.

And, once again, she was alone.

The couch disappeared the instant that she got to her feet. Evangeline walked easily on both feet, another sign that this was still a dream. While she was awake, her right ankle was too swollen and painful to support her weight. At that moment, she was trudging through the empty space, searching for her mate. Her ankle was the last thing on her mind.

Where was Maddox?

"Maddox," she shouted, waving her hands through the pale smoke. "Maddox! Where did you go?"

"Where you can't touch him."

Evangeline went still at that unwelcome female voice.

It was light and clear, almost cheery, despite the force behind the words. Power underlined the statement, reverberating through Evangeline's skull. She couldn't even be sure that the words had been spoken out loud, or that she had heard them in her head.

She couldn't see anyone. She had no clue who was there with her, especially since it wasn't Maddox.

But that voice?

Evangeline knew it almost as well as her own. It was the voice in the back of her head that often warned her about trying too hard to remember. After all, some things were best forgotten.

She clenched her fists. The same voice used to follow her in her dreams, inevitably turning them to nightmares. Right after her accident, it endlessly mocked her, causing setback after setback in her mental recovery. Eventually Evangeline had to make a choice: her memories or some peace.

So for three years she dealt with the nagging sensation that there was something she forgot. As soon as she gave up, the voice disappeared.

Was… was this what it was all about?

Maddox.

Evangeline gasped, taking in a lungful of the dense purple smoke. The gasp became a choking fit that left her short of breath and extremely dizzy. She tried to fight her way through it.

Where was she? What was going on? Last thing she remembered, Evangeline had gotten so hungry that she asked her captor for a meal. She made sure it wasn't laced with a sedative by telling him to taste it—but it wasn't in the steak.

It was in the water.

She stopped pushing at the smoke.

Holy shit. The bastard had drugged her again!

Was this a dream? It had to be. Coming up with a fantasy where Maddox groveled and begged her forgiveness? A dream where she gave in to her insane urge to touch the deranged shifter? A nightmare where the mocking voice reminded her again and again that she was worthless and should've died in the crash?

Evangeline felt the old, familiar anger returning. For too long she'd done everything she could to claw some independence back. Nobody—not her parents, not Adam, not Maddox... not this bitchy voice—was going to take that from her.

"What is this? Who are you?" she demanded. "Why can't I see you?"

"You shouldn't be here."

No shit. "I don't *want* to be. Maddox kidnapped *me*. I want nothing to do with him. I only want to go back home!"

A disbelieving scoff echoed all around her. "What do you think you're playing at? I can tell when you lie. Sure, you want to go home, but despite everything I've done to you, you still feel the connection. Don't deny it," the female voice snapped when Evangeline was about to do exactly that, "I know better. Are you trying to take my mate away from me?"

Mate? What mate? "I don't know what you're talking about."

"Maddox is mine. You're wasting his time. He only gets one mate and that's *me*."

The voice seemed to grow closer. Or maybe it was just louder.

A heartbeat later, the smoke parted like the red sea, revealing a statuesque beauty with straight black hair, caramel-colored skin, and a pair of wicked purple eyes narrowed in obvious hate.

Evangeline could have forgiven the purple smoke. But the eyes? There was no denying it now. The voice that haunted her these last three years might belong to her conscience or even her battered self-esteem. But since it just manifested as a Para, she was beginning to understand that it might be more than that.

She was dealing with a witch.

"Look at you," the female witch sneered. "A knock-off version of me. Do you really believe that he could ever love you when I exist in his world?"

"He's the one who said I was his mate," retorted Evangeline. "Not me."

"My Mad is confused. His wolf has led him astray. One of the downsides of dealing with shifters, I'm afraid. The animal is led by base instincts and its nose. But the man... he's in control of the heart. And Maddox loves me. He *belongs* to me."

The witch made it look so easy, gliding through the smoke as she pointedly circled Evangeline. Nothing stopped the witch from prowling; it was as if the space only consisted of the two women and the smoke. She moved effortlessly, her glare constantly on Evangeline.

Evangeline found it difficult to even stay standing, the weight of the magic suddenly too much for her. But she was nothing if not determined. She refused to believe that she wanted anything to do with Maddox. She definitely didn't accept that she was his mate.

That didn't mean she was going to let this witch talk to her like that, either.

"Back off, Broomhilda."

"You're nothing but an Ant. You don't scare me."

"Yeah?" Evangeline's outrage was almost tangible. She shoved at the air in front of her. It did nothing to scatter the smoke, but the force managed to knock the witch back on her heels. "You're forgetting something. I might be a... an Ant, but this is still my dream. I conjured you up. I can make you disappear."

The dark-haired witch laughed. Considering the nasty look on her face, her laugh shouldn't have sounded as pretty as it did. "I'd love to see you try it. You caught me off-guard once. It won't happen again."

Oh?

Evangeline pushed a second time.

The witch was right. It didn't work.

She stalked forward confidently, slapping aside the rush of wind as if batting away a gnat.

"I own your dreams, human. I see your fantasies, know that you think my mate is yours. You might not want to admit it, but I *know*. Enough. It's gone too far now. Leave Maddox alone."

Was she serious?

Evangeline openly gawked at the other woman. "You got it all wrong, lady. I think you're missing some very important information. In case you didn't figure it out, he *stole* me. I didn't ask for any of this."

"He's confused," snapped the witch. Her face twisted, her beautiful features vicious. "He's convinced himself that he's in love with you. He's wrong."

"You want him?" offered Evangeline. "Take him."

The witch's ruby red lips quirked upward. "I'm working on it. You're just a complication I didn't need right now. The dreams should have kept you off his radar. At least I didn't waste all of my diamonds. You clearly don't know anything about him—as you shouldn't."

"What do you mean? Of course I don't. I never met him before last week!"

"That's right."

There was something in the way the witch said that. Her voice went even higher, almost piercing. She was lying, Evangeline realized. But why would she lie?

Why would this witch come to her in her dreams to warn her to stay away from Maddox?

Why would she have haunted her for years?

Evangeline said the first thing that popped in her head. "You're just jealous."

"Of you? Please. We both know you're nothing but Maddox's mistake. Don't take it so hard, *Angie*."

Evangeline's jaw tightened. When she spoke, she did so through clenched teeth. "Don't call me 'Angie'."

The witch's purple eyes glittered maliciously. "Maybe you're right. Maybe you don't want him. Besides, whatever he says, whatever he thinks... there's no true mate bond between the two of you, nothing to tie you together. As soon as he comes to me, he'll realize what he's done."

Because she couldn't deny that she was dreaming —however whacked her consciousness was to create this vision—Evangeline let herself submit to the compulsion toward Maddox that she'd been denying since the first time she locked eyes with him at Mugs.

It didn't mean she was giving up. It didn't mean she had any intention of telling the overwhelming brute that his caveman tactics might have struck a chord with her. She couldn't come to grips with the idea that a man she met less than a week ago was destined to be her lifelong mate. And that was if she ever got over the whole, you know, abduction thing.

Still, she was lying to herself if she continued to deny an attraction that she'd felt from that pivotal moment.

"Who says I don't want him?"

That... might've been the wrong thing to tell the witch.

The air crackled with magic. The purple smoke thickened, turned heavy, went dark. The wind picked up, making Evangeline feel like she was standing in the center of a tornado. Her hair slapped her in her face, stinging her eyes. She threw up her hands to protect them.

"You can't," hissed the witch. "He's *mine*. We're going to be together as soon as I get rid of *you*!"

Evangeline gulped. The pressure was back, pushing against her, forcing her to bend her knees. Her right hip twinged; the ache that never quite went away was a memento from her accident. Thank goodness her ankle held out otherwise she'd be flat on her face on the invisible floor.

Her stubborn streak returned with a vengeance. She refused to give the deranged witch the satisfaction of seeing her weak. Forcing herself to straighten, she said, "I'd like to see you try it."

"No. You wouldn't." The witch's expression was eerily calm, a juxtaposition to the elements surrounding her. As the wind picked up its pace, roaring around Evangeline, the magic gave the witch a wide berth. Not one perfectly straight piece of hair was out of place as she strode even closer, erasing the gap that existed between them. "You listen to me, human. One last chance. Get out. Get out now. You're just a mistake Maddox will regret once I've bonded to him. He'll look back on his time with you and his wolf will want to tear out your throat for being a distraction. And that's if I don't lose my temper and finish you off first myself."

A burst of purple exploded over the witch's head, showering her in violet fireworks. Evangeline buckled, dropping to her knees when she recognized the flash of purple power.

It was the same flash she had seen in every single dream that forced her to relive the crash that nearly killed her.

The witch's clear, haunting voice lifted high, carrying over the rush of the wind. "You survived me once. Are you lucky enough to do it again?"

The witch lifted her hands. She held them in front of her, keeping her palms facing each other with about a foot of space between them. Her fingers started to take on a pale lilac glow.

"Is it worth it?" she wondered. "Ask yourself that. He'll hate you for the rest of your life. Considering Maddox's wolf is an unpredictable beast at the best of times, that's assuming he even lets you *have* a life. Come, come... are you that desperate to have someone love you?"

Evangeline tilted her head back, glaring up at the witch. "I already have someone who loves me."

Her mother, her father... Adam. Sure, they didn't cause her to dance along the thin line that existed between anger and hate, attraction and something so very primal, she almost—*almost*—understood why Maddox felt like he had to abduct her, but she had no doubt that they loved her even so.

A glowing orb the size of a softball hung between the witch's hands. The color darkened to lavender, throwing garish purple shadows across the hatred in her face.

"Good," she bit out. "Remember that."

Before Evangeline could duck, the witch threw the orb right at her.

It struck her dead in the chest.

22

Choking, Evangeline's eyes sprang open as she suddenly came to. An instant later, she shot straight up in the bed, panting as if she'd just finished running a marathon.

Apart from the mild ache in her ankle, she didn't feel any pain, though her hands were wrapped around her middle, cradling her chest. Poking her side, probing her rib cage, her first instinct was to check for an injury.

There weren't any. Her skin was unmarked.

Her heart was still racing, though.

And that's when she noticed the man sitting in the corner.

Maddox.

Of course he was there.

He looked like hell. Some time while she slept, he

had dragged a big wooden chair into the corner across from the bed. He was perched on the edge, his elbows on his thighs, his hands folded aimlessly in front of him. His hair was longer than it had been, or maybe that was because he'd been anxiously running his claws through it. Strands stuck up all over the place. The scruff on his jaw was so thick, it was more like the beginning of a beard.

Purple bruises shadowed a pair of dull, golden eyes rimmed with red. He was watching her closely, barely blinking. His body language screamed he was alert while his eyes were glazed over. It seemed as if he hadn't slept for days.

Wait—

How long had *she* been sleeping?

"Wha—" Her voice was thick with sleep, yet rough, sounding more like a croak. "What time is it?"

"You were out even longer this time." Maddox untangled his fingers, then ran an anxious hand down his face. "Almost fourteen hours, and for most of it you were twitching, crying out in your sleep. You kept calling my name."

That was a revelation, and not one that Evangeline wanted to hear about—or explain.

Maddox must have sensed her reluctance. Leaning forward in the chair, he said softly, "What were you dreaming about, Angie?"

"What's going on?" she whispered, ignoring his quiet question. Her dreams were her own, as crazy and inexplicable as they were. Now that she was conscious again, the witch's threats seemed like nothing more than a manifestation of her confusion. And, on the off chance that some crazy witch managed to infiltrate her dreams, she refused to tell him about it. As protective as a shifter could be, he would try to fight the witch for her.

What if it turned out her dream was right? That Evangeline wasn't his mate, and that witch was? If Maddox went to these lengths to capture her to prove that she *was* his, what would he do if it turned out he was wrong?

Better that she keep her secrets. God knows that Maddox had plenty of his own.

Like this room.

She... she shouldn't be in *this* room.

Evangeline didn't want to face it. If she thought she could slip into a dreamless sleep, she'd close her eyes and pretend that this wasn't happening. Any of it. But her dreams were often even harder to live through than her reality. Especially this strange new one where everything she thought she knew was questionable, and Evangeline didn't know what to believe anymore.

That was just another thing she struggled to accept.

"Where— where are we? Where am I now?"

Because one thing was for sure: this much bigger room wasn't the same one he put her in while they were at the secluded cabin. That was obvious from her first glance. But... but she recognized it all the same.

Well. Kind of.

It was her bedroom, but it wasn't. Small details were off. The walls should be sage green instead of this soft mint shade. There was a nightstand on each side of the bed; in her apartment, she only had one on the left side. The lampshade was a vaguely different shape. The wall art featured soothing photos of sweeping countrysides. At home, she posted frames that showed bright city landscapes.

It was like a facsimile of the bedroom she'd spent months getting just how she liked.

But... but why?

How?

She was shaking. Covering her mouth with her hand, she didn't know if she was going to start sobbing or simply throw up. Throwing up was definitely up there on her list of options. Because this... this was too much. To be torn from a dream where she'd been threatened and manipulated into admitting that, despite all of her denials, she might kind of, sort of have feelings for her abductor only to wake up to... to *this*—it was just too damn much.

She had to ask. She had to know.

"How did you know what my room looked like?" Evangeline whispered.

"What do you mean?" Maddox frowned. "This *is* your room."

That didn't make sense. Did he change it around while she was sleeping? Her head still felt dizzy and foggy. It was too hard to understand what was going on. "My apartment? How did you get inside? I have wards... and a key—"

Maddox tightened his grip on the chair's arms. The wood creaked a second before one splintered off. Tossing it to the carpet—it was beige, just like before— he got up and started to pace.

A flash of anger had her sinking back into the pile of pillows behind her. He threw her a look of hunger, a look of despair when he noticed, then purposely kept his distance while scowling, as if her reaction had personally pained him.

His voice was low. Rough. "You don't understand. I thought this would help... this is *your* room, Angie. *Our* room. The room we used to share before you forgot all about me."

Evangeline didn't know what to say about that. She couldn't deny that she didn't remember Maddox; no matter how much it hurt him to hear her admit that over and over again, she couldn't force herself to remember. If she could, she would've filled in the nagging gaps years ago.

Maddox continued to pace like a caged animal, his heavy steps barely muffled by the thick shag carpet.

"Ang... if the room in your apartment looks anything like this, that has nothing to do with me. Maybe— maybe you remember more than you think."

The big holes where her memories should be had been a source of aggravation for Evangeline ever since she woke up in the hospital and couldn't remember anything about the year that led up to the crash that nearly killed her. At the time, she had a hell of a recovery to look forward to. Her parents were against using any magic to help heal her injuries; they meant well, but their wariness when it came to anything paranormal led to an extended recovery time while Evangeline relearned how to use her entire right side. They told her that her missing memories were the least of her worries. She'd get them back in time.

Three years later, she was still waiting.

Frustration welled up inside of her. She wanted to scream.

Because the truth was that she just wasn't sure. Monday morning, she knew one thing. Since then, her whole life had changed because Maddox insisted she was his mate.

How could she tell him time and time again that she wasn't his when she couldn't *remember*?

Maybe she was. Fresh on the heels of that vulnerable dream, waking up in a room that was as familiar as it was strange, Evangeline wasn't about to discount anything. Maybe she was his mate—

No.

No.

It wasn't possible. It couldn't be. And not only

because Evangeline hated the idea of having her choices ripped away from her.

Her mother would have told her. If she was mated to a shifter, her family would've known. She wouldn't have pushed Evangeline toward every eligible bachelor in East Windsor before finally having success with Adam Wright—

Would she?

For the first time since she woke up and discovered Maddox had abducted her, Evangeline began to really wonder.

Maddox loped across the wide room, his stride eating up the steps before he would turn, throw a helpless glance toward the bed, then stalk again. She was agitated. So was he.

"I brought you here on purpose. The cabin didn't help because you never made it there before the accident. You didn't know it. Fine. But this... this is our home and I thought— I want you to *remember*... can you tell me that none of this is familiar? That *I'm* not?"

Desperation flashed in those golden eyes of his.

The same eyes that had been eerily familiar from the start.

Evangeline gulped. "You know it is. I just told you. My room... my bedroom looks almost exactly like this. But, please, just listen to me: this isn't *my* home."

"It is—"

Why wasn't he listening? "I lived in Woodbridge

before I had to move back home, now I'm in Grayson. I know I've never been here before."

"No," retorted Maddox. "You don't *remember* it. You moved in with me more than three and a half years ago. We'd been dating for six months by then and you decided to put your house up for sale so you could live here. This became your home. Our home."

Three and a half years ago. That fell firmly in the space where she couldn't remember anything. Same thing as the six months prior. If what he was saying was true, she could have lost an entire relationship after her accident.

No. *No.* It couldn't be. This was Stockholm Syndrome hard at work. She was, for some unknown reason, drawn to this shifter. She wanted to believe that he was good, that he had a reason for everything he'd done so far. If they really had a history she couldn't remember, she could blame his mating instincts and possessive shifter nature for how he just *took* her, disregarding all laws and decencies like, oh, maybe telling her that she used to be his mate instead of just running off with her.

It couldn't be. Any man she loved—any man she chose—would treat her better than a possession that he could grab at will.

"There's no way—"

"You just don't remember," he insisted. "You will, my mate. Whatever it takes, I won't stop until you remember everything."

Evangeline flinched. The way he said that—*my mate*—with such fierceness, such conviction... he was never going to drop it. Didn't matter how she tried to reason with him. The witch was right. Maddox was convinced that Evangeline belonged with him.

To him.

She pulled herself up, resting her back against a thick oak headboard that was way too close to the one she had at home. "This has gone far enough. Look, for the last time, I'm not your mate. I don't know why you think I am, but you have to understand that. I won't tell anyone that you abducted me. It was an honest mistake... just let me go and you can find your real mate. Because it's not me. It can't be me. I—"

"Angie."

She trembled. There was something about the throaty way he said her name. She'd given up on getting him to call her anything else; deep down, she *liked* it, even though she knew she shouldn't. A chill coursed through her, making her shudder. She tried to ignore it.

She had to. No matter what he said—what he believed—Maddox already belonged to another. The witch was willing to fight for him, and Evangeline wanted nothing to do with that. So it didn't matter what he was doing, what he was saying, or the fact that having him in this room felt right for some reason.

A throb started at the base of her skull. Her vision seemed tinged with purple as she lowered her head.

She tried to deny it. Accepting the faint purple aura meant she had to admit that that had been a real witch threatening her, not just a figment of her drugged subconscious.

Evangeline rubbed her eyes, then probed gently at the back of her head.

23

"Are you okay?"

His mate glared up at him. "What? Oh. Yeah. Just a headache. Probably from the knock-out drugs you slipped me with dinner. I'll be fine."

"You sure?"

"Trust me, I'm used to it. I've been getting headaches since this accident I was in. Don't worry about it."

He refused to feel guilty for doing what he had felt like he had to, even if her casual mention of the accident that ripped her from him cut deep. When the bond was cemented, his claim secure, he'd make it up to Evangeline—*all* of it. For the rest of their lives, he'd treat her like the queen she was. They just had to survive this bumpy patch together.

Maddox thought about offering her some more aspirin, realized that she'd totally cut off her nose to spite her face again—or, in this case, let her head throb just to stick it to him.

He gentled his growl, careful not to aggravate her headache. They had to have this discussion. Maybe that made him an even bigger bastard, taking advantage of her pain, using it as a distraction to move closer to her, but Maddox was okay with it.

He'd make it up to her. He promised.

Edging toward the foot of the bed, he asked softly, "What do you know about shifters' mates?"

"You only get one," she mumbled, refusing to meet his gaze. She continued to rub her head. "But that doesn't mean—"

"It's you," Maddox said.

He couldn't keep the distance between them any longer. Daring to sit on the edge of the bed now, he went slowly, trying not to spook her. He reached for her hand, not surprised when she pulled away before he got too close. There was a spark whenever their skin touched, the bond attempting to re-ignite. He kept going all in but Evangeline was still denying him—and that *hurt*.

Almost as much as the determined way she said, "It can't be."

"I know you think I'm a crazy paranormal bastard, but I've spent my whole life searching for my mate. It's you, Angie. It's always been you. And I can prove it."

She leaned away from him, the air shifting as her scent changed. Maddox sniffed. He could've sworn that he caught a hint of something sweet, something unnatural before. Now, her warm vanilla scent soothed his soul, and he breathed deep, picking up on the emotional notes coloring her scent.

He didn't smell any fear coming off of her so that was a good sign. It was more like… sadness. Sadness mingled with regret, with a hint of confusion thrown into the mix. Maddox gazed earnestly at her face, at the way her thick waterfall of long, dark hair fell forward like a curtain. Slowly, because his mate was acting so uncharacteristically skittish, he raised his large hand and pushed a lock of hair behind her delicate ear.

His mouth opened slightly in surprise. There were tears in her eyes, a touch of salt stinging his senses. Evangeline lifted her hand up and roughly wiped at her face before turning away from him again.

Without another word, she slid across the sheets, perching her long, lean body on the edge of the bed. She turned her back on him.

Maddox was stunned.

He could deal with her anger. Her fire. Her spirit. He hated the idea that she would run from him, but even her escape last night had been expected. He'd hoped for recognition when she realized he'd moved her from the cabin to their home in Wolf's Creek. He didn't get that, but he was okay with confusion. She was working through it.

He thought he was making strides.

But this overarching sadness? When Evangeline was so distraught, she couldn't even think of a way to fight back again?

Shit.

He really *had* broken his mate, hadn't he?

Maddox longed to wrap her up in his arms, hold her close, whisper that he loved her and that, if he could, he'd wait forever for her to come back to him on her own.

But they didn't have the time. As Colt so kindly—okay, maybe not so kindly—reminded him when they talked after he settled Evangeline in the bedroom, Maddox had started the clock. He was a fool if he thought that no one would think to check Wolf's Creek for him and Evangeline.

The move in the middle of the night had been a calculated risk. He was determined to make her see that they belonged together. In his haste, Maddox had fucked up any goodwill he had earned when Evangeline let him feed her dinner. He'd be lucky if she ever accepted anything from his hand ever again.

Still, he had to try. He'd come so far already... there was no other choice.

"What's wrong, sweetheart?"

"I'm not your sweetheart," she retorted. No heat, though, only a deep resignation that made his wolf sit up and howl a sad, lonely song. "And I'm not your mate. When are you going to give up on this and let me go? You've got to know that your true mate's out there waiting for you. Stop wasting your time with me when I'm nothing but a *mistake*."

There was venom in the way she spit out the last word. Maddox didn't understand it, and decided not to question it. There was a reason he started this conversation and, fuck it, he was going to make sure she knew.

Time was running out. He told her he had proof.

He had to show her.

"You're no mistake, Angie."

"Stop. Just stop—"

He couldn't. "Shifters know their mates at first sight. At first sniff. But it's not as simple as that. I didn't take a whiff and say, 'yeah, she's the one' just because you smelled good. It's a little more... *obvious* than that. I knew it was you because, for the first time in my life, my body was ready to take a mate. Do you understand what I'm telling you?"

Evangeline hesitated, as if she was about to tell him to stop again, then she surprised him. Instead of arguing, she simply shook her head.

It was as close to a *go* sign as he was going to get.

"I knew you were my mate because you were the only one that could ever do *this* to me." Maddox moved quickly. Before she could react, he took her hand gently and hovered it over the bulge in his jeans. He waited for her to struggle, to yank her hand back. When she didn't, he placed her palm against his aching hard-on. "I can only mate with my mate.

And that's you, Angie. So no fucking mistake, alright?"

Evangeline stiffened. Once she got a feel of how hot and hard he was, Maddox expected her to pull away—but, to his shock, she didn't. After a few seconds when he held his breath, she pressed her palm down against his cock, applying enough pressure that he wanted to grunt and groan.

Questing fingers stroked lightly against the denim as she explored his length. Afraid he might spook her—terrified he might be dreaming—Maddox bit back another groan. A few soft touches from his mate's hand and he was about to start coming in his jeans like a schoolboy.

"Oh, wow," she breathed out, her voice gone husky. "I shouldn't be doing this."

He knew that voice. Whenever she was ready to go to bed, her eyelids became heavy and she started to sound like she smoked a pack a day.

She should definitely be doing this, Maddox thought. He leaned into her hand, the most he allowed himself to do in case he scared her into stopping. This was more than he could have hoped for and, after all these years without her, it took everything he had to hang onto his control.

Before he lost it entirely, he flared his nostrils. If he scented any type of worry or fear, he would stop himself. He would follow her lead every step of the way, just like he had before.

When the intoxicating musk of Evangeline's arousal filled his senses, he gave a sudden jerk. He couldn't keep his moan back.

Evangeline went still, her fingers resting lightly against his erection. "I'm sorry. I've never— am I doing this right?"

Through the haze of overwhelming sensation, it got through to Maddox that Evangeline sounded like an uncertain virgin with the practiced touch of his wife. Her hands knew what she was doing even if her mind didn't.

She still didn't remember, didn't know that he was her husband *and* her mate. He should be frustrated, and he definitely was, but that wasn't all. In an instant, when her meaning sunk in, Maddox was so fucking happy, it felt like his heart was about to leap out of his chest.

She hadn't been with anyone else since him. She hadn't even been with that Adam fucker.

Not that it would have mattered. Just like when she admitted to him during their courtship that he'd be her first, Maddox knew he didn't have any control over what—or who—Evangeline did when she wasn't bonded to him. But, hell, it was great to hear that they were still each other's one and only.

It was a reminder that fate had gotten this right. This woman was meant for him, just like he belonged to her. Deep down, Evangeline must know that. Her body did. Maybe her heart did, too. He just needed to get her head on board.

Later.

For now, he had his mate's hand on his cock and that required all of his attention.

Maddox let out a deep-throated moan. "Ung, Angie, sweetheart, nothing has ever felt so good before."

The tip of her tongue peeked through her lips as she added a little more pressure. Just the way he liked it.

She didn't remember him. But, he realized with more hope than he'd had since he first poured the sedatives into Evangeline's coffee, that didn't mean she'd *forgotten* him. It was a small distinction.

Maddox would take it.

And that's when his ears caught the sound of gravel crunching underneath a set of tires. An engine died. A few seconds later, a car door opened. Maddox reached with his senses, closing his eyes to catch the heavy footfalls of a pair of boots heading up his walkway.

He took a deep breath and scowled. "Damn it!"

Evangeline was a human. She had no idea that someone was approaching the house and figured Maddox's sudden mood swing had something to do with her exploration.

She yanked her hand back, embarrassment turning her cheeks pink. "I shouldn't have... I'm sorry. I don't know what came over me."

"It's not your fault," Maddox said hurriedly. He felt the loss of her hand all the way to his soul. His poor balls wanted to fall right off. But that wasn't his Angie's fault, and he tried like hell to show her that he meant that. "We've got company."

Human company, he knew.

Male human company, his wolf supplied.

The beast was already baring its teeth in warning. It had its mate in their bedroom and another man was closing in on Maddox's territory. His wolf was eager to defend what was theirs.

The man tried to think rationally because there was only one logical reason why a male Ant had breached his boundaries. It had to be the cops, coming to ask him about Evangeline.

Fuck!

He knew time would be short, but he'd expected more than this.

Maddox had tried to be careful. He waited until the middle of the night to drive Evangeline over. He hadn't sensed anyone around when they arrived and it only took him less than a minute to carry her inside. He hid Colt's truck in the garage. He refused to turn on any of the lights, relying on his wolf's superior night vision instead.

None of that had mattered, though.

Someone had seen them. Someone had snitched.

Well, tough shit. They didn't have any proof that Evangeline was there. And, if Maddox had anything to say about it, it would stay that way. He wouldn't let anyone take his mate away from him, not until they were formally bonded and the laws *said* they couldn't.

He turned to tell Evangeline that she would have to stay put when the look on her face stole the words from him. His heart sank as he sniffed the air. Yup. That was panic, all right.

And not all of it was coming from her.

Maddox could tell that Evangeline was already regretting the charged moment that had just passed between them. She glanced at her hand as if she couldn't believe it belonged to her, then forcefully crossed her arms over her chest. It was a shield, a barricade, and Maddox felt his erection deflate. To be so close to release at his mate's hands and have it ripped away by an Ant—

Maddox let loose a torrent of muttered curses and growls that said his wolf was in total agreement.

Kill the Ant.

Take his mate.

Claim Evangeline.

Good fucking plan.

Maddox's control had been shaky ever since he took Evangeline's hand and placed it on his cock. The instant he sensed another man in his territory, the last of it snapped. His wolf was fully in charge as he leapt over the bed, got up, and pulled Evangeline into his arms.

In the back of his mind, he remembered her

sprained ankle and, using his strength, pressed her along his body while keeping her dangling just off the ground. With one arm around her waist and the other around her back, he breathed in her scent before doing something he'd been dying to do for three years.

Slanting his mouth over hers, he pressed their lips together. Since he caught her off guard, her mouth was open slightly in surprise. He took total advantage of that.

This was no gentle, coaxing kiss. He thrust his tongue into her mouth, drinking in her taste as he got inside of her the only way he could. He kissed her hungrily, so focused on the sensation that it took him a few seconds before he realized that she was actually responding.

Evangeline was kissing him back.

It was like no time had passed at all. The passion in her embrace as she relaxed in his arms before she gripped the material of his t-shirt and brought him even closer. The way she caressed his tongue, then pulled back to place small kisses to the corner of his lips before diving back in for more. She writhed against him, then started to climb him like he was a tree.

It was only when she started to wrap her legs around his waist that Maddox remembered that, while she was his mate, she still didn't believe him.

Even if it seemed like her body knew exactly who he was.

Before he lost his head entirely and threw her to the bed, Maddox pulled back. They were both panting. Evangeline's cheeks were flushed, her lips swollen and red. She looked dazed and Maddox figured he did, too. Kissing his mate was like coming home at last. The fact that she kissed him back? He felt his bond stretching out toward her and, *finally*, he felt an answering tug coming from Evangeline.

Hope flooded him. He leaned back in to steal another kiss when the doorbell rang, shattering the moment.

His wolf grumbled deep inside his chest and the lust in Evangeline's eyes cleared. She started to squirm in his arms, pushing against him.

"Put me down," she whispered.

That husky, sex operator voice of hers shot straight to his cock, bringing it back to life. He felt his sac tighten but refused to give in to the temptation. Taking his time—and, okay, maybe he took advantage of their position to purposely rub his chest against her breasts once or twice—Maddox gently set her on the edge of the bed.

She immediately put as much space between them as she could. As soon as she scooted to the other side, Evangeline used the back of her hand to wipe her mouth.

"Don't," he growled.

She stilled. "Don't what?"

"Don't wipe me off of you. Not... not now. The wolf won't like it."

Evangeline's lips thinned. She dropped her hand, fire blazing in her eyes. "Screw the wolf."

Maddox stretched his hands. His claws shot out. "Don't tempt the beast, Angie. One word from you, one sign you'd welcome him, and that's exactly what would happen."

Talk about mixed signals. The acrid stench of fear filled the air, only overshadowed by the flood of arousal from between Evangeline's legs. She was turned on, though she clearly didn't want to be.

That was one of the only reasons why Maddox was able to calm down and force his shift back—

The doorbell rang again.

—and *that* was the other.

He had to answer. He knew he did. If he wanted to allay any suspicions that he had Evangeline with him, he had to put on a show for the cops. But the last thing he wanted to do was leave his mate alone in this state. She was confused and upset and would be able to obsess over what had happened if he left her by herself.

Time alone was the last thing he wanted her to have. Something told him that, if he *did* go, she might not be there when he came back. Maddox could already see the gears working in her head. She'd escape if he gave her the chance. He had no doubts. Sprained ankle and all.

He had to find a way to make her stay put. And tying her to the bed was out of the question.

Huffing angrily, Maddox ran his hands through his shaggy mane. "Stay here," he told her, praying she would listen and knowing deep down that hell would freeze over first. "I mean it, Angie. I can't be held responsible for my actions if you try to escape again."

He realized his mistake the second the words left his mouth. Horror filled her expression as she recoiled away from him, seeking sanctuary among the pillows at the head of the bed.

Maddox rushed to reassure her. "No, no, no. Not you, Angie, never you. I would die before I hurt you, you gotta believe me. But that man out there—he's gonna try to take you from me. You know I can't let him. I'm... I'm hanging on by a thread here. If I have to worry about you running again, I don't know what'll happen out there."

It was low. He knew it was. His Angie had always been so compassionate, giving up everything she had for someone else. It was so fucking wrong of him to use her heart against her, but Maddox had to play any hand he was dealt. If it meant she stayed... it would be worth the look of resignation that dashed across her beautiful face.

There wasn't a single hint of her arousal lingering in the air any longer.

"I'll behave."

"That's my girl."

24

Maddox had no choice but to trust her.

Remembering what happened in the cabin, he didn't bother locking her in the room. If she wanted to leave him, he wasn't going to force her to use the window and risk further injury to her ankle. She could walk out. It wouldn't matter. As soon as he was done with the cop at his door, he would find her again. Maybe then she would finally understand that she'd never be able to get away from him.

There was a mirror in the hallway. Evangeline had picked it out at a yard sale shortly after they moved in together. It was fancier than anything Maddox had in his old bachelor pad and the sight of it made him frown as he checked his reflection. The gold inlaid on the edge, the roses carved into the design, it was too good for a rugged shifter.

Just like his Evangeline.

Maddox checked his eyes—gold but not glowing—and his teeth—pointy but not long enough to worry the human—before making sure that his fingers had nails, not claws, and his back was straight, not hunched. His wolf was lurking right on the edge. It wouldn't take much to switch forms, but his beast kept prowling inside his chest. Even it realized that being in its two-legged shape would make this easier.

After giving the bulge in his jeans one sorry pat, adjusting it so that his hard-on wasn't so damn obvious, Maddox exhaled and opened the door before the Ant had the chance to ring the doorbell for a third time.

Just like he expected, the man who stood on his porch was from the Grayson PD. Tall and lanky for a human, the cop was at least a decade older than Maddox. A touch of grey started at the edges of his thick dark hair, his tanned skin lightly lined. Still, he had a friendly sort of air to him, despite the serious way he regarded Maddox.

"Good morning, sir."

"Morning."

"Are you Maddox Wolfe?"

Maddox nodded.

"Please step outside, Mr. Wolfe. I'd like to talk to you, if you don't mind."

Yeah, right. Like he had a choice.

He made sure to keep the door open behind him as he stepped onto the porch. For one thing, it told the cop that he had nothing to hide. For another, he was able to sense Evangeline easier this way. He would know if she left the room with enough of a head start to be able to block the door before the cop discovered her inside.

Maddox offered the Ant—his nameplate said Diaz—a tight-lipped smile. When it came to the police, a shifter couldn't be too careful. He didn't want to give Diaz a reason to reach for one of the weapons on his belt because he "felt" threatened.

"Can I help you with something, Officer?"

"I've come about an Evangeline Lewis. Is that name familiar to you?"

The cop watched him with a gleam in his dark eyes that Maddox took as a dare. Okay, so this guy had come prepared. He knew exactly who Maddox was and all about his relationship to Evangeline. For whatever reason, Diaz was testing him.

"Of course I do," Maddox answered. Probably not what the cop expected him to say, but he was proud to admit the truth. "She's my mate."

"She's also missing."

"Tell me something I don't know. I've been trying to find her ever since they let me out of the Cage, but no one will tell me where she is."

"Are you sure you don't know where we can find her? Her mother's frantic. It seems Ms. Lewis hasn't been back to her apartment in a day or two and that's very unusual. We've tried contacting friends and family. You're the next one on my list. Can you help me?"

Keeping his expression neutral was harder than he thought. Diaz seemed earnest but Maddox called bullshit. If he didn't suspect Maddox, he would've tried talking to him first by reaching out to Colt; that was the only number left in his file at the Cage. Plus, Maddox only nabbed Evangeline early yesterday afternoon. The cops couldn't know for sure that she was actually missing already.

Could they?

Maybe.

There was no deception coming off of the cop. Didn't matter. Diaz was up to something. Maddox was positive. While they might not have proof that Evangeline was with him—otherwise he'd be back in silver shackles and she'd be ripped away from him again—they were as certain as they could be. Now all they had to do was trick Maddox into confessing.

Ha. Not likely.

Maddox wasn't about to waste his limited time beating around the bush, either. Officer Diaz could dance around the subject all he wanted to see if he could get Maddox to trip up, but Maddox had his unpredictable mate to worry about. The quicker he got this over with, the quicker he could get back to her.

"I've been searching for her for more than a week myself, Officer. I'm sure you already knew that, just like I'm sure you know that I've only just been let out of the

Cage myself. It's a no-brainer that the first thing I would do after getting out would be go after Evangeline. But, if you know anything about my story, you'll know that my bond with her was severed. It's why I thought she was dead. It's why the warden finally signed off on my release. I'm rehabilitated, right? So, yeah, I know she's out there. If only I knew where."

"Really? That true?"

There was something in the way the Ant asked that. Somehow, Diaz knew he was lying. But, unless Maddox confessed, the cop couldn't prove anything. This wasn't a real interrogation. Not yet, anyway.

It was like high noon in Dodge City. Two gunslingers facing off, their hands on their weapons just in case. No one knew who was going to make the first move. Diaz wasn't ready to simply take Maddox's word for it. Maddox refused to admit to anything.

The sound of a car door slamming cut through the standoff. Maddox broke eye contact first, glancing over at the cruiser parked along the curb. Once he determined that it was safe to take his stare off of the shifter, Diaz followed Maddox's gaze.

A second cop came storming across the lawn.

This one... this one Maddox recognized. He'd dealt with him on a couple of occasions when he was in the Cage and always got the impression that the guard didn't like him. He realized he was wrong as the blonde officer came rushing toward him. This Ant didn't just dislike him—that was *hatred* clinging to his uniform.

It put Maddox's back right up. "Wright?" It was a growl. "What are you doing here?"

Wright's good-looking features twisted into an ugly grimace. "That's Officer Wright to you, asshole."

Maddox had to give Diaz credit. For an older guy, he was fucking quick. Before Maddox could launch himself at Wright, bristling at the rage coming off of the livid cop, Diaz inserted his body between the two, pressing his hand to Wright's chest to force him to take a couple of steps back.

"Cool it, man."

When Wright tried to lunge around him, Diaz stopped him again, more forcefully than he had before.

"I said cool it. Bennett let you come on the ride-along if you agreed to stay in the cruiser. You gotta back down. I got this."

Wright shook him off. "Fuck you, too. What would you do if one of these bastards made off with Connie, huh?"

Diaz obviously didn't like that. Wright's taunt must have gotten through to him because, dropping his hand, he didn't try to stop the other cop again.

Wright took that as his cue to whirl back on Maddox. "Where the fuck is my girlfriend?"

Maddox heard his claws unleash with a menacing *snick*. He curled his fists so tightly that the points sliced right into his palm. The small jolt of pain grounded him and he was able to keep his voice calm. "I don't understand what you mean."

"The fuck you don't. Eva! I'm here, babe. Where are you? Answer me!"

Wright took a step toward the house, then stopped when he realized that, while he was a big guy, Maddox was so much bigger. There was no way he could go through Maddox, and when he tried to feint and get past the shifter, Maddox turned his body just enough to ensure that Wright couldn't see anything inside the house before reaching behind him and slamming the door shut with his bloody palm.

Wright growled. The fucking Ant actually growled at him. "I know you have her," he spat out, stepping up to Maddox until they were toe to toe. "Give her to me now, you animal."

"Even if I had her, I wouldn't. She's not yours."

"Fuck you, Wolfe. She's not yours, either."

"She's my mate—"

"Mate, my ass. You don't have a bond with her. 'Cause, if you did, you'd have known she survived the crash. You would've been there for her these last three years like I was. Me. Get it through your thick skull. She's *mine* now."

Maddox's whole body tensed, then froze.

Half of his attention was back in the house, waiting to see what sort of move Evangeline would make. The other half was on the uniforms in front of him and the guns they had strapped to their hips. He wasn't going to make any sudden movements that would allow them to draw their weapons and use the *Claws Clause* to their advantage. Bonded shifters without their mates could be put down if they posed any threat and he'd told them he didn't have Evangeline with him.

Rehabilitation wouldn't mean anything if he lost his shit now.

His conversation with that prick Wright was almost on autopilot. He could tell the Cage guard was trying to goad him, bringing Evangeline up like that. Right. As if he believed that this guy even knew his mate. If he did, he would've known how much she hated being called 'Eva'.

But the way Wright snarled 'mine' roused Maddox's wolf, the possessive need to assert his claim over his mate almost unbearably hard to resist.

And then the wind shifted. His nostrils flared, automatically searching out the scent of his sudden rival. Because there was no denying that Wright was telling the fucking truth. Maddox knew that scent. He'd smelled hints of it all over Evangeline before her scent came back and overpowered it. With a stifled growl, he narrowed his gaze on Wright's nameplate.

A. Wright.

"*Adam*," he snarled. He knew in an instant that he'd made a huge mistake. Didn't matter. He couldn't have stopped his reaction if he wanted to.

This was the man who had tried to steal his mate from him?

Wright's shit-eating grin was *huge*. "Eva tell you about me? She remembers me, you see. Can you say the same? What kind of bond do you think you had with her if she forgot you so easily?"

If Maddox hadn't been too busy kicking his own ass for slipping up in front of Diaz, he would've turned on Wright. That—and timely intervention by the other police officer when Diaz realized Maddox was going to lunge at Wright again—was probably the only thing that saved the Ant's life.

Diaz grabbed Wright by the shoulder and hauled him about five feet away from Maddox's front porch. Did he forget that Maddox was an alpha wolf? The distance wasn't anywhere near far enough to keep their conversation quiet. Though Diaz dropped his voice to a whisper, Maddox's shifter senses picked up on every word over his angry panting.

"Adam, what the hell are you trying to do?"

"He's got her, Lou. I know he does."

"We've got to do this right, you know that, too."

"She needs me."

"Sure she does, but do you think it's a good idea to rub his face in the fact that you knew his mate when he was locked up in the Cage?"

"What's he gonna do? He wolfs out, you shoot him. Plain and simple."

"I can't—"

"That's the beauty of the *Claws Clause*, Diaz. Yes, you can."

Then, before Diaz could get another word in,

Wright stomped back over to Maddox, hand out, pointer finger extended.

"You weren't supposed to get your paws on her. I watched her from afar, took care of her while she recovered. When it seemed like you might go after her again, I kept her safe from you. It was easy, too. Fucking animal follows its nose, right? So I hid her scent trail, made you work for it. But you got to my girl anyway. Tell me. Tell me, Wolfe. How did you find her?"

Maddox's gaze strayed back over to Diaz's gun. It was a struggle to keep his voice steady, but he did it by forcing himself to remember that he couldn't bond with Evangeline if he had a chest full of silver bullets.

"I didn't."

Truth. Maddox hadn't found her.

Colton had.

"You're lying," spat out Wright.

Diaz shook his head. "He's telling the truth."

"How the hell would you know? You a witch or something?" Then, as if realizing how he had spoken to a fellow officer, Wright regained some composure. Wincing, he said, "Sorry about that. You know I don't honestly think you're one of *them*."

Of course he would apologize to Diaz. Because, to an Ant, accusing a human of being a Para was the lowest of the low.

Diaz didn't seem to care. He waved Wright off before jerking his thumb over his shoulder at the waiting cruiser. "It's fine. Don't worry about it. But do me a favor? Get back in the car. You're not helping either one of us here."

It seemed as if Wright wasn't going to listen to the other officer for a moment before he huffed and started to back off. He must have felt incredibly guilty over his low blow to give in so easily.

It was Maddox who wasn't ready to end this. It was reckless and stupid and basic macho bullshit, but he wasn't done with the man who thought he deserved Evangeline just yet.

"If she was yours, wouldn't she have come out when she heard you here? You're making enough racket to wake the dead, Wright. And I don't see her. So if you're right, and she's here, I guess she'd rather stay with me than come running to *you*."

That stopped Wright right in his tracks. His momentary calm? Gone.

"How do I know that you don't have her chained to a bed somewhere?" sneered Wright. "Anything to keep her from trying to escape. That's how you animals operate, right? With your precious 'mates'."

Okay. At the beginning of this confrontation, there was an invisible line drawn in the sand. Ever since the cruiser pulled up to his house, they had all been dancing around it, even tiptoeing up to it, but no one had dared cross it.

Until then. Every one of them knew at that

moment that Adam Wright hadn't just stepped over it. He had fucking flown right past that line.

Maddox's eyes flashed, burning brightly like liquid gold. That... *that* was a challenge.

"Do you think I would do that?" he snarled. His fangs started to lengthen, his face turning sharp as his features began to shift. "Do you really think I would *chain* up my *mate*? I *love* her!"

In one fluid motion, Diaz yanked his gun from his holster. "Stand down, sir. Show me your hands. Now."

Maddox held up his hands. Thank fucking Alpha they were human hands. As angry as he was, shifting more than he already had would have been a very big mistake. Even his wolf knew that.

Didn't stop him from having the last word. "I would never hurt her. *If* I knew where she was."

If she was still where he left her.

The closed door mocked Maddox, Wright's taunts about Evangeline ringing in his ears. While it kept her from showing herself—or letting that bastard Wright peek inside of the house—it also cut him off from his mate. He couldn't sense her as easily through the wood, not when he was so preoccupied with keeping his cool in front of these cops. Had she run again? He needed to know.

"Is there anything else I can help you with?" he asked, trying to hurry them along.

"Yeah, you can let us in so I can check your place out for myself."

There was no way in hell he was going to let that happen. This cop wanted to pretend he was playing by the rules?

Well, fine. Maddox could do that, too.

"You got a warrant, Wright?"

"I told you, it's Officer Wright. And if you were innocent, you'd let me in without a warrant."

"No. If I were *stupid*, I'd let you in without a warrant."

"Wright—"

Wright ignored Diaz's warning. He poked Maddox right in the chest and was fucking lucky he didn't lose that finger. "You want a warrant? I'll get a warrant. But you better be here when I get back, Wolfe."

"I've nothing to hide, *Officer*. I'm not going anywhere." At least, he thought to himself, he wasn't going anywhere until he was sure being home again wouldn't be enough to help jog Evangeline's memories.

"If she's in there, I'll bring you up on kidnapping charges so fast, your head'll spin. And if she's not..." Wright might not be a shifter, but his sudden grin was so shark-like, Maddox almost started second-guessing him. "If she's not, then I'll put you back in the Cage."

"You can't—"

"I can. And I will. Ordinance 7304, asshole. You're still nothing but a shifter without his mate. Maybe this time I'll suggest putting you down." He sniffed angrily. "They never should've let you out again. Your kind should all be locked up."

"Okay, that's enough. Wright, get back in the cruiser before I tell Bennett what you've been up to."

When Wright made like he was about to argue, Diaz reached for the walkie clipped to his belt.

That shut the other cop up. With one last hate-filled glare thrown at Maddox, Wright turned on his heel and marched back over to the cop car. Climbing into the front seat, he slammed the door behind him.

Diaz waited until the echo from the slam died down before he nodded over at Maddox. He looked embarrassed. "He'll be trying every judge he can within the hour. I don't blame him, either. He's going to do everything he can to get his girl back—just like I would expect you to do the same. I know I would for my Connie."

Then the dark-haired officer leaned closer and did the last thing Maddox ever expected. With a secretive little smile, Diaz dropped his glamour long enough to let the inky blackness of his gaze fall away until Maddox was looking into a pair of strikingly violet eyes.

Fucking hell, he *was* a witch. Which meant that he knew what he was talking about when he said Maddox was telling the truth before since most witches could sense a deception the same way that Maddox could scent emotions. Diaz probably also knew that every other denial about knowing Evangeline's location was an out and out lie.

Shit.

"Officer, I—"

"I'm sure we'll be back the second he gets his hands on that warrant. Wright's a good cop and an okay guy, but to fuck with a bond? Humans don't understand. I'll stall for as long as I can. Do what you have to do."

"Why are you helping me?"

Officer Diaz's eyes were back to their black color as he studied Maddox closely. "Because you were telling the truth when you said you loved her." He nodded over at Maddox. "I'm sure I'll be seeing you soon. Good luck, sir."

Maddox stayed on his front porch until even he couldn't see the tail end of the police car. He glanced around, feeling eyes on him. A blue-haired biddy across the street from him was peeping through her curtains. Maddox lifted a hand and waved, not even a little surprised when she dropped the curtains and disappeared from the window.

Huh. Looked like he found his snitch.

There was a newspaper at the end of his driveway. Since he hadn't lived in this house in three years, he knew it had to belong to his neighbor. He took it anyway, just because he needed a few more moments before he went back inside the house and looked for Evangeline. He clung to those moments, like a drowning man trying to stay afloat in a sea of denial. She couldn't have run out on him again. Her ankle was still tender, he reminded himself. She promised to stay—

Deep down, he knew she was probably already gone. No matter. He'd find her, and he would have to be quick about it, too.

The clock was back to ticking. Maddox either needed to be bonded to Evangeline before Wright came back, or they had to be in the wind until he could get her to remember him. Either way, he made his decision at that moment. Evangeline had to remember him. If the house wasn't going to do the trick, he would have to turn to the more drastic Plan B.

Sorry, Colt.

The clock had already run down. They were completely out of time.

25

Maddox walked back into the house, tossing the stolen newspaper onto the table by the door. His hands were shaking.

Okay. The whole exchange with Diaz and Wright couldn't have been more than ten minutes. If Evangeline still didn't remember her life with him, then she wouldn't know the path to take out of the back door to get very far. No way she went out through the front. That limited her possibilities. He could track her.

He *would* track her—

Maddox drew up as he caught sight of his dark-haired angel sitting at the kitchen table with her head bowed. So certain she was gone, he never even tried to sense if she was still in the house. It was probably the first time since he was a pup that someone had caught him off guard.

"Angie!"

Her head jerked up. Her expression was strained, a sad smile tugging on her lips. "You sound so surprised. What? Didn't expect to see me here?"

Maddox blinked quickly, afraid to shut his eyes for even a split second in fear she'd disappear. His answering grin was crooked, full of relief. "I'm not gonna lie. In my head, I was already halfway out the back door after you."

"Smart." She sighed, leaning into the chair, tilting her head up so that she was looking to the ceiling. "I was going to run."

He wanted to be grateful that she hadn't escaped, but... well, he had to know. He'd expected her to run, too. "Then why didn't you?"

"The perfume."

"Perfume?"

"Right after you went to answer the door, I hobbled behind you. I wanted to see who was out there, and then I was going to sneak out the back once I saw they were safe and you were preoccupied. But then I heard Adam... that *was* Adam Wright out there, wasn't it?"

Maddox didn't want to cringe when she said that name, but he couldn't help it. He started to pace the lengths of the kitchen, keeping an eye on the table. If she tried to get up, he'd be on her in a heartbeat.

"I won't let him come back for you," he grunted. "I don't care what he said out there."

"I couldn't believe him—"

"He thinks he can take you from me."

"When I heard him say—"

"He knows you're my mate and he's still trying to come between us."

Evangeline huffed. "Jeez! Can I just say something?"

"I'll fight for you first, Angie. I promise, I—"

"*Maddox.*"

That word, that one single word on her lips... it was enough to stop him in his tracks.

She said his name. She finally used it.

His grin came back. And it was even wider than it had been only moments ago when he realized she hadn't left him.

"Finally," Evangeline muttered. "You're just as bad as he is. If you don't want to hear what I was going to say, maybe I should leave after all."

"I'm sorry. I'm so sorry, sweetheart."

Letting that *sweetheart* slip past her unmentioned, she sighed, unsure what to think. In the last couple of days she had had so much thrown at her—but there was one thing she was sure of and that was Adam Wright. She was absolutely positive that he would come for her eventually. Only she thought it was because he wanted her, not because he wanted to keep her *from* someone else.

Looking back on the past five weeks, how much of

it was a lie? Twenty minutes ago, she was questioning her sanity when it came to the strength of her response to a shifter who had *kidnapped* her, for goodness sake. She refused to even entertain the idea that any of his crazy story could be true.

But now—

"The perfume," she murmured. That stupid perfume in the signature purple bottle. Then there was Adam's insistence that she put it on daily, and the satisfied way he told her that the girl who sold it to him guaranteed it. Purple—the official color of the witches. How hadn't she seen that? She shuddered. Her gut had warned her against wearing the perfume. Had she listened? *Nope*. "It had to be in the perfume."

"What do you mean, Angie?" His voice was calmer than it had been, the amber-colored sheen that rolled over his glowing eyes dimming down to a simmering gold. "What about the perfume?"

"Adam gave me perfume on our first date. He told you he found a way to cover my scent—it had to be the perfume. He made me put it on every day, always making sure I wore his gift. I thought it was his way of showing he cared, but it wasn't about that at all. He was covering my scent on purpose long before we met at Mugs..."

Her voice trailed to a close. It was hard, working out what that could mean when she was still so lost, so confused. The truth was standing there, staring her right in the face, a gorgeous brute of an alpha wolf shifter who said he wanted to be with her forever.

But hadn't Adam promised her the same?

Evangeline could feel the beginning of one of her headaches pulsing at the back of her skull. Gritting her teeth, she struggled to finish her thought.

"If he had the perfume made... then that means that he already knew there'd be a reason he'd need it. That *I* would need it. He knew about *you*." Evangeline's chin wavered, but she would be damned if she gave in to the emotions rushing through her. Or the pain. God, it hurt. She raised her hand, probing at the back of her head as she turned to look up at Maddox. "How?" she asked. "How did he know? That's why I stayed. I couldn't leave without asking you because..."

Maddox waited to see if she would continue speaking. Good luck. Evangeline didn't even know what she was trying to say right then.

Clearing his throat, his voice coming out as a hoarse rasp, Maddox said softly, "Because?"

"Because I'm beginning to wonder if..." She shook her head. "If..." She sighed, defeated. "I don't know."

THERE WAS NO WAY IN HELL THAT MADDOX WAS GOING to leave it at that. He tread carefully, knowing that one wrong word would have her shutting down. Her scent had taken on a darker edge and he couldn't tell if it was a physical hurt—or an emotional one.

Sometimes betrayal could be more painful than anything else.

Except for a shot from his claws, he amended. Because when he got his paws on Wright and confirmed Evangeline's suspicions about the perfume, Maddox was going to do a lot more damage than wounding the cop's pride.

But that was later. This moment was for Evangeline. For his mate.

He could feel it. This was important. They were on the edge of something big and, if he fucked this up, it could set him all the way back. They didn't have time for that.

"What's on your mind, Angie? Listen to me. You can tell me anything. You have to believe that."

She gulped. Maddox tracked the movement of her throat, barely daring to breathe. "I... I think I'm beginning to."

He wanted to roar in triumph. Good thing he knew better than to do just that. Evangeline was clearly vulnerable, but she was *there*. For the first time since he found her, he began to believe they'd get their forever back.

For the first time, he thought she might be ready to actually listen to him.

Crouching down at her side, Maddox took her hand in his. It was cold and clammy. Wrapping his fingers gently around hers, he offered Evangeline his warmth.

"I told you. You're my mate. It wasn't luck that I found you at the coffee shop that day. I was already looking for you." He took a deep breath. A tinge of salt in the air, that terrible sadness again, interspersed with a jagged line of pain. He felt his gut twist. An echo of that ache hit him as he realized how much she cared. "He hurt you."

"He betrayed me. I thought Adam cared about me—" She shivered. "All this time, he was just keeping me from you. Why would he do that? I don't get it. And I need to understand."

Wright's hatred for Maddox was deep. It wasn't new. This went back well before his time in the Cage. There was jealousy, too, of course there was, but the hatred... Maddox had a sudden suspicion.

"He hates me for being your mate when he wants you, but I'm betting there's more to it than that. I think... I think he blames me for the accident," Maddox admitted. "Why wouldn't he? You were so close to death— shit, Angie, I spent three years convinced you *were* dead. I think he blames me for taking you away in more ways than one."

She glanced down at him, her expression bewildered. "The crash? How is that your fault? I... maybe I should go talk to him. Adam might have an explanation. Maybe he can explain this better so I understand."

"No!" Maddox barked. Evangeline flinched and he tried to hide his sudden surge of anguish. "Let me. You don't need that cop, not now, not ever. You want to know why he blames me? Probably because I was with you when you crashed."

Evangeline's answer—"No, you weren't"—was swift, and it was wrong.

Maddox nodded.

She hesitated. When he expected another denial, she surprised him by saying softly, "That was you?"

His heart gave an unexpected jolt. A tinge of fear filtered into her scent and she quickly squashed it. He was glad; he much preferred her fire and her anger to his Angie being afraid. She was looking at him differently now, as if seeing him for the first time.

Maddox chose his words carefully. "Do you... do you remember the accident at all?"

"Yes... no—I don't know." Evangeline seemed to finally realize that he was holding her hand like a vice. She slipped out of his grip before raising her fingers to cover her eyes. "Something is going on here that I don't understand. Between what happened in the bedroom, and the dreams..."

Maddox found it charming that she blushed crimson behind the shield of her hands at the mere mention of the bedroom, but shoved it aside at the mention of her dreams.

That was the important thing. Paranormal bonds—

especially when the Para was a shifter—were a source of magic. And magic traveled through dreams.

Could it be that he was finally opening her consciousness in some way, coming one step closer to getting her to see the truth? "What about them?"

"I don't remember you. I... *don't*. But there's been a hole in my memory so long, I can't tell you what else I don't remember. But—I've dreamt of you, I think." She was blushing even harder now. It was fucking adorable. "It had to be you. Those golden eyes were always so familiar. And when I dream about the accident... You say you were there and maybe you were. Because I know this: I wasn't alone. They tell me I was, but I've never believed it. Not really. I came out of the accident alone, but someone protected me when we went over the side."

"That was me," he murmured. "I wrapped you in my arms when I heard the tires skid. I could take a lot more damage than you could, but it knocked me out anyway. We were separated by the time I regained consciousness at the scene. I would never have left you alone, Angie. They told me you were dead, that's the only reason why I took this long to find you. The bond was gone. I didn't know."

She went on as if she hadn't heard him. "What happened to me?" Evangeline took a deep breath and impulsively met Maddox's heated gaze straight on. "I feel like everyone knows the truth but me. You. Adam. *Her*. Why don't I remember?"

"You have to believe me when I tell you this. This... this thing between us, it isn't new. We were mates before. Remember, Evangeline," Maddox pleaded. Pride? What pride? He was so fucking close. He growled low in his throat, an order. "Remember us. Remember *me*."

Evangeline scrunched up her face. "I'm... I'm trying."

Even though it was the one thing he didn't want to bring up to her, he pounced on the only advantage he had. "You said you remember someone with you the night of the crash. Tell me about that. What exactly do you remember?"

"In my dreams, I'm not the one driving. I... We were going somewhere. I remember I was happy. Excited. And then..."

"What, Angie? What?"

Maybe he pushed her too hard. Maybe she wasn't ready to see what happened after all.

All Maddox knew was that, as he waited desperately for her answer, the only one he got was Evangeline's sudden scream. The jagged line of pain he sensed inside of her blossomed into a crevice that nearly split her in two.

Her hands flew to her temples, her eyes screwed shut as she cried out once, then curled up in the chair as if trying to protect herself.

Maddox's only thought was to protect her from the unseen threat. He jumped to his feet, his heart thudding so loudly he expected it to burst free from his chest. Leaping to her side, he was there as Evangeline's body gave a jerk before she went completely limp in her seat. If he hadn't moved as fast as he had, she would have crumpled to the floor.

She looked like she was dead.

Flashbacks of that night rushed through Maddox.

"Evangeline," he roared. "No!"

He hurriedly scooped her up into his arms, holding her close as he fought his panic. His wolf howled its grief, wanting to nose at his mate's cheek to see if she was all right. He refused the shift, needing to hold her close as she lay like a corpse in his arms. Corpse—*no*, he wasn't going to think like that. She wasn't dead. He couldn't let her be.

Closing his eyes, he tapped into his beast and relied on its senses.

Okay. *Okay*. She was still breathing. He could hear her wheezes, soft and gentle. He flared his nostrils. The air surrounding Evangeline was a blend of her mouthwatering vanilla scent, the tickle of sweet baby powder, and a sharp tang that screamed *pain*. Whatever it was must have been agonizing to have such a flavor; it left a bitter taste in his mouth. Maddox was almost grateful that she was out. Unconscious, yeah, but that meant she wasn't in pain any longer.

That was a good thing.

Now, if only he could convince himself that any part of what had just happened was good.

It was the baby powder that he couldn't get out of his nose. As he carried his mate from the kitchen to their bedroom, he left the stink of her pain behind him. But the baby powder clung to her, a faint overlay to her natural scent. He knew that smell. It was the smell of magic—it was the mark of the witches.

There was only one way to know for sure. Leaning in, Maddox carefully lifted her left eyelid and stared. Because instead of the forest green he adored, a streak of vivid purple colored her iris before her eye rolled back in her head and she exhaled softly.

Maddox let go of her eyelid before laying her on their bed and giving her space, his head whirring at his discovery.

Evangeline was human. One hundred percent as way too many people had told him lately. But the essence of baby powder and the violet swirling in her eyes...

Colt was right. Evangeline had been touched by a witch.

Shit.

26

Colton knew he shouldn't be there. He promised himself he wouldn't return, no matter how loudly his wolf howled. No good would come of it. Besides, Maddox was relying on his help. How could he help his brother when he was too busy following his dick?

He sat in his delivery van, gripping the steering wheel so tightly his knuckles were white. The temptation to leave the van and head into the store was too strong. He'd always prided himself on his control. Sure, his temper was legendary and he tended to shift at the drop of a hat, but that was all part of who he was.

What he *wasn't* was some lovesick pup who sat in vans, mooning at displays of crystals, incense, and supplements all because he lost his fucking mind somewhere in Grayson.

It was the stupid town's fault, he decided. One

chance encounter—one stupid delivery—and now he was cursed to hide among the Ants because he just couldn't help himself.

After accidentally stumbling upon Evangeline all those weeks ago, Colt never expected to have to come back. Except then Maddox sent him back twice more to pick up Evangeline's scent. He hadn't been able to, but that's when he found *her*.

It was supposed to be a job. Just another commission: a simple dresser that he might have painstakingly labored over for two weeks in between visiting Maddox in the Cage and securing his brother's release. Then came the innocent brush of her hand against his arm as he attempted to deliver the dresser and the sudden shock of his first erection. It surprised him so much that he dropped the dresser, crushed his ankle, and probably scared the shit out of his client.

His client, he repeated to himself. Because that's all she was. That's all she could be, no matter what his wayward dick thought.

Colt yawned, leaning his head up against the headrest. He spared only a second to rub the fatigue out of his eyes before his gaze was locked on the shopfront again. He couldn't look away, not until he got a glimpse of that inky black hair, that honest smile.

Just a glimpse. Just a sign that she was doing okay and he could get back to searching for Cilla.

When he got his hands on that wayward witch, it was going to be a struggle not to snap his teeth at her.

Priscilla Winters was his last hope. He'd spent the last twenty-four hours calling in any favor he had, hoping he could track her down. Just because Luciana said that a witch wouldn't be able to help, that didn't mean Colt actually accepted that.

Cilla was an old friend of Maddox's. If anyone would be willing to help him, it would be Cilla. At least, if she felt the same guilt over Maddox's fate as Colt did, she would.

Though he'd rather gnaw off his foot than admit it to Maddox, Colt long suspected that Cilla might have had something to do with the crash that destroyed his brother's life. It was an open secret that she'd been in love with Maddox since they were teens. Back when Maddox first found Evangeline, Cilla was visibly upset at the news before later being happy that her childhood friend had discovered his mate at last.

Colt knew better.

Twisting the key in the ignition viciously, he started the van. He had to get out of here before he made another mistake.

Pulling out onto the street, he couldn't stop himself from thinking back. It was all his fault. He'd never gotten along with Cilla and it pissed him off that she thought she could come and go as she pleased, visiting the Bumptown when everyone knew the witches owned Coventry. There wasn't a single witch living in Colt's Para community.

He liked it that way.

So when he saw Cilla strutting around like she owned the place? He couldn't stop himself from throwing Maddox's upcoming wedding in her face. In one afternoon, Maddox would be finally married and formally bonded. Cilla would never get a chance with him.

The next night, Maddox's truck ran through a guardrail. Mere hours after a quick courthouse wedding, Maddox and Evangeline were on their way to the cabin for their honeymoon.

They never made it.

Colt was the first one called to the scene to check on Maddox. Law enforcement didn't want to go through the Alpha of the pack, so Terrence was out. Colt was there to watch as Evangeline was rushed away in an ambulance and Maddox was strapped down in case she didn't survive.

And he was there to pick up on the scent of baby powder that lingered on the mountaintop.

Magic.

The officials said it was an accident. A sudden rainstorm coupled with a pitted old guardrail and his brother's tendency to speed. Even Colt believed it, second-guessing his nose.

Who knows? Maybe there really *is* another reason why he caught a whiff of baby powder on the breeze.

Colt spent three years trying to convince himself that his arrogant taunts toward Priscilla Winters had nothing to do with the crash that nearly killed Evangeline. Maddox was a shifter; he would've survived that and more. But Evangeline was human.

It was supposed to have been an accident. Nowadays? Colt wasn't so sure.

Especially now that he was almost positive a witch had something to do with the state of his brother's bond with his mate.

Was it a certain witch? Until he tracked down Cilla, he wouldn't know for sure. He didn't even try asking Luciana for help in that regards. A coven was almost as close-knit as a pack. They never turned on their own.

Hell.

Colt yawned again, trying to shake off his exhaustion. He blinked once, twice, keeping his attention on the road ahead of him.

When was the last time he slept? Between trying to keep up with orders, driving down to his father's latest construction site to keep him from suspecting that something was up, and continuing his search for Cilla, he was more tired than he'd ever been before.

Sarah Wolfe, most likely acting on her mate's tip, had called and offered to bring fresh meat to Colt's house. It killed him to have to turn her down. One sniff and Sarah would know that Maddox had been around. As much as he disagreed with his brother's insistence that they keep his parents out of it for now, he gave his word. It was one thing to shower Maddox's scent off of him before heading out to see his father. There was no way he had the time to clean his house of any sign that Maddox had been living there.

Though, he thought snidely, maybe if Colt didn't spend the only free time he had stalking some poor unsuspecting human, he'd be able to get a little housekeeping done.

Human.

Not a witch.

Too bad another of my kind has already got her hooks in you...

That thought had him jamming his lead foot on the gas pedal, swerving around some little old lady in her sedan. She surprised him by flipping him the bird.

He bared his teeth in the rearview mirror.

Tires squealed, the scent of burning rubber against asphalt seeping in through the gap in his window, stinging his nose. The little old lady took off, igniting Colt's predator's need to chase.

Just as he was about to slam his boot on the accelerator, speeding down the road after her, he felt a buzz against his hip. It was distracting enough that the sedan peeled away, disappearing down a side road while Colt slapped at his pocket.

It was his phone.

Pulling it out, he saw the number, cursed under his breath, then jerked on the wheel, parking the van in the first spot he could find. It was in front of a fire hydrant and he knew he couldn't stay long. Better make this quick.

He answered with a grunt. "Yeah?"

"Colt? It's me. We have a problem. How's your hunt for a witch going?"

Colt wanted to groan. He knew Maddox had a one-track mind, but he hated being reminded that he couldn't do the one fucking thing his brother asked of him. Admitting that he couldn't get a single witch to hear him out sucked. It was even worse when he filled Maddox in late last night, telling him about his meeting with the head witch.

He even got Dodge to agree to tag some of his contacts. No dice. If it killed Colt, he was going to find out what the witches had against him.

Just because he hated them all, didn't mean they had to take it out on *him.*

"I haven't been able to find Cilla yet, but I'm still trying." Or, he told himself, he would be once he got the hell out of Grayson.

"Cilla? You mean Priscilla? I thought you gave up on looking for her when she wouldn't answer. She's probably too busy with her personal clients. Right now I just need any witch."

Colt was so tired that he slipped up. Shit. "Not my fault none of the damn witches want anything to do with you *or* me. Cilla's the best plan I got. I figure she might be willing to help us. You know, shared history and all."

Shared history. Yeah. That was the nice way to put it.

Maddox's growl reverberated through the speaker. "Last I knew, Cilla went lone witch." Lone witch was the same as a lone wolf to a shifter: she gave up on her coven, striking it out on her own. "Who knows if she's even still around? Forget about her—there's gotta be someone local who can help. And Colt? We gotta be discreet. I've already had cops at the house and you'll never fucking believe it: one of them is an old Cage guard."

After visiting Maddox for years, Colt knew all of the guards. "Which one?"

"Wright."

Colt nearly crunched his phone. "I hate that Ant."

"Get in line, bro. Because Wright? He's not just a cop. He's *Adam*."

"You've got to be shitting me. The guy who tried to shack up with Evangeline?"

"One and the same," snarled Maddox. "And that's not even the worst of it."

"What do you mean? And make it quick, okay? I'm parked illegally. You probably don't want me catching the attention of the police right about now."

Maddox didn't, so he filled Colt in as fast as he could. Clear and straight to the point, he told Colt all about Evangeline's spell. How, just when she was on the verge of finally—*finally*—remembering something, her nagging headache turned into something she couldn't handle. Maddox's mate collapsed, her vanilla scent mingling with baby powder. As if that wasn't a big enough clue, when Maddox peeled Evangeline's lid back, her green eyes were flooded with purple.

Fucking witches.

"So, yeah, you were right, and Alpha knows I hate telling you that, little brother. Some way, somehow, a witch did something to her head. It's gotta be old, too. She told me she's been getting those headaches since the crash. It's got to have something to do with the broken bond, right?"

Colt let out an angry exhale. "That makes sense to me."

"I'm going to tell her."

What? "I wouldn't. I think it's still too soon. She's just starting to trust you — what if this fucks up everything you've done so far?"

Before Colt talked Maddox into just running off with Evangeline—desperate times called for desperate measures—Maddox had come up with the idea of confronting Evangeline with the truth. If he laid out all of the physical proof he had, wouldn't she have to believe him?

Colt didn't think so. He thought it would work out better if Evangeline recovered her memories on her own. Maddox reluctantly agreed.

Seems like he was reconsidering that plan.

"It's a risk I have to take," Maddox said firmly. Okay. Not reconsidering; Mad already had his mind set. "I can't sit here and wait for her to remember. It's hurting her and that's killing me, Colt. And I know you don't have a mate so I can't expect you to understand. If I could take the pain from her, I'd do it. But I can't. I can't do anything. I don't want to be helpless. I don't want to be at the mercy of that prick coming back and taking her away from me. She's my wife," Maddox snapped. "It's time she knew that."

Colt was silent for a moment. The jab about not having a mate—

"Okay. Fine. Do what you have to. I'll call you when I can get my claws on a witch. Enough diamonds and maybe one of them will be willing to help."

"Money's no object, Colt. Get it done."

"Will do."

It took sixteen hours before Evangeline regained consciousness again. Whatever the witch did to her, it hit her harder than Colt's sedatives.

Maddox stood watch over her for every one of those hours. He dragged his chair so that he could sit at her bedside. He kept his elbows propped on his knees and his head hanging, his chin resting on his chest for the few ten-minute catnaps he permitted himself to have. His ears twitched anytime he heard a car approaching, panicked that it might be Wright returning with that damn warrant.

How was he supposed to make her remember when she spent all of her time unconscious? It was closing in on almost three days since he carried her away from Mugs. She'd spent more than half of it where he couldn't reach her.

It was better than her being in pain, but not by much. At least, while she slept, she was healing. Her ankle—helped along by some ice and whatever healing he could share through their fledgling bond—was looking much, much better.

Maddox forced himself to eat if only because he would need his strength if Wright tried to take her from him. His only focus was on waiting for his mate to come back to him again.

He lost track of time. The lights were still off, the shades pulled low. It could be late afternoon, early evening... he had no idea. Time stretched on as Evangeline lay there, eerily still.

No twitching this time. No crying out. She slept like the dead.

Her scent changed first. The lingering cloying aroma of sickly sweet baby powder dissipated first, her warm, rich vanilla scent overpowering it. She let out a soft sigh, then turned from her back to her side.

Whether she meant to or not, she turned her body so that she was facing Maddox directly.

Evangeline opened her eyes, blinking slowly. Her hand reached up to her head, running her fingers through the tangles in her long hair. Maddox didn't sense any pain radiating off of her; seconds later, she sighed and dropped her hand.

No headache.

Good.

Maddox cleared his throat, drawing her attention over to him. "Just putting it out there, that had nothing to do with me. I didn't drug you."

Evangeline swallowed roughly. "I... I know. I, uh, I actually remember. We were talking and..." Her eyes darkened, a mixture of despair and anger flashing across her pale features. She lost all color while she slept, her lips thin and cracked, her eyes dull. "It's the headaches. They used to be that bad, but they were getting better. Now they're worse."

"I'm sorry."

"I'd say it's not your fault, but stress does trigger them..." She shook her head. "I'm feeling better now. It's just... can I have some water?"

Maddox's chest felt light, as if a huge fucking weight had been lifted. Barely three days ago, Evangeline swore she would never consume anything he gave her. Now? She was asking him for a drink. Probably because the magic left her mouth dry, and she had to be dehydrated after how long she was out. It didn't matter.

"Wait here." There was a manila folder resting at his feet. Maddox scooped it up, tossing it on the chair after he stood. "I'll be right back."

He ducked downstairs, grabbing her a glass of water, before rushing back into the room. It didn't even look like she had moved an inch.

"Here you go."

Evangeline took the glass, sipping it slowly. It took her a few minutes to drain the contents. By the time she was done, she was already looking a little better.

She held the empty out to him. "Thanks."

"More? Or do you want me to get you something to eat? You've gotta be starving."

"Not right now. I'm still feeling a little queasy. Maybe later?"

Maddox nodded. "You just let me know. Whatever you want, it's yours."

As soon as the words escaped him, Maddox wanted to take them back. He gave his mate the perfect opening to demand to be let free again. Not that he would do it—he couldn't, not when he was so damn close—but it would hurt him to have to refuse.

But, to his surprise, Evangeline just nodded. "That's fine. I'm usually not too hungry for a while after I get one of those awful headaches."

"You still get them often?"

She looked down. Her hands were folded in her lap, but she noticed a thread pulling from her pale pink tee and absently pulled at it. Maddox needed to do something about getting Evangeline to change. The closets and drawers were full of her old clothes. When Colt came to take care of the place shortly after the accident, Maddox refused to let his brother throw any reminder of Evangeline away. Didn't matter that she was supposed to be dead and Maddox was never getting out of the Cage. He liked the idea of their home being left just the way it was, like a shrine to their mating, no matter how brief it was.

Now, Maddox was glad for his stubbornly sentimental streak. The clothes were more than three years old, but they were hers.

He told her that, surprised again when she accepted what he said with a distracted nod. Knowing he was stalling, Maddox asked her if she wanted to use the shower, even offering to carry her to the bathroom so that she could keep off her ankle.

Later.

A nightgown to change into?

Later.

Some aspirin?

Later.

Eventually, Maddox ran out of excuses. He could tell that she was lost in her own thoughts. And while he would've given every last penny he had if she would only open up to him like she had been before the headache became too much, Maddox decided it was time.

She wasn't going to remember on her own. Being around him, feeling the slight tug of the bond trying to forge again, even returning to her own home... if none of that was going to make her memories come back, maybe this would.

Maddox returned to his chair. He grabbed the manila envelope, removing the two pieces inside of it.

Sitting down at her bedside again, he handed the bigger certificate to Evangeline.

She took it.

Her eyebrows rose. "What's this?"

"Look at it. I mean really look at it. Maybe this will finally prove to you that I'm not full of shit."

IT WAS A MARRIAGE LICENSE.

Her stomach dropped.

In utter disbelief, she read it again.

Certificate of Marriage.

This certifies that **Maddox Wolfe** *and* **Evangeline Lewis** *were united in marriage on this day...*

Her gaze lowered to the four handwritten scrawls along the bottom. She could just about make out Maddox's signature, and the one below his that looked like it read Colton Wolfe as the witness. The one next to Maddox's, though? She knew that one.

"That... that's my signature." Evangeline glared accusingly up at Maddox. "What the hell's wrong with you? You forged this? Just when I thought— I thought I was..." She refused to tell the bastard that she was beginning to think about sticking around a little longer, trying to understand just what there was between them. Not now. Not after *this*. "There isn't a single honest judge in the world who'd sign off on this so if you think, for one second, this is gonna trap me here with you—"

"Look at the date," he interrupted. He used his pointer finger to underline the date printed on the license.

She did.

"Three years ago... wait a second, I *know* that date. That's the date of my accident."

"*Our* accident." Maddox reminded her.

"You weren't there," she argued, tearing her gaze away from his muscular chest. Her voice was shaky, her head spinning. It was getting harder and harder to separate her blanked memories from the dreams that constantly haunted her, especially when Maddox kept insisting he was in the car when she crashed.

And that wasn't the only thing he wouldn't let go of, either.

As if Maddox could sense her hesitation, he gentled his rough, raspy tone. "We're bonded, Angie. Mated. But we're also married."

Then, before she could argue, he handed her the other sheaf he held carefully in his hand. With shaky fingers, she gripped it, turning it over only to discover that it was a photograph.

The world stopped.

Just *stopped*.

It was Maddox, but he seemed different. Softer somehow, his golden eyes reflecting life and love instead of cold determination. His tanned skin was healthy, his hair shorter than it was now. He was smiling.

He wasn't alone.

A white dress. Evangeline was wearing a white dress.

A wedding dress.

The Evangeline in the photo looked different, too. She was *happy*. Leaning into the embrace of the big shifter who managed to dwarf such a tall woman, his arms were wrapped snugly under her chest, her fingers intertwined with his. This was a picture of two people on the happiest day of their lives and their beaming grins proved it.

She had a wedding band on the ring finger of her left hand.

Evangeline gulped. When she woke up in the hospital, all of her jewelry was gone. They gave her a sealed bag with her necklace, earrings, and a bracelet in it when the hospital discharged her.

There was no ring.

"I... I don't remember any of this."

"I know, and it's okay. I'll help you remember. I promise. And, if you can't, we'll start over. You're my wife—my *mate*—and I love you. I'll always love you. Whatever happened, we can start all over again."

He didn't get it. The buzzing in her skull was starting up, the precursor to the mother of all migraines, but Evangeline shoved it all aside. No. Not now. Not when she had to focus.

"No," she snapped, the word coming out louder than she intended. Maddox's eyes widened, but at least the warning signs of her headache seemed to fade. "You don't understand. I remember everything else. Everything! Everything that happened in my life up until about a year before the accident, then everything after they left me out of the hospital. But I don't remember *you*."

He kept his expression flat, his voice neutral. "I know, Angie. I know."

"But... how is that possible?" A terrible, awful suspicion crept in. Why hadn't she thought to ask this before? "How long have I known you?"

He pursed his lips.

"Damn it, Maddox. *How long*?"

It took him a few seconds to answer her. When he finally spoke up, she caught a hint of fang. Her shifter was trying to hide it, trying to stay calm, but his wolf was riding him and it was riding him *hard*.

"You lost little more than a year. That's about how long we were together."

Evangeline's mouth opened. No words came out.

Maddox seemed to understand. "I found you about a year before the accident. I knew you were mine right away, but you insisted on dating. We were mated about six months in, and then you insisted on human marriage before I claimed you as my bonded mate. We got married, just like you wanted. You even took me home to meet your parents."

Everything inside of her seemed to screech to a halt.

"My... my parents?" Evangeline felt her heart lodge in her throat. "You met my parents."

"I did. Took 'em ages before they got over the fact I was Para."

Did they, wondered Evangeline. Because something was very, very clear to her. Her dad didn't like to talk about the accident and she understood that. But her mother? She spoke to Naomi almost every day.

When she grew frustrated about the things she couldn't remember, her mother was the one who told her about her life during those missing moments. Her job at the publishing house, her home in Woodbridge, her everyday existence. It helped her retain her sanity, knowing she had someone who could fill her in when she came up against a blank wall inside her whole mind.

Not once did her mother ever mention that Evangeline was with anyone—especially a paranormal who she was *married* to.

"She never told me. My mom never told me." The photo slipped from trembling fingers. "Why wouldn't she have *told* me?"

"I don't know."

Yeah. She didn't know, either.

But she could guess.

Tears sprang to her eyes. Confusion, betrayal, shock... a motley of different emotions came crashing over her, weighing her down. She could feel Maddox watching her closely, gauging her reaction.

The sympathy mixed with love in his gaze somehow made it so much worse. How could she process all of this when Maddox was looking at her with so much expectation?

She couldn't, that was for sure.

"I think you should go."

Maddox stiffened on the edge of the chair. "Ang?"

She nodded. "Please, Maddox. I... I think I'd like to be alone right now."

27

To her surprise, Maddox nodded. Gathering up the marriage certificate and the photo, he slipped them back into the manila folder.

"I didn't want to do this," he said, and there was enough regret in his tone that she believed him. "Wright forced my hand. I wanted you to remember on your own... I'm sorry, Ang. I really am."

Then, before she could say anything, he leaned down, brushed the back of his hand across her cheek, then left her alone in the room.

She felt the burn of his flesh against hers long after he was gone.

The image of Evangeline in a wedding dress, holding tightly to Maddox as if she never wanted to let him go? That stayed seared in her mind even longer.

She didn't know what to think. Her initial reaction to deny the validity of the marriage license—to accuse him of forging her signature—had come from the last remnants of her certainty that Maddox had made this all up. The moment it slipped out, she didn't even believe it.

It was like she thought she *had* to.

But even that was wrong—because of the dreams.

She'd been having dreams about a shadowy figure with glowing golden eyes since right after her accident. Long before she met Maddox at Mugs, she dreamed of him, erotic dreams that made the virgin she thought she was blush. But then, before Adam and the other cop interrupted them, she grabbed hold of Maddox's cock and it seemed *right*. Like she'd done the same exact thing a thousand times before, his moans and his pleasure music to his ears.

And that wasn't all.

The despair at waking up and finding out that he had just *taken* her from Mugs had blinded her to the fact that she'd felt a pull to Maddox from the first moment they locked eyes.

He repeatedly told her that she was his mate. That there was a special bond between them, a tether put in place by fate. She was the one woman he was meant to love, meant to sleep with, meant to breed with.

In her dreams, they did that. A lot.

Then there were the recent visions that seemed so real... Memories? At first, Evangeline thought they were fantasies. Now? She wasn't so sure. It was like déjà vu. She felt like she'd lived those scenes before but, without the memories to back them up, she dismissed them.

She had to start paying attention.

The room. The bedroom that so eerily resembled the space she created for herself in Grayson. She'd only lived there for months, though it felt like a lifetime. Was it possible? Could she have celebrated her newly won independence by subconsciously decorating her room like the one she left behind—*and couldn't remember*?

Adam.

Apart from the wedding picture—which could've been faked, just like the marriage license, they *could've* been faked—Adam was the biggest piece of proof she had. He was the one she could believe. And he was the one who said out loud that Maddox and Evangeline used to have a bond.

Used to.

Did they still?

Sitting on the edge of the bed—her bed— Evangeline reached deep inside of her. It felt strange and kind of silly, but maybe there was something to it because, after a few seconds, she felt this kind of knot down low. Without knowing what it was or how she was doing it, she tugged at it.

There was an answering pull a second before a feeling of warmth rushed over her. Breathing deep, she could've sworn she got a whiff of Maddox's scent: musky and earthy.

Was that the bond?

Evangeline didn't know.

So what *did* she know?

She knew that Adam wanted to make her his own.

That Maddox wanted to make her his mate again.

That the witch wanted her to stay away from Maddox.

Okay.

That begged another question: What did *Evangeline* want?

She was so sick and tired of every part of her life being out of her control. For far too long, every aspect of her life had belonged to someone else. When would it be her turn to live it? She'd cheated death, come out on the other side healthy if not entirely whole.

She always thought she was missing something.

Glancing around the room, thinking of how desperately Maddox implored her to remember, Evangeline had to ask herself if *this* was what she was missing.

Him.

What did *she* want?

Maybe it was crazy. Maybe she needed space, needed time. Needed to get her head on straight. The dreams were messing with her, the headaches making it difficult to focus on something so important. Evangeline felt like she was on the precipice of something huge.

All she needed was a push.

Or to jump.

What did she *want*?

Just once, she was going to be the one who decided.

If she accepted her dreams as memories, the visions that she had these last few years as more than just fantasies... there was a lot less missing than she thought. If Maddox was the man of her dreams, then...

It was worth a shot. And, well, it wasn't as if she hadn't secretly harbored a desire to do exactly this ever since he told her she was his mate—and then the nasty witch said she wasn't.

That decided it for her.

Evangeline swung her legs over the edge of the bed, gingerly testing her ankle. There was an awful twinge if she put too much pressure on it. Shifting her weight to her good side, she limped across the room.

It took her a second to realize that she hadn't had to guess. Maddox offered her a nightgown, subtly slipping it into their conversation that, as this was their old room, all of the clothes inside used to belong to her. When she went to one particular dresser, yanking out a lacy white nightgown without even thinking about it, she paused for a second, completely stunned.

Maybe... maybe that was her problem. Maybe she was thinking *too* much.

Maybe it was time to let her feel.

She wanted Maddox.

Maybe she shouldn't.

Maybe she'd fallen under his spell.

Maybe this was fate—

Taking careful steps so that didn't aggravate her tender ankle, Evangeline tried not to think about what happened the last time she took a leap of faith, either. The actual leap left her injured, easy prey for the alpha wolf that chased her.

Her hand closed on the doorknob. She tugged.

Maddox hadn't locked her in.

Good.

Because this time? She wasn't running from him.

She was going right to him.

Maddox should be sleeping.

Impossible.

He could hear Evangeline moving around in their old room so he knew she wasn't sleeping, either. He picked up on the slide of the dresser drawer opening and let out a relieved huff. She'd at least listened to him when it came to the clothes being hers. She was finally changing out of the t-shirt and shorts she'd been wearing for days. He was glad that she was getting comfortable, and only hoped it didn't mean that she was getting ready to leave after all.

Now if only he could've stayed in that room with her...

Just like Colt kept a spare room in his Bumptown house for when Maddox stayed over, Maddox's home in Wolf's Creek had a guest room for the times a packmate needed a bed for the night. He was lying in there now, grateful he had the foresight to put a king-sized bed in that room, too, but it didn't matter how big the bed was when he had to sleep in it alone.

It was all his fault. What a fucking moron. After taking his time, trying to build up some kind of relationship with Evangeline, he shot it all to hell by showing her the marriage license and their wedding photo. And while it seemed like a good idea when he asked Colt to get the envelope together, his brother had warned him to take it slow.

Yeah. Slow. Slow as a rocketship, maybe.

He had to come up with a Plan C. Plan A was a colossal failure, Plan B was a train wreck. With Wright breathing down his neck, he needed to—

His body went rigid, his ears cocked toward the door. Was that a doorknob turning?

Shit. Evangeline *was* leaving him.

He'd gone to bed in his jeans because he was too lazy—and too frustrated—to change. He stripped off his shirt, then flopped on the bed. Good. That meant he didn't have to stop to pull on clothes before he ran after her.

Maddox climbed out of his bed, only to slip back into it as noiselessly as possible when the knob to his door turned.

Evangeline eased the door inward, stepping inside of the room after a moment's hesitation.

The shades were drawn, the lights off. A sliver of moonlight illuminated his mate enough to see that she had changed into a frilly, lacy white nightgown that revealed her curves and showed a mile of her long, lean legs. Her feet were bare and she tiptoed soundlessly into the room.

At first, he thought she was just checking to see if he was sleeping. He kept his eyes cracked open just enough that he could see her, but she didn't know he was awake. Maddox watched what she was doing.

To his ever-loving surprised, Evangeline pulled the blanket back and slipped in next to him.

Maybe she was lonely, he thought. Or scared. He tried not to remember that, in all of the time since he took her with him, she hadn't been able to fall asleep on her own: she was either dosed or she fell unconscious. Sleep never came easy to her. Maybe that was why—

Evangeline's hand whispered toward him. "Maddox, you awake?"

He grunted. It could mean yes, or it could mean no.

"You said... you said I could."

Maddox said a lot of things. With Evangeline's scent drifting toward him, he felt cozy, relaxed, and so fucking happy just to have her near him. Then he breathed again, caught a hint of arousal on the still summer air, and nearly gave himself away.

No fucking way.

She didn't mean—

Hesitant at first, then growing bolder, she started to run her finger up and down his length, teasing his cock, waking it up. It didn't take much. One whiff of her scent—her wet, intoxicating scent—and he was so hard, it hurt.

Through gritted teeth, he managed to grunt out, "Angie..."

"So you *are* awake," she said huskily.

"What are you... unh, that feels so fucking good—sorry. What are you doing?"

"You said I could touch you."

"Oh, sweetheart, you never have to get my permission." Maddox was careful not to move too quickly in case she stopped her gentle exploration. He went from his side to his back, allowing her the full spread of his body. "I'm all yours."

"It's kind of tough with your jeans in the way," she said after a moment.

She didn't mean—

She couldn't mean—

Maddox wasn't about to ask her. Before she could repeat herself, he slipped out of the bed, shucking his jeans and his boxers in less time than it took for Evangeline to scoot closer to the center of the bed.

His erection was wide awake. Suddenly, so was Maddox.

He lay back down. Evangeline immediately placed her head on his stomach, her body molded to his side as she reached out for him again.

The instant she circled his cock, touching her thumb to her pinky, Maddox felt a jolt that had his cock jerking, pre-cum already leaking from the tip. Her soft touch, her gentle stroke calmed him at the same time as she teased him into a frenzy.

Was he really asleep? Could this be a dream? It seemed like one.

"Angie..." he groaned again.

Evangeline lazily traced every vein, every ridge on his erection. "Shh," she told him. "I'm remembering."

So was he. This took him back to their first time together, right after Evangeline finally put him out of his misery after months of waiting and jerking off so much that his palm felt like it had rug burn. She was twenty-three, he was twenty-six, the two of them virgins fumbling around in the dark.

As Evangeline continued her gentle exploration, Maddox decided he'd be lucky if he lasted even half as long as he had four years ago.

Wait—

What was he thinking? Just because Evangeline was touching him, he was thinking three steps ahead, already imagining himself balls deep inside his woman.

"Ang—"

She lazily ran one finger against the top of his cock. He couldn't keep his groan back.

With eyes that shouldn't be so innocent, Evangeline

looked up at him. "Do you want me to stop?" she asked in that sex kitten voice of hers.

Oh, he should. He should want her to. For Alpha's sake, he drugged her, kidnapped her, terrified her, and lusted after her. She deserved so much better than him. If he was half the man he should be, he would tell her to stop so that he wasn't taking any further advantage of her.

But that was the problem. While he was half a man, he was also half a beast.

"Never," he barked.

He was so painfully hard that her simple touch was sending sparks of pleasure jolting through his entire body. Ever since he found her in the coffee shop, his dick had been standing at attention.

This was something new. His mate had her hands on him, stroking him much more delicately than the thousands of rubs he'd given himself over the last few days. The pressure started mounting, the beginning of his orgasm drawing his balls up tight.

Her breath fanned his belly. He was seconds away from exploding. This was no dream.

Curling his hands into tight fists, he refused to give in to the sensation. He wanted to see what else Evangeline was going to do. One thing was for sure: he had gone to bed alone. She'd purposely made her way into his bed.

Was there a reason?

"I can feel you're close, baby. Don't be embarrassed

about it. Let it go. I remember how quickly you recover. You'll be ready again in no time, hmm? And then we can get to the good part."

As if her words were a trigger for his release, Maddox's whole body jerked as thick jets of hot semen spurted out, covering his stomach. She giggled, then brazenly pulled her nightgown up and over her head. Wadding it up into a ball, she swiped at his chest until she'd gotten rid of the last bit of his cum.

"There you go. All nice and clean."

Maddox was stunned by the amazing sight of Evangeline's bare breasts bouncing gently in front of him. Holy shit, she wasn't wearing a bra. This time he had to pinch himself to make sure that he wasn't dreaming.

The pinch hurt. This was all real. Didn't mean he had half a clue what was going on here.

"Evangeline, what are you doing?"

"My mate," she answered before boldly reaching for his cock again.

The stupid thing didn't know when to stay down. At her touch, it stiffened and rose, like a dog begging for more.

Too bad it wasn't getting anything else. Not from Evangeline. Maddox was an asshole, but he wasn't a *fucking* asshole.

"Angie," he groaned her name as she gave him another experimental tug. Grabbing a pillow, he covered himself before moving out of her reach. "You can't."

"Are you telling me no?"

"I'd rather die, but you don't understand." His mind racing, the scent of her heady arousal doing a number on him, Maddox scrambled for an excuse that wouldn't leave his mate believing that he didn't want her. He wasn't that much of a dick. Between showing her the marriage certificate and now, something had switched inside of her. Instead of swearing that she never wanted to see him again, now she was giving him a handjob and propositioning him like she used to.

If he thought she was serious, that she really meant this, he'd be on top of her in a heartbeat. But as much as he dreamed of a wet and willing Evangeline, he knew he'd be the world's biggest asshole if he took advantage of her.

And then it hit him. "We can't because I don't have any condoms here."

Maddox might have been willing to do anything to have his mate back with him but, despite what Evangeline accused him of, he wasn't delusional. He hoped for this, he prayed for this, but he never expected that she'd ever let him touch her again. So condoms? Not on the list of things he had Colt prepare for him.

Boy, was he regretting that oversight now.

Maddox was the one who always insisted on the condoms. He had to. Even though he and Evangeline had been each other's one and only so diseases weren't an issue, unplanned pregnancy was. Because a shifter could only be with their fated mate—and because mating ensured future generations of pups—any time there was unprotected sex, pregnancy was not only possible, it was almost guaranteed. When they first started mating, he and Evangeline both agreed to wait until they were a little older before they thought about starting a family.

That wasn't the only reason why Maddox refused to go bareback. To claim his mate, Maddox had to do two things: bite her in a claiming bite at the exact moment he released inside of her. The temptation would have been too strong to claim her if he knew she was willingly accepting his seed and the possibility of carrying his child. She'd been adamant that she didn't want to be claimed until after they were married.

It was the biggest regret of his life. But if he listened to her now, claimed her, then had to hear Evangeline say one more time that she wasn't his... it would kill him. What the Cage didn't accomplish, what the silver collar didn't manage, she would do with a simple denial.

So, as much as he was delighted to have Evangeline in his bed again, he wouldn't dare go another step further without any protection.

"What if I said I didn't care?"

"I'd say that's a quick turn around. Remember your ankle? You messed it up trying to escape, and now you want me to believe you changed your mind about me?"

28

She bit her bottom lip. Maddox wanted to slap himself in the head. Here she was, warm and willing and in his bed, and what did he do? Force her to confront the shitty thing he did that led her there.

"I'm sorry, Ang—"

"No. Don't be. You're not wrong. Three days ago, I would've rather broken my leg than even think of doing this... but I'm beginning to remember. I think—I have this... I don't know... this *hunch* that this is the answer."

Hunch. Maddox's wolf sat up. A hunch to a human was like his instincts. Maybe she wasn't sure that taking this step—taking this amazing, wonderful, *final* step—could bring back the rest of her memories. But if she could sense something was there between them...

"Angie, I—"

"Shh. Please, let me finish. I have to... I have to say

this before I lose my nerve. Okay? Some kind of tie is here. I've been trying too hard to deny it. *Something* is here. I... I feel it inside of me. I think I always have. I'm your mate, right? It's what you've been telling me for days. What if doing this together is what helps put it all in place?"

It sounded like a dream come true to him.

Still, he had to ask. He had to make sure she understood that regaining her memories might not be the only thing she got out of this mating.

"Are you ready to have my pup? Because that could happen. You *are* my mate. My body knows it. I release inside of you, you could very easily get pregnant. Knocked up. Get it?"

To his surprise, Evangeline didn't even quail. With a bold grasp, she took his cock in her hand and squeezed.

She fucking *squeezed*.

He almost nutted right there.

"I've lost the last three years of my life. *Our* life together. We were married. That cabin... you were supposed to claim me there if the accident never happened. I kinda guessed... now I *know*. Tell me, Maddox, baby: how many pups could we have had already?"

Oh, *shit*. He wanted to. He wanted to so bad. The image of his wife swelled with their pup—was this payback?

Was this torture what he got for taking her the way he had?

And *baby*... she hadn't called him *baby* since seconds before the crash. It was her pet name for him. Big and brawny and a dangerous alpha wolf, and Maddox was always her baby.

He gulped.

"You're killing me, Angie. You know that, right? I'm trying to be the good guy here—"

"Too late for that, I think." Her husky laugh went straight to his throbbing cock. The damn thing started to weep against the pillowcase. He didn't blame it one bit. "You already kidnapped me. Maybe we should cut straight to the ravishing now?"

Who would have thought she'd be the one trying to seduce him?

Relying on the one thing he could think of to talk sense into her, he said bluntly, "If I fuck you, I'll claim you. You'll be mine forever. What do you say about that?"

"I... I remember we had this talk before. You wanted to claim me, and I said we had to get married. Well, you definitely proved that part earlier, didn't you? 'Til death do we part... to me, that's the same as forever. I claimed you. Now it's your turn to claim me."

Wrong answer. Or, rather, the right answer if the question was how to get Maddox to throw the pillow away and lunge for her without any further hesitation.

All he wanted to do was sink right into her but, in

the haze of his lust-fueled mind, he managed to remember what his size could do to Evangeline if she wasn't ready for him.

He slipped his big hands between them, running two fingers up her slit, testing how wet she was. From the arousal perfuming the air, he expected to find some moisture, but she was so hot and so slick, he managed to fit two fingers inside of her without even trying.

She was tight. So fucking tight. There was resistance as he slowly slid in and out, stretching her slightly as he moved his fingers just enough to fill her. Evangeline gasped every time he went back inside, pausing to rub her clit with his thumb so that she continued to get wetter and wetter.

Her pants were the same as they were back then. Just like she used to, Evangeline took charge, maneuvering his hand so that he was rubbing her right where she liked him to. He hadn't forgotten the way his mate liked it, and as she rode his two fingers, he felt her muscles clench as she came on his fingers.

Holy shit. She was *totally* into this.

There was no turning back now, though Maddox knew he would hate himself forever if he didn't give her one last chance to back out.

His voice hoarse, his wolf coming to the front so that they could do this together, he asked her, "Had enough?"

"One orgasm?" she teased. "Is that all you got?"

Not even close.

Once he managed to fit three fingers in, he knew she was as ready as she was going to get. Later, if she let him do this again, he would take his time. He would pleasure her lazily with his tongue, nibble her clit just the way she liked, fuck her for hours until she was crying with frustration. She always came the hardest when he took his time, though she never used to have any complaints when he went hard and rough and fast.

Which was a good thing because, as close as he was, that was exactly what she was in for.

He placed the tip of his cock to her entrance, his wolf keening in his throat. Over the course of the last three years, he'd relived what it had been like to thrust his cock inside of her pussy, his fantasies the only thing that kept him going through the lonely, awful nights in the Cage.

With one thrust, Maddox was seated all the way inside of Evangeline. It was a hundred times better than he remembered. The way she gripped him, how hot she was, how incredibly tight. She squeezed him so much, it took him a second to regain control before he exploded before he'd even had the chance to stroke in and out once.

He wasn't the only one who needed a moment. Evangeline let out a low, throaty moan when he entered her, shifting just enough to let him know that she was feeling every inch of his length.

"You okay?"

"I know we've done this before, but, uh, it's been a while for me. I just have to adjust—" She let out a rush of air, breathing in, getting used to his size. "It, wow, this feels amazing."

Maddox felt his chest puff out. If just sliding inside of her once got a *wow*, wait until he really got moving. He braced himself on his elbows, careful to keep his weight off of her, drawing out until just the tip was left inside. Then, when she was ready, he slammed back in.

Once he got going, he didn't stop.

Evangeline's tits bounced as he mounted her, thrusting with everything he had. He dipped his head low, aware from the flash of concern on her face when he got close that he had shifted enough to worry her. He could feel his fangs lengthening, but he knew he would only use them for the claiming bite.

It had been forever since he proved to Evangeline that he knew how to work around his fangs. Once he took her breast between his lips, lathing her nipple with his tongue, she forgot all about his glowing eyes, his extended fangs. He didn't know what happened in the time since he left Evangeline alone in that room, but the woman who came to him knew exactly who he was—*what* he was—and as she fell prey to the pleasure he gave her, the only expression she wore was one of bliss, never fear.

He wanted to go forever, but he already knew he wasn't going to last. After making sure she got off a second time, rubbing her clit forcefully in time to his powerful thrusts, Maddox knew that he wouldn't make it that much longer.

One last time.

He'd give her one last time to change her mind.

Maddox needed to make sure she was still with him. It was one thing to mate her. She could take it back tomorrow and, sure, it would fucking hurt, but he'd understand. If this was just another way for her to convince him that she was harmless before she tried to run, he could forgive her using his body this way. He totally deserved to be treated like a plaything after everything he did to her.

But bonding?

It was forever.

"Are you sure?" he panted. His fangs were the longest they'd ever been without entering into a partial shift, aching to plunge into her skin. "If you changed your mind, I can still stop. We don't have to do this right now. Give me the word and I'll put out. I don't have to bite. We have forever, Ang, and I'll take your word for it. You don't have to prove anything to me."

They had mated countless times before, but the urge to bite—the urge to claim—had never been as strong as it was in that moment. Just like Evangeline wouldn't sign the bonding license until they were officially married, Maddox refused to claim his mate until they were legal and bonded.

The marriage license was safe in the top drawer of his nightstand. Fuck the bonding license. He needed to make Evangeline irrevocably his. The government wouldn't decide that. His claiming bite would.

But only if she wanted it.

Her little breaths as she came down from her last climax were music to his ears. And even they paled in comparison to the way she moaned out her answer.

"Don't you dare stop. Claim me, baby. Do it now. Make me whole."

That was a tall order. He had no way of knowing if claiming her would help her regain her memories. It would strengthen the bond—he was almost positive that it would—but that didn't mean everything would go back to the way it was.

He fucking hoped so, but he didn't know.

Call him a selfish bastard. Maddox didn't give her even a second to reconsider her answer. The bond wouldn't let him. With one last thrust, he shuddered and emptied himself into her. It was the first time his wife accepted his seed without anything between them and that realization sent his orgasm into the atmosphere. At its peak, he buried his mouth into the supple curve where her neck and her shoulder met and struck.

His fangs slid into her flesh like a hot knife through butter. Maddox had hoped that she wouldn't feel any pain and from the way her pussy clenched down on him and her fingers dug into his shoulder blades, he figured she got as much pleasure out of the claiming bite as he did. Her blood was hot, rich and tangy, and he decided it was only right that he had some of her inside of him while she had him inside of her.

Evangeline let out a squeak of surprise, then a low throaty moan as her muscles clenched, squeezing his cock. It sent another jolt of pleasure through Maddox.

When he had finished, when there was nothing left to give her, he lapped leisurely at his bite, sealing it for her. His cock was softening, the force of the claiming enough to drain him for now. It wouldn't last. He'd be ready to go before long, but it took a little wrangling of his hips to keep the connection.

He left the tip of his cock inside of her, desperate not to leave her heat. Evangeline didn't seem to mind. She snuggled into him, pressing her lips to his left pec, before closing her eyes.

He tucked his mate into his side, wiping her sweaty brow, running his palm gently over her hair. The long dark strands were everywhere, tangled and knotted from the mating. As she snuffled, snoring softly, her breath blowing on his overheated chest, Maddox urged her closer.

Their breathing slowed, the scent of sex, of lust, of Maddox and Evangeline filling the air. It was fucking delicious and, as he calmed his racing heart, he let it settle over him.

Evangeline was quiet. He was almost sure she had fallen asleep right after he claimed her. She would need the rest—she was a human, and the claiming would knock her on her ass for a bit as her body changed to be a match for Maddox's—and he was secretly proud of himself for boning her into unconsciousness.

A few minutes later, though, he heard her murmur his name.

"Yes, sweetheart?"

"I just wanted to ask you something."

"Anything."

Her hand slid across his belly. To his slight disappointment, it didn't travel south, but drifted upward instead. She laid her hand over his heart. "You have a tattoo. When I saw the date, I was so confused. I thought it was the date of my accident. I... I remember a little. You didn't use to have it."

His heart gave a joyful beat when she said that she remembered a little. Holding onto the thread of hope that her recent memories were the catalyst for their bonding, Maddox leaned over, pressing a kiss to the top of her damp hair.

"When you were in the hospital... when they told me you died, they gave me a choice. Cage, no memories of you, or death. I couldn't live without you, and I couldn't live without my memories of you, but the pack... Colt... I couldn't die, either. Maybe it's because I knew you were still alive, even if our bond was gone. I spent three years in the Cage, missing you. Loving you. One of the other guys gave me the tat. Of course I picked that day."

She was quiet again. Maddox almost thought he

had put her to sleep with his story when she whispered, "Why's that?"

"That day... it was the best day of my life. The worst, too, 'cause I thought you had left me. But the best because, even if it was only for a few hours, you were my wife."

Maddox wrapped his arm around her, tugging her into his embrace. They fit like a glove.

"Now it's the second best day," he told her.

"What's the first?" she asked shyly.

Did she not know?

"Tonight, when you finally became my true mate."

29

For the first time in years, Evangeline slept peacefully.

She didn't have a single dream, and when she woke up the next morning, wrapped in Maddox's arms and his musky, manly scent, she knew exactly why.

Why would she dream up a fantasy man who lurked in the shadows of her consciousness when she had the real thing right there with her?

Her lover.

Her husband.

Her *mate*.

Maddox was still sleeping. Man slept like the dead. His senses were extraordinary, though. If he so much as caught a hint that she might be in danger, or that she might need him, she did not doubt that he would be up without a second's hesitation. She'd seen him do it a thousand times before—

Evangeline went giddy. Because that certainty didn't come from her last few days with Maddox. It came from a year's courtship where she met and fell in love with an alpha wolf shifter named Maddox Wolfe.

Evangeline Wolfe.

She was Evangeline Wolfe.

She blinked. Only yesterday, that realization would have had her testing her ankle as she tried to run away from him—run away from the feelings that he brought about in her. Now, though?

It was a whole new day.

Day—

Trying her best not to wake him, Evangeline slipped out from under his arm, creeping toward the edge of the massive king-sized bed. Inch by inch, she went at a snail's pace, careful not to catch Maddox's attention. A single memory—more vivid than the others—was running through her clear head. She held onto it, determined not to let it slip away.

She was so used to losing them. It was as different as it was nice to be able to call it up and *keep* it.

She remembered this room. She remembered that the mattress was perched on a high box spring so there was a bit of a step before her bare foot hit the floor. She grabbed the crumpled quilt that was balled up near the end of the bed. Wrapping herself up with it, like a makeshift toga, Evangeline gently tiptoed across the room. The last thing she needed was one of their neighbors getting an eyeful of her tits when she lifted the window shade.

Slowly, slowly, Evangeline tugged on the shade, wincing when the plastic jerked out of her hand, slapping into the top of the window frame as it rolled shut. Sunlight streamed in through the glass, bathing the room in a bright light that highlighted Maddox's naked form. His legs got tangled up in a sheet sometime after he fell asleep, leaving most of him revealed.

Evangeline stopped and stared.

God, he was *gorgeous*.

It was the first time she'd been able to see him sleeping. With his eyes closed, his face relaxed, he seemed softer. She took this moment in time to study him without being hypnotized by his beautiful golden gaze.

She took in the cutting edge of his jaw, cheekbones as sharp as knives... the dark shadow of a stubble he could never fully shave clean. Worry lines were missing when he slept, his forehead smooth, his mouth slightly open as he snuffled and snored.

He let out a rush of air, his hand reaching out. Even in his sleep, Maddox searched for her. His fingers flexed, twitching, his body tensing when he realized that she was missing. She watched as he flared his nostrils, trying to find her scent. He exhaled softly when he assured himself that she was still close.

He didn't need his eyes to see her when his other

senses could pick up on her presence. Good. That gave Evangeline a precious few seconds to climb in the bed before her shifter mate slowly roused himself out of sleep.

His eyes were bright, the gold a burnished shade that brightened when he found her only a couple of inches away from where his palm lay flat on the sheet. He stretched, his fingertips brushing alongside the edge of her bare hip.

"Morning," he rasped out. "Sleep well?"

"Best night in a long time."

"Me, too," Maddox murmured.

And then he smiled.

It was the first real smile he'd given her since he was trying to seduce her at the coffee shop. She'd been oblivious to his tactics then, though now she knew better. Looking back on it, she was kind of shocked that it hadn't worked.

That smile? It turned him from gorgeous to drop dead sexy with the simple curve of his lips.

Evangeline had to resist the urge to roll toward him, laying her cheek against his chest. With the sheet pooled around his waist, his sculpted body was a temptation that, as his wife, she no longer had to pretend she didn't want.

Maddox being super attractive had never been the problem. His insistence on what she knew to be false —the lengths he had gone to convince her otherwise

—was what had been the biggest obstacle between them. Between that and her missing memories, the two of them were doomed at the beginning.

Then he had shown her the wedding photo. That, added to the few glimpses into the past that she managed to recover, Evangeline knew better now. He was her husband. After last night, he was her bonded mate.

It was time he knew that, too.

So, rather than touch him like she was dying to, Evangeline lifted her hand, shielding her eyes.

"Something wrong, sweetheart?"

"Kinda. The sun's, um, really bright out today."

"Oh. Sorry. How did— Never mind. Here, let me get the shade."

Maddox hopped out of the bed, stalking naked across the room. Evangeline enjoyed the vision of that tight ass moving away from her so much that she almost forgot the reason why she pointed out the glare.

He reached up, tall enough to grab the shade without going up on his toes. His delicious ass went taut, the muscles on his back rippling as he yanked it down, turning the room into a dim shadow.

"Better?"

Much, but that wasn't the point.

"Not really," she lied. "Do... do you have an extra pair of sunglasses I can borrow?"

He frowned, as if he could sense her deception, but

that didn't stop him from trying to give her what she asked for. Maddox's hand slapped at his hip, reaching for a pocket in a pair of jeans that were tossed somewhere in his haste to disrobe last night. It took him a second to remember that he was naked, then even longer to realize that she wasn't asking him for a pair of shades because she actually *needed* them.

His mouth dropped. He hesitated, hope warring with caution, before he said, "You... you remember?"

Evangeline nodded. The giddy feeling from when she woke up? It manifested in a bubble of laughter that had Maddox crouching low, then pushing off of the carpeted floor. He landed in the bed easily, barely jostling her. She giggled, her laugh turning into more of a surprised shriek as Maddox's arm wrapped around her, tugging her into his warm embrace.

"Angie, you remember!"

She wiggled until she was facing him. "Some... more this morning, too. I wasn't kidding when I told you that last night. I mean, some things are more vivid than others, and I know I'm still missing a lot. That day, though? I remember that day because it was the day you told me I was your mate."

Maddox winced. "I don't know why I ever bother pretending to be a human. The first time, you called me out on being a shifter. This time, I barely lasted a couple of days before my wolf took control."

"You're a Para, Maddox. I don't ever want you to be something you're not. Even when you stole me, I understood *why* you thought you had to, even when I thought you were crazy for thinking I was your mate."

"You *are* my mate."

"I know." Evangeline slipped a hand between their bodies, caressing the bite on her shoulder. It was halfway healed; with their bond finally intact again, Maddox must have taken the pain from Evangeline, lending her his increased healing properties. Come to think of it, her ankle was feeling better, too. "Now everyone else will, too."

Maddox eyed her closely, his eyes gleaming with a mixture of possessiveness and concern. "How are you feeling?"

"Great," admitted Evangeline. Laughter bubbled up and out of her again. "For the first time in a long, long time, I feel great."

It wouldn't be easy. There was the fact that Evangeline still wasn't completely whole, a possessive witch out there somewhere, and Maddox had technically gone against the *Claws Clause* by taking the subject of their mating into his own paws.

Then, of course, there was Adam.

She had to do something about Adam.

For now, she was safe and she was loved, and the man who risked everything—including his own life—because he loved her even more than that was holding her close. Evangeline ducked her head, brushing her lips over the tattoo over his left pec.

That had been the best day of his life, he told her, then the worst.

Together, they had hit the highest of highs and the lowest of lows. It wouldn't be easy, but the best things never were. She had a hard road ahead of her as she continued to recover that lost year.

But at least she would have her mate by her side. And Maddox had been right. If she never recovered their time together, that was fine. They had each other now. With the future ahead of them, they had all the time in the world to make new memories.

Better memories.

Together.

As if he thought that she was a dream he might wake up from, Maddox was hesitant to let her out of his sight. They showered together, and while Evangeline was interested in a repeat of last night when he hoisted her up so that she wasn't putting weight on her still tender ankle, Maddox refused. He flat-out told her that he could sense how sore she was between her legs. Angry at himself that he'd been rougher than he meant to, he swore he wouldn't take her again until she felt better.

She couldn't lie. As a wolf shifter, he would know. Besides, her poor pussy was aching—but it was a delicious ache.

God, she missed him. With so many of her memories slowly returning, with the knowledge that she'd been dreaming of Maddox all of this time, Evangeline finally understood that *he* was what had been missing all along.

She still couldn't understand how she could have forgotten the love of her life. It made no sense to her, especially since Maddox assured her that the only reason it took him as long as it did to find her again was because he believed she was dead.

As soon as Maddox claimed her last night, the bond snapped back into place. Just like she hoped— just like she suspected—her vulnerability as Maddox gave her his claiming bite had opened her up to him. He'd been calling for her with his end of the bond since the beginning. Once Evangeline dropped her guard, tentatively reaching back, the mate bond connected. There was no going back now.

With fuzzy memories becoming clearer and clearer, she only felt relief. In the end, Maddox had told her the truth right after she woke up to the reality that he had whisked her away.

It really *was* her choice.

Once they were showered and dressed—Evangeline marveling with delight as she went through a wardrobe she hadn't seen in years—Maddox insisted on leaving the house behind. It was closing in on two days since Adam threatened to return with the warrant. Just because he hadn't yet, Maddox argued, didn't mean he gave up.

Evangeline thought she knew Adam very well. Whether or not he knew about Maddox, that she'd actually been *married* when the car crashed... it didn't matter. Adam still thought of her as his girlfriend. No way was he going to let this go.

Maddox had a point. The laws were very clear. By taking her, he broke one of the biggest ones of all. Ordinance 7304 was a human's only assurance that they couldn't be forced into a lifelong bond with someone because they lacked the magic to protect themselves. So what if she was ready to accept Maddox as her mate? According to the *Claws Clause*, he could be facing death if anyone caught them together and he admitted that he did steal her away.

It was a good thing that there was a pretty simple fix to that solution. In Para circles, the bonding license was like a "get out of jail free" card. With the notarized certificate that said that Maddox and Evangeline were bonded mates, the laws regarding unbonded mates no longer applied. She wasn't completely human anymore—as a Para's mate, she was technically a Para herself now—and the bonding license gave Maddox every right to use his paranormal abilities to protect his mate.

That was why a bonding license could only be given to a pair that pledged under oath that a bond existed. Laws and rights flew out the window when they got their license notarized. It meant *everything*, especially since bureaucratic red tape ensured that a bonding license could only be signed after the couple presented themselves in front of a Para office who could tell if they were lying.

To keep Maddox from the Cage—or worse—the first thing they needed to do was go and get their bonding license. Every Bumptown had an office onsite to take care of that, so at least they didn't have to take a trip to the D.P.R. In and out, they could have the license by mid-afternoon if they hurried.

There was a tiny problem when it came to that, though. Because Evangeline was, well, drugged and sedated every time he moved her, first from the coffee shop to the cabin, then the cabin to their old home, Maddox didn't know about her phobia when it came to riding in a car.

Turned out, with the memories of the crash more vivid and realler than ever, her phobia only grew worse. Just the idea of willingly climbing inside of Colton Wolfe's truck for the hour trip to the Bumptown from Wolf's Creek erased her euphoric mood.

In fact, it nearly caused a nervous breakdown.

She just couldn't do it. Maddox didn't push it, either. He told her they could figure something out, and if Adam showed up before they got the license, they'd figure that out, too.

The only thing was, with more and more memories becoming clearer, Evangeline remembered Maddox.

She remembered his personality, his likes, his desires. How he wore shades because he didn't want to deal with humans judging him for his beast, even though he radiated such a dominant power, most people recognized him for what he was—a born Alpha—without such an easy clue.

She remembered his position in the pack, his former role as foreman at his father's construction company, and how he doted on his younger brother. Maddox was loyal and he was stubborn and he was strong.

If Adam came with the might of the Grayson PD behind him, Maddox wouldn't be carted off to the Cage that easily. He would fight for her, and one of the two men in her life would be hurt.

Evangeline could be stubborn, too. And while she might feel like throttling Adam herself, she wasn't going to let anything happen to him until she gave him the chance to explain what he thought he was doing. Because he loved her, she had no doubt that he loved her, and with fresh memories filling her brain, Evangeline knew people did stupid things when they were in love.

Which was why she asked Maddox if he still had that baggy full of white powder.

Sugar-free sugar, her ass. Her Maddox had a sweet tooth and he'd never give up the real stuff. But she gave him credit. As an explanation for what he was doing when she nearly caught him dosing her coffee, she had to admit he thought quick.

Evangeline never thought she'd see the day that she'd gladly swallow a laced drink. But if it came down to a choice between waiting around for Adam to show up or getting the protection a bonding license would afford her mate, she knew what she had to do.

30

Maddox was getting better at figuring out how much of the drugs to use.

Just a pinch this time. A teensy tiny drop in a glass of water that Evangeline swallowed with a nervous chuckle and a shaky, "Bottom's up."

It took a little bit longer for it to affect her. By the time they cleaned up breakfast, then grabbed a few changes of clothes from the musty closets—Maddox because he needed to be prepared in case he had to shift, and Evangeline because he had every intention of bringing her to the cabin for a belated honeymoon—Evangeline was starting to yawn.

Maddox stayed close to her. When she gave the sign that it was affecting her, he swooped her up in his arms, slung the duffel bag holding their clothes over his shoulder, then slipped out of the house.

It was the middle of the afternoon. He was taking a

huge risk, heading out in the daylight with a noticeably sleeping Evangeline stretched out in a bridal carry. His nosy ass neighbors would call the cops in a heartbeat if they caught sight of them together. He didn't give a shit. So long as he got to Colt's Bumptown before Wright found him, he'd be fine. No Ant police officer would ever dare separate a bonded shifter from his mate inside of a Bumptown.

Wolf's Creek was about a half an hour's drive from the opposite direction. He kept to the speed limit, not wanting to catch the attention from his local police department. The boys in blue were another kind of pack; Wolf's Creek might be an integrated community, equal parts human and Para, but the cops would partner up with Grayson PD if Wright called in a favor. Maddox's best bet was to cross into Para territory.

Everything worked according to plan. He brought Evangeline to Colt's house, shooing Dodge away when the phantom made an appearance to tell Maddox that Colt was out for the day. Dodge wanted to stay and say hi to Evangeline—as a phantom, he had perfect recall, and he said he was happy to tell her any number of embarrassing stories about Maddox that she might've forgotten—but Maddox told him to come back later. It had been less than twenty-four hours since he claimed her, and though she proudly wore his bite, it was going to take some time before the possessiveness dialed it back a little.

So maybe he shouldn't have snapped his teeth at

Dodge. He was such a pain in the ass, Maddox always seemed to forget he was not only dead, but transparent, too. None of his threats would work on the ghost. Didn't stop him from trying. Eventually, Dodge grew bored with teasing Maddox and drifted back to where he came from.

Maddox waited for his mate to wake.

It only took another hour. The sedative had been enough for her to miss the entire drive over, and she seemed sheepish that it had been needed. Maddox brushed her worries aside. He was so in awe that she wanted to get the bonding license squared away enough that she willingly went under because, otherwise, her phobia regarding a car ride meant that they'd have to wait.

Maddox would do everything he could to support her in the future. He totally understood the source of her fears, and was willing to help her any way he could. Therapy? Sure. Hypnosis? Okay. Asking a witch for help? Well, the head witch had already been way overpaid by Colt. Maybe she knew someone.

And if it meant that Evangeline never could ride in a car again, then he'd fucking shift and give her a ride on his back if that's what she wanted. She was his life. His world. And, about an hour after she woke up, groggy but happy to see him, Evangeline was his fully bonded, fully claimed mate.

No one could take her away from him—

—at least, that's what he *thought*.

The Para who notarized their bonding license was a Dayborn vampire. Dayborns were a subset of the Vampire Nation; considered the "good" vampires because they didn't *need* blood like their Nightwalker counterparts, Dayborns were more like Ants than other Paras. They had a few strengths—like most Paras, they could tell when someone was lying, even though they couldn't lie themselves—with their most noted being an ability to walk in the sun. They had milder temperaments than the vicious Nightwalkers, mercenary witches, and growly shifters. They were also unusually efficient.

After a couple of quick questions, an analysis of their blood—another trick that only a Dayborn could do—to prove that the mate bond was there, and a couple of signatures, Maddox had their bonding license tucked in the same manila envelope that held the marriage certificate.

A copy of the bonding license was also uploaded to the Web. The Web, with its uppercase 'w', was an online database that served Paras only. It was the same database that the Ants at the D.P.R. used to check on a paranormal's status. From the moment the Dayborn affirmed that it went through, Evangeline's file had been updated to say Evangeline Wolfe, shifter's mate.

He couldn't wait to rub it in Wright's face.

Maddox tucked the manila envelope under his arm as he led Evangeline out of the Dayborn's office, bringing her back out into the busy Bumptown streets.

The office was along Sunset Boulevard, the vampire part of the settlement, about a fifteen minute's walk back to Colt's place, on the edge of the Zoo.

It was beautiful out. He had his mate's hand in his, the proof of their bonding clasped under his arm, and the summer sun was shining. Evangeline was chatting happily about all of the sights she saw; the Bumptown was clearly something she hadn't recovered her memories on and she marveled over how distinct each neighborhood was.

Maddox was just telling her about Cemetery Row—where Dodge spent his time when he wasn't with Colt—when his mate stopped dead in her tracks. At first, he thought she was staring at a bear shifter out for a roam in her fur. But then he noticed the patch of smoke about fifteen feet in the distance. Long and narrow, it was about the size of a full-length mirror, without any color to it at all.

He sniffed. It didn't smell like fire—it didn't smell like *anything*—so he couldn't understand what the smoke was about. That's when Evangeline shuddered, taking her hand from his as she covered her mouth with her fingers.

"Oh, no," whispered Evangeline. "Not now... not again."

She was staring at the smoke. *Again*, she said. What did his mate know that he didn't?

"Angie? What's going on?"

"It's her. She's followed me here."

The hair on the back of his neck stood straight up at her pronouncement. Evangeline's voice was flat, the sort of emotionless tone she had when she didn't know who he was or what he was capable of.

His stomach clenched. The smoke was billowing toward them, but there was nothing to distinguish it from any other patch of dense fog. It had no scent—

Wait.

It had *no* scent.

Like Evangeline had no scent when she wore that stupid fucking perfume Wright gave her.

Magic. He reached out, grabbing her elbow. "Come on, we have to go."

She didn't react. It was like she hadn't heard him. She continued to stare at the patch of smoke, growing thicker as they watched. Shadows moved in the colorless smoke. Was that a hand? A torso? Legs?

Was there someone in there?

He hesitated too long. Before he knew it, the smoke rushed toward him, wrapping him up in its tendrils. It did something to his wolf, turning it borderline feral. He lashed out, forcing his beast back, maintaining his shape only because he knew, if he let his wolf out, Evangeline would be caught in the crossfires. With the smoke muffling all of his senses, his wolf might attack its mate first, not realizing she wasn't a threat until it was too late.

He couldn't keep his claws back. Letting go of Evangeline's elbow a split second before they would've sliced her to ribbons, Maddox howled, then shoved at his wolf. It was wild, snarling, and spitting, its hackles raised.

And that's when he heard Evangeline scream.

Her scream was high-pitched. Terrified. Pure fear in a single sound. It had the power to make Maddox's focus turn deadly. Whatever this smoke was, it was no match for an enraged alpha wolf.

"Angie!"

His nose was bombarded with an array of overwhelming scents. The smoke might have blinded him, but his sense of smell had always been exceptionally keen. Warm vanilla to his right—*Evangeline*. Baby powder nearly dampened his senses, it was so strong. That was the magic.

There.

A hint of spice, coated in frost. Only one person in the world had a scent that reminded him of cold heat.

"Priscilla!"

A laugh filled the smoke, echoing around him. His body tensed, his muscles locked as he swiveled to and fro, searching for the witch.

He didn't see her, but he heard Priscilla Winter's notably clear laugh, then her girlish coo, "Miss me, my love?"

My love. Maddox shivered at how easily she called him that. He thought back to the countless amount of times both Colt and Dodge teased him, pointing out

But Cilla knew she wasn't his mate. She had given

up on her stupid, unrequited crush when they were kids—

Hadn't she?

"Priscilla," he growled, "what the fuck do you think you're doing?"

"Something I should've done years ago," she retorted. "Now, listen to me, Maddox. You've had your fun and I've been patient enough... but, *tsk, tsk*, you never should've filled out the bonding license. Not when we both know you're mine."

"Bullshit."

"Maddox," cried Evangeline. She sounded shaky and scared and, while he could sense her nearby, he couldn't see her. "Where are you?"

She obviously couldn't see him, either.

"I'm right here, sweetheart," he called out.

"I wouldn't call her *sweetheart*, my mate. You know how jealous I can be."

"Cilla, you—"

The witch snapped her fingers. He heard the crack, then felt the rush of power that came with it.

The smoke was suffocating; he couldn't break out of it, fight through it, or find Cilla hiding inside of her magical shield. A flash of light danced across the dense covering, blinding him for an instant, the only sign that Cilla wasn't as cheery as her voice would have let either of them believe.

"Don't think that piece of paper will stop me, either. The bonding license means nothing to me, not when my name will be on it before long. You've forced my hand, Maddox, but you'll have forever to make it up to me. I just wish I didn't have to take care of your pesky human sooner than I wanted to. Pity. I was having so much *fun* with her."

Cilla's cheery *fun* was punctuated by another scream from Evangeline.

Maddox growled. "If you lay one finger on my mate—"

He'd kill her. Childhood friend or no, he'd strike Cilla down in a heartbeat if she continued to threaten Evangeline.

Another flash, like lightning across a midnight sky. "*She* is not your mate," retorted Cilla. "*I am*."

Maddox had known Cilla for years, since he was a pup and she was a witchling. She could be recklessly stubborn, the type of woman who refused to take *no* for an answer without a good reason behind it.

He stepped closer, leaving about a foot of space between him and Evangeline. Threatening Cilla never worked, but sometimes—when he was desperate—he could reason with her. "You're not my mate."

She was obstinate. "I will be."

"You know that's not true. I only get one mate, and she's right here with me."

"She *was*."

Maddox went still, his angry wolf suddenly on alert. He could sense Evangeline trapped in the magic smoke right next to him but, keeping his eye on the threat he could perceive in front of him, he didn't dare turn away from where he thought Cilla was. "What?"

"You want her?" Another laugh from the witch. He didn't know what it was about it, but it sent shivers coursing down his spine. "Come and get her."

A clap of thunder rolled overhead. A wave of almost unbearable pressure slammed down on Maddox, nearly sending him to his knees. He forced himself back up, searching through the smoke, instinct warring with panic as he realized that he couldn't sense his mate at his side any longer.

His hand closed on air. Cilla laughed once more, her high-pitched chuckle closer to a cackle by the time the wind carried it away.

The smoke disappeared next, as if it had never been.

That wasn't the only thing that was missing.

Evangeline was gone.

Magic. He couldn't track magic.

Maddox felt a wrench in his chest, like his heart was being ripped in half. That was his bond being tested. Priscilla had stolen into the Bumptown like a thief in the night, cleaving Maddox in two as she grabbed Evangeline and disappeared with her.

Her last mocking taunt rang in his ears. *You want her? Come and get her.*

It was fucking impossible. His nose could follow Evangeline's scent through time itself, but not when magic was involved. With Cilla placing a spell over their bond, dampening it, he couldn't even rely on his connection to Evangeline to follow her.

It was like the night of the crash all over again. Only, this time, he knew Evangeline was still alive.

But for how long?

Beneath the sickly sweet baby powder stink that warned of Cilla's inherent paranormal power, Maddox caught a whiff of another underlying stench. It was dark and viscous, like hot tar, and he recognized it from a few of the inmates he crossed paths with in the Cage. The demented, the disturbed, the Paras who crossed over to the bad side, who gave up on their instincts and did as their cold, empty hearts demanded.

Those were the dangerous Paras who were locked up, not because they were unstable due to a lost bond, but because they were incapable of bonding with anyone. Sociopaths who had unbelievable power, whether it was shifter strength, vampiric abilities, or magical powers. They were the true danger to society, humans and paranormals both.

Evil. That's what Maddox used to call that stench. Pure evil.

And it clung to every inch of his childhood friend.

Maddox knew then that it wasn't as simple as Cilla being jealous. She might think that she was doing this because Evangeline was the one thing standing between her happily-ever-after with Maddox, but there was more to it than that. She had somehow fixated on his mate, using her as an excuse to indulge in the darkest of magics, all in the name of a long ago crush.

And now Cilla had Evangeline.

He burst through the Bumptown, dashing past shifters who knew better than to stop him while he was on the verge of rampaging. Every Para sensed his urgency, moving out of the way before he ran them down. His wolf clawed at the inside of his chest, eager to break out, convinced it could find its mate.

Maddox just managed to stay in his human form. He needed to. No way could he dial a phone with claws, or get his message across with yips and snarls.

He bolted toward the truck he left parked in front of Colt's house. As he raced, he yanked out his phone, jabbed his thumb into the redial button. Wind whistled through his ears, the echo of the phone ringing dulled as he poured on the speed.

Answer, answer, answer—

A click.

"Colt?" Despite his speed, he wasn't out of breath at all. "Where the fuck are you?"

An annoyed huff. "Hello to you, too, Mad."

"Cut the shit. I'm not fucking kidding. Where are you? And don't tell me you're in the Bumptown 'cause I'm here and you're not."

"I had to go out of town. Didn't think I needed permission—"

Maddox cut off Colt's smart ass answer with a roar that reverberated through the cell phone.

"O-*kay*. You've got my attention, bro. What's up?"

The truck was about ten feet away. Maddox leaped for it, nearly ripping the door off the hinge with the grip of his yank. "She's got my mate, Colt. She fucking took her."

"What? Who?"

"Priscilla. Now, don't make me ask again: Where. Are. You?"

"I'm in Grayson," Colt said hurriedly. "What can I do to help?"

Grayson. That worked. Quickly, he rattled off Evangeline's address. "That's Angie's apartment building. Sixth floor. It's the eastern most window if you're looking up from the street. I don't know if Cilla would bring her there, but it's worth a shot. Cilla said to come and get her. It means she's going somewhere I know. I'm about an hour out of Grayson, half that to Woodbridge. Cilla used to live there. I'll check that out, you check Angie's place. If that doesn't work, I'll go back to Wolf's Creek."

Colt didn't waste any time asking Maddox any stupid fucking questions. "I'm maybe ten minutes away from that street. Five if I let my wolf out."

"Go fur," ordered Maddox.

"Already yanking off my jeans. I'll keep my phone

in my pocket, carry the jeans in my jaw. When I get there, I'll call you back, let you know what I find. Shoot me a text if you need to."

"I'm getting in the truck as we speak. I'll be skin for now, but I'll let you know if that changes. Find her, Colt. Please."

"I'm on it. We'll get her back, Mad."

"I'm fucking counting on it."

31

"Wake up. Oh, come on, no one stays out that long after a simple transportation spell. Either you're faking it, or you're a weaker version of me than I thought. Goddess knows you're an Ant so I didn't hold much hope for a worthy opponent. But this is ridiculous."

Evangeline tried to ignore the menacing voice snapping at her. She was still feeling a bit shaky as she lay sprawled out on her side on a hard floor. Her head wasn't hurting, which was a damn miracle, and she kept her features expressionless as she pretended to sleep.

The clear, familiar voice filtered into her ears from somewhere above her. She thought about risking a peek, making sure it belonged to the witch she thought it did, then decided not to. The longer she could pass for being out, the more time she bought.

Too bad the witch didn't agree.

A heavy sigh, followed by the *clack-clack-clack*ing of high heels across the floor.

"Maybe I should kick you and see—"

Evangeline couldn't help herself. Her eyes popped open.

The voice turned smarmy. "That's what I thought."

Now that the jig was up, Evangeline pulled herself into a sitting position. The witch stood in her living room—

Wait.

This was *her* living room. In *her* apartment.

She looked around. Everything was exactly as she left it the fateful morning she headed over to Mugs for a drink. The only difference? The witch looming just in front of her coffee table, and the large circle of diamonds that was spread out on the floor.

She couldn't even count how many of the precious jewels—all different shapes and sizes—were piled upon each other. At least three inches thick, it made a circle around eight feet wide, taking up most of her living room. Evangeline had been dropped right in the middle of the circle.

As if she needed another clue apart from the purple eyes and the transportation spell that this Priscilla was a witch, now she found herself surrounded by diamonds.

That, uh, didn't bode well at all.

Because she almost didn't want to know, she didn't ask. Instead, she said, "Who... who are you?"

It was another stall tactic. Knowing that she had to rely on Maddox to find and rescue her now, Evangeline was trying to buy time. She didn't know this Priscilla—at least, that's the name Maddox has called her—not really, but she was intimately familiar with the witch who haunted her dreams.

There had to be a reason why the witch had finally chosen to step out of the shadows and into the light. Considering her comments to Maddox, it didn't take a super genius to figure it out.

She'd been warned. Even Evangeline had to admit that. The witch had warned her.

It wasn't supposed to happen, though. There was no denying that she was Maddox's mate—or that he was hers. So what was wrong with this witch?

She was flat-out delusional.

Simple as that.

And delusional people with the power to back up their delusions were nothing but trouble.

Evangeline glared up at her. Pricilla looked exactly the same as she had when she visited Evangeline in her dream two nights ago. Pin-straight black hair that fell past her shoulders, creamy caramel-colored skin, a face that might have been sculpted by the masters themselves, all capped off with a pair of exotic Para eyes.

There was insanity and the promise of retribution in her lovely purple witch's eyes.

"Don't you recognize me?" she purred.

Evangeline looked away. Confused, scared, and alone, she didn't want to fall into the witch's gaze in case she got lost in there.

"I saw you in my dreams."

"Very good." Sarcasm laced the witch's cheery tone. "So glad to see we're on the same page. Now, please, don't be too afraid. I want you to look at me. *Angie*, look."

There was power in the command. Evangeline was unable to resist the order.

Priscilla smiled. "I can see it in your eyes. Despite my best efforts and a good deal of my precious diamonds, you've regained some of your memories. Not enough to make you a threat, but some. Tell me, do you remember *this* me?"

The witch's form went hazy, a soft lavender smoke obscuring her from head to toe. Then, as quickly as it came, it fluttered away.

Evangeline gasped.

She did remember this witch. "You're the witch who set up my wards. You said your name was Ms. Winters."

"It is, but I prefer Cilla," she said before snapping her fingers. Her hair went from dark to light, her skin paling considerably. Her grin widened. "I wore this face when I sold your cop boyfriend the perfume."

Evangeline knew this was probably the worst time in the world to be worried about that. Still, she couldn't stop herself from blurting out, "So Adam was working with you, too?"

The witch looked scandalized. "Me working with an Ant? Hardly. With enough diamonds, a human can buy my services, but I'd never team up with one. Let's just say, we had the same goals. Your cop wanted a spell to keep you hidden from a shifter's nose. I didn't want Maddox to track you down."

Evangeline opened her mouth to ask another question.

Cilla's eyes flashed angrily, the first crack in her armor of faux pleasantness. "Now don't you dare ask why. You might not be a witch, but you charmed him all the same. He was convinced you were the woman for him just because you made his dick hard. Big deal. I make males—Para and human—desperate for my touch every single day. That doesn't mean I deserve their love, or even want it. You don't deserve Maddox's. Only I do."

She'd said as much when she arrived in a cloud of smoke at the Bumptown. Evangeline was still struggling to understand.

"Why are you doing this?"

"What? And tell you now before your wolf in shining armor comes to rescue you? Please. I'd only have to explain my brilliant plans all over again when he arrives and I really do hate to repeat myself."

That wasn't what Evangeline thought. From her impression of the witch, it seemed as if all she wanted to do *was* talk. And if she got her to talk, then maybe she could get her to slip up and say something that she could use.

"Brilliant plans?"

"Oh, yes. Getting your mother to hire me to do your wards was no accident. You've been a pain in my side for far too long now, human. I always knew that troublesome bond would break through my spells and I needed to be able to get to you whenever I needed to. Sacrificing you in your own apartment... it just had a nice ring to it." Cilla paused, then giggled at her own joke. "Ring? Get it. Ah. I kill me—actually. No. I guess I'll be killing you. Oops."

Evangeline always wondered if her mother's fear and hatred when it came to the paranormal races would ever have any repercussions. Trapped inside of a circle of diamonds, facing off against an insane witch in her apartment... that was definitely some kind of repercussion.

Hearing that the circle was needed for some kind of *sacrifice*—

No. Terror filled her veins, already knowing that she was looking death in the eye whenever she glanced at Cilla's narrowed gaze. Then again, she was to supposed to have been dead once before. She survived. With Maddox's love and his support, she survived;

even when the bond was broken, she never truly forgot him.

He would come for her. She just had to keep Cilla talking until he did. Evangeline had never been the type of woman who was going to be be the damsel in distress, waiting to be rescued. Just this once, though, she was going to make an exception.

In a world where paranormals and humans lived side by side, sometimes the Para had the upper hand. The Web might list Evangeline as a Para now, but she was human where it counted. She was no match for Cilla's magic.

She needed Maddox. For a million different reasons, she needed her mate.

Purposely dropping the topic of her mother, Evangeline grasped for something to say. A second later, she had it. "You said something about your diamonds and my memories. What did you mean?"

Cilla hesitated, torn between wanting to gloat and wanting to wait until Maddox undoubtedly tracked them down.

Like Evangeline, she had no doubt that he would be there.

Belittling the captive Evangeline seemed to be Cilla's best choice. Rolling her eyes, she snapped, "Don't be so stupid. You must have figured it out by now."

"I wouldn't have asked if I knew."

A scoff. "So, then you *are* stupid."

If that's what she had to hear. "I guess so."

"It's your fault, you know."

"Mine? How?"

"If you'd have died like you were supposed to, I never would've had to use half of my hard-earned diamonds to snip the bond on your side. It took more power than I had without a coven on my side, and I never was able to scrub your memories completely clean. No matter what I tried, you kept trying to think about *my* Maddox."

Evangeline was stunned. She'd had her suspicions, had been working toward the conclusion that the accident had everything to do with her missing bond and her lost memories, but... "Wait. *You're* the one who did this to me?"

"Oh, yes. The accident, too. Well, can you call it an accident when I purposely used magic to lead the truck off the side of the mountain?" Cilla waved her hand. "Ah. Semantics."

"You *bitch*—"

"Flattery will get you nowhere, human. You'll see that when my mate finally gets here." Cilla stilled, a whisper of an anticipatory grin curving her lips. "Speak of the devil. Seems like someone's coming."

Evangeline gasped. It was so much faster than she expected. How long did it take for the transportation spell to work?

Maddox.

Snapping her fingers, Cilla told her, "I've dropped

all wards in the building. We wouldn't want to make it difficult for Maddox to find you. After all, I did dare him to."

Another snap, followed by a devious chuckle. Electricity pulsed in the air, lightning crackling off of the ring of diamonds that surrounded Evangeline. If she squinted her eyes just so, she could see wavy lines—heat lines—stretching up from the jewels about a split second before a four foot high, semi-transparent barrier exploded from the top.

"Just in case you got any ideas of breaking free before he got here. Now, if you'll excuse me. I've got to be ready to make my entrance."

Cilla winked out with a barely there *pop*.

Evangeline had to test it. She had to know. Reaching out, she touched a finger to the barrier. She let out a yelp, cradling her poor finger to her chest. It felt like she'd been shocked all the way to her toes. No way was she getting out of there without some help.

Help arrived less than a minute later.

The door swung inward, the power of the hit nearly knocking it off the hinges.

Evangeline pulled herself up to her knees. Through the haze of her prison, she caught sight of a naked body with tanned skin, dark hair, and an animalistic warning growl. She dared to climb higher, her heart in her throat. She wanted it to be Maddox so bad that it hurt, but, at the same time, she didn't want him getting caught in the witch's crosshairs.

As soon as she could see over the diamond's reach, Evangeline felt disappointment slug her in the gut. That... that wasn't Maddox. A second later, a jolt of recognition had her even more afraid.

That wasn't Maddox.

It was his brother.

Evangeline remembered him.

Colton Wolfe was Maddox's beloved younger brother. He was closer to her age, and while Maddox was courting her to be his mate, she got to know Colt very well. She used to think of him as the brother she never had. They got along just fine.

But what the hell was he doing there?

He hadn't changed much in the last three years. Still with a face so pretty, she wanted to just pinch his cheeks and make sure he was real, and an angry look in his icy blue eyes that warned anyone from trying. He stood in the ruined doorway of her old apartment, chest heaving, eyes narrowed in hate.

And he was naked.

Maddox must have sent him. If Colt had shifted shapes, switching back to two-legs would've incinerated any clothes he was wearing. He didn't seem to be bothered all that much by it, though, as his gaze fell on Evangeline in her diamond prison.

The ring of diamonds? Yeah. That pissed him off.

"A cage," he rumbled, more to himself than to her. His voice was deeper than she remembered, and there was a dangerous fury in his tone that had her shrinking back. "That bitch put you in a diamond cage."

A roar tore out of his throat. Arctic white fur sprouted along his tanned arms as he ran into the room. "Cilla! Where are you?" He stopped with his back to the windows, giving all of downtown Grayson a hell of a view as he called for the witch again. "Cilla, face me!"

Cilla appeared in a wisp of pale purple smoke. "You rang?"

The purr in her voice sent chills up and down Evangeline's spine.

Cilla had no reason to keep Maddox's brother alive. Evangeline was bait for Maddox; as soon as Cilla got what she wanted or she realized that she *wouldn't*, Evangeline knew the witch would be gunning for her. And it wasn't like she could escape. The diamond ring made sure of that.

But Colt didn't have to get involved. The witch was looking for a victim and here he was, signed, sealed, and delivered to her completely naked.

She had to warn him.

"Colton," she shouted. "Colt! Don't do this! Get out while you can. She's crazy!"

Colt didn't seem to think that Cilla was that big of a threat. At Evangeline's shout, he turned toward the diamond circle again, total surprise replacing the abject fury twisting his pretty, pretty features. His icy blue eyes softened just enough to make him look like the younger man she once knew. "You remember me?"

"Yes! You're Maddox's brother—"

"His little brother," sneered Cilla. Her purple eyes dipped low, a coy smile curving her lips. "Or should I say *big* brother. Oh, Colton, I had no idea what you've been hiding."

He spun back to face Cilla. His face went hard. "Don't you fucking look at me," he warned.

Her eyebrow quirked. Not out of anger, strangely enough, but out of curiosity. "How quaint. All you animals never seemed to care about nudity before. What changed?"

Colt didn't say anything. He didn't have to.

Cilla peered closely, her purple eyes turning dark as she—despite Colt's warning—looked him over. A shock of laughter slipped out of her. It was clear and sweet and too nice to belong to such a nasty woman.

"Oh, that's *rich*. After all the years you told Maddox that you'd be happy without a mate tying you down, Fate tagged you anyway. *And* she's like me. Oh, Colt, honey, Fate must hate you even more than she hates me. Honestly, you should thank me for what I'm about to do. I'm certainly doing you a favor in the long run."

Before he could react, Cilla conjured a ball of deep purple magic between her palms. It was about the size of a softball, compact and deadly. The witch jerked her arms back, then shoved it right at Colt.

A quarter of the diamonds ringing Evangeline

exploded with a deafening pop. Through the echo of the loud noise, she still heard it when the magic struck Colt right in his chest. He swallowed a howl of pain, but he wasn't able to catch it. The orb hit him dead center, lifting him off of his feet and throwing him backward out of the window.

His body burst through the glass, leaving jagged shards to mark the spot where Colt hit it. An instant later, a thud seemed to rattle the whole building.

Cilla poked her head out of the window, stared down below, turned and shrugged. With a devilish smile, she peered over at Evangeline.

"He should've been a cat shifter. Maybe then he would have landed on his feet."

32

The wolf wanted to take over. Maddox nearly gave in to the urge.

Only the fact that his top speed as a wolf hit fifty miles per hour while his truck could go a hundred if he pushed it kept him from handing the reins over to his beast. He didn't care if he broke a thousand laws in his pursuit of his mate. He had the fucking bonding license in the manila envelope serving as his passenger. With that, nothing and no one could stop him.

He'd barely been a couple of minutes into his drive when Colt called him. He was standing right outside of Evangeline's apartment building in Grayson, his ass hanging out as he paced along the edge of the wards. He didn't even stop to throw his jeans on, quickly making the call to tell Maddox there was a light on in Evangeline's window.

Someone was in there, he explained. Maddox

immediately did an illegal U-turn, abandoning the road to Woodbridge. He needed to get to Grayson.

Colt was just asking him for new orders when he felt the wards go down. Both Wolfe brothers knew it had to be a trap. If Evangeline was home alone, she never would drop the wards of her own free will. If Cilla was there—whether she still had Evangeline with her or not—it was a blatant invitation.

Maddox told his brother to wait. He'd be there in twenty no matter what he had to do. He didn't want to risk Colt facing off against this version of Priscilla without him.

Colt said no.

Actually, what he said was, "I owe that bitch," before disconnecting the call. And Maddox knew, deep in his gut, that his brother wasn't going to stick around and wait for anything.

Which meant that Maddox had to push the speedometer as far as it could go. At one-ten, the truck started to whine in protest. And one-twenty, it started to rattle. Smoke—dark smoke, not the pale purple magic shit—started to billow out a few minutes later. He pushed Colt's truck even harder, promising himself he would replace it as soon as he had Evangeline back with him.

He started to make all kinds of fucking promises if he could only get his mate back.

The truck made it all the way into Grayson, but the tires squealed, the transmission seizing when he was forced to come to a sudden stop when he hit a nasty traffic snarl right in the middle of the downtown.

Leaving the truck where it was, Maddox bolted in the direction of Evangeline's apartment building.

And that's when he discovered the source of the traffic.

A crowd of people was milling in the street in front of Evangeline's home. Maddox counted three cop cars —no sign of Wright yet, but that could change at any second—and two news vans. Blood and magic filled the air. Maddox sniffed, recognized whose blood that was, then pushed his way through the crowd of Ants.

Colt was lying bare-assed naked on his side, his body bloody and broken in the middle of Evangeline's street. Chunks of asphalt littered the space around him, torn up from impact. Maddox's head jerked upward. There was a Colt-sized hole in the window.

Maddox's heart stopped, only beating again when he heard a weak snarl coming from his brother, followed by, "Mad, tell these Ants to leave me the fuck alone."

Maddox dropped to his knees. Blood splattered his face, his neck, his chest, wounds slowly healing on the side that didn't look like hamburger meat, but Colt's eyes were open and alert.

Thank fucking Alpha.

"Colt, what happened? How badly are you hurt?"

"Might need... might need another minute before I can kick that witch's ass."

Another minute? Colt looked like, in another minute, they might need a hearse instead of an ambulance. "Cilla did this to you?"

"Unh, yeah. You're right. She's got Evangeline up there with her. She's got your mate."

Maddox glanced toward the busted window on the sixth floor. He was too far to make out what was being said clearly, though he heard a soft female voice. Purple shadows rolled across the jagged teeth of the broken glass.

"Stay here."

Colt grunted. "Give me a second. Healing's got to kick in any second now. I'll be your back-up. The cops here won't do shit since both Cilla and Evangeline are considered Paras. You can't go up there alone."

Like hell he wasn't.

His brother was lying broken and bloody on the asphalt, surrounded by a growing crowd of gawking humans. Colt's snarl kept them from getting too close, but Maddox was the Alpha.

He got low, locking eyes with Colt. His brother's eyes went glacial, a hint of a whine slipping out through gritted teeth. It was a show of dominance, pure and simple. When Colt was a hundred percent, he was no match for Maddox. After being thrown through a window, he didn't have a prayer.

"Stay. Here."

Colt tore his gaze away. "Then you get that fucking witch. Make her pay."

It was an order. Any other time, Maddox would've gone for Colt's throat if he thought he could issue an order to an Alpha right after a dominance challenge. Only, this time, Maddox was more than happy to accept it.

He braced Colt's shoulder, his ears picking up the wail of the sirens in the not too far distance. Maddox needed to hurry. Evangeline needed him, and it was essential he took care of Cilla as soon as possible. If the Ants called an ambulance for Colt, they were all in for a hell of a surprise when they tried to get him on a stretcher.

Maddox squeezed Colt's shoulder before rising to his feet, glaring at the window where his mate was facing off against an unpredictable witch.

"You got it."

The wards were still down.

Good. It made Maddox's race up the stairs easier.

The door was open when he reached the sixth floor. Since he'd never been inside the building before, he'd been worried about picking the right one. He ran straight toward it, coming to a screeching halt when he went a few feet past the open threshold.

The first thing he saw was Evangeline. She was curled in a ball on the floor. A ring of diamonds surrounded her, with a barrier that extended past her torso.

It was a cage.

Cilla had trapped his mate in a *cage*.

The growl tore out of him, followed by a snarl of a wolfish demand: "Let her go."

Evangeline's head jerked up, hope and despair fighting a battle on her lovely features. Considering she had to have been a witness to the way Cilla launched Colt through the sixth-floor window, no wonder she couldn't express how happy she was to see him. She was probably terrified that he would be next.

Not gonna happen.

As soon as she saw him, Cilla rose up from the couch, folding her hands primly in front of her black and white suit.

"Maddox." She waved. She actually waved. "It's so nice to see you."

"Let. Her. Go."

Cilla smiled coyly. "You don't honestly think that Alpha nonsense is going to work on me, do you? It never worked when we were kids, and I don't think we should start now. Mates must always be on an even footing. Wouldn't you agree?"

"No," snarled Maddox.

"No?"

He gestured at Evangeline, enraged that Cilla would dare put his mate in a cage. "I would never think my mate is my equal. My Evangeline is so much better than I was, than I am, than I'll ever be. And you took her from me!"

The smile slid off of Cilla's face. Her expression went stormy. "She's not your mate, Maddox."

"She's *always* been my mate."

"What about me?"

"What about you?" he snarled. "You're nothing to me now that you've crossed the line and *caged* my mate."

"Nothing?" Cilla recoiled as if he had slapped her in the face. "I used to be your best friend."

"When we were kids! If you were my friend, you never would've tried to hurt the woman that I love. And, for that, I'm sorry, because you *used* to be my friend, Priscilla." The fury inside of Maddox was surprisingly controllable because, for once, his wolf wasn't fighting him to be more vicious than the man wanted to be. To his beast, there was hierarchy, and there was pack, and, most importantly of all, there was the mate bond. No one—absolutely *no one*—could be allowed to fuck with the mate bond. "The laws are clear. You tried to take my mate from me. Whatever your reasons, whatever you thought you were going to do... it doesn't matter. You took my mate. You have to pay for that."

With a scoff, Cilla held her hands up. "You say that now. But she's *not* your mate."

The bite on Evangeline's neck said otherwise.

"Cilla, stop this shit. Don't make this harder than it has to be."

She lifted her chin, unafraid. "Do you see my diamonds, Maddox?"

How could he miss them? "You turned them into a cage for my mate. Of course I see them."

"There's so many of them. Thousands. Hundreds of thousands. Do you know how long I had to work for that many diamonds? What I had to *do*? Diamonds don't come cheap, but it was worth it if I could have you."

Maddox froze. A fresh wave of that dark stench—pure fucking evil—rolled off of Cilla, stretching out toward him, unfurling past him as he reached for Evangeline's huddled form. "What are you talking about?"

"For years... almost fifteen years now, I scrimped and I saved and I whored myself out for anyone with a diamond. Lone witch, they called me, all because I worked on my own, saving every gem I earned. Diamonds amplify a witch's power, I'm sure you know that. And I needed as much strength as I could get if I was going to create a bond."

Glancing over at Evangeline, Maddox saw that his mate had gone pale. He forced himself to focus. "Colt asked Luciana if it was possible. She said no."

"Anything is possible with enough diamonds." Cilla tucked a lock of her long, black hair behind her ear, a serene smile at home on her beautiful face.

"Even taking an existing bond and transferring it where it belongs."

Evangeline gasped. "You... you can't do that."

Cilla's brow furrowed, almost as if she had forgotten about Evangeline and loathed the reminder.

Maddox had to draw her attention back to him. "I won't let you do that."

"You can't stop me." Cilla pointed at him. "I spent years working to learn how to trigger a mate bond, but this human came along and ruined everything before I had the chance. Cutting your bond when she refused to die in the accident I orchestrated, stealing her memories so she didn't even remember you... I did it all so that I could work on giving you a second chance, letting you have the mate you deserved... then *she* ruined everything again! When the magic rips her soul out of her, I'll snatch it, and I'll take her side of the bond, too. It's a perfect solution. No more pesky Ant, and the two of us will be mates like we were always supposed to be."

Maddox couldn't believe what he was hearing. That Cilla was the reason behind the crash, and his going three years without his mate. And she actually thought *she* could replace Evangeline.

He shook his head in disbelief. "You're out of your fucking mind."

"No. I've just finally figured out how to get what it is that I want." She smiled again, utter insanity etched into every line of her face. "Isn't that the beauty of the

Claws Clause? Humans wanted to control mate bonds so badly, they left it wide open to interpretation. When it comes to bonded mates, anything goes, right?"

For once, Priscilla was absolutely right.

The dark stench had a bitter note to it that ruffled Maddox's wolf's fur. Cilla wasn't inherently evil, though that bitter note had a hand in making her that way. And, Maddox knew, putting her down was no longer just her punishment. It was inevitable.

And that had been *before* he knew she was the reason he lost three years with his beloved Evangeline. Or had to stand there while Cilla threatened to try and kill her again.

No fucking way.

Maddox could do whatever he wanted to regain his mate now that they were a licensed bonded pair. And to see Evangeline free from terror, free from fear, free from a fucking *cage,* there wasn't a single line he wouldn't cross.

"I'm sorry, Cilla. I never meant for it to end this way. But if it's a choice between your life and Evangeline's, my wolf and I are in agreement on this. You brought this on yourself. When you die, the magic dies with you. The threat to Evangeline dies with you, too. It has to happen like this."

He moved toward her.

Cilla shook her head royally. "You'd never hurt me."

He would. He'd regret it for maybe a moment, but

for a lifetime with Evangeline, there were precious few things he wouldn't sacrifice. And he hadn't been kidding when he said that she brought this on herself.

The *Claws Clause* was clear. Any threat to his mate deserved to be dealt with in whatever manner he saw fit.

A life for a life.

Maddox flexed his hand, his claws unsheathing without a warning. Though his fangs made his words seem harsh, danger rolling off of him in waves, he tried to gentle his voice as he called out to his mate, "Look away, Angie. You don't need to see this."

Out of the corner of his eye, he watched as Evangeline gulped, then ducked her head into her chest, turning her back on Maddox and the witch.

He took another forceful step toward Cilla.

She stepped back, throwing her hands up. "Mercy."

"Mercy?" Maddox's voice was deathly quiet. From the way Cilla gave a full-body tremble, he knew she heard his echo—and the promise in the single word. "Where was your mercy when you tried to kill my mate? Or when you ripped our bond apart and let me think she was dead for three years?"

"I only did it because I love you!"

"Yeah? Well, I'm doing this because I love *her*."

"Maddox, no, please—"

He stalked toward her.

Cilla had it coming.

The *Claws Clause* was clear.

She would only be a threat if Maddox showed her mercy.

He knew the moment that Cilla realized that her pleas were falling on deaf ears. She looked crushed, but she recovered quickly. A nasty expression turning her face ugly, she sneered, "If I can't have you, then she can't, either."

Cilla snapped her fingers.

Crack.

Evangeline screamed.

It was the only thing that could've ripped his focus off of Cilla and she *knew* it.

The barrier dissolved like so much smoke, but Evangeline never got the chance to leave the ring of diamonds. The remaining jewels burst into flame, crackling three feet high, surrounding Evangeline with dark violet sparks that shot toward her.

Maddox didn't even stop to think. He ran right through the magic fire, scooping his mate up in his arms, shielding her from Cilla's revenge.

The fire licked at his body, singing his clothes, blistering his skin. The scent of burning hair filled the air, added to the baby powder smell of Cilla's power and the sharp tang of Evangeline's sudden fear. He had to save her. Maddox didn't give a shit what would happen to him. He was a shifter. He could take it.

While holding tightly to Evangeline, he reached up, tucking her long hair beneath her shirt. Then he urged her to fold her body in tight before bowing his body over hers.

"I've got you," he promised.

She choked on the heat from the flames, shuddering in his embrace. When she found her breath again, she nodded. "I know. You always have."

"And I always will," Maddox promised.

He crouched low, pushing off of the hardwood floor with as much power as he could. Maddox leaped over the flames, hearing the sizzle as the sparks hit the soles of his shoes. He landed with a grunt, immediately moving out of the magic's reach before checking that Evangeline was unharmed.

He dashed across the room, laying her out on her couch. Running his hands over every part of her he could, Maddox didn't back off until Evangeline murmured repeatedly that she was fine. She was okay.

Once he finally believed it, and he was sure that she was safely out of the reach of the flames, Maddox got up and turned his attention back on the witch.

Smoke started at her feet, pale purple tendrils wrapping around her legs, twisting her torso, wafting toward her fingers. As Maddox stared over at her, his chest heaving, his wolf desperate to strike, the smoke continued to climb, passing her throat, covering her face.

The whole thing—from Cilla's threat and Evangeline's scream until he watched her get cocooned in the magic cloud—might have taken a minute. Maybe less.

After using the last of the diamonds in her circle, Cilla was almost completely tapped out. Instead of taking advantage of Maddox's distraction and using it to escape, Cilla stayed where she was, conjuring the smoke.

He could hear her chanting under her breath, still casting.

It would be harder to pull the magic into her without her precious diamonds. Cilla had sacrificed the last of the stones with her failed assassination attempt. All she had left was the magic that came from being a born witch.

It would be enough to hurt Evangeline.

He thought about what her spell did to Colt. He thought about the look of relief on Evangeline's face, as if she doubted that he would come for her. And he thought about the promise he made to his brother before he raced inside the building.

Get that fucking witch.

Make her pay.

Maddox lunged toward Cilla, swiping down. His claws met resistance. He sliced through something. He knew he did. Witch's blood—a combination of the rusty, iron tang and sweet baby powder—perfumed the air. It splashed on the floor.

But when the smoke finally cleared, there was no sign of Priscilla Winters anywhere except for a few drops of blood and the charred remains of destroyed diamonds.

EPILOGUE

"It's been twelve hours already. How much longer do you think he'll be out?"

"I don't know, baby," Evangeline said softly. His wolf preened at the affection in her husky voice. And after hearing Wright call her *babe* so easily, like he had the right? It felt pretty damn good to be her *baby* again "That stuff you drugged him with is kinda strong. Remember what it did to me?"

He knew his mate didn't say that to make him feel guilty—which was good because he abso-fucking-lutely refused to regret a single one of the drastic measures he had taken to get her back. If he'd sat on his claws, waiting for the bond to snap into place instead of completely ignoring the *Claws Clause*, Evangeline wouldn't be with him.

But Colton wouldn't be down for the count, either.

Yeah. What happened to his brother? Maddox might not regret how he got Evangeline back, but his shoulders were hunched, weighed down by the guilt he harbored over Colt's near brush with death.

It had only been one week since Cilla threw Colt out of the window, though it seemed like Maddox was still trapped in that terrible moment when he burst into Evangeline's apartment. The scent of Evangeline's terror was seared into his nose, the sight of Colt's broken body on the asphalt below burned into the back of his mind. His brother's shifter nature meant that he regenerated much more quickly than a human; as strong as his wolf was, Colt was on his way to being healed.

Maddox... wasn't. He had to fight the urge to pull Evangeline into his arms whenever she moved more than a few feet away from him. Seeing her vanish like that so soon after he claimed her had messed him up and *bad*. It would take a long time before he got over it so it was a good thing that they had forever.

If it wasn't for him being partly responsible for Colt's injuries—no matter that Colt hadn't listened when he told him to hang back—Maddox might have just given in to his wolf's demand that he run off with his mate, hiding her away so that he knew she was safe and protected. But he couldn't do that. Not yet.

Not until Colt was back on his feet again.

The hospital finally released Colt yesterday morning, though Maddox thought it would be fairer to say that the medical staff kicked his brother out. He didn't blame them, either. The entire time Colt was in the hospital, the orderlies, nurses, and doctors insisted that he be strapped to the bed. Since it was a mixed hospital with a shifter ward, the straps were made of treated silver—and, okay, maybe they *were* necessary. The sedative the paramedics gave him at the crime scene had worn off sooner than expected and Colt wolfed out as soon as he realized that he'd been brought in.

Three drug-laced darts to his backside knocked him out long enough for them to wrap a pair of silver cuffs on him and strap him to his hospital bed. He fought like a demon when he regained consciousness again. Luckily, the silver kept him human and in one place, even if it did nothing to stop his growled curses and angrily muttered threats.

So, yeah. Colt wasn't a fan of hospitals.

He had to go, though. Maddox insisted. A shifter's regenerative abilities meant that he should've been halfway healed by the time the ambulance pulled up to Grayson General. During the first rounds of tests, the doctors diagnosed four cracked ribs, a fractured tibia, and a broken hand. Pretty severe injuries, but nothing that would put Colt out of commission for long. Except for one thing. He was healing at a fraction of his usual speed. And fuck if they could explain it.

It was the magic. With Cilla still gone, there was no one who knew what it was she hit Colt with. It had to be something powerful to almost take out an alpha wolf like that. Luciana was contacted, the head witch meeting the ambulance at the hospital, but even she was at a loss. Maddox had howled in rage, Luciana escaping from Colt's room before the other shifter woke back up. She said something about dragging Cilla back herself, but Maddox's wolf wasn't too picky about which witch paid for her crimes. Luciana was lucky to get out before he lost it entirely.

Which was good in retrospect since he didn't really need the entire might of Coventry on his head like that.

Six days later, when Colt threatened to go all Big Bad Wolf on the human nurse checking his vitals that morning, the head of Grayson General's security team escorted Colt out personally. They used a hospice van to transport Colt to his Bumptown before the hospital staff washed their hands of their ornery patient. Maddox was glad. The harsh stink of the industrial-grade cleaners wasn't enough to hide the sickness, death, and decay that permeated hospitals. Colt could recuperate at home where Maddox could keep a better eye on him. And he wouldn't resort to silver cuffs to do it.

Of course, that didn't mean he was going to let Colt get back to work like he obviously expected to. Six days in and the right side of his body was barely serviceable. The fracture in his leg had healed enough that he could step lightly on it, but that was about it.

Pulling rank, going Alpha on Colt, Maddox put his brother right to bed. Sure, Colt complained about it, but it wasn't like he could fight back—and not just because his wolf was submissive to Maddox's. Just like the silver collar had done to Maddox back when he was still in the Cage, the silver in the hospital straps left Colt as docile as he'd ever been.

And that scared the ever-loving shit out of Maddox.

He didn't let that stop him. As Alpha, he needed to be stronger, faster, and more devious than the rest of the shifters in his pack if he wanted to stay in charge of it. He might not be the official Alpha yet—that was still his father—but in Colt's house, he was the dominant beast and he was going to act like it.

It wasn't just the pack hierarchy, either. This was family; he'd always been responsible for his younger brother. So Maddox did what he had to do to keep Colt from hurting himself while he was recovering. Colt was in even worse shape than anyone thought if his own wolf hadn't detected the liberal amount of sedatives that Evangeline had sprinkled in last night's dinner.

Considering Colt's size and shifter metabolism, Maddox gave her triple the amount to dose Colt's plate than what he had used for Evangeline. It, uh, definitely did the job.

He expected his brother to wake up, snarling and foaming at the bit when Colt realized he'd been drugged. Except it was going on twenty-four hours and Colt hadn't even twitched.

Maddox paced. He had too much nervous energy and he had to keep moving. "Do you think I made a mistake?"

Evangeline got up from her perch by the window, crossing the room and meeting Maddox in the middle. She laid her hand on her mate's arm. He immediately stilled.

Just her touch had the power to calm him. He closed his eyes for a moment, breathing in her scent, letting it wash over him.

"Maddox, honey, you did what you had to. You know that, don't you?"

"Colt's gonna—"

"Colt's going to understand. If he tried to get up, he'd only end up hurting himself more. And I know you big, tough shifters like to think you're infallible. You can still get hurt like the rest of us. He was thrown through a window by a *witch*. Six floors high, Maddox, right into the road. It's going to take time for him to heal."

"I know." Frustrated, he ran his free hand through his shaggy mane of hair. "It's just, I hate feeling so helpless. It's all my fault—"

"It's not. It was *her* fault," Evangeline argued, her expression turning dark. Didn't matter that, without Cilla's interference, Evangeline was regaining more and more memories every day. If looks could kill,

Evangeline would manage what Maddox just missed—Cilla would be a dead witch at last. "She'll get what she deserves in the end. I don't want you to spend another second thinking about her and what she did. I won't let her win. She owned my memories for too long. Forgetting her will be poetic justice."

Maddox exhaled. "You're right. I know you are." Bending down, he stole a quick kiss. It felt wrong asking for more while Colt was lying unconscious a few feet from them, but he needed that at least. Pulling away, he ran his tongue over his lips. "How did I get you to be my mate again?"

"Luck," she said, punctuating the word with a small kiss of her own right on his chin. "Love." Another kiss, this one on his cheek. "And a touch of fate, I think." And a final lingering kiss on his mouth.

"Hey, fellas. Knock, knock, alright?" There was a ghostly hand reaching through the wood, waving slightly as Dodge interrupted the pair. "I hope you ain't doin' nothin' I can't do in your brother's room, Mad Dog."

Maddox scowled as he reluctantly moved away from Evangeline. "Cool it, Dodge. You know I hate that name."

"It's still better than Hounddog, ain't it?"

Evangeline stifled a small chuckle. There hadn't been much to laugh at since that day at her apartment, but Dodge always managed to lighten the mood.

"Did he just say 'knock, knock'?" she asked, making

sure. "He's a ghost. He floats right through the walls. Why is he knocking?"

"Dodge thinks he's charming. It's his way of acting like he's giving us some privacy in here," Maddox muttered in explanation. Raising his voice enough to be heard, he called, "Come on in, you peeping tom. Lucky for you we still have our clothes on."

Evangeline elbowed her mate in the side as Dodge drifted through the wood, a strange expression on his face. At first he was wearing his usual cocky smirk, his derby tilted forward to hide one of his electric blue eyes. Once he had fully passed into the room, he lifted his hand, resetting his phantom hat so that Maddox could tell that something wasn't right. Frowning now, his brow furrowed as Dodge looked over at Colt. It was almost as if he was seeing his best friend for the first time.

Maddox felt the wisp of humor flee from the room. Dodge was Colt's best friend, but Maddox had known the ghost for almost twenty years. Something wasn't right.

He nodded over at him. "Hey, Dodge. You okay?"

"Yeah. Me? I'm fine. Just... just thinkin' about something. Anyway, it seems Colt's got himself another visitor."

"Again? The witch was already here." Luciana had balls, he'd give her that. The head witch stopped by last night to check on Colt. Like the time in the hospital, though, she left when Maddox snapped at her. He had decided she knew more than she was telling and it pissed him off. As far as he was concerned, until she was ready to help Colt, she could stay the hell away from him. "If she came back, tell her she can slink away again for all I care."

"Well, that's the thing, Mad. It, uh, it ain't her."

Dodge was Colt's only friend. None of the pack would dare enter Colt's territory unless they were trying to challenge him while he was healing—which was the same thing as signing their death warrant. Maddox would kill to protect his brother and every shifter in the area—packmate or not—knew it.

It couldn't be anyone else. Maddox made sure of it. He had even gone so far as to be the buffer between Colt and their parents; that's how much the guilt got to him. It was bad enough that he finally had to admit that he was released from the Cage, but the worst part was having to tell them that Colton had been thrown out of a window trying to save Evangeline.

Sarah was dying to dote on her baby boy. To calm her, Maddox promised, once Colt was back on his feet, she could come mother him all she wanted. And, yes, he would bring Evangeline to his parents' den so that Sarah could see for herself that her older son was finally happy and whole.

But if it wasn't Dodge, the witch, or his well-meaning parents... it couldn't be anyone else.

Unless—

His claws unsheathed with a soft *snick*, his lips twisted in a possessive snarl.

"Who is it?" he asked Dodge. "If it's Wright, you better scare him off before I do. I told him to stop sniffing around here."

Evangeline sighed. "I keep hoping Adam will give up."

"Fucking *Adam*," sneered Maddox.

Apart from seeing Colt back to his full strength, there was nothing he wanted more than to challenge the human cop once and for all. Evangeline refused to let him. He didn't blame her. The outcome was inevitable: Maddox would tear the Ant from limb to limb and, because of Wright's connections and the damn *Claws Clause*, Maddox would be put down in a heartbeat.

Evangeline didn't want to lose either one of them. But that didn't mean she was keen on seeing her ex again, either.

After the crime scene was cleared and their statements had been taken, Evangeline and Maddox went straight to the hospital to be with Colt. Wright followed them there, cornered Evangeline while Maddox was filling out paperwork for his brother, and tried to convince her to press charges against Maddox for the kidnapping.

Evangeline immediately invoked the *Claws Clause*; now that they were officially bonded, the bond between them superseded any other laws. Wright tried to plead his case, explaining why he lied to her. She wouldn't budge. Once he left, his tail tucked between his legs, Evangeline immediately found Maddox and told him what had happened. Her description of the devastated look on Wright's face was probably the only thing that kept Maddox from hunting him down. That, and the fact that Colt had suddenly come to while he was halfway toward the exit. The orderlies and security team needed his help more than Wright needed to be taught a lesson.

The Ant took it as a sign that he still had a chance. Wright showed up at the Bumptown last night while Maddox was busy coaxing—well, *threatening*—Colt into eating his spiked dinner. Evangeline had been downstairs, washing dishes and catching up with Dodge when Wright knocked at the front door.

Evangeline turned him away. By the time Dodge popped into Colt's room and got Maddox, Wright had already disappeared. Only Evangeline's murmured *please* kept him from shifting on the spot and chasing after Wright's cruiser.

Taking care of Colt was important. At the same time, his mate needed him, too. So he stayed.

Wright's betrayal cut her deep. Knowing that she was a mated—and married—woman, he still tried to build a relationship with her. Wright had been a Cage cop. He had known all about Maddox from the beginning.

Evangeline was still coming to grips with her mother's meddling, too. They'd had a long, tear-filled conversation the night after Cilla snatched Evangeline. Naomi Lewis confessed that she kept the truth about Maddox hidden because she blamed him for the accident that nearly killed Evangeline three years ago. All she had wanted was to protect her daughter.

That was Maddox's job. And, he vowed, he would spend the rest of his life doing so.

Naomi was forced to accept his place in her daughter's life; she had no choice, not now that they had both a marriage license and the bonding license. She was his mother-in-law and Maddox forgave her because, in the end, Evangeline's happiness was all that mattered.

Wright could jump off a bridge for all he cared.

As if she could sense that he needed her, Evangeline reached out her hand. He clasped it in a grip like a vice. Pulling her near him, Maddox folded Evangeline in his arms and rested his chin on the top of her head.

Dodge scowled, a spasm of pain dashing across the shadows of his nearly transparent face before he shook his head. His expression closed off suddenly, only to be replaced by a familiar grin. "It ain't the cop, either," he told them. "You don't gotta worry about him coming back. I tracked him down last night and told him if I saw him skulkin' around the Bumptown again, I'd go haunt him myself." Dodge shrugged. "Don't think he liked the idea I might see somethin' I shouldn't. He'll stay away."

Evangeline stiffened. "Oh, Dodge. You didn't."

"Don't you feel sorry for him, Angie," Maddox said. He lowered his head and pressed his nose against the crook of her neck and shoulder, nuzzling his bite. "He went after a mated woman. You're *mine*. Far as I'm concerned, bastard deserves worse than Dodge getting an eyeful of his dick."

Evangeline slapped lazily at Maddox. "Your brother has company. Stop that. Leave me alone."

"Never," he swore, even as he straightened. He turned his flashing gaze on the ghost. "Well?"

"Well what?"

"It's not pack. Not the witch. Wright would have to be a fucking moron to come back. Who's out there?"

Dodge thought about it for a second. His lips quirked slightly, his sudden grin devilish. "I think it might be best if I let her tell you herself."

Then, before Maddox could argue, he floated back through the closed door and winked out of sight. Considering his grin slid off of his hazy face a split second before he did, Maddox decided Dodge wanted to escape the happily mated couple more than anything else.

He nearly followed Dodge out of the room; only his protective instincts held him back. He didn't want to leave his mate or his softly snoring brother unprotected. And while he could bring Evangeline with him, Colt was passed out on the bed. He wasn't going anywhere any time soon.

Instead, he let go of his mate, stroking her back

gently before resuming his agitated pacing from one side of the master bedroom to the next. Every time he passed her, Evangeline murmured soothing words under her breath, keeping him sane and his wolf calm.

Maddox caught the scent an instant before he sensed a stranger approaching. The thud of a nervous heartbeat echoed in time to a pair of heeled shoes tapping gently up the stairs. He smelled soap, a twinge of sweat, and a faint wood-burning aroma. It wasn't acrid, so it wasn't fear, and he recognized it as determination.

Determination and something else.

There was something off about the scent, though. It was faint, sure, but fainter than it should've been; it didn't get any stronger, not even when he could sense the stranger standing outside of the closed bedroom door. It was definitely muted, almost like it was close to missing the way that Evangeline's had been while she wore that damned and enchanted perfume.

Maddox had a few seconds to put two and two together before the soft knock echoed around him. Sometimes you got four. And sometimes you got—

"It's open. Come in."

—a witch.

It wasn't just that the woman who moved slowly into the room was cloaked in magic. She *was* magic. Maddox didn't need his wolf's nose to tell him that. Her vivid purple eyes were more than enough of a clue.

She was probably of average height; compared to Maddox and Evangeline, she was petite. Her skin was a rich olive shade, her witch's eyes striking against the tone. She had hair that fell past her shoulders, a tumble of loose curls that were so black, they were nearly blue. She kept her head held high as she stopped just inside the door, though she gulped when her gaze fell on Maddox, then Evangeline.

Then, as if she were drawn to him, she turned to look at Colt. In an instant, it was as if no one else was in the room.

Maddox cleared his throat. The rasp caught her attention. With a jerk, she tore her gaze away from Colt. If possible, her purple eyes seemed to glow a little brighter. He didn't sense her using any magic, but there was no denying what she was.

What was an unknown witch doing at Colt's house?

"Who are you?" he asked. So maybe it came out more like a snarl. After what Cilla did, he wasn't feeling too kindly toward any witches—and this one was a stranger. "What are you doing here?"

"Maddox!"

"What?"

"Don't pay my husband any mind," Evangeline said. "I'm still trying to teach him manners."

The look that flashed across the witch's face wished Evangeline luck. Maddox bristled, torn between waiting for her answer and simply calling Dodge back to escort the human out of the Bumptown before he did something he regretted.

He didn't get the chance to throw Cilla out of a window. Maybe he could take his revenge out on a different witch.

He must have given his thoughts away because the witch took a step back. She recovered quickly—he'd give her credit for that—and stepped toward him. Not too close, because it was clear that he guarded his personal space fiercely. Except for his mate, everyone else gave him a wide berth. The witch was no different.

Maddox gave her credit for that, too.

"My name is Shea. Why am I here? Well, that's kind of a long story." She swallowed, looking for the words. "My grandma finally convinced me that I should just come over here. You see— oh, goddess, I can't believe I'm about to say this—"

"Just spit it out," growled Maddox.

"Maddox!"

"What? I don't have time for this. Colt's lying there, he won't wake up, and you expect me to listen to some witch's rambling? Luciana was bad enough, but she's the head of the coven. This one's got no reason to be here."

Evangeline joined him by his side. She obviously heard the frustration in his grumble, the desperation he could never hide from her. It wasn't about the witch. They both knew that.

She took his hand and squeezed it. "He'll wake up

when he's ready. It's just taking his body a little longer to recover than we thought, that's all."

The witch—Shea—made a small noise in the back of her throat. "So he's not healing. I was afraid of that."

"A witch did this to him." That one? That was totally a snarl. He couldn't stop it from escaping. "The magic is messing with his shifter abilities. Unless you know better than Luciana, you should probably just go."

A small smile. It was fleeting yet sad, and Maddox realized that the shock of her wearing her witch's eyes rather than a glamour hid the fact that she was pretty. She didn't hold a candle to Evangeline, no one could, but she was pretty enough.

And she looked as if she would rather be anywhere other than where she was.

"I wish I could. Sorry. I didn't want to come—"

"Then what *do* you want?"

"What do I want? For you not to bark at me, for starters. Please don't think this was my choice. Any of this. It's not." She inhaled deeply, winced noticeably, then placed her hand against her side as she exhaled slowly. She purposefully met his alpha stare. "It's getting worse for me, too."

"Oh." Next to him, Evangeline covered her mouth with her hand. "*Oh.*"

Pain. Despite the way Shea kept her scent muted, it spiked when she winced, fading as she controlled her breathing in an effort to fight through it. She'd hidden it well, but she was hurting. Inhaling deeply, Maddox realized that that was the reason she had muted her scent. Shit. How was she even still standing?

Glancing over at Evangeline, wordlessly asking for permission, he waited until his mate had nodded before he hurried over and scooped the hunched witch up in his brawny arms. She went rigid as soon as he grabbed her, swatting angrily at his arms as he crossed the room.

He took her by surprise. Maddox never even gave her the chance to curse him, moving quickly before easing her into the high-backed chair next to Colt's bed.

Maddox had dragged the wooden beauty up from Colt's workshop shortly after they moved Colt to his room. His wolf was too anxious to sit and Maddox hadn't used it; instead, he paced the lengths of the room, watching over his brother. Evangeline said the chair was too uncomfortable to sit in for long and usually sat by the window—as far from Colt as she could get while still being near to her own mate.

Maddox knew she was lying and didn't argue. She was only thinking of him. On top of everything else that had happened, the strain of seeing his mate tend so closely to Colt had caused Maddox to snap. As soon as she entered the room, surrounded by Colt's scent, Maddox lunged at his weakened brother, only stopping when Evangeline rushed forward and grabbed his arm before he could do any damage.

Since Colt had tried to accept the challenge, even injured and half-groggy from another hospital-grade sedative, they both decided that it was time to put him all the way under while he healed. That's when Maddox remembered the sedative he used on Evangeline.

The witch looked like she could have used some of the same drugs. In spite of Evangeline's claims, the chair was one of Colt's masterpieces which meant that it looked pretty but, more importantly, was a great piece of furniture. Once Maddox placed her down, Shea immediately curled up against the high back, her hand rubbing her side.

Maddox snuffled. Her mild scent clung to his clothes. It didn't matter that Evangeline had given him her blessing. It made his skin itch to be so close to another woman, his wolf howling for its mate.

His fangs punched out, a wild rumbling growl starting deep in his chest and filling the silence in the room. Evangeline immediately opened her arms, welcoming him into her embrace.

After giving her one big squeeze, assuring himself she was still there and transferring her scent back to him, Maddox kissed her on the top of her head.

Then, with the fierce stare of a predator looking at lunch, he turned back to Shea.

Her eyes were drawn to Colt's drugged form again. Before Maddox could stop her, she shakily reached her hand out toward the bed. Shea bit her lip, hesitating, the tips of her fingers hovering an inch above Colt's blanket-covered leg. Her brow furrowed. Taking a deep breath, she dropped her hand.

The instant she made contact, she let out the smallest sigh of relief. Followed by a very fierce, "Shit!"

That shook Maddox. "What just happened? Why are you touching my brother?"

The witch didn't say anything at first. When he heard a soft, muffled snort coming from his mate, Maddox glanced back at Evangeline. Her shoulders were shaking, sudden amusement filling her forest green eyes.

His wolf let out a warning grumble. "I'm missing something and I don't like it."

"He's your brother?" asked Shea. She pet Colt's knee awkwardly before leaning into the wooden seat. "You... you look different from him."

Maddox barely resisted the urge to shake the witch. Yeah. Of course they looked different. Maddox wasn't half dead, Colt didn't have a scar wrapped around his throat, and no one had ever called the elder Wolfe brother *pretty*. Baring his teeth at Shea, he snapped, "I'm fucking sure. That's Colton, my younger brother. You seem to know him well enough to touch him. *How*?"

"Well, that's where it gets a little bit weird. You see—" She shrugged apologetically. "I think we might be mates."

While Evangeline let out an adorable snort mixed

with laughter behind him, Maddox blinked. Once. Twice. His wolf tilted its head quizzically to the side. The man had no answers for it. He closed his eyes and, echoing Shea from before, he cursed under his breath.

Shit.

AUTHOR'S NOTE

Thank you for reading *Hungry Like a Wolf*!

Wow. So, I started this book as a NaNoWriMo project in 2015. I wasn't really sure what I was going to do with it when I hit the 50k word goal that year, but I've always been a fan of paranormal romances, magic, ghosts and witches, and everything like that. While my *Mirrorside* series is full of fantasy, I'm limited to Greek mythology (which I also adore). My *Hamlet* series is a contemporary series full of mystery, murder, romance, and secrets. With the *Claws Clause* series, I wanted to create a world that would actually kind of fit seamlessly with ours today. I got the idea of the D.P.R. from a visit at the D.M.V. and the rest is history.

Because of the way this book was designed—with Maddox and Evangeline essentially having a second-chance romance in the confines of the fated mate trope—I reference to their backstory a lot. In case you didn't

Author's Note

know, I already wrote that story: *Mates*, a 25k prequel novella that shows you how they first got together three years before this book.

And, while the next book in the series is obviously Colton's story, I also have a Christmas story that features Evangeline and Maddox that shows where they are a couple of months after this story: *Of Mistletoe and Mating*.

Keep clicking for a sneak peek at Colton's book, *Season of the Witch*—out now!

xoxo,
Jessica

SEASON OF THE WITCH
SNEAK PEEK AT THE SECOND BOOK

Colt's hatred of witches was legendary. Most of the witches in the area—and that didn't include his Bumptown anymore because, well, *hatred*—regarded him as an enemy. Not because he ever acted on his dislike, but because his temper and his stubborn nature meant he never hid it, either.

When he was younger, it had to do with their magic. He just couldn't understand how, with one flick of a finger or a wave of a hand, a witch could cancel out his brute strength, inch-long canines, and razor-sharp claws.

Right after the almost-fatal car crash, when the truck carrying Maddox and Evangeline toward their honeymoon careened off the mountain, Maddox got thrown into the Cage. Every time Colt visited his brother over the last three years, he was only reminded that witches were a traitor to other Paras.

The paranormal prison was warded. *Witches*. The glass partition separating the brothers in the visitors' room was enchanted to be Para-proof. *Witches*. The covens were even responsible for the silver collars used to leash the shifters locked inside. Even after Maddox was freed, the ring of ruined skin remained, the terrible scars a memento of his time forced into the silver collar.

Fucking witches.

Then Priscilla had ruined Maddox's life, broken Evangeline, and tried to murder Colt when he confronted her. The lone witch was twisted, obsessed with the idea that she could use her witchcraft to create a bond with Maddox. Cilla thought magic could trump fate; with enough diamonds, she could get rid of her competition and make herself Maddox's mate instead.

He had hundreds of reasons to hate witches, and his family wondered why he just couldn't accept one as a mate?

He might've been able to get over his knee jerk reaction about falling in lust at first sight with a stranger—he *was* a shifter and, unfortunately, finding his mate had long been a possibility even if he'd never actually looked—but a *witch*?

No.

No.

Not even one as kind and as sweet and as caring as his.

Now, when it came to Nightwalkers, he wasn't alone in his dislike. Of all the different types of paranormals—shifters, vamps, phantoms, witches, and othersiders—Nightwalkers were universally despised. They were dead, though they didn't appear that way except for their strangely silver eyes and their pale skin. As a whole, the turned race of vampires were vicious and cruel, their lusts only tempered by their blood-drinking and, if they could find one, their betrothed.

Not many people wanted to tie themselves to a Nightwalker unless they liked to be used as a pincushion. A Nightwalker could offer pleasure with its bite, but there was a cost. Non-Nightwalkers could grow addicted to the high a Nightwalker could offer, becoming a Donor who existed solely to give blood and wait for their next fix. A Donor only loved the feeling, never the corpse; they could never be a vampire's blood-bonded mate.

In the past, most Nightwalkers were solitary by nature, only relying on the humans they could feed from. Since Paras were forced out into the open, individual Para quirks were more tolerated. Sure, the drinking had to be done behind closed doors, but nowadays there were synthetic blood shops and blood banks even in mixed towns.

There were even a couple of Nightwalkers living in his Bumptown; not many, since there was definitely something in their make-up that made them more reclusive than other Paras.

They settled together in a corner referred to as Little Transylvania. Though Colt was abso-fucking-lutely positive that the vamps in his Bumptown didn't have anything to do with the bodies, he decided to run past their hidden corner and sniff around after he made it back to the Bumptown.

His wolf needed the exercise. And Colt needed to focus on something that wasn't Shea Moonshadow.

To make matters worse, right before he left, his mother had cornered him to ask if she would see him Thursday for dinner. Before he could snap at Maddox for involving their parents, he put two and two together and realized that Thursday—the day Maddox wanted him over to eat—was Thanksgiving.

No wonder Dodge had looked at him like he was an idiot for not understanding why Maddox was pushing the whole family dinner thing.

His mother was waiting for Colt to finally make Shea his mate in truth. She wanted her boys to settle down and nagged in that loving way Sarah Wolfe was known for. Luckily, Terrence stepped in and told his mate that Colt wasn't a pup anymore.

When Sarah snapped her teeth at her mate—the only member of the pack who could challenge the Alpha without it being a true challenge—Colt tucked his tail between his legs and dashed out the back door.

He narrowly missed running into Ralph, waving off

the unnecessary offer of a ride back into town before he kicked off his shoes and shifted on the spot. His t-shirt and jeans exploded into tatters as the over-sized, white arctic wolf appeared where the boyishly handsome twenty-seven-year-old Colt had been seconds before.

He ran the entire way home. Sure, he'd have to find a way to get his truck back tomorrow, pick up his discarded boots, too, but that was *tomorrow*.

Tonight was for his wolf.

Of the two Wolfe brothers, Colt had always been the most in tune with his beast. Not lately. Both halves of him were locked in a constant battle as they fought over his... his mate.

Five months later and Colt couldn't stop thinking about her.

He couldn't stop fantasizing about her, either.

Shit.

Just as he crossed onto the wooded land that surrounded the perimeter of his Bumptown, he couldn't hold back any longer. In mid-stride, the wolf shifted back to his two-legged shape, revealing a very naked, very aroused male.

That wasn't so unusual. From the moment he woke up in his bed and discovered that she was there, that she was touching him, that she knew she was his mate, Colt struggled to deal with his hard-on. It was like his damn cock had a mind of its own. No matter how Colt tried to convince himself that he wasn't going to mate her—that he *couldn't*—his cock went stiff at just the slightest thought of her.

Her curls.

Her smile.

Her *tits*.

The head bobbed, pointed skyward as Colt went down on his knees. It was cold out, November on the east coast, and he felt the chill like a caress on his overheated skin. How many times had he stroked himself, praying for some relief, wishing he could tame his wayward cock without going to Shea and sacrificing his stubborn pride?

Finding another woman was out of the question. He couldn't have Shea—he was too stubborn, too hard-headed, and he'd lost any chance of getting inside of her a long time ago. No matter what, though, she *was* his true mate. The one fate picked out for him. He couldn't have Shea, but he wouldn't take anyone else.

So he jerked off. A lot. Considering how many times he'd brought himself to come in the last five months, it amazed him that he'd never masturbated before he found Shea. Male shifters couldn't even get an erection until they chanced upon their true mate—another reason why he knew Shea was supposed to be his—and it seemed as if he was making up for lost time.

Taking just a second to make sure no one else was close enough to see what he was doing, Colt wrapped his hand around his shaft. It was hot, it was hard, and a bead of pre-cum was already forming at the tip of the mushroom-shaped head.

He gave it a vicious tug, then another, every rough stroke like another punishment. He refused to find any type of gratification in the act. It was another biological urge, one he didn't have the strength to ignore. When the friction started to burn, he increased the pace, throwing back his head and moaning when the quick jolt of pleasure overtook the pain.

Come spurted out on the frozen grass. He wiped his hand against his bare ass, chest heaving in the brisk night air. His cock twitched, still semi-hard, and he took a deep breath, struggling for control.

He took a deep breath and snuffled back through his nose.

He'd been too preoccupied with his quick orgasm to use his nose. When his ears and his wolf assured him that he was the only living creature around him, he left it at that. The deep breath he just took? The stench of carrion, of rotten meat, blood, and death that nearly slapped him in the face... he was right.

He was the only *living* thing around.

Nightwalkers stunk like that. Once you caught your first whiff of the dead vampires, you never forgot it. Only... he wasn't anywhere near Little Transylvania.

Colt shifted back to his wolf, choosing fur over bare skin. Not that he gave a shit if someone caught him with his cock out when he wasn't tugging on it. Shifters always came back from their animal shape without any clothes on. Far as he was concerned, nudity was definitely more of a human hang-up.

But, as he dashed over the wooded terrain, four paws were faster than two legs. His wolf lifted its muzzle high, tasting the blood in the air, following it to the edge of the boundary that butted up against Colt's immediate territory.

His wolf kept its mouth open, tongue lolling as he sampled the scents, processing them. It belonged to a Nightwalker, one who was long gone and unfamiliar to him. But... that wasn't the only scent he caught as he got closer.

Human. That was a human female scent wafting toward him, nearly covered up by the copious amounts of blood.

He spurred his wolf to go faster.

AVAILABLE NOW
SEASON OF THE WITCH

I won't—

Colton Wolfe has never liked witches.

There's something about their magic. With a snap of a finger, a witch can cancel out his brute strength, razor-sharp claws, and inch-long fangs. It just isn't natural. The Para-proof wards constructed by witches always made his fur itch, and it has bothered him for years how they betrayed all paranormals by selling their services to the highest bidders.

Then a witch nearly killed him and his dislike turned into full-blown hate.

His brother thinks his anger is unhealthy.

Available Now

Following his brush with near-death, Colt refuses to even talk to any packmates. Dodge, his best friend and a ghost, can't even get through to him. Colt keeps himself confined to his workshop, shutting every one out. His wolf is just about rabid and he keeps his beast locked up tight.

His wolf wants its mate. Colt won't admit it, but he does, too.

Only Shea is a witch.
And Colt hates all witches—
Doesn't he?

I can't—

Shea Moonshadow is a healer first, a witch second. Considering her magic has a way of backfiring on her whenever she tries the simplest of spells, she sticks with what she knows will work. Her herbs and her poultices have never failed her before.

Now if she could only say the same about her brother.

Hudson is a Donor, a blood junkie who gives blood to vampires in exchange for a high only a dangerous Nightwalker can give. When he gets in over his head, he does what he's always done: runs to Shea for help.

She can't say no. She's never been able to say no.
Not to Hudson.
Not to anyone.

And that's how she finds herself pledged to a blood-bonding with an obsessed vampire.

When a dangerous group of Paras move in on Colt's territory, going after humans and paranormals alike, the Grayson Police Department recruit him to take on the vicious Nightwalkers. If it's bad enough that Colt gets saddled with an old enemy, it's even worse when he discovers that his almost-mate is in it up to her adorable purple eyes.

He might've put off claiming his mate. But no way in hell is Colt—or his wolf—going to let some Nightwalker scum take Shea away from him.

---

* *Season of the Witch* is the second full-length novel in the *Claws Clause* series. It's the story of a grumpy wolf shifter hero and the sassy witch who has cast a spell over him. With danger, intrigue, and heart, watch as Colton submits to the one woman meant for him.

Out Now!

AVAILABLE NOW
TRUE ANGEL (CURSE OF THE OTHERSIDERS #1)

What do a talking cat, a 70-year-old virgin, and a human woman searching for her sister have in common?

More than you would think...

In a world where paranormals live side by side with humans, mortals take one look at Camiel and think that he's an angel... until his black wings unfurl and it's all, "*Oh, no! Demon!*"

Yeah. Not quite.

Cam is an Othersider. Which, okay, just means that he'll eventually be one of the two... just not yet. Formally known as the Fallen, Othersiders walk—and, yes, sometimes fly—among the humans, knowing that their every step, their every move, their every *thought*

Available Now

adds to their tally. If he's good, he'll finally earn his halo.

If he's bad...

He's working damn hard to resist any urges to be bad.

It's a good thing he has his auditor at his side. Dina might look like a neighborhood stray, but it's the cat's job to help Cam get the points he needs to go from Fallen to Angel. And it's working... until Cam meets Avery.

Avery is human, she's in trouble, and Cam decides that she needs her very own guardian angel. If he can help her save her sister from the feral shifter that ran off with her, then maybe he'll finally prove that he's a good guy.

If only it was that easy. Because Othersiders? There's a reason why they're stuck on Earth, working hard to prove where they belong: they're cursed.

So when it comes to falling in love? There's one rule.

Don't.

Now Cam is losing his feathers at an alarming rate. In the middle of his mission, Dina disappears. Avery is a temptation he can't ignore, and when he doesn't, that's when all hell breaks loose.

Literally.

****True Angel** *is the first in a new series by the author of the* Claws Clause. *Think* The Good Place *but set on Earth,*

Available Now

where every action means our hero is one step closer to earning his halo or his horns. And when he meets his fated mate, he realizes that he'd take either if it meant that he could have her by his side for all eternity.

Releasing January 29, 2021

Out now!

STAY IN TOUCH

Interested in updates from me? I'll never spam you, and I'll only send out a newsletter in regards to upcoming releases, subscriber exclusives, promotions, and more:

Sign up for my newsletter here!

For a limited time, anyone who signs up for my newsletter will also receive two free books!

ABOUT THE AUTHOR

Jessica lives in New Jersey with her family, including enough pets to cement her status as the neighborhood's future Cat Lady. She spends her days working in retail, and her nights lost in whatever world the current novel she is working on is set in. After writing for fun for more than a decade, she has finally decided to take some of the stories out of her head and put them out there for others who might also enjoy them! She loves Broadway and the Mets, as well as reading in her free time.

JessicaLynchWrites.com
cursetheflame@gmail.com

ALSO BY JESSICA LYNCH

Welcome to Hamlet

Don't Trust Me

You Were Made For Me*

Ophelia

Let Nothing You Dismay

I'll Never Stop

Wherever You Go

Here Comes the Bride

Gloria

Tesoro

Holly

That Girl Will Never Be Mine

Welcome to Hamlet: I-III**

No Outsiders Allowed: IV-VI**

Mirrorside

Tame the Spark*

Stalk the Moon

Hunt the Stars

The Witch in the Woods

Hide from the Heart

Chase the Beauty

The Other Duet**

The Claws Clause

Mates*

Hungry Like a Wolf

Of Mistletoe and Mating

No Way

Season of the Witch

Rogue

Sunglasses at Night

Ghost of Jealousy

Broken Wings

Born to Run

The Curse of the Othersiders

Ain't No Angel*

True Angel

Night Angel

Lost Angel

Touched by the Fae

Favor*

Asylum

Shadow

Touch

Zella

The Shadow Prophecy**

Imprisoned by the Fae

Tricked*

Trapped

Escaped

Freed

Gifted

The Shadow Realm**

Wanted by the Fae

Glamour Eyes

* prequel story

** boxed set collection

Printed in Great Britain
by Amazon